TRASH

TRASH

The Rubbishman's Ball

Chip Clements

ISBN: 9798394604706
Book and cover design by Deborah Daly
MADE IN THE USA

"Every man has his folly,
but the greatest folly of all is not to have one."
—Zorba the Greek

"A cornered cat will turn into a lion."
—Old Armenian Saying

"Winning isn't everything,
it's the only thing."
—Vince Lombardi

1

(Los Angeles – March 1985)

Nazareth Agajanian **wove through the smoke and din** of the ballroom, the packed crowd of garbage haulers, recyclers, landfill guys, all the families carousing at the Annual Rubbishman's Ball. He felt warm and alive, the booze working its magic. The bid deadline from the City of Los Angeles loomed a month away, like a cliff on the horizon. But tonight he would forget all that, reaching out, touching hands, smiling at old friends, the man in his element—the Pope of trash.

The mandolin struck a chord and the band fired into a song. Like a wave, the raven-haired women broke onto the dance floor, hands clasped in a line, feet flying in unison, gold jewelry sparking in the cascade of light from the mirrored chandeliers.

Naz sat at his table and watched them. Like Christmas

tree ornaments, they glittered in his eyes. A beautiful young woman yelled out to him from the front of the line, "Dad! Come on!"

The other dancers picked up the chant, "Come on, Nazareth!"

Naz slapped the table and said to his wife beside him, "Well, Mayda, my people need me."

"According to you, everyone needs you," she said, waving to a friend at another table. Her short curvaceous body, now slightly padded by thirty years of marriage to Naz, was stuffed into a black cocktail dress, her hair quaffed and sprayed hard as lacquered wood. Light glinted off the rhinestones that rimmed her eyeglasses, magnifying her soft brown eyes.

Naz squeezed an elderly man on the shoulder as he walked by the far end of the table.

"Don't get hurt out there, Nazareth," his father, Harry, said, a smile creasing the eighty-year-old face.

"With women, you always get hurt," Naz said, as he patted his father on the cheek.

Naz caught his daughter's glance and smiled. It was good to see Carina dancing again, after all that had happened. Naz shook off the memory of the accident and strode onto the dance floor. Tufts of gray hair flowered out from the throat of his pink tuxedo shirt. At fifty-five, he had thickened some around the middle, but he was tall and carried it well. His once heavy mat of black hair had thinned some. More flesh, less hair, it all evened out to Naz.

He smiled into Carina's eyes. She stood close to five-ten in spiked heels, and had a hawk-like nose that gave her a beautiful, yet exotic look. Gold earrings and necklace flashed against hair that fell in waves to her shoulders.

Naz took his daughter's hand and waved his white handkerchief in the other. His blue eyes were electric against his olive skin in the pulsing light. Then, he danced, arms aloft, and the line of women moved with him, now dropping, now twisting, floating on the light and the night and the roaring rhythm.

Then, in a rush, it was over, the last chord hanging in the air with the smoke. Naz bowed, arms extended as if embracing the world. The dancers came up panting and hugged him, strands of dark hair, wet with sweat, stuck to their temples.

Carina laid her hand on his shoulder. "Just like I thought," she said, catching her breath. "You've lost a step."

Naz smiled. "My ass," he said.

In the back of the room, two men sat at the bar. Alex Hart ran his hand through his hair until it lay back over the starched collar of his shirt. He had square, muscular features and intense brown eyes. His gaze turned to the dance floor and fell on Naz. His jaw tightened. "The great Agajanian," he mumbled, "God's gift to trash." He tossed down the rest of his drink. "I offered him a good price, way above market. Any sane man would've jumped at it." Alex rattled his ice cubes at the bartender.

"Pride cometh before the fall," Joe Kirby, Alex's attorney, said, cleaning his wire rimmed glasses on a napkin. "When we beat him on the L.A. bid, it'll finish Pacific Rim once and for all."

"This guy you've got to bury with a stake in his heart," Alex said. He snorted to clear his nose, which was scarred across the bridge. A white suit and tailored black western shirt fit tightly to his muscular frame. At forty-five, he was nearly as fit as he was during his football days at USC.

Back at the Agajanian table, Naz hollered over the music at his father, "Remember when they had that Miss Rubbishman's Ball thing and we wanted Carina to enter?"

"She could still be winner," Harry said, biting into a celery stick.

"It's demeaning to women," Carina replied.

"What?" Mayda said. "To look beautiful and have everyone love you?"

"You should enter, Mom. Give them a thrill."

"Don't think she couldn't," Naz said. "Gives me one every night."

Mayda threw a napkin at Naz. He just let it hit him in the face and smiled.

Carina got up, kissed her grandfather on the cheek and said, "I'm going to the bar, *Babig*. You want a drink?"

Harry patted her hand and raised a glass of milky liquid. "I still have *oghi*."

Naz said, "Get him another one. I seen him drink ten of those."

As Carina approached the bar, she spotted Alex and turned her shoulder to him. Their brief fling had ended a couple years ago, and not well.

"So, how's life at Pacific Rim?" Alex said.

She turned, "Alex, I didn't see you."

Alex smiled. "Must be the lights."

She ordered drinks, then said without looking at him. "I hear you're expanding the evil empire. Who was it this time—Rapid Disposal?"

"The Bedrosians saw the golden ring and grabbed for it. Your father needs to take off the blinders."

"Sees pretty well, you ask me," she said. The bartender handed her a drink.

"How's your bid coming?" Joe Kirby said.

"What bid?" she replied.

Alex turned to Joe and said, "Good. She's good, Joe. You think we might have a position for her?" Alex reached over and brushed a smudge of makeup off the shoulder of Carina's dress. "You know...something under me maybe."

"Fuck off, Alex." Carina turned, drinks in hand.

"Is that a no, Ms. Agajanian?" He grabbed her arm.

"Let go of me!" she said, pulling her arm away. Her drinks splattered the front of her dress and the glasses shattered against the bar. Heads turned from nearby tables.

Joe said, "Come on, Alex."

Alex shouted, "And you tell your father...."

Naz burst in between. "Tell him what, Hartunian!"

"It's OK, Dad," Carina said. "Let's go."

"You touch her again...." Naz said.

"Oh, God Almighty is talking to me, Joe! Well, listen to this, God Almighty." Alex poked Naz in the chest with each word, his eyes black. "You're out of the landfill! Got me? Out!"

The band ground to a halt. Men rose from their chairs.

"Better celebrate tonight," Alex yelled. "You'll never win that L.A. bid. And without that Naz, you're going down!"

Naz yelled back, "I don't need your shithole dump!"

With the last word, Naz pushed Alex, who lunged back, fists doubled up. Joe Kirby caught Alex in a bear hug and wrestled him off.

Alex whirled and pointed at Naz. "You'll be back picking up cardboard off the street!"

Naz watched Alex storm off, then put a hand on Carina's shoulder. "You OK?"

"You didn't need to rescue me."

Naz smiled at her. "I just didn't want you to hurt him."

"God, I can't believe I ever liked that guy," she said.

"Everyone makes mistakes," Naz said as he guided her toward their table. The crowd was returning to their seats, and the band started back up.

"What was that all about?" Mayda asked, as Naz and Carina sat down.

"Nothing." Naz drained his scotch.

"It's the bid isn't it?"

Carina dipped a cocktail napkin in her water glass and wiped at her dress. "God, my best dress."

"Alex threw us out of the landfill," said Naz.

Mayda said, "What!?"

"Forces us to use the county dump—expensive," Carina replied. "Hurts our bid."

Harry tapped Naz on the arm with his cane. "The old days in Fresno," he said. "The Hartunians, they buy with money, or they take."

Carina said, "City didn't do us a favor with that

short, thirty-day bid deadline, either. Looks like some-one's got it wired."

"I wonder who?" said Mayda, with a sideways glance at Naz.

"No one's got it wired," said Naz. "We can make thirty days. Carina's just got to type faster."

Mayda said, "The Harts have the biggest landfill in California, and bought out most of our friends. They can't share a little?"

"This ain't exactly a little, I told you." Naz jabbed the butt end of a cigar in his mouth. "One of the biggest deals in the history of L.A.—a twenty year contract. Five…six hundred million dollars. Hartunians win this, you can kiss our ass goodbye. They get all our L.A. accounts, fatten their wallets so they can lowball other bids with predatory pricing. It's over."

"There's a happy thought," Carina said.

"But we ain't going to let that happen. Right?" Naz looked around the table but all he got back were blank stares.

Mayda ran a fresh coat of lipstick around her mouth. "We should have sold to them."

Naz groaned. "Let's not go through that again."

Mayda said, "We are like one of those picata things they hang from the tree."

"It's piñata, Mom," said Carina.

"And the Harts swing the bat," said Mayda. "And when they hit us, we break open, and all we have spills over the ground, and those vultures eat it."

Naz picked a piece of tobacco off his tongue and tossed it at the ashtray in the middle of the table.

* * *

The rear door of the hearse creaked open. With a groan, Charles Goodnight rolled off the moldy mattress and crawled out. A security light cast metallic shadows across the yard and silhouetted the buildings of Pacific Rim Recycling. Mist hung in the cool night air. Charlie shuddered.

"God, Black. I'm gettin' old."

The dog lifted his head from the front seat and peered out the open window at the familiar voice, then started chewing between the toes of his front paw.

Charlie's throat rattled with mucous and he coughed and spit. He could smell the odors of stale beer from the glass pile, pigeon crap, and from somewhere, sweet mock orange blossoms. He staggered in the dim light, stiff and hunched over. Dirt covered his shoes and pant legs making it hard to tell where the earth ended and Charlie began.

Splaying his feet out of the way, he peed into the packed dirt. He glanced up at the play of headlights along the guardrails of the freeway overpass, the traffic heavy, even at night. "Poor bastards, Black. Bumper to bumper to nowhere."

Black's tongue lolled out and he panted.

Charlie looked at his reflection in the car window, cast in the light of the street lamps overhead. The cracks in the glass made a jigsaw puzzle of his face. Gray hair, thick as hay, hung down his neck, covering skin burned by years in the sun. Bloodshot eyes peered out past a nose etched with capillaries. He smiled into the glass, and picked at something between his teeth, what he had left of them.

"We got the shortest commute in all LA. Don't we, Black. Zippo. That's our commute. Oughta get a fuckin' reward from the air pollutin' district for that."

He patted the hood of the hearse that had been his home for the last seven years, petrified in a corner of the yard. A 1959 Cadillac with flat whitewall tires, broken transmission, all faded to a dull gray, as dead as the bodies it had hauled over the years.

Charlie cracked open the door and the dog bounded out, all ninety pounds of him. The Black Lab. The Black. The dog yawned and trotted over to where Charlie had peed. He snorted, then ripped at the dirt with his front paws, spraying the side of the Coup de Ville.

"Hey!" Charlie yelled. "Knock it off. You're wreckin' the paint job!"

Then Charlie heard a sound, tires on gravel. He peered through the dark and saw a car creeping along outside the perimeter fence, its lights off. Charlie froze but not Black. With a soft woof, the dog bounded off.

"Black," Charlie yelled in a whisper, but the dog was a torpedo on its run. Charlie saw a small flame light up a man's profile. The flame leapt up. Something in the man's hand. Charlie tried to yell, but nothing came out.

The man drew back his arm and just as he started to throw, Black blasted into the cyclone fence. The man jerked away, startled, and the flaming bottle flew wide of its mark. A roar of fire exploded in the yard, engulfing an old fork lift. Charlie threw his arm across his face. Black barked and attacked the fence. Charlie saw the man topple backwards, get up and stumble into the car, the door closing as it tore away.

Charlie ran to his car, rummaged through some junk, and grabbed a fire extinguisher, the only thing in his world that actually worked. Perhaps some residue of his days in the Navy—an all pervading fear of fire. Charlie pulled the pin and blasted the fire with foam. The heat seared his face, and he had to turn away, but the foam was working. He gave it another shot from the extinguisher and the fire was out, smoke and the smell of burned rubber drifting up from the smoldering forklift.

Black came trotting back, and Charlie patted the dog on the head, his hands shaking. The dog smelled of gasoline. "Good boy! Scared the shit out of 'em. Yessir. You got him, Black."

As the dog rolled in the dirt, Charlie meandered back to the hearse, reached into the glove compartment and pulled out a pint of Old Overholt that had a couple good belts left in it. He took one and sagged against the car, knowing he would get blamed for the fire. He was supposed to be watching out, but nothing like this had ever happened before.

His hands wouldn't stop trembling. He had felt the tension around the plant for the past month, the mutterings among the men about "the bid" swirling like litter on the wind. Charlie didn't like change and this firebomb was the beginning of it. Sooner or later, he'd have to call Naz and report in. He wondered if he had a dime for the pay phone, and hated the thought of wasting good money on a phone call.

Charlie took another swallow of whiskey and settled

down in the front seat of the hearse. Black hopped up beside him, dusty, panting, his eyes alive, ears still twitching, hoping for another sound in the darkness. Charlie threw an arm around his dog.

*   *   *

Carina stood in front of her bathroom mirror, smoothing cleansing cream on her face. She was tired from the Ball, and moved with well-rehearsed motions. She twisted her hair and clipped it on top of her head, then dampened a wash cloth. As she wiped off the cream, reality set back in. Not even the music, the dancing, the grip of her father's hand, could hold off the darkness for long.

The spidery legs of fear crawled up inside her. The fear that she would never be happy again, that the memory would haunt her, never truly forgotten, just hiding, only to well up at some unexpected moment and steal her breath away. And here it was, again.

He almost never took loads to the landfill. But when one of their drivers came down sick, Galen had jumped into the cab of the eighteen-wheel semi-truck full of trash. She remembered watching him pull out of the yard, the profile of his face through the cab window.

He could have sent one of the reserve drivers. If only he had, it wouldn't have been Galen standing there at the landfill when that truck filled with demolition debris dumping next to him, its bed raised 35 feet in the air, had toppled sideways in the soft earth. The other driver walked away—Galen didn't. His body had been crushed, even his beautiful face.

Carina swayed unsteadily and braced herself against the counter top. Looking in the mirror, she surveyed her hollow cheeks. She'd lost weight since the accident.

"Upright and taking nourishment," she said, straightening her shoulders. It was one of Galen's old expressions. A bittersweet smile spread across her face. See, there he is, still clinging to her life. They say a broken heart gets stronger in the broken places, but she knew it never forgets the breaking.

She looked over at a picture in a frame on her dresser. Galen Minasian, standing in the raised bucket of one of the loaders, arms spread wide—bigger than life. And so much like her father. Who'd have thought there could ever be another Nazareth Agajanian. Well, now there wasn't. She closed her eyes for a moment.

Carina dabbed eye makeup remover on a cotton ball, and gently rubbed it over her eyelids. It felt cool, soothing. She thought of her father and the relief Galen had provided him, the void he had filled. A son at last, even if only a son-in-law. But so much more. When Galen was killed six months ago, it not only took away her fiancé, it stole her father's future, his protégé, his link to the long line of Armenian life, to his unborn grandchildren.

She felt the familiar pressure that had haunted her as long as she could remember. Her parents had wanted more children, but then there was the infamous pap smear, when even her father knew that the hysterectomy was the only option for Mayda.

And that was that.

Only one child—and a girl, at that.

No matter what she did, no forklift driving,

swearing, drinking; no construction boots or hard hat was ever going to change that. Her father had trained her well. But he could never change her into the son he really wanted. In her father's eyes, her greatest achievement had died at the landfill.

Carina brushed away tears. God, she was tired of feeling like this. She clenched her teeth and thought of Pacific Rim. Even if she wasn't a man, her father had to admit that she was the future, as hard as it was for him to swallow. She could see it coming: curbside recycling, composting yard waste, power plants that made renewable electricity from trash, and everything on computers—even their secretary, Mrs. Avakian, would have one. Carina smiled at the thought, well, maybe not Mrs. Avakian.

She'd show her father. She'd write the best damn bid the city had ever seen. Little Miss God Almighty would show Alex Hart and the rest of them.

Carina flicked off the light and walked out of the bathroom.

* * *

The phone rang. Naz reached out and grabbed it in the dark. Mayda groaned next to him, and rolled to the far side of the bed.

"Yeah?" he said into the phone. Naz listened for a moment, then bolted up in bed. "What!" he yelled, flicking on the lamp.

Mayda groaned again. "Jesus, it's the middle of the night!"

"Charlie! Listen to me! Don't do nothing. I don't

want the cops snooping around, checking our god-damn registrations….You all right? OK. I'll deal with it in the morning." Naz hung up.

"What?" Mayda said, as Naz climbed back under the covers.

"Nothing."

She reached out and touched his arm. "What?"

"Someone tried to set the plant on fire."

"Just like Big Bear. They wouldn't sell to the Harts."

"That was an accident," said Naz.

"Right in the lake? Right in front of everyone?"

"It crashed, that's all. Happens all the time with those small planes."

"They said something was wrong, something was cut. . ."

Naz could see tears pooling in her eyes and took her by the shoulders. "No one's getting hurt. Now go to sleep."

He tucked the covers around her as she rolled away.

"Be careful, Nazareth."

"Careful's my middle name."

"And Mt. Ararat just flew to Paris," Mayda said, her voice muffled by the pillow.

Naz lay back and stared at the ceiling.

2

Black whimpered and sniffed Charlie's face. The old derelict didn't move, his face ashen, no sign of breath. Black barked and whined. He pawed Charlie's shoulder.

A minute went by. A minute thirty.

Not a flutter. Not a twitch. His chest quiet as stone. His face a mask.

Two minutes.

Black hovered over Charlie.

Slowly, the old man's lips parted, and a moan escaped, "Blaaaaaaack."

The dog barked and nudged Charlie with his nose.

Charlie rolled over on his mattress, took a deep breath, and hugged his dog. "Fooled your ass!"

It was a survival trick Charlie had learned as a child when he would get beat up at school—to pull deep inside himself. Then they could pound away at him, but it wouldn't matter, he was someplace else. He had perfected

21

the technique in the Navy, with all those macho assholes. Charlie would challenge the toughest to contests of holding their breath. Piece of cake. Charlie had become a guru of hibernation. Those yoga masters in India had nothing on him. He could slow his vital signs to virtual zero, all for a pint of alcohol or a carton of cigarettes.

Charlie and Black crawled out of the hearse and into the predawn grayness that edged Pacific Rim. The plant sat amid dilapidated warehouses. Nearby, the river gurgled by in its concrete channel under the freeway bridges converging on downtown L.A.

The cluster of metal buildings that made up Pacific Rim was arranged like a squared off letter "C." The office, such as it was, sat at one end. Along the long side of the "C" was the sorting plant where mixed trash was run up and over a series of screens, magnets, and conveyors that ran passed workers who separated out the recyclable material into a series of bunkers and bins down below. Opposite the office, was the area where they compacted the left over garbage from the sorting system into big-semi-trucks. This residual garbage was then hauled to the landfill for disposal. The recyclables were baled and loaded into trucks for hauling to domestic markets, or sea containers for shipment overseas. An open paved area in the center of the yard allowed the trash trucks to maneuver into the recycling building to dump their loads. Streaks of rust stained the corrugated metal walls, and a cyclone fence topped with concertina wire surrounded the site.

Charlie had run out of his cure-all, Old Overholt, and as he ambled across the yard, he rubbed his hands on his pants to try to quiet the shakes. He wondered what today's trash might bring.

Charlie was a small man, and even store-bought clothes had never looked right on him, hanging from his scrawny limbs. Now he had to make do with whatever he could sift out of the trash. His current outfit included a sweatshirt, a pair of oversized jeans hanging down over his heels, and red Converse All Star basketball shoes with the tongues torn out. On his head he wore an orange hard hat, the "Safety First" nearly faded away. He was the only one who wore a hard hat in the plant. It made him feel special. Besides, it offered some protection from the pigeon shit dropping from the rafters.

*   *   *

Naz bolted awake in the dark of the bedroom, sweating and disoriented. He groaned and lay back down on the bed, trying to shake the anxiety. The real fight for the bid had started with that firebomb at the plant. In addition, he desperately needed the second re-financing of the house to go through, and quickly. That infusion of cash would keep Pacific Rim pumping, and more importantly, cover the $100,000 bond that the city required for anyone submitting a bid. Normally, the bank would cover the bond with a ten percent deposit from Naz—but not in his current precarious financial position. With all his debt and IRS troubles, even the ice-cream man wouldn't give Naz credit. No doubt the Harts had someone's ear in the city on that one. Squeeze out the small guys with a killer bid bond.

Gray light dappled the room, and Mayda's black hair lay tussled on the pillow next to him. Naz ran his hand along the curve of her hip and it reminded him of a time thirty years ago. He had driven Mayda to a cove, tucked under the cliffs of Palos Verdes. Already light-headed after a few beers, they had scrambled down a rocky path in the dark to a secluded crescent moon beach. She sat tucked into the blanket as Naz started a fire of driftwood. How Mayda's brown eyes had glistened. With the swells of the Pacific crashing in shimmering lines of foam and the gulls crying from the ledges above, they had made love for the first time.

He remembered the clean, warm smell of her skin, his heart pounding as he kissed her full breasts, the catch of the air in her throat. And the slow, gentle ride that was as natural as breathing.

Naz sighed and let the memory drift away. Mayda moaned softly in her sleep. He kissed her cheek.

Naz walked down the gold-carpeted stairs into the living room. He punched on the tapedeck and an Italian aria flew up and filled the room, and he quickly turned the volume down so as not to wake Mayda. He loved the arias, even though he couldn't understand the words. He just floated on the emotion, and that was even better, especially on a rocky morning like this one.

Once he had the pot of coffee brewing, he lit his first cigar of the day.

Mayda woke to predawn light coming through the bedroom window. She could hear the opera from downstairs and smell the first waft of cigar smoke. It was Naz in the air around her, floating, soothing—her Naz. God he was a beautiful pain in the ass.

Out the bedroom window, Mayda saw a winter drizzle falling and it felt cold in the room. She pulled her knees up and tucked the covers under her chin.

Sometimes she wondered why she put up with it,

with the risks, with the fear that often haunted her. She preferred the known universe of family and friends and warm conversation, sweet cookies and soft linen sheets. Naz could sleep on a plank, and be tough, almost cruel at times; yet she had seen him save a drowning bee in their fountain by dipping a leaf under it and lifting it to safety. He couldn't stand to watch a living thing struggle, unless it was a competitor. That was different, and he'd tear their eyes out to protect the family business. She understood that as well.

Her brother-in-law, Jack, could kill a lion with his bare hands, but Naz was the ultimate fighter, not the biggest, not the strongest, but the most stubborn. And there was safety in that, something grounded and eternal. Arguing with Naz was like arguing with a rock. Naz would stand for what he felt in his heart and would fight to the death for it. And if he ever lost that fight, she would go down with him.

She heard Naz, singing along with the Italian aria, reach for a high note and butcher it, and she smiled.

*   *   *

Charlie passed the charred hulk of the forklift and walked into the recycling building. He saw the familiar, stooped figure of Harry Agajanian poking through the garbage with his cane. Naz's father showed up every day at 5:30 a.m. rain or shine. It was in a junkman's blood.

Harry was five-and-a-half feet tall and seventy-seven or eighty years old, depending on whether you believed the American immigration records, or him. Charlie had heard bits and pieces of the story; how Harry had escaped the Turks in the genocide back in 1915 or whenever it was, floating down some river to freedom with a bullet in him. But Harry never talked about it. Charlie could just sense the pain in Harry. He knew a thing or two about pain himself. But it wasn't just the pain that tied him to Harry, it was the brotherhood of survivors. He and Harry, they would be the last ones standing—if it ever came to that.

A halo of silver hair rimmed Harry's bald head giving him the look of a monk. He dressed in the same khaki work clothes he wore twenty years ago; his pants held up with red suspenders. They were well broken in, like everything else about him.

Charlie yelled, "Anything good in the trash this morning, Harry?"

"Always good in trash!" Harry knocked some cardboard aside with a beautiful cane made of polished burl wood with a gold handle in the shape of a duck's head. Naz had given it to him for his birthday. Harry pointed his cane at the burned forklift. "You have visitor?"

"It's because of the bid, ain't it? The one from City Sanitation I been hearin' about."

"You got good ears. Not like mine. No more I hear nothing."

"I'm just, you know, wonderin'...what if we lose? I mean, I don't think Naz could ever lose, him knowin' more about trash than anyone, but say on a long shot, somethin' goes wrong? Hell, stuff can go wrong, right?"

"Don't worry, Charlie." Harry tapped Charlie on the chest with his cane. "We win."

"I can drive a forklift," Charlie said. "You tell Naz. Security ain't the only thing I do."

"I tell him," Harry smiled at Charlie, his gold front tooth glinting in the light.

"Maybe we can make rocket fuel out of the trash," Charlie said, "Like that new movie, Back to the Future. I'll bet my old Caddy would even run on that stuff."

"Sound crazy, but one thing I know," Harry said.

"Yeah, what's that?"

"You never know."

"Makes sense to me," Charlie mumbled, "I sure as hell never do."

Just then, the Mexican crew started arriving, parking their cars and trickling into the building. They stared at the charred forklift and mumbled among themselves, then climbed onto loaders, and mounted the elevated conveyors to take their positions along the sorting line. Engines fired up. Conveyors whined. The blood of Pacific Rim started flowing.

The first garbage trucks came in off the night routes grinding down the access road and onto the weigh scales. Then, backing into the building, they groaned and bucked as they disgorged their loads.

Charlie glanced across the tipping floor.

"Goddammit!" he screamed, startling Harry.

As the load whooshed out of the truck, everyone saw the new jumper cables twisted like red and green snakes through the pile. Naz had set strict rules against personal salvaging, but like the other rules at Pacific Rim, it went right out the window when something was to be had.

Like vultures, the men swooped in. Usually, Charlie

would've seen the load coming and been in better position. He knew the roll-off containers, the big, truck bodies that special trucks could pick up on their backs. He had memorized their dings and dents and graffiti, and followed their migrations out to the customers and back like an old whale watcher, and he knew the good loads.

He would have been onto this load from the auto parts store, but talking to Harry had distracted him and, at his age and condition, Charlie just couldn't swoop like the others. He spotted a pair of jumper cables and grabbed it, but so did Rodrigo, the lead equipment operator. Charlie wrapped his end of the cables around his forearm, and the tug of war was on. Rodrigo had Charlie by fifty pounds, and Charlie had Rodrigo by twenty-five years. Not a good combination for Charlie.

"Let go, you cocksucker!" Charlie screamed.

Rodrigo planted his feet. As Charlie leaped around like a terrier at the end of a leash, the workers baited him.

"You get 'im, Charlie!"

"Where your *cojones*, Charlie?"

"Fuck you! You assholes," he shouted back.

Charlie was a long and masterful student of the science of losing, and he could smell it coming better than anyone. So Charlie did the only thing he could—he made a suicide charge. Rodrigo let Charlie pass by like a wounded bull, and when his charge reached the end of the cables, Rodrigo jerked Charlie's feet out from under him. Charlie landed flat on his back on a pile of vegetable crates.

Then came the soft growl. Rodrigo saw the dog just in time. He dropped the jumper cables as Black toppled him.

Charlie groaned to his feet, grabbed the jumper

cables, and limped off. "Black!" he yelled. "Black! Come here!"

Black let go of Rodrigo's arm and trotted up to Charlie. As they walked back to the hearse amid a chorus of insults and threats, Charlie raised his arm and, without turning back, gave the men the finger.

Naz's Lincoln Continental, with 200,000 miles on it and 200,000 to go, roared into the yard just in time to catch Charlie's final act. Naz slammed on the brakes, and leapt out. The license plate read, "TRASH."

"What the hell's goin' on here?" he yelled, a half-chewed cigar flying around his mouth. One of the workers said, "The dog bite Rodrigo."

Naz groaned. Same old shit. Maybe he should firebomb his own plant, take the insurance and be done with the whole thing. On second thought, he didn't have insurance.

Naz told Rodrigo to tow the scorched forklift out of sight. Let the others know it was just faulty wiring. No problem. Then he walked toward Charlie's hearse.

The derelict was a holdover from the days before Naz had bought the abandoned factory and turned it into a trash recycling plant. Every time Naz had shown up with the real estate agent, Charlie would be out sweeping with a broken down broom, or pretending to mend the cyclone fence, anything to look useful.

Naz carried a soft spot for the downtrodden, and when he'd bought the plant, he just didn't have the heart to toss Charlie out. And in the long run, Naz had figured, it might not be so bad to have someone on site twenty-four hours a day, especially someone he didn't have to pay, at least not regular. And even if Charlie couldn't guard his own ass, the dog was another story.

That's how Charlie became Vice-President of Security, and Black his First Assistant, or maybe it was the other way around.

The truth was that more worthless junk was stolen from the plant by Charlie than anyone else—busted pallets, broken TV sets, rusted spools of baling wire, balding tires. But Naz knew that most of it was still stashed in the dilapidated shipping container that squatted in the dirt behind Charlie's car. So technically, nothing was really stolen, just relocated.

Naz glanced at Black sprawled on the passenger seat of the hearse. He leaned on the door and peered in at Charlie. "Not enough excitement for one day?"

Charlie was rubbing Vaseline on his arm. That was the only medication he ever used, except, of course, for alcohol, which he usually took internally. "Asshole just about ripped my arm off."

"Stay out of the trash, you won't get hurt."

Charlie grimaced at a tender spot on his elbow.

"Last night," Naz said, "You were shitfaced."

"No, Naz, I swear. I was takin' a piss, and I hear the car creeping along. Then Black jumps on the fence, and the bottle explodes. The forklift's on fire. I grab the extinguisher and blast it."

"That's the official security report?"

"Yeah."

"We keep this between us, OK?" Naz handed a five-dollar bill through the window. "Buy your partner some dog food."

"Thanks, Naz."

As Naz walked away, Charlie waved the bill at Black. "ALPO!"

* * *

"Jesus Christ!" Alex said, bursting into the office. Kail Hart, Alex's father, looked up slowly from the papers arranged neatly on his mahogany desk.

"Good morning, Alex," he said, sliding his pen parallel with the edge of his blotter. A wooden boat model sailed the polished surface of the credenza behind him.

"What the hell were you thinking?" Alex whispered, glancing over his shoulder, as if someone might be listening.

Kail smiled and rose from his chair. He was still fit, well-proportioned, more like fifty-five than the seventy-plus he actually was. An impeccable, dark blue suit framed a starched white shirt open at the collar. His short gray hair was trimmed so it lay back smoothly, his nails polished clear. He turned and peered out the window at the huge landfill canyon and the long lines of garbage trucks queued at the scales. This was Hart Industries of America—HIA.

"We needed to get their attention," Kail said.

"With a firebomb?"

"They're still bidding."

"Their bid is bullshit." Alex paced the room. "Their pricing will be sky high! Using the county dump, with that gate fee? They'll be ten dollars over our rate."

"They're persistent. I have a longer memory than you."

"They're strangling. I put the IRS onto them. Their

equipment is falling apart. He can't raise the hundred grand for the bid bond. And on top of all that, I had that little chat with Zaven Petoyan. He's going to pull his loads from Pacific Rim. Their cash flow will plummet. The hole gets deeper and deeper."

"I talked to the corporate counsel for Global," Kail said. "He made it quite clear to me that they're looking at this Los Angeles bid as the linchpin of our merger. No contract, no 3,000 tons a day—no merger."

"You gave me the job, remember? It says 'President' on my name plate. The Board said they have total confidence in me."

"They do, Alex. As long as you win the bid. And they are nervous with the merger pending. I'm sure I don't need to remind you that losing the city's tonnage could be the beginning of an ugly trend, one that could ripple out, inspire others. We can't ever show them that we're vulnerable."

"So without even consulting me, you go off half-cocked and risk the whole thing by bombing Pacific Rim?"

Kail turned from the window. "I've told you many times. It's easier to throw a brick than to catch one. I'm afraid you still don't have the killer instinct."

Alex pressed his lips together. "You can't ever let go, can you?"

The senior Hart sat back down at his desk without looking up. "I suggest you save your venom for the enemy." His gaze lifted to Alex and he smiled.

Alex stormed out.

Kail picked up a framed photo on his desk of older son Alex, and younger Michael as boys standing on either side of him. All smiles.

He never was able to connect with Mike, a quiet, sensitive boy, more like his mother. Not interested in the trash business, he had gone off to a liberal arts college in New England and stayed there as a drug and alcohol addiction counselor. Rarely to be seen again.

Alex was a different story and relished the family business, often skipping school to help paint bins, or change truck tires. Yet Kail had always expected more of him. Perhaps he had failed him in some ways as a father, especially after Alex's mother passed away. Maybe he was too tough on him. At times, he wishes they had been closer.

But there was little room for that now, with all they'd worked for on the line. And it was too late anyway.

He adjusted the picture frame and went back to his paperwork.

Back in his office, Alex closed the door and slumped on the couch. If his father wanted hardball, he'd give him hardball.

Naz Agajanian wasn't the problem. His own father, the great Kail Hart, was. Alex was confident he could beat Pacific Rim on the bid. It was no contest, in spite of his father's concern. Even if by some act of Divine Intervention Naz won the bid, he could never pass the performance test with that piece of shit plant of his. Naz couldn't bluff his way through this one. No, the bid was safe, but his father would never give up control, would never step aside unless he were pushed.

Then the old vision roared up behind Alex's eyes.

Twelve years old, in his backyard. The weight of the padded gloves on his hands, the rubbery mouthpiece between his teeth. The air hot and humid, smell of the grass. The face of his younger brother weaves into view, then slips away against the ropes of the makeshift boxing ring.

"Come on, Alex!" his father yells. "Chase him, cut off the ring. Throw some punches, for Chrissake." Alex grimaces and stalks his brother. Fear in the younger boy's eyes. Alex throws a left jab into his brother's gloves, then a soft right that glances off his brother's forehead.

"Go down, Mikey!" he whispers through his mouthpiece. He hits his brother hard on the shoulder. Then he sees his brother drop his gloves and gaze past him. He turns to see his father climb into the ring, pulling on his gloves.

"Get out of the ring, Mike," his father says. "You call that boxing?" He turns to Alex. "You won't hit him? Maybe you'll hit me." His father circles to his left, raising his fists.

"I don't want to fight you," Alex says, arms hanging at his sides. His father punches him in the stomach. Pain, gagging for breath, doubled over, covering his mid-section and struggling to stay on his feet. "I don't want to fight you!" he yells in tears.

"You don't want to fight anyone," his father says calmly. He throws a jab that snaps Alex's head back. "Never going to make a man of yourself that way. Here, take a shot at me." His father sticks his chin out, hands down. "Come on. Hit me!" As Alex cocks his right arm half-heartedly, his father punches him hard in the face.

Back in his office, Alex jerked on the couch. Unconsciously, he touched the scar across the bridge of his nose.

3

The men on the sorting lines at Pacific Rim turned at the slam of the car door and watched Carina Agajanian, with her long legs and cascade of black hair, emerge from her red El Camino and walk into the office.

She walked past the counter in the reception area that doubled as kitchen and noticed the vile-looking coffee sitting in a brown crust, and the creamer spilled on the floor. She shook her head. Charlie.

Carina glanced in Mrs. Avakian's office, not much more than a converted closet, and waved to their ancient secretary, who was busy on the phone taking down a message in her precise shorthand. Mrs. Avakian smiled and nodded back. Carina eyed the plate of dried figs and squares of baklava that Mrs. Avakian always brought in. She grabbed a fig, and plopped it in her mouth. The sweet flavor erupted. Good old Mrs. Avakian.

Mrs. Avakian's office stood like an island of order in the sea of chaos that was Pacific Rim: equipment catalogs alphabetized on bookshelves, an in and out box with nothing in the "in" section, and a pile of neat documents in the "out." And this was at seven in the morning. Carina knew that without Mrs. A. they would drown.

Carina dropped her purse on her desk and gazed out her office window at the view of a nearby high-tension tower and rusted flatcars on the railroad spur down behind the abandoned cold storage warehouse. Those flatcars had been there forever, carrying nothing now but rust and graffiti.

The walls of Carina's office were hung with posters of smiling grime-faced race car drivers, cars side-to-side in the curves, aerial photos of a speedway at night, the lights blazing down on the oval of blurred color. Various automobile bric-a-brac, ranging from a mutilated piston to an autographed steering wheel, was scattered across her shelves. And there, conspicuous in the center, sat a racer's helmet, black with a tinted visor. Not just any helmet—her helmet.

A year ago, Carina barely knew stock cars existed. To her, it was just a bunch of fat guys from Alabama full of testosterone and beer, blasting around and around in a cloud of dust and exhaust. But Galen had dragged her down that one Sunday night to the dirt track in the South Bay. When they had wedged themselves in the bleachers between a bunch of rednecks from Pomona and a leather-jacketed Hells Angels gang from Lancaster, she knew she was in the wrong place—until the engines started. In that moment, she became a stock car fan.

The combination of sound, power, light and speed enthralled her; the bleachers vibrating from the roar, the dirt flying, the cars banging in the turns, the smell of fuel, fire, carbon, the wonderful animal adrenaline of it all. It was perfect.

She had even gone as far as signing up with Galen for racing lessons, finished her classroom work and solo trial laps, and had run hundreds of simulated race laps against her instructor and Galen. And she was good. The instructor had said so, and he was a man of few words and no bullshit, unlike so many of the other men in her life.

The phone rang on Carina's desk. "Pacific Rim," she answered.

"Miss Agajanian?" said the upbeat voice on the phone. "I was expecting your secretary. This is Bernard Dashman."

Carina sagged onto the edge of her desk, one leg still anchored to the floor, and mouthed "shit." The IRS. She took a deep breath, searching her library of excuses, stalling, then said, "Yeah. Mr. Dashman. How are you doing?"

"Listen Miss Agajanian, I'm sure you know why I'm calling."

"Wouldn't have a clue."

"Your last three payroll tax payments are overdue. Twenty thousand for January. Twenty thousand for February. And last but not least, twenty thousand for March."

Carina decided to go right to her strong suit. Putting a little breath in her voice she said, "Listen, Bernie—it's all right to call you Bernie?"

"Uh...."

"Bernie. I really appreciated your meeting with us

last week. You know we're good for the payments. It's just that cash flow is incredibly tight, but that's only temporary."

"Look, Miss Agajanian...."

"Carina."

"Yes, uh...I know you mean well, but...."

"You know we're like a family here, Bernie. My Dad won't lay off anybody, especially guys who've worked here half their lives. I tried to tell him we can't afford to carry people, but you know how he is."

Dashman's voice softened. "I'm not sure he appreciates the gravity of the situation."

"Bernie, can't you work with me on this? Cut us just a little slack?" She heard him hesitate.

"I'd love to, uh, work with you," he replied, "but unfortunately, my supervisor has already laid down the law. You're so far behind there's very little negotiating room left." He paused. "The best I could possibly do, and I'm sticking my neck way out for you, is ten thousand by Friday, or enforcement is going to take it out of my hands and put liens on your bank accounts."

Naz walked into Carina's office, lost in thought, twirling a cigar in his mouth. He was wearing a Hawaii shirt and shorts.

"OK. You have my word," she said. "Ten thousand by Friday. I appreciate it, Bernie." She hung up. God, she was really tired of this. It was like slogging through deep mud.

Naz snapped out of his reverie and frowned. "$10,000! Where the hell are we going to get that?"

Carina glared at her father. "We owe sixty! You think I like this?"

"You do what you gotta do. Just do it better next time."

"Better!" Carina yelled. "I'm getting tired of lying!"

"It's not lying, it's saving the company!" Naz said.

"You never listen!"

"I'm listening now!"

"That's not listening! You can't wait to scream your next thought at me!"

"Jesus Christ!," Naz screamed at her.

Naz had been waiting for the right moment to tell her about the firebombing, and realized this wasn't it.

"Look at this place!" she yelled. "We're strangling because we're under-capitalized."

"No shit?"

"If it weren't for goddamn baling wire, the whole plant would fall apart," Carina yelled. "There's never enough of anything around here to do it right."

Naz pulled the cigar out of his mouth and pointed it at her. "I've been doing this since before you were born. You don't tell me what's right!"

"Well someone has to tell you, or we'll all be out on the street!"

"Hey, the door's right over there!"

Carina screamed, "Nothing I say means anything to you! It never has." Tears in her eyes, Carina stomped out, nearly knocking over Mrs. Avakian.

Naz roared past Mrs. Avakian the other way, stormed into his office and slammed the door.

The sound boomed around Naz's office. He heard Carina's car drive off, and he took a few deep breaths. He sat down at his desk, then threw a pencil across the room, "Goddammit!" It bounced off the fake wood paneling and fell to the linoleum floor.

Women could be such a pain in the ass, especially ones you're related to. Make one innocent comment and a bomb of emotions goes off in your face. It was like walking through a mine field. But what could you do? Nothing. That's the killer. Occasionally, you could fix it. Shouldn't you be able to fix it? But most of the time it was fucked beyond repair; at least for a while.

Naz looked out over his desk. He subscribed to the "pile" theory of document management. Piles of manila folders and papers covered every surface and spilled over to the floor. Each was crowned with its own special paperweight, souvenirs plucked from the trash over the years. A toy garbage truck, half a bowling ball, a shell from an anti-aircraft gun, rumored to still be "live", or so Naz would tell visitors when he was trying to shorten meetings.

Black and white photographs peppered the wall behind his desk, horse-drawn wagons with trash piled high and men in hats holding the reins. In one photo, a young boy sat behind the wheel of an ancient forklift: Nazareth Agajanian. The photo menagerie was Naz's personal rubbishman's Wall of Fame.

And above it all, a framed photograph of *Agri Dagi*, Mt. Ararat, the holy mountain of Armenia. It was the symbol of his homeland, the mountain where ancient tradition says Noah's Ark came to rest after the flood. His father could hardly look at it without getting tears in his eyes. At those moments, Naz would put his arm around his father's shoulders and say, "The mountain is with us."

But now, alone, Naz looked at Mt. Ararat and felt the

crushing weight of it all. If he lost this City of L.A. bid, he would lose not just the contract, not just the family business, but Mt. Ararat itself. Naz slumped in his chair and held his head in his hands.

Twenty minutes later, Carina walked in and handed her father a bottle of Tums. "Thought you could use these. I popped a couple myself on the way back."

Naz took the bottle. "Thanks," he said.

"Sorry about the, uh, discussion. I just get frustrated," said Carina.

"After we win this bid, things'll be different," said Naz. "Hell, we might even be over-capitalized, if there is such a thing. Then you can try all your fancy ideas, composting, turning trash into dog food, shooting it into space. Who knows?"

"I'll remember you said that." She started to go.

"One other thing you should know," Naz said. She turned back, waiting for him to continue.

"Someone tried to firebomb the plant last night. Got one of the forklifts."

"What? Why didn't you tell me!"

"Apparently, our Vice-President of Security was taking a leak when it happened, but the dog scared them off."

"You think it was Alex?"

"Maybe old man Hartunian got tired of the way Alex was handling it."

"Jesus Christ."

"I had Rodrigo tow it out back, and check it for parts. Your grandfather knows, too," Naz said. "No use telling anyone else. It'll just scare them more than they already are about losing their jobs if the bid goes bad."

"I know the feeling," Carina said as she walked out.

Naz popped his cigar in his mouth and got up from his chair. It squeaked and dropped a bolt to the floor in protest. Place was falling down around him. He gazed out the window and watched a battered pickup truck pull onto the scale, the vehicle sagging under its load of flattened cardboard. It was one of Naz's small army of scavengers. Naz had dropped a re-built transmission in that truck about a year ago for virtually nothing. But the man came in every day with a ton and a half of cardboard and would never go anywhere else. Naz got used oil and tires for other guys, you name it. Whatever it took to keep them rolling. It all added up. To Naz, the loyalty of men like these was priceless—especially now, when he was down and hurting.

Naz wiped some dust from the windowsill. The Consolidated Fibers deal six years ago, that's when the slide started. The whole affair had settled in like cancer. It would go into remission, and then come back with a vengeance. There were times he wanted to rip out his own mind.

Goddammit, if he'd only grabbed the Consolidated offer when it was on the table. Five million dollars. It hurt his heart to think of it now. The wastepaper market was booming. All the trends looked good—virgin pulp pricing, the buying patterns of the Asian mills, domestic consumption.

Riding a wave of prosperity, the Consolidated Fibers Paper Mill was expanding and short on wastepaper supply. And here he was, sitting on 15,000 bales of cardboard and a nice little wastepaper collection operation. He had all the printing plants, the big downtown accounts and the street scavengers coming in droves.

That's when he had built the house in the hills behind Glendale, 5,000 square feet with the long circular drive, five bedrooms and four baths, the guest house, pool, Jacuzzi, and outdoor grill for cooking the shish kabab.

That's when he was rolling and had some leverage. He had bought twenty acres of spec land in Corona, turned around a stagnant wastepaper operation in Modesto, bought controlling interest in a south-central L.A. scrap metal yard. It was a sellers market and he cut long-term delivery deals with mills in Taiwan, Japan and Korea, with guaranteed floor prices and revenue sharing upsides.

And deliver he did, 4,000 tons a month, then 7,500 and finally 10,000. The banks were throwing money at him, offering lines of credit below market rates with no points, just to get in on his next move. There were nights when half the Armenians in LA, from Boyle Heights to Montebello, were drunk on *oghi* in his front yard, and the other half smoking cigars around the pool as the music of the mandolin, flute and drum bounced off the chaparral covered hills.

And above all, the joy of seeing his father Harry, sitting in a wicker chair by the pool, tapping his cane to the music, the father of it all, 10,000 miles from Armenia, 30,000 days from what he thought had been the end of his life.

Naz had the upper hand. He knew it. Consolidated knew it. So he did what any smart businessman would do, what Consolidated would do…he held out for more.

No one saw it coming.

At first, Naz thought it was just an anomaly, a couple of bad reports on the Asian market, a little dip in demand, but then it snowballed into an avalanche. Overnight, the

Asian mills stopped buying, the export market went to hell, the domestic mills went into oversupply, and the price of wastepaper fell through the floor. Shit, it fell through the basement.

Suddenly, he was scrambling.

Consolidated wouldn't return his calls. His 15,000 bale inventory dropped from a value of $1.5 million to zilch. And just like that, the opportunity was gone. And this time, the market rebound was a long time coming. Too long, as it turned out.

He liquidated his holdings and consolidated everything, such as it was, into Pacific Rim. Still unable to stop the bleeding, he did the only thing he could. He cheated.

He knew he wouldn't get away with shorting the IRS on payroll taxes for long. All he had needed was a little breathing room. His back was not only up against the wall, he could feel the bricks coming out through his teeth.

Goddamn, that Consolidated deal!

Back in his office and back to reality, Naz took a deep breath and sighed. Then the idea crept back into his mind, the one he'd been mulling over for months. Just maybe, the ace in the hole he needed for the bid. He would work some more on that later. But now, he had to create some shit even to make it to the bid. Luckily, no one could create shit like he could.

"Mrs. Avakian!" Naz yelled.

"Coming Nazareth!"

Naz glanced down at the cluster of pink slips on his desk...termination notices for four of his laborers, good ones. All had worked for him over five years—damn hard workers, and part of the unofficial, extended family at Pacific Rim. He closed his eyes and dropped his head. Sometimes, you got to do what you got to do, no matter the cost.

Mrs. Avakian scurried in with her steno pad, just like she had for almost two decades. She reminded Naz of a trained squirrel, with her small, pinched face, and flat brown hair.

"We got to find $10,000 for our IRS pals," Naz said.

"Unless you know something I don't," she said, moving a pile of paper from a chair and taking a seat in front of his desk, "We don't have it."

Naz twirled the cigar in his mouth and raised his eyebrows at her in a knowing glance. She nodded and said, "We're going to sell another piece of worthless equipment."

"The Cat backhoe. Tell Jack to drag the sonuvabitch out and put it beside the scale house."

"After this, we're down to your car."

As she walked out, Naz stared at the pink slips. "Fuck it," he whispered, then tore them up and tossed them in the wastebasket.

* * *

Later that afternoon, Carina's nails clicked on the Selectric typewriter keys, her back to the door of the office. Suddenly, she felt a presence in the room like the breath of an animal on the back of her neck. The smell of heavy aftershave. She turned, startled.

"Zaven! What a surprise," her throat tightening.

The big man wore a rust-colored silk shirt unbuttoned

to mid-chest. A heavy, gold bracelet hung from a wrist that looked like a two-by-four with a hand on it. His pants fit tight, and his big thighs pulled the pleats flat. Close-cropped black hair flowed down his neck like fur. His bulk alone was threatening, but it was the eyes that always set Carina on edge...like dark pools that had no bottom. He reminded her of something nocturnal, a reptile that hunts at night. A tremor ran down her back.

Zaven Petoyan dropped a pair of large, gold hoop earrings on her blotter.

"What are these?" Carina said, not touching them. Armenian women knew their jewelry, and these were expensive.

"For you."

"I can't take those."

"Why not? They ain't stolen."

"Look, Zaven...."

"I seen you last night, at the Ball," he said. "You dance pretty good."

"It runs in the family," Carina said, revolted by the thought of him watching her dance. She felt his eyes running over her body, but fought down the urge to bolt for the door. She knew her father and all of Pacific Rim walked a delicate line with the man her father had once saved from the streets. At this point, none of them gave a rat's ass about Zaven and she knew the feeling was mutual. But they needed each other. Zaven needed Pacific Rim for quick easy dumping for his collection routes along the industrial corridor flanking the river, each truck saving over an hour per load compared to the long haul to dump at the Hart's landfill. That meant more time on the routes, more accounts serviced and more profit. And Pacific Rim needed the tipping fees from Zaven's 300 tons a day, about a quarter of their total volume, and the revenue from the cardboard and other recyclables they sorted out. But to Carina, if felt like sleeping with the enemy.

Zaven picked up a picture of Carina and Galen that was sitting on her desk. "Tough about Galen. But everyone's got to move on, sooner or later." He set the frame down facing away from her. "Maybe I'll give you a call."

"I'm afraid I'm pretty tied up these days. The bid, you know." Carina saw Zaven perusing the papers scattered on her desk, and she nonchalantly reached out and stuffed them in a drawer.

Zaven nodded as if remembering. "That's right, the bid. Good luck on that."

"We'll be all right."

Zaven leaned over her desk. "You need any help, you let me know." He patted her on the shoulder, his hand lingering. She stared at his hand, then his face.

"Your dad around?" he said.

"In the plant."

As he walked out of her office, he turned. "Those earrings'll look good on you."

She watched him walk into the yard, and heard her mind loud and clear: don't ever turn your back on Zaven Petoyan.

Naz stood on the baler platform. He could feel the machinery around him, its throbbing hydraulics like his own pulse. He peered down into the baler chamber. "OK, Jack. Get out of there and let's give her a shot."

Jack Oseppian, Naz's brother-in-law, grabbed a railing

and sprang up out of the baler pit. Jack was married to Naz's older sister, Sophie, which should win Jack the Medal of Honor, or at least a Purple Heart, as far as Naz was concerned. Jack wiped his hands on a rag. His thick upper arms and shoulders carried down a long torso to legs that looked like they could hold up a bridge. His brown eyes were alert and closely spaced, a cropped beard shading his jaw. With his clean flannel shirt and work boots, he looked like a lumberjack out of a Sears catalogue.

"That should hold her for awhile. But she really needs a whole new ram," Jack said, his voice soft yet with an edge, like something hard swathed in cotton. "Sure miss Galen. He was something around equipment."

Naz grimaced. He missed Galen in everything. He could still hear his laugh echoing around the plant. See his smiling face. "After we win the bid, we'll buy a new goddamn baler," Naz said.

"Hope she holds, Naz."

"Me, too. Just baby the sonuvabitch."

Naz glanced up and saw Zaven approaching across the yard, his legs splayed out to allow the heavy thighs to scrape past each other, his face rigid and eyes glaring, a smirk on his face. He watched Zaven squint into the shadows of the building, his head rotating like a tank turret. It would be easy to think a gorilla like Petoyan would be dumb as a sack of hammers; but Naz knew different. Zaven was a survivor from the time he was a street urchin living on what he could steal from the good recycling accounts. And by the time he was a teenager, he had gotten good at stealing. Naz had finally caught him taking cardboard from one of Pacific Rim's bins behind a printing plant. Instead of turning him over to the authorities, or beating the hell out of him, Naz had seen the upside potential in the young delinquent, and "sponsored" him, so to speak—sending Zaven out as an official scavenger, picking up recyclables at accounts too small to service with a regular Pacific Rim truck. With the good prices Naz paid him for his deliveries, Zaven prospered. The kid had real promise, business sense, and tenacity. Within a few years he had his first trash truck, and he would build it from there.

Naz knew all along that the street part of Zaven ran deep, like it did in most of the trash guys, and that everyone had to cover their own ass, protect their turf to survive. In fact, he admired all that. Still, he was surprised when Zaven became more and more secretive, untrustworthy, even threatening as his little empire grew. Maybe it was like the chickens that Naz's mother raised in the back yard. The youngest, lowest ones in the pecking order became the most vicious once they had grown older and bigger and had others below them. Well, Zaven was a big man now in money, power and pure girth. And there were no word of thanks to Naz for saving his ass, no favors returned, not even a cigar. Since loyalty was high on Naz's scale, Zaven's stock had plummeted.

"Hey, Naz!" Zaven yelled, "How are ya?"

"You know damn well how I am," Naz shouted back. "For shit. That's how I am." The cigar bobbed in his mouth as he talked.

"Aw, come on, Naz. I'm your best customer." Zaven's mouth tipped up in an innocent smile, but his eyes stared, unblinking. He held out his right hand.

"Don't give me that friendly crap," Naz ignored the hand.

"What's the problem around this place?" Zaven said. "I drive all the way down to this garden spot and everyone treats me like a leper."

"Pay your bills, and I'll treat you like the fucking Queen of England."

"Your gate fees are way out of line!" Zaven yelled. "I'm bringing you rich loads here." Zaven pointed at one of his trucks rolling across the scale. "I don't mind you making a little profit, but forty dollars a ton is bullshit."

Naz ripped the cigar out of his mouth. "I should be charging you eighty for the garbage you bring in here!" he said.

Even with the noise of the machinery, the workers could hear the exchange, and they watched from their perches on the equipment. Zaven's head twitched to the side, his jaw set and his fists clenched.

"You owe me $15,000 in tipping fees! Naz screamed. He punctuated the last word by launching a poke at Zaven's chest.

Petoyan's hand shot up and grabbed Naz's wrist. Through gritted teeth, he spat out "Fuck you, pal! I'm pulling out all my tonnage. You and your plant can rot...."

Naz swung from the waist with a left hook, but the punch just glanced off Zaven's shoulder. Zaven's right arm cocked just as Jack slammed into him from the blind side, low and hard. The blow caught Zaven in the rib cage, knocking the wind out of him and sending him down hard. He gasped for breath as Jack restrained Naz, who was flailing wildly, trying to get a piece of Zaven.

Like a wounded bear, Zaven rolled to his feet, arms

wide, as if to crush the whole plant. Naz's men scrambled from their workstations. Rodrigo, the crew chief, appeared first at Naz's shoulder, the rest formed a ragtag but formidable group behind.

Zaven pointed a finger at Naz. "Someday Jack won't be around to save your ass." He spat on the ground. "Or your army of wetbacks." He turned and walked toward his pickup truck.

Carina yelled at Zaven from the doorway of the office, "Don't forget to weigh out!" Zaven fixed her with a brutal glare, piled in his pickup truck, gunned the engine and roared off.

Black raced out from behind Charlie's hearse and attacked the front tire of Zaven's truck. Zaven swerved into the dog and clipped him with the fender, sending Black sprawling in the dirt, stunned.

Charlie ran at Zaven, trying to punch the car as it rocketed past. "Cocksucker!" he screamed. Charlie turned to Black, but the dog was already up looking for the car. Charlie patted his dog's head. "You'll get him next time." Charlie glared after Zaven's pickup as it disappeared down the access road.

Carina appeared behind Naz and laid a hand on his shoulder.

"That sonuvabitch," he muttered.

"Dad?"

"Thinks he can —"

"Dad. Come on."

"What, goddammit!"

Carina caught his gaze. "Come on, it's late," she said. "I'll buy you a Stoli at Elena's."

"Without Zaven's tonnage, could be the last one I ever have."

Carina said, "It ain't over till the fat lady sings."

"I hear her warming up in the wings," he said.

She listened for a second. "That's just the compactor blowing out it's hydraulics."

Naz smiled. "All right. Fuck it."

Carina put her arm around her father and they started back across the yard.

*   *   *

All was quiet during the graveyard shift at the Hart Industries Material Recovery Facility, except for the sound of a solitary truck approaching. Security lights shone from the observation deck, silhouetting a lone figure that looked out over the floor of the massive operation.

Alex and his father had built the recycling plant next to their landfill to siphon as much tonnage as possible away from Pacific Rim, and to prepare for the L.A. bid they knew was coming. Alex himself had rammed the permitting and plan checks through the city bureaucracy in record time. It paid to have contacts. But this was no junkyard like Pacific Rim. It had a black glass façade, decorative masonry, a visitor's center, and a recycling exhibit with miniature cranes and magnets that school kids could operate. There was a talking tree made out of aluminum cans, and a metal sculpture of children on a swing that Alex had commissioned some local artist to create out of junk pulled from the trash. That sculpture had cost him \$50,000. All told, he'd sunk twenty million dollars into the plant.

Inside the building, that was as large as three football fields, it was all state-of-the-art with a chemically-enhanced misting system to knock down dust and odor in the tipping area, hardened concrete floors, a menagerie of equipment, conveyors, screens, air classifiers, an eddy current magnet to recover aluminum cans. It was the Taj Mahal of recycling.

Looking out over his domain from his glass paneled office high above the floor, Alex remembered the Gala Grand Opening when the L.A. City Councilmembers ate it up, literally and figuratively. Ice mountains of shrimp rising in front of the baler, black-tie waiters circulating among the brand new loaders and forklifts with trays of mushrooms stuffed with crabmeat, Swedish meatballs, a jazz band playing on the loading dock. Alex knew how to work the politicians, make them feel like champions, like they had actually built this marvelous plant.

In truth, Alex wouldn't have bothered with recycling at all if it weren't for the clamoring of the goddamn environmentalists, and more importantly, the ranting of the City Council about their recycling target. In reality, recycling made as much difference as a pimple on a bull elephant's ass. No one made money recycling. There was no gold in garbage. The gold was in picking it up and burying it—that was the bull elephant.

From his high vantage point, Alex watched the lone roll-off truck pull into the building. One of his special loads, this one came from the plant in South Gate that manufactured catalytic converters for automobile exhaust systems. The truck dumped its recycling load of office paper and cardboard, then pulled out. The door rolled down.

One edge of a metal ingot stuck out of the pile and glinted under the lights. Alex gestured to his man on the floor below, who waded in and dragged the heavy object out. He placed it on the feed conveyor to the baler and dumped some cardboard behind it. The metal ingot and cardboard rode up the conveyor and dropped into the bale chamber that was already loaded half-full. The hydraulics kicked on and the rams compressed the cardboard into a tight bale around the ingot. The worker forklifted the bale into a loaded shipping container, closed the rear doors and seated the locking bars with a clang.

Alex sat down at his desk. He unlocked a drawer in his credenza and pulled out a leather binder. Opening it to a master spreadsheet, he checked the listing of his special "accounts" and their deliveries. Disgruntled, underpaid custodians were not hard to find, most of them long-tenured and looking at retirement near the poverty line. Not a pretty sight. A few nights of risk would turn that all around and set them up for the rest of their lives. So far, it had gone flawlessly.

There were twelve in total, operating on and off over the past year smuggling advanced computer circuit boards, composite resins for aircraft components, platinum ingots, and other items—all wired into the black market overseas through the paper mill in Taiwan. The shipments were marked, the special bales recovered. It was a piece of cake.

He punched some numbers on his calculator, looked at the total, and smiled. Not long now, maybe another month, he'd have the money he needed to influence certain members of the HIA Board of Directors and take down his father. He'd already laid the groundwork, the fix was in.

Alex knew he had to look out for his own. After all these years, the battles fought, the victories won. Sure, there were the promises. The "passing of the torch" speeches. Yet his father still held all the stock.

He knew the smuggling scheme was a huge risk. If discovered, it would blow the lid off everything and essentially bury him, and perhaps the whole company. But his father left him no choice, racing ahead with the mega-merger that would leave himself with a fortune and Alex with a herd of corporate ax-men and bean counters breathing down his neck.

By the time his little black-market deal was over, Alex would have a couple million socked away. Then he would go after the boxing king and his merger.

Alex snorted to clear his nose.

*　　*　　*

The dealer's hands fluttered like doves and the cards slid across the green velvet table. Although his face was calm as stone, Jack Oseppian had to fight to keep his hands from trembling. He sat in the back room of the casino down in the industrial bowels of the city, at the "no limit" table reserved for select players that the owner knew.

The waitress brought another scotch on the rocks, his fourth. Jack tipped her five bucks and took the drink down in a swallow. He could feel the alcohol working, rounding the sharp edges of his nerves, his dilemma.

Money.

He needed it, and needed it bad. For the past year, maybe more, it felt as if someone had opened a vein in him and was slowly sucking him dry. The mortgage payment, private school for the girls, the pool man, the maid, the gardener, the new car, copper plumbing, and always Sophie's spending—furniture, remodeling the kitchen, although she didn't even like to cook. Naz called the kitchen the most expensive can opener in the world. And if Pacific Rim lost the bid and went under, Jack would go down with it like one of those Roman galley slaves chained to his oar.

He felt helpless against such a falling tide. His only hope—the black jack table. Here, he found order. For all his compulsion, his obsession, he kept himself in check with his system, and he played it religiously. He was a master card counter, maybe he had one of those photographic minds. Even with four decks in the sleeve, Jack could track the face cards, gauge the odds of getting one on a hit, of the dealer busting.

But Jack had been losing all night. Hell, he had been losing for weeks. He had never suffered such a string of bad luck. The cards just wouldn't fall. But he knew that all it took was one hand, one good hand, like the first nudge of a rudder, to turn the entire ship of luck. Here, miracles were possible, but he needed one now.

His first card was coming. If he saw another four or five, he was going to fold. Instead, the king of spades.

Funny, how Naz never trusted him with the higher level decisions, the thinking stuff—like the bid. No, he was just Jack, the loyal brother-in-law, the mechanic, the muscle. Maybe his curse was that he could fix anything with a length of wire and pair of two-bit pliers. Maybe if he wasn't so good with his hands, Naz would recognize him for his mind. It didn't seem right, after all Jack had done for Naz and the family.

The dealer threw Jack his second card, face down. Jack lifted the edge and glanced at it—a second king. His heart quickened, and he looked at his pile of chips.

They called it "scared money" in the trade...money you couldn't afford to lose. And conventional wisdom said never play with it. It was as if the cards could smell your fear and the good ones stayed away. Jack had never played with scared money before. That was part of the system. But he couldn't turn to Naz for money again, and yet he couldn't climb out of the hole without a major move. Scared money was all he had left. Those chips represented a chunk of the college funds for his daughters, $10,000—money he could never earn back. But if he could double it in one strike....

Jack felt in his gut that this was it. He had told himself a thousand times not to trust his gut—to trust only the cards, his system. But now he could get ahead for once, get some leverage, create a hedge against the uncertain future.

The dealer drew a seven. Bad for the dealer, good for the table.

Jack shoved his entire pile of chips into the center of the table. Then he took out his checkbook and wrote a check for $40,000 and slid it over with his chips.

That got the attention of the pit boss, who drifted over from a nearby table. The man surveyed the check, glanced at Jack and nodded to the dealer. The dealer dealt Jack a card.

*　　*　　*

Ten minutes later, Jack stood in the casino parking lot. His pallor was ashen and he felt hollowed out, like a cadaver after all the organs have been removed. He couldn't remember where he had parked his car, and wasn't certain he wanted to find it.

He should have won. All the odds were screaming in his favor. He had a twenty count—and the dealer showing that seven. Then he had watched as the dealer drew a queen for a count of seventeen. Perfect. The dealer had to hit that seventeen and all the odds said he would bust, screamed he would bust.

Goddamn, that four of hearts.

Jack leaned against a light pole. In his mind, he ticked off the names of those he could hit up for loans, but he had already burned too many bridges. After the last bail out, he had sworn to Naz that it would never happen again.

Jack wandered across the parking lot, climbed into his car and sat behind the wheel, staring out the window. He reached into his coat pocket and pulled out the business card the pit boss had slipped to him as he had pushed back from the table. Alex Hart's card. Nothing written on it, no note, no message —but Jack could read it loud and clear. They must have been watching him.

He should tear up that card right now, Jack thought. He turned it in his fingers, then tucked it away.

4

Harry Agajanian knelt in the warm earth, working
the trowel among the cucumber plants, dislodging
weeds, loosening the soil. A wide-brimmed hat shaded
his face and the patch of ground in front of him. He
picked up a clod of clay and tossed it against the fence.
This soil required so much work, not like the wondrous
dirt in Fresno that fell apart under the plow, full of nutrients and rich humus.

Harry let his mind wander as his hands worked.

Fresno, 1933. God, she was beautiful—his Armi. He
could see her down by the river, her body wet and tight
in her swimming suit. All of them laughing and drinking homemade *oghi* out of milk bottles, the feel of her
bare thigh brushing against his.

And then the shadow falling over them, over their
lives—Kail Hartunian. While Harry grunted on his scrap
route, hefting 55-gallon drums of glass and cans, bundles

of cardboard into his old truck, Kail was already learning to work the system, attending City Council fundraisers, greasing palms, hiring someone's favorite nephew, brown-nosing the old Armenian guard. Harry knew that the only thing Kail Hartunian didn't have was what he wanted more than anything—Armi Papparian, the beautiful young woman with the almond-shaped hazel eyes, like liquid amber, the boisterous laugh. Harry remembered that day how he and Kail had argued at the river, others separating them before it came to blows. Armi's eyes filled with fire and tears. Words spoken.

Harry turned his attention back to his plants. He checked a tassel of blossoms, turned brown before they could pollinate. He felt guilty, letting his plants suffer through his distractions over the bid. He must water more.

Another memory flashed in his mind—the ceremonial "first crush", the traditional start of the grape harvest. Stomping in the press at the local winery, the music playing, all of them holding hands and dancing in a circle, laughing, slipping on the skins. And Armi next to him, her grip firm in his, holding up her dress, the grape juice splashing up her legs.

And then again, climbing over the side of the press, uninvited, Kail. Harry remembered the hard edge to his eyes, how Armi's grip on his hand had tightened. And then Kail losing his mind, flying across the circle at him. Harry tackling him, both down in the slush, punching. Blood in his head, blood in his mouth, blood in the grapes. Yet later, when Armi was dabbing his cut lip with Mercurochrome, her face so close, then kissing him on the cut, it had all been worth it.

Harry glanced up to the sky and felt the warmth on his face. He was blessed with two suns in his life, this one shining down, and Armi. He couldn't live without either one. A bee landed on a cucumber blossom, sucking the nectar. Harry put his callused hand up and the bee crawled on to it. He brought the bee up to the next blossom and it crawled onto the tiny flower. Harry rose slowly on complaining knees, thinking of getting a little nectar of his own.

*   *   *

Naz paced behind his desk, occasionally glancing out the window. Carina would be in soon. He agonized over why he hadn't told her earlier, but in the same breath he knew exactly why he hadn't. He didn't want to argue with her for days over a decision he knew was right. She was struggling to put the bid together. Not because she wasn't capable, but because she had never done it before. He couldn't risk letting her go it alone any longer. There was too much at stake.

Still, he could feel his stomach tightening. He knew his daughter. This would not go down easy. She was hard-headed, same thing Mayda always said about him. Naz smiled. She was a chip off the old block, and that was OK with him. He popped a Tums in his mouth and crunched it. The lime flavor shot up behind his nose as he heard her car door slam, then the office door.

"Hey, Carina," Naz shouted from his desk.

She strutted in. "Was that our backhoe going out the gate?" she said. "The one with the cracked head gasket?"

"That was $10,000 from South Central Recycling for the IRS payment, the one you promised."

"You mean the one that stayed our execution."

"That, too," Naz hesitated, looking for a way to open the real conversation.

Carina looked at her father. "What?" she said.

"About the bid," said Naz, rolling the cigar in his mouth. "I thought maybe, you know, just thinking, you could use…."

"Don't worry, I got it handled."

Naz winced. The longer it went, the worse it got. He spit it out. "I hired a consultant."

Carina just stared at him.

"You know," Naz went on, "to help on the bid package."

Carina flashed a startled, hurt look at her father. "Jesus, Dad!"

"What? You're the one complaining we're under-cap-italized, we never do it right. Well, here I bring in some help, and now you don't like that."

"Thanks for the vote of confidence."

"It's too big a job for one person."

"You mean it's too big a job for me."

"I didn't mean that," said Naz, realizing the conversation was taking one of those ugly turns. Why did she always take everything so personally? She's a woman, he thought, that's why.

"This guy's experienced. How many presentations you made to the City Council? He saved Union Disposal when they were going to lose that contract because they had no recycling plan. And he kept Haig Katangian open when he had that spill and the toxic boys were all over his ass. This guy comes highly recommended."

Carina stared at her father, hands on her hips, eyes flashing. "I wouldn't take Haig Katangian's recommendation for a taco! But no, it's OK for me to lie to the IRS! It's OK for me to type up the recycling reports! It's OK for me to make the goddamn coffee, or the chickenshit curtains! But it's not OK for me to prepare the bid!"

Naz screwed up his face. "You made the curtains?"

"God!" Carina turned her back on her father and headed for the front door.

Naz looked at Mrs. Avakian, "What can you do?" he said.

"Better," she answered, with a steely glare. Naz rolled his eyes and disappeared into his office.

Just as Carina reached the front door, it burst open and a young man tripped in, grabbed onto Carina, nearly toppling her. His briefcase flew and popped open, spilling papers.

"Sorry," he said, scooping up his documents, "that last step." Carina took him in at a glance. Tall, angular, blond hair, light blue eyes, in a starched white shirt, red tie, and blue blazer.

"I'm here to meet with Nazareth Agajanian?" he said with a smile that flashed perfect white teeth, under a straight nose. The guy looked like he'd be more comfortable riding a desk at IBM; the guy who is supposed to save them.

"I'm Denny DeYoung," he said, sticking out his hand. Reluctantly, she shook his it. At least he has a firm grip, she thought.

"Right over there," Carina motioned to her father's office and followed the consultant in.

Naz walked out from behind his desk, took his cigar out of his mouth and grasped the young man's hand in both of his. "Glad you could make it. Denny, right? You get coffee?"

"Uh...."

"Mrs. A's getting it," said Carina.

"You met my daughter, Carina, I see."

"Yes, sort of."

"Good, good," he said. "Sit down. Jack's on his way. He's the Operations Manager."

Carina flashed her eyes at her father. Operations Manager? Where the hell had he gotten that one? She wondered what title he had made up for her—administrative assistant, Girl Friday?

Naz motioned to Harry sitting in the corner, looking like one of those old guys who pushed shopping carts piled with junk.

"Denny, this is my father, Harry Agajanian, founder of the Company. Dad, this is Denny DeYoung. He's here to help us on the bid." Harry waved his cane at Denny. Denny nodded back.

"You found us OK?" Naz asked Denny.

"Sure, fell right into it." Denny glanced at Carina. She rolled her eyes.

Denny continued, "Actually, I know the area a little. I worked with the railroad at the switch yard across the river on a Spill Contingency Plan."

"Yeah, they can use it. Bastards spill shit all the time over there," Naz said lighting his cigar. "But I ain't seen nothing' this morning, so maybe your plan's working."

Denny flashed Carina a quick, friendly smile.

Save it, she thought.

They all glanced up as Jack walked into the office and nodded at the group. Carina could see by the half-belligerent look on his face that Jack was about as happy as she was about the new consultant.

"Jack," said Naz. "Meet Denny DeYoung. Denny, Jack."

Denny popped out of his chair to shake hands with Jack, who then sat and began scraping dirt from under his fingernails.

"We got some work to do," Naz said as he peeled a roll of Tums and offered one to Denny. "No thanks," Denny said. "I already had breakfast."

Carina couldn't help a smile. Most people were intimidated by her father. At least Mr. IBM had a sense of humor.

Naz crunched one of the tablets. "Plugs the holes."

Carina watched Denny open a day planner filled with plastic tabs, ruler, pen and pencil holder, a calculator, business cards, things to remember, things to do. Well, she thought, it was one thing to be organized, another thing to know the trash business, a standard roll-off from a lowboy, a disc screen from a trommel, and high-grade office pack from white ledger. At Pacific Rim, organization was not as highly touted as experience and instinct. You could organize bullshit till you went blind, but it was still bullshit.

"OK, let's get right to it," Naz said. "I brought Denny in because we need help on this bid." He couldn't help a quick glance at Carina. She stared right back at him, and crossed her eyes.

Naz cleared his throat and continued, "He's familiar

with the city, and from what I hear he writes damn good, and we could use that, too. And I'm not taking nothing away from Carina. She got a good start on the bid and we all know the great job she does here, from handling the books, to driving a forklift, to uh…making the curtains." Naz winked at Carina, who stared back as if she were about to leap over the desk and claw his face off. He knew the look.

Naz said, "I'm not going to sugar coat this thing. We're the underdog on the bid."

"There's a surprise," said Jack.

Naz clipped off the soggy end of his cigar with a pair of scissors. It made a sickening plop in the wastebasket. "As some of you know, me and Carina had a little discussion with Alex at the Ball a couple nights ago. To make a short story shorter, he threw us out of the landfill…but he was going to throw us out anyway."

Carina said, "And the Zaven Petoyan thing, too."

Jack tapped Denny on the knee. "We'll be down a little tonnage for a while." Jack turned to Naz. "That reminds me. I haven't seen Ajax or Spartan for a couple days either."

Naz grimaced.

Harry tapped the desk with his cane. "Hartunians."

Denny jotted down a note. Carina figured this was not quite what he expected. Welcome to Pacific Rim.

Naz said to Denny, "They shortened their name to Hart when Kail moved into LA, thought it sounded more 'American.' That asshole will sell out for anything, even his own name."

Denny said, "I've been up against the Harts before, as an expert witness in a lawsuit regarding their leachate collection system at the HIA landfill. Forced them to spend another two million dollars for the upgrade. Let's just say I'm not one of their favorite people."

"Join the crowd," Carina said, feeling a faint blush of camaraderie that she quickly squelched. "Now he's pissed because we won't sell out to him."

Naz explained, "He knows we've got the prime location. We've got him worried and he wants to put a little heat on us."

"A little heat my ass," Jack said. "No way we make it without his landfill and he knows it."

"We'll make it," Naz said flatly. "And he ain't so sure as you, otherwise why'd they try to bomb the plant?"

"Bomb the plant?" Denny said.

Carina added, "Our ace security force foiled the attempt." She shot a sarcastic look at her father.

"So," Denny said, "They assume you'll have to haul to the county landfill and pay ten dollars more a ton," Denny said. "Ten dollar loss per ton, 1,000 tons a day. At that rate, you may not have the reserves to last the month till the bid is due."

Carina stared at Denny. Shit, maybe he knew something after all.

"A month?" Naz said. "Try a week."

Carina added, "And even if we did make it, that ten dollar hike will kill our bid number."

"Who says they never taught you nothin' at UCLA?" Naz quipped.

Jack started cracking his knuckles, one at a time. Carina leaned her head back against the wall. Just once she wished her father would take her seriously.

Naz spread his arms up in front on him and said,

"Big picture. We got a couple advantages, we're small, we can move fast, maneuver, none of those Wall Street vultures looking over our shoulder. We got low overhead."

Carina laughed. "Now, that's the truth."

Naz continued, "But HIA, they got a ton of overhead. That palace they built out there, fountains, marble shit everywhere. And even with all that, they don't give a rat's ass about recycling. They own the landfill, for Chrissake! All recycling does is take stuff out of their landfill. They don't want that! That's why they're weak on the recycling side. They can't compete with our markets. We've been working with the mills for sixty years. Stuck with them through it all. We know what to pick, how to pick it, and who to ship it to. And look at Carina with that new glass sorting system. No one's got that."

Denny piped in, "All that combined, more material recycled, higher prices from the mills, you can drop your bid two or three dollars a ton right there."

Carina glanced at Denny. OK, so he knew a little about the business and he can do math in his head, so he had a sense of humor, some balls, might even know what he's doing, he's still not in her league. At a time when they've got no money, why throw away ninety dollars an hour, or whatever his fee is?

"Excuse me, Mr. Agajanian," Denny said.

"Naz."

"Naz. Even assuming you can survive for thirty days, aren't you still in trouble on the bid? Like Carina said, there's no way you're competitive with the high county landfill gate fee tacked on to your bid price."

"I got something working on that front, too. Cousin

of mine runs a landfill for the Indians out in the desert. He'll give me the 'family' rate."

"You don't mean Saroyan?" said Carina. Naz just smiled. "That's 200 miles away," she said. "What sense does that make?"

"Two fifty," Naz said. "You just worry about the bid package. Let me worry about the landfill. I got a contingency plan."

Carina leaned over to Denny and whispered, "In case you haven't noticed, our whole operation's a contingency plan."

Naz stretched his arms over his head and yawned, his eyes suddenly taking on a glassy, tired look. "OK. Everyone get out of here now. Carina, you show Denny the plant."

"Hey, I've got a lot to do," she said. "Let Jack take him."

"You take him! You're going to be working with him on this thing." Naz looked at Denny. "She knows everything about the operation. She'll dig out anything you need. You organize the sonuvabitch, make it look good, you know...professional, better than HIA. We got thirty days to finish the bid. He looked at a calendar tacked to the wall of a buxom young woman leaning against a bulldozer. "Make that twenty-nine. You be ready to go day and night. Maybe we should pump you up with a thermos of espresso and a bottle of *oghi*."

Denny smiled. "You're just trying to turn me into an Armenian."

"Worse things could happen."

Carina marched toward the office door, but Denny

reached around and held it open for her. She hesitated. That was the first time someone, anyone, had held the door for her in a long time.

As they walked out into the yard, Denny stopped at his car, an old, but well maintained Jeep Grand Wagoneer with real wood paneling on the side. He popped open the rear hatch and Carina glimpsed the perfectly ordered trunk, with a tool kit, flat tire inflation bottle, flashlight, even a box of tire chains. Well, if it ever snowed in LA, he'd be ready. Denny pulled out a white hard-hat, and offered her a second one.

"No thanks," she said. "Those things really mess up my hair." She took off across the yard, but Denny caught up, adjusting his hard hat.

"I've heard about your operation," he said. "You run at a high throughput for such a small plant."

"Look, uh, Denny. It wasn't my idea to hire you, OK?" She continued walking, but Denny touched her on the arm, stopping her.

"I know this must feel like an invasion of your turf. But believe me, I…."

Carina looked Denny in the eye. She had to admit, the guy was sincere, for what that was worth. "I don't know how much help I'll be," she said. "After all, Dad hired you because he thought I couldn't handle it."

"If it's any consolation, I've got the feeling you could handle it."

"Thanks for the vote of confidence. Now let's go before the sun sets."

"Lead on," Denny said, his face slightly fallen.

She took him through the plant from start to finish in

a business-like manner, from the scales where the trash trucks weighed in, to the tipping floor in the building where they dumped. Then on to the heavy screen that allowed the small stuff, mostly dirt, rocks, bits of paper and plastic, and broken glass to fall through, while the bigger material ran over the screen onto the elevated conveyor. There, workers pulled out recyclable material as the trash rushed past. Carina pointed out the baler that crushed the recyclables into 1,500-pound bales the size of large desks, and onto the loading dock where the bales of newspaper, cardboard, aluminum cans, and plastic bottles where shipped out. They watched as a forklift driver loaded a double stack of newspaper bales into a shipping container.

"Headed for Japan," she said. "Dad goes over once a year on a good will tour. Comes crawling back barely alive, but you know it's just from too much of a good time. And no one gets deals like my dad."

Denny reached up and pulled a crushed plastic 7-Up bottle out of the paper bale. "Don't want to ruin your record." He smiled.

Despite herself, Carina smiled back.

Finally, she took him over to the massive compactor. Its hydraulic ram groaned as it packed another charge of garbage into the back end of a semi-truck. "Four hundred horse," she yelled over the whine of the machine. "This is the garbage residue we can't recycle. Twenty-three ton payload. Puts us right at the maximum axle load limits."

She pointed to an idling piece of equipment. "You know how to run a loader?"

"Can't say as I do," said Denny.

"Figures," Carina muttered under her breath as she hopped up in the loader cab and shoved it in gear. She lowered the bucket and pushed some trash onto a conveyor.

"You've been around equipment, I see," Denny yelled to her in the cab.

She hopped down looking at her hand. "Split a nail. Goddammit." She bit off the tip of the polished red fingernail and spit it on the ground. "Come on, I'll show you my pride and joy." With that, Carina led Denny over to a system of vibrating screens and conveyors, an overhead magnet, and high pressure air separator. Shards of glass fell off the final discharge belt into a bin, while out one side flew bits of paper and plastic and bottle caps—all the light stuff, and out the other side, mostly rocks and dirt—the heavy material.

"Glass recovery system," Carina said. She reached into a bin and brought up a handful of glass cullet, glistening like gemstones. "It doesn't look like much in volume, but this stuff is heavy. Until we got the machine, all this was going to the landfill. No one else on the West Coast has got one. Not even the Harts. Gives us an additional five percent on our recycling rate for the glass and even more for the dirt and rock."

Denny asked, "What do you do with it?"

"The dirt and rock we take to the aggregate guys." Carina replied. "Or, as a last resort, to the county dump, free of charge, where they use it to cover the trash. The environmentalists hate that this counts as recycling, but to me it's one of the few good things the government ever did."

"Impressive," Denny said, looking in the glass bin. "What's the end use for the glass?"

"Mostly in asphalt paving. It increases the roughness coefficient of the surface, better traction."

Denny said, "I've seen sample sections of that. I like the way the road glitters at night in the headlights. Kind of magical, you know?"

Strange comment for an engineer, she thought. Maybe he wasn't all bad.

As they walked over to the back wall of the plant, Denny clipped the top of his head on an I-beam. Carina smiled. This guy needs a hard hat. "Here's the most important part of the facility," she said, following him through a door. They gazed out on a small plot of land and neat rows of vine-like plants, with thin tendrils gripping coated wires strung between posts, large jagged leaves.

"My *Babig's*...grandfather's garden. They're all heirloom, too. A guy in Glendale grows the seedlings from the original seeds from Armenia. It's as close as *Babig* can get to home. Sweetest cucumbers you've ever tasted, too."

"Your grandfather came over from Armenia?"

"Nineteen fifteen. He lived through the *Megz Yeghern*—the great catastrophe, the genocide. He made it to Fresno and that's where it all started. The junkman. That's where he ran into Kail Hartunian, too, sixty plus years ago. You're not the only one got crosswise with HIA."

Suddenly, Carina froze. Among the cucumber vines, she saw a hazy figure working between the rows with a hoe. Then she recognized him and tears cornered in her eyes—Galen.

Denny looked at her. "Are you feeling all right?"

Carina closed her eyes hard. Opened them. The vision was gone. "Sure," she said, turning away, and steadying herself against an I-beam.

Denny said, "Speaking of gardening, the city's putting on a composting demonstration tomorrow morning. Maybe you could give me your opinion of this new equipment they've developed. Could be something for Pacific Rim in the future. The times are changing...."

"Try telling that to my Dad," Carina said. "Organics are the next target in the waste stream for recovery! He thinks it's all bullshit."

"But you don't."

"Look, there's some people going to be there I just don't feel like seeing, that's all."

"You mean the same ones I don't feel like seeing?"

She raised her hand to shield the sun from her eyes and looked at Denny.

"We'll stick together," he said. "So even if the Harts are there in force, better to know what they've got, right? Good intel for the bid."

"Alex will be gloating," Carina replied. "The big sponsor. The man who makes things happen."

"So he pays for it, and we try to steal an idea or two," Denny said, as he straightened a stake.

"Yeah, OK," she said. "I'll meet you there."

"Great," said Denny.

Carina winced. This Denny guy looked like someone who would say 'great' all the time.

He glanced at his watch. "I better pick up what corporate data I can, so I can get started on the bid package tonight. Site plan, equipment specs, org chart."

"Org chart?"

"Organization chart. You know, of the company."

"Oh, sure. Got one framed right here in the Board Room." Carina laughed out loud, and God did it feel good. It had been a long time.

* * *

While Carina was taking Denny on the plant tour, Naz called Mrs. Avakian into his office. He was feeling jumpy with the bid deadline closing in, and so much on the line. Pacific Rim was not exactly the bastion of secure operations. Half his guys didn't even have a green card. The entire work force was a security risk. So he had decided to keep his next operation a little more covert, and had not shared it in the team meeting. Although his inner circle was beyond reproach, he'd decided to keep them all out of it; no need to go beyond the bare essentials, in this case, Mrs. Avakian.

Naz's secretary walked in and he closed the door behind her. She sat in a chair in front of his desk, her back straight as a piece of rebar, and he paced behind.

"How many years you worked for me Mrs. A?"

"Nineteen, Nazareth."

"In all those years, I ever asked you to do anything illegal?"

"All the time," she said.

Naz cleared his throat, "Well, uh...I'm going to ask you to do another one." He noticed the gleam in Mrs. Avakian's eyes as she opened her steno pad and sat poised with her pen. People thought she was an old lady, but Naz knew that was just the exterior. Inside was someone who was tough, could bend the rules, and who would do anything for him. He trusted her completely.

"Mrs. A," Naz said. "The L.A. bid don't mean nothing if we're dead before we get there. And this county landfill deal will kill us." Naz licked a cigar as he rolled it in his mouth.

"I'm all ears," she said.

"You know all those accounts HIA stole from us last year with low-ball pricing?" Naz said. "Johnny Bedrosian just about went out of business, they took so many of his roll-off accounts. But they ain't the only ones can steal accounts, right?"

"Eye for an eye," said Mrs. Avakian. "So the Bible says."

"Right!" said Naz, slapping the top of his desk. "God's an Armenian!"

"Well," she said. "That would explain why we're still in business."

"So," Naz continued, "The Hartunians steal our accounts...we steal them back. Just the good ones. The ones with the recycling programs. Clean corrugated and office mix, in separate bins. Nice."

"Not exactly the high road," she said.

"This is nothing!" Naz shouted. "We're not bombing their plant. We're not running other families out of business! We're just taking back what is legally ours!"

"As my father always used to say, 'You eat the bear, or the bear eats you,' said Mrs. Avakian.

"And it's our turn at the table," Naz said, a little smile slipping out. "I want you to start a second set of books. I'll give you the HIA accounts, maybe twenty-five or thirty of them, and you coordinate everything with Manny. He'll do the driving, just him, not a word of any of this to anyone else."

"Yes, Nazareth."

"Each night he can pick up five or six of HIA's roll-offs containers when no one's around. We'll figure out the collection frequency so Manny grabs them right before HIA picks them up, when they're full of clean cardboard and paper. He'll haul them back here, dump them, then fill them up with our left over garbage and deliver them back to the HIA accounts. We get the recyclables, they get the trash. What do you think?"

"Looks like we're going to eat some bear," she said.

Naz could have kissed her.

5

From the top of his hill, Alex surveyed the cornerstone of the family empire, the 500-acre landfill carved into a giant canyon in the rolling hills thirty miles east of Los Angeles. Four parallel lines of trash trucks queued at the scales and others crawled up the access road to the dumping area.

A few trucks were diverted off to the side and Alex watched them pull into his new recycling plant. He looked across to the other side of the property, where the earth movers ripped long scars into the side of the hill, swallowing ten-cubic-yards of dirt into their hoppers. He watched them shuttle over to the working area, and lay a blanket of dirt over the packed slope of recently deposited trash.

When his father first brought him as a boy to this huge canyon in what was then the rural countryside, he had marveled at it. Winter rains streamed down over boulder-strewn cuts in the side hills and washed the dusty leaves of the sycamore trees clustered along the creek bottom. Alex would build little dams with rocks and look for tadpoles in the water. The canyon was dotted with live oak trees that grew along the shaded side of the ridges.

Down in the arroyo in a little side canyon off the main landfill, Alex could see his Tudor-style mansion. Everyone, especially his father, thought Alex was out of his mind, building his own mansion virtually on top of the landfill. But Alex had known exactly what he was doing. The greatest threat to any landfill was the encroachment of development—people. Sooner or later, the whispers of dissent would start, growing to a roar. NIMBY—Not In My Back Yard! That argument nearly always worked because the owners of the landfills lived world's away in tony San Marino, Brentwood, or Pacific Palisades.

By living closer than anyone else to the landfill, Alex had shut up the NIMBYs forever. The landfill *was* in his backyard!

It didn't hurt of course that the prevailing winds blew toward the other side of the landfill and Eagle Heights, or that Alex's broken nose severely limited his ability to smell. So even if there was an odor problem, maybe his girlfriend Julia would know, but not Alex.

The Oaks, his father named the canyon site. But now the oaks were there only in name, the trees long since cut down and buried in their own canyon to make room for the trash. Later, it officially became the Hart Industries of America Regional Landfill; HIA for short.

Now, after nearly forty years, he still loved it, but in a different way. The oaks were long gone, but in their place

1,500 trucks a day crawled up that same grade where the trees once grew. At $300 per truck on average, that was $450,000 a day. He let the number hang in his mind. Every two days or so, a million dollars. And still, it was not enough.

He turned at the sound of the two-way radio in his pickup. "Alex, it's Jerry. Alex it's Jerry, over."

Alex grabbed the radio mic, "Yeah, Jerry."

"You better come down to the cut-off wall. We got a problem."

"What kind of problem?"

"I'd rather tell you when you get here."

As he drove down the hill, he thought about the bid. Sure HIA had other sources of trash, but the City of L.A. was the jewel. The thought of it sent a chill through him. He knew that if by some freak HIA lost, it could be crippling. Like a river that shifts its course after an earthquake, the flow of trash could be altered forever by the shakeout from the bid. He cleared his nose and spat out the window.

Alex pulled up at the mouth of the canyon, the lowest point of the site. He climbed out of his pickup, and walked up to his foreman. "So, what's so important that I had to drive all the way down here?"

The small man just motioned with his head and walked over to the top of a long wall that ran like a dam across the arroyo. Alex hopped up next to him. Jerry pointed to the plastic head of a pipe sticking up out of the ground down in the arroyo below. "I went to pull a groundwater sample out of that new downstream well about fifteen minutes ago."

Alex could feel the chill starting again, the slippery slope of something going wrong. These environmental monitoring programs were nothing but trouble. Between the bureaucratic bigwigs in Sacramento and the lunatic eco-freaks who thought every goddamn gum wrapper should be recycled, they'd passed so many regulations that the real players, the facility operators, spent more time filling out reports than operating—monitoring air, groundwater, noise at the property line, gas generation. He even had to develop a seagull abatement program. The neighbors in Eagle Heights over a quarter-mile away worried that a bird would pick up an infected needle and drop it in their baby's crib.

Jerry continued, "Funny thing was, I didn't find any water in the well. Not a drop."

"Perfect," Alex said. "No leachate. Dry as a tomb."

"I found something else," Jerry said. "Gas. Blew the cap clear off the well as soon as I loosened it. Nearly took my head with it."

"So what? All landfills generate gas. A little got in our groundwater monitoring well. That's all."

"Means our gas collection system is failing." Jerry played in the dirt with the toe of his boot. "The gas is slipping under the cutoff wall, and moving out past our property line." Jerry pointed. "See those eucalyptus down in the arroyo, all those brown leaves? The landfill gas is killing their roots, and it's going to get worse. City inspector sees that…."

"How can the gas get under the wall?" said Alex. "The concrete goes all the way down and anchors three feet deep in the bedrock."

"Gas must be down deep, in the fissures in the granite. Your dad was right. We should have sealed that rock first. Too late now. We got a couple hundred thousand tons over it."

Alex frowned. "Can't you just draw more vacuum on the gas wells?"

"Won't work," answered Jerry. "We'd just suck more air in through the surface of the fill."

"Goddamn environmental bullshit!"

Jerry fidgeted with the clasp of his watchband. "What do we do?"

"Not a damn thing," said Alex.

The response startled Jerry, and he said, "Judging by those trees, the gas is migrating toward Eagle Heights. If it gets there in explosive concentrations, could...."

"All we have to worry about now is winning that L.A. bid. Then we'll do whatever it takes to control the gas. But if word of this gets out now, it'll kill us. Regulators will be crawling all over, smelling gas everywhere. I can see guys in moon suits taking air samples in every basement in Eagle Heights. And that for sure will bury our bid."

Alex turned to his foreman. "Who knows about this?"

"Just you and me."

"Good," Alex said. "Let's keep it that way. I want a lid on it, a tight lid."

Alex walked back to the jeep, Jerry trailing along.

"You and me's not the problem," Jerry said. "It's the city inspector, Ms. Singh. She's a stickler, the one who made us put in that well in the first place, and her next site visit is coming up."

"Don't worry about it. She won't be out here," Alex said. "You just cap that well good and tight."

"OK. You're the boss."

Alex drove off. He picked up his car phone, fumbled through his address book, and dialed.

* * *

Charlie jerked awake in the middle of the night with a cramp in his thigh. He hobbled out the back door of the hearse, limping around in the dark. He turned at the sound of a truck approaching up the Pacific Rim access road, probably one of the loads coming in from downtown. When the truck roared right past the scalehouse without weighing in, Charlie felt a flutter in his gut. Following the truck through the pools of light spilling across the yard, he glimpsed the HIA insignia on the side of the roll-off container and he was on the move with Black trotting after him.

What the hell was Manny doing in a Pacific Rim truck, Charlie thought, picking up one of HIA's roll off containers? Charlie could smell it: Naz was up to something. Living hand-to-mouth for so long had honed Charlie's survival instincts. The two things he knew for sure were fear and opportunity. He felt both now.

The truck pulled into a corner of the tipping floor. Charlie hid in the shadow of the sorting platform. The truck body tilted up and with a whoosh, the load slid out. Charlie couldn't believe what he saw. It was all high-grade... six, seven tons of computer paper, and white ledger, clean cardboard. There was at least $1,500 sitting on that floor.

He watched while Manny positioned his truck, now carrying the emptied HIA roll-off container, under the load-out conveyor and then turned the system on. Garbage from an old load, with all the recyclables pulled out, disgorged off the end of the sorting line, filling the HIA roll-off container with worthless trash.

As Manny drove back out into the night, Charlie moved like a shadow over to the pile in the corner. Hell, Naz would never miss a little computer paper. It's already stolen anyway.

Charlie wheeled over a canvas mail cart that had somehow made its way to Pacific Rim from the post office, and started chucking stacks of computer paper into it. With each handful, Charlie's breath quickened. "Holy shit," he said to himself over and over. He was in a feeding frenzy. He weighed each armful in his mind, and multiplied it by the price per pound. Charlie couldn't quote a word of Shakespeare or the Dow Jones average, but he knew to a penny the value of the commodities of his trade. He grunted as he heaved a handful of computer paper, thick as two New York phone books, into the bin. Twenty-five pounds was worth three dollars and seventy-five cents—an armful of cardboard, another two dollars and fifty cents. The cash register kept ringing in his mind.

When the cart was full, he wheeled it off toward his shipping container. Looking up the access road, Charlie saw Manny coming in with a second load, again bypassing the scale. Charlie smiled.

He had hit the mother lode.

*   *   *

Alex hammered the cue ball and it exploded into the racked balls, sending them skittering around the pool table. The twelve-ball hung on the lip of the corner pocket. Alex nudged the table and the ball fell. The phone rang in the corner of his game room and he picked it up.

"Yeah," he said, then smiled. The pit boss at the casino had alerted him the night before, so Alex was expecting this call. He loved people's weaknesses, especially when they were addictions, because then he knew that it wasn't a matter of "if" but only "when" he'd be able to take advantage. He knew Jack Oseppian was in deep. He'd seen him at the casino from a distance and followed the tide of chips flowing away from him at the table. On a hunch, Alex had his people monitor Jack's fortunes as they spiraled down, and told them when to plant the seed of Jack's "salvation."

"Yeah, Jack...yeah. Sorry to hear that, yeah...hey, everybody's been through bad stretches...I'm here to help. No problem. Two hundred grand? That's quite a chunk, Jack. I'd have to see something of equivalent value...yeah, OK, you think about it. Maybe we can come up with a 'win-win' situation."

Alex hung up the phone and smiled. He rosined up his cue stick. This was going to be good. Jack was hooked. A little advance money, a little good faith, a pat on the back, and he'd have the inside man he needed, his insurance policy for the bid. Unlike Jack, Alex didn't like to gamble. He preferred a fixed game.

Alex sighted down his cue stick. He tapped the cue ball, it caromed off the rail, kissed the 3-ball and dropped it in the pocket.

6

The man pulled the five-gallon can of chlorine bleach out of the trunk of his car and walked over to the dumpster. He peeled off the sealed safety cap. Lifting the dumpster lid, he carefully buried the open can upright in the wastepaper. He heard the groan of the front loader coming down the dark alley, picking up its route of wastepaper from the small row of print shops and offices. He saw the headlights and the shadow of the hydraulic forks raising the first bin, the one in which he'd earlier buried the container of ammonia.

He knew what would happen when the Pacific Rim truck picked up that next bin, the one with the bleach, and dumped it on top of the ammonia. He walked to his car, killed the car lights, but left the engine running.

The truck pulled up and slid its forks into the second container, lifted it up over the cab, and dumped the contents into its body. The man watched and waited. On

87

the breeze, he smelled just a hint of ammonia. The truck ground its gears and pulled forward.

The blast lit up the night and shook the man's car. Chunks of metal and flaming trash rained down. He watched the driver leap out, his shirt on fire, and roll around in a muddy puddle. He had missed several nights earlier with the Molotov cocktail when the dog had surprised him at Pacific Rim, but this time he was right on target.

He pulled away from the curb and drove a block before he turned his lights on.

*   *   *

The light towers of Dodger Stadium caught the morning sun and peeked over the hill at the gathering of environmentalists, corporate waste managers, city staff, and the local press, huddled in the field in Elysian Park. In front of them, a large machine straddled a pile of grass, leaves, and tree trimmings.

Late as usual, Carina huffed across the parking lot in high heels toward the gathering in the field beyond. She had dressed up to meet her mother for breakfast at the local café. It was a periodic event that she soldiered through to please Mayda. But this morning the conversation had definitely been spiced up by the Pacific Rim truck explosion. Her mother had been more paranoid than ever.

Carina stepped off the pavement and her heels sank into the soft grass. She remembered her boots back at the office. "Shit," she swore under her breath, continuing on, tip-toeing on the balls of her feet.

Carina scanned the crowd and saw him. Denny stood an inch or two above the rest. It figured that he would be right on time, probably got there fifteen minutes early to be safe. She had never been fifteen minutes early for anything in her life.

Denny turned from the crowd and their eyes met. He smiled and waved. The thought popped into her mind—golden retriever. That's what he was. Her future hung on the talents of a happy dog.

As she neared Denny, one of Carina's heels spiked into the ground, she stumbled and the shoe pulled off her foot. Denny grabbed her as she tumbled into him. Heads in the crowd turned to check the commotion. She looked into his eyes, one shoe on, one nylon soaking in the dewy grass, blew the hair out of her face and blurted, "We've got to stop meeting like this."

Someone said, "Shhh." Carina noticed that Denny flushed, like a little boy.

He whispered, "I'll get your shoe."

Carina balanced one foot on top of the other until he came back with the mud-coated high heel. He cleaned the mud off the heel with his hands, gave the shoe to her, and wiped his hands on the grass.

"Sorry about that," Carina said. Without thinking, she reached out and steadied herself on his shoulder, slipping the shoe on. She was startled at how easily she had performed that little act of familiarity, and let go of him.

"You always wear high heels to field demonstrations?" he said.

"Only when it's muddy."

Carina focused on the demonstration in front of

them and her eyes locked on Alex Hart's. Startled, her breath caught. He smiled at her, then turned to a formidable-looking woman next to him, Barbara Miller, president of the Los Angeles City Council.

Even though Carina's affair with Alex had ended three years ago when she called it off and eventually connected with Galen, she still felt a twinge. There was a certain current to Alex that could sweep you away. And she had been in a rebellious period, angry at her father for trying to run her life—so she had let the current carry her for a short time. She realized soon enough that it wouldn't work. Alex would never see her as an equal. When he asked her to pack his clothes for a short trip they were taking up the coast, the die was cast and she was out the door.

But Alex wasn't used to rejection and had turned vengeful, looking for opportunities to get even. As far as she knew, Alex didn't even like Barbara Miller, but watched as Alex put his hand on the Council President's forearm and whispered to her.

Instinctively, Carina moved a little closer to Denny.

Barbara Miller moved in front of the group, the large compost machine looming behind her. She wore a clean-tailored pantsuit, her auburn hair closely cropped. She was thin, probably anorexic, Carina thought, but powerful and cold, like her skin was made of plaster. Maybe Barbara was Alex's type after all.

"It's always a pleasure for the City of Los Angles to team up in a private-public partnership for the betterment of our environment," the Council President said in a voice loud and clear and comfortable in command. "At considerable savings to city taxpayers, Hart Industries of America, and in particular its president, Alex Hart, has graciously co-funded the development of the Evergreen Compost project." The group applauded politely as Barbara and Alex exchanged a smile. "But seeing that actions speak louder than words, let's get rolling."

With that, the machine rumbled forward, scooping up a mixture of grass and yard trimmings with a series of augers, grinding it and packing it into an eight-foot diameter, heavy plastic bag that extruded out the back as the machine crawled ahead. Soon, the bag was loaded, a 150-foot long sausage, complete with air distribution pipes, water lines, and ports for temperature probes.

Carina was impressed. No odor, no dust, no blowing debris, no flies. Thirty days in that bag, and voila, compost. This was just the kind of thing Pacific Rim should be doing, but her Dad was skeptical of new technologies, to say the least, and thought anyone who worked for the city didn't know jack shit. He was partly right, but only partly. Here was a world beyond Pacific Rim, a world that in the end could support them, or leave them behind.

She stole a glance at Denny. The sunlight caught his blonde hair and softened his face. He had good bones, as her mother would say, meaning chiseled features with solid brows, prominent cheeks, and a strong jaw line. "What do you think?" she yelled over the grinding of the machine.

"It's too expensive for yard waste," he said. "Simple row composting will still beat it. But for the more problematic material, food from restaurants, manure, sludge from the wastewater treatment plants—this could be effective."

Good answer, she thought.

After fielding questions, and with a round of applause for HIA and the city, the demonstration finished.

"Come on," Denny said, reaching out his hand to Carina. "Let's catch Barbara Miller."

"I'm not that hot on seeing the person she's with," Carina said.

"Me neither, but she's crucial for the bid. You know she'll be working behind the scenes. We can't just let Alex waltz off with her."

"Yeah, you're right." Carina took Denny's hand in a firm grip and he half held her up as they dodged slower moving people and hustled toward the parking lot.

Oh, if her mother saw her now, Carina thought, she'd have enough ammunition for six months. Armenian men never held a woman's hand in public, not a girlfriend's, not a fiancee's, not a wife's, not even a lover's. The men were too busy walking five feet ahead, and no one had arms that long.

Carina squeezed Denny's hand a little harder, hobbling over the curb, bringing her mind back to business. Denny was right. Connections were critical, and although her family had a ton of them on the streets, they had few on the political side where the big decisions were made.

Alex held Barbara Miller by the elbow, and was quickly escorting her off the field, as Carina shot up beside them, puffing slightly with exertion.

"Ms. Miller? I'm Carina Agajanian, from Pacific Rim Recycling." Carina offered her hand. Barbara turned and shook it after a slight hesitation.

"I'm sorry...?" she said, uncertain.

"You know, the facility off 9th Street?"

Alex smiled and said to Barbara, "The small transfer station down by the river."

"Running twelve hundred tons a day with a thirty-five hundred ton permit is not exactly small," Carina shot back, her eyes flashing.

Barbara said, "I'm sure Mr. Hart meant no disrespect, Miss...?"

"Agajanian."

"Yes. Well, you should bid on our recycling and transfer contract."

"We fully intend to."

"That's wonderful. I'm sure you'll give HIA a run for their money," she said with a frozen smile.

"Well give them more than that," Carina said. "We're fifteen miles closer to the center of the city's wasteshed and—"

"Nice meeting you, Ms. Agajanian," Barbara Miller said. Then she shook Alex's hand and smiled. "Thank you, again, Alex, for the contribution to our environmental programs."

"Anything for the city," he said with a nod.

As she drove away, Alex turned to Carina. "I saw one of your trucks in the news, not the good kind unfortunately. But accidents do happen—even to the best of us."

"That was no accident," she said.

Alex smiled. "I don't think I've met your friend."

"Denny DeYoung meet Alex Hart."

The two men shook hands, eyeing each other. Carina could see by the tension in their fingers that they were both gripping hard.

Alex studied Denny, a questioning look on his face.

"I know you, don't I?"

"Regional Water Board hearings, about two years ago."

Alex nodded, and a knowing smile twitched at the corners of his mouth. "You're that consultant. The leach-ate guy. Cost me a million dollars."

"Two, I believe."

"What's a million here or there between friends?" Alex said. "By the way, Mr. DeYoung, we've got quite a workload coming up with the merger. New assets, expansion, the future's wide open. What you saw today is just the tip of the iceberg. We can always use a good consultant, and I trust Ms. Agajanian's impeccable judgment in men. Do you have a card?"

"Didn't bring any with me," said Denny.

Alex said, "Never knew a consultant who didn't always have a card in his hot little hands."

"My plate's pretty full at the moment, anyway," Denny said.

Alex smiled at Carina, "I'll bet it is. Well, hey, thanks for coming out for the demonstration."

"It was a slice of heaven," said Carina.

Alex glanced at Carina's feet as he walked away. "Nice shoes."

They watched Alex climb into his black BMW and drive off.

Denny said, "What was that about the truck in the news?"

"I'll tell you later. Let's get out of here," Carina said, and started marching across the parking lot. Then she stumbled, catching herself against a car. She jerked her shoe off, the high heel had snapped at the sole. She took off the other one, walked over and hurled them into a dumpster. Then, in her nylon-stockinged feet, muttering to herself, she huffed toward her car, grimacing as she stepped on small stones.

* * *

Pacific Rim lay like a graveyard under slabs of neon light. As Charlie walked to his truck-size shipping container, he could hear Black panting at his heels. He took the key from around his neck, turned it in the padlock, and opened the door. He flicked on his flashlight as Black squeezed past into the familiar surroundings. Charlie closed the doors behind them, and set the locking bar that he had bolted on the inside.

Junk was piled head high on both sides forming a cramped aisle to the back. Copper plumbing fittings here, old electric motors there, a refrigerator box filled with rags, a jumble of porcelain toilets, bed frames, bits and pieces of the ass end of society all awaiting a new life.

Charlie turned on a construction lamp, hanging on a hook overhead, while Black curled up on a ratty beach towel in the corner. Charlie sat at a battered wooden workbench. "That's a good boy, Black." The dog's tail flopped at the sound of his name. Charlie picked up a welder's mask, slid the strap over his head and with a quick nod, flipped the visor down. Now he was in his own world, behind the mask. He lit the acetylene torch, and it popped to life.

Welding may have been the only good thing Machinist's Mate Charles Goodnight got out of the Navy. Sure, there were guys at Pacific Rim who could rough weld a buck wall, but if the job required real skill, Charlie was your man.

Charlie used the torch to cut a small leaf shape from a sheet of scrap metal. Then he picked up a soldering stick and melted it with the torch, welding the leaf to the twig-like branch of a miniature maple bonsai tree made of copper, zinc and tin. Along a dusty rack on the wall, fifty completed trees caught the light from the torch. The smell of hot metal hung under the lamp in a cloud of blue smoke.

Charlie let his dream rise like a bathysphere from the deep. He would have a little shop and he would make trees and maybe tune in the Dodger game on his radio, listen to Vin Scully's melodic voice, take a swig or two of Old Overholt for good measure.

If he could sell each piece for twenty dollars, he would have a thousand dollars. The number exploded in his head like a piñata. If he could only snag a little luck as it drifted by. A man had to have a little luck. Once you got it, you could ride it as fast and far as it would go, until it ran out. Charlie's had run out the day he was born into the family with eight kids, and a mother who died of stomach cancer two months after the last one, Charlie, was born. She got out. Charlie didn't.

He gazed over at the dog. Besides his discovery of Naz's stolen loads, Black was the only other piece of luck Charlie could ever remember. New Year's Day, five years ago, he'd taken his last ten bucks and bought a pint of Old Overholt at Fong's grocery store. He'd had enough left over for a package of Hostess cupcakes.

Charlie remembered swilling down half the pint

as he walked along the rail spur. And then, under the bridge, Charlie saw the near starved, black puppy, a writhing field mouse trapped in his paws. When Charlie picked him up, the mouse scampered away and the puppy squirmed to get after him. Charlie looked around for the mother, but they were all alone.

"Wait a minute," Charlie had said, holding him against his chest. "Look what I got for you." He pulled out the pack of cupcakes and tore open the cellophane with his teeth. The puppy looked at him, cocking his head. Charlie stuck a finger into the cupcake and held the creamy filling up to the little guy's nose. A pink tongue shot out and licked the cream. He stopped wriggling and put his full concentration on Charlie's finger.

The dog was thin, dirty and cold. With a twinge of sadness, Charlie realized the mother was probably gone, hit by a car or who knows what. Charlie tucked the little fellow inside his coat and fed him the two cupcakes on the walk home. From that day on, Black's loyalty had been unflinching. So had Charlie's. And as it turned out, that puppy had grown into the only power Charlie ever had, the only thing of Charlie's that anyone ever respected.

Black snorted in his sleep, and Charlie broke from the warmth of his reverie. He glanced with soft eyes at his dog, then back to his sculpture. Sparks flew among the maple leaves.

* * *

Naz drove south on the Harbor Freeway, as light rain fell from the flattened sky. Bright orange flares of gas licked at the clouds above the refineries of Wilmington. He pulled off and drove into the harbor, its cranes silhouetted against the sky; ships slumbering against the docks. As the car powered through the puddles, he followed the road that paralleled the main rail line.

The road narrowed past a boat yard, with cabin cruisers up on cradles, racks of dinghies and rusted gear. Then Naz spotted his destination and pulled off the road. Coal dust hung in the mist and the air smelled of salt, rotting seaweed, and diesel fuel. Naz walked past the "No Trespassing" signs into the rail yard. A gantry groaned as it dug its scoop into a mountain of coal and sent tons of the black rock shooting out its conveyor arm and into the hold of a ship. The heavy machinery set the air vibrating.

A switch engine jockeyed empty coal cars, reforming a train 120 gondolas long. It stretched over a mile down the track to the east, where four mainline locomotives hissed and ticked and waited to pull the empties back to the mine in Utah.

There was something about trains that Naz had always loved, so solid and certain. He used to bring Carina down here when she was little, just to see, and maybe get a friendly engineer to let them climb into the cab.

Naz dodged puddles as he made his way over to the rail yard office, where a light shone in the window.

Half an hour later, the locomotives roared to life and pulled. In chain reaction, the shots rang out as each coal car coupling boomed taut down the line. As the train crept forward, Naz stepped up onto the coupling of the last car.

He huddled against the metal to get out of the rain, as the train pulled him through the darkness toward his car.

He rode in a trance, his mind lost in the bid. Carina had mentioned to him about the composting demonstration and Alex's attempt to lure Denny away from them. Naz figured the offer must've looked pretty good to his consultant and wondered if he could really count on him—how easy it would be for Denny to sabotage the bid, leave out some critical item. Well, he couldn't do much about it now. Denny was his man, and he'd win or lose with him.

He grimaced at the thought of how the Harts continued to chip away at him. First, the IRS, then the firebomb at the plant, Zaven pulling out his tonnage, and now the truck blast. And after that last one, Naz was ready to fight fire with fire, but it was Naz's father, Harry, who had counseled patience. Harry knew that if they got caught retaliating, it was all over. After all the blows, the losses, his father still wasn't bitter, and could even smile. Naz could only dream of such restraint and resilience.

Thank God, the bid was less than three weeks away. He could never survive a long war of attrition. If they could just hang on, the pieces of his plan were coming together, even if he was the only one who knew it. He would tell his team when they had to know, but not before. The only thing that was certain, was that nothing was certain, especially the long shot he was playing. So much could go wrong. But he had no choice. You took your best shot—and this was his.

Naz jumped off the back of the slow-moving train onto the gravel of the track bed and walked to his car.

As he drove off into the night, Naz hummed a folk song about a dark woman from the hills, and when she danced around the fire and her skirts flared, the old men glanced at the bare flesh of her legs and dreamt of a time when they were young.

7

Two weeks raced by, as Naz badgered and screamed and swore and downed an entire bottle of Tums. Pacific Rim screeched and stumbled in chaotic preparation to meet the specifications of the bid. Fences were mended, craters in the access road patched, handrails reinforced, and safety signs posted. The skylights were even hosed off for the first time in memory, and natural sunlight filtered through the dancing motes of dust. More importantly, a thirty-foot extension was welded to the end of the sorting line, allowing another twelve sorters to man positions.

Naz's collection truck drivers were wearing thin, working overtime hours he couldn't afford. After the truck explosion, Naz told them they had to inspect each bin before they could stab it with the front loader forks and dump it in the truck. This added hours to their routes, but no more incidents occurred. He suspected that to the

Harts, Pacific Rim looked hopelessly out of the competition, and to tell the truth, he thought they might be right.

Ever since the bid request had hit the streets, Naz had been so preoccupied that he had failed to notice that Jack was even quieter than normal, not that it was easy to spot given that Jack usually said about as much as a tree.

And so it was one day, that Naz walked by Jack, who was replacing the propane tank that fueled one of the forklifts. Jack caught his hand in the bracket and yelled out. Naz leaped over and braced against the tank, creating a little space

Jack backed off, grabbing his hand. "Son of a bitch."

Naz clamped the tank in place and turned to his brother-in-law. "You all right?"

Jack grimaced, looking at his bleeding thumb.

Naz reached out. "Here, let me see it."

Jack jerked away. "It's all right."

"Don't look all right." Naz pulled a handkerchief out of his picket and offered it to Jack.

"I said, it's all right. Goddamn forklift. Shit's so rusted…."

Naz looked more closely at Jack. They were all under a lot of pressure, nerves like old brake linings were wearing thin. But Jack of all of them usually maintained an even keel. Naz said, "Maybe you should get some lunch. Take a break."

Jack tested his thumb to see if anything was broken.

Naz put his hand on Jack's shoulder. "Come on, Jack. Let's grab a cheeseburger at Ronnie's."

"I got too much to do," Jack said, wiping blood off his thumb with a rag. "I'm all right, Naz."

Naz pursed his lips, then nodded. "I'll bring one back for you. Ketchup and grilled onions?"

"Yeah, OK."

As Naz walked off, he glanced back and saw Jack pick up a wrench with his good hand and tighten the nut holding the propane tank. He thought again of the times Jack had approached him about playing a larger role at Pacific Rim, maybe General Manager, or something. Naz knew the value of Jack—the hardest worker he knew, a natural mechanic, street-smart, loyal, a good soldier—but he was no leader. Carina was the leader, even though she was a woman, which had its own challenges.

When this was all over, Naz swore to himself that he'd give Jack a bonus. But for now, he'd get him a double cheeseburger, and that would have to do.

*   *   *

Ever since the composting demonstration, Carina had felt the tug of camaraderie with Denny. Maybe nothing more than the temporary bond formed by the battle against a common enemy. Nonetheless, she was starting to relax behind the feeling that she wasn't all alone in putting the bid package together. And in fact, she had realized that her Dad had been right—she never could have done it all herself. She had to admit, that even amid the chaos of Pacific Rim, Denny was managing to pull together the bid.

She was surprised at how well he had adjusted to the free-for-all atmosphere with his need for order and his structured engineering training. She had reviewed his draft bid documents, organized in fifteen sections in a fat binder. It started with a cover letter and an executive summary, followed by sections on methodology, facilities, scheduling, references, insurance, and so on, ending with another section on minority and women-owned business outreach. Denny had also included an envelope for the $100,000 bid bond, an envelope that lay conspicuously empty.

And somehow, Denny had even cobbled together the now infamous org chart, fitting the people and functions of Pacific Rim into little boxes connected by lines of authority. Although she knew that in reality the company ran more in the "putting out fires" mode, the org chart looked good.

Carina walked out of the office and surveyed the activity in the yard. Denny approached with his clipboard and said, "How are the repairs coming along?"

"From what I've seen," Carina said, "We're using our duck tape and WD40 formula to perfection."

Denny shot her a quizzical look.

"If something moves and it's not supposed to, we tape it. If it's supposed to move and doesn't, we lube it."

"The elegance of simplicity," Denny said.

"The elegance of a shoestring budget is more like it."

As Denny headed for the storm water clarifier, she noticed his easy, long-legged gait. If someone would just dress him right, Mr. IBM wouldn't be a bad looking guy. She walked back into the office. She was behind in pulling together the financials, and with the bid date looming closer and closer, she wondered how the tide of red ink would look to the city. Then again, with a little creative accounting help....

"Mrs. Avakian!"

"Yes, Carina," the secretary called out from her office.

"How's that Profit and Loss statement looking?"

Mrs. Avakian stuck her head out of her office, holding a ledger. "I haven't exactly got us in the black, but at least the red is turning pink."

Carina laughed. "At this point, pink is good."

Between updating the scale weighing system, running out for parts, handling another call from the IRS, and various other tasks, Carina saw little of Denny in the days that followed. Sometimes they'd pass in the hall, Carina coming out of her father's office, Denny going in, arms loaded with documents. She liked the clean smell of him as he swept by.

Finally, the bid was only seven days away, as bit by bit, weld by weld, with baling wire and black coffee Pacific Rim was becoming a real player.

The stolen loads of recyclables from the HIA accounts kept rolling in late at night. Just that bit of good material gave Naz the financial boost to keep his head above water, or at least his nose.

*   *   *

A cool afternoon breeze rippled the water in the channel and sent wavelets lapping up against the hull of the big powerboat. The condos of Marina Del Rey rose up behind, purple bougainvillea spilling over the railings, and blue canvas awnings ruffling in the wind.

Alex Hart hosed down the afterdeck of his fifty-foot cabin cruiser. Even with his sunglasses, it was bright in the cockpit with the sun glaring off the wet fiberglass. The water splashed up over his Topsiders and felt cold on his bare ankles. He wore an old pair of jeans, a yellow polo shirt, and a maroon USC windbreaker.

A movement caught his eye and squinting into the sun he saw a slim female figure walking down the dock towards the boat. Alex turned the water off and coiled the hose. Very few people made him nervous, but Barbara Miller was one of them. God, he was beginning to hate these little rendezvous, but he realized they came with the territory. He needed her to exert her power at City Hall, to tilt the playing field his way, strong-arm the Board of Public Works, slant contracts in HIA's favor with insurance and bonding requirements that eliminated competition, applying subtle pressure on colleagues. In return, he stocked her re-election war chest with contributions from his suppliers, equipment contractors, shipping lines, and of course the fat white envelope with $10,000 that was delivered to her each month. He kept her in power, and she wielded it his way. This was her second term in office and her future was bright and rising. Among the power brokers, her name was already being mentioned for Governor. And once she climbed that pinnacle, all of California would open up to his reach, although he could only imagine how much blood she'd extract from him for entry into that arena.

His whole deal with her was clean, except for the personal entanglement. Somehow, he had let down his guard, gone along for that first ride and now he couldn't get off. She not only worked her magic on his enemies, she worked it on him. Was it the black widow, he wondered, where the female mates with the male, then kills him and sucks his carcass dry?

She wore a wide-brimmed straw hat pulled low, hiding her face. As she approached, Alex cleared his throat and said, "You should've worn boat shoes."

"The city didn't issue me a pair." Her voice was smooth and confident.

Alex motioned her over to the portable steps on the dock. He held out his hand as she tottered up the first step, then lifted her over the side and carried her to the companionway. He ushered her into the cabin and she sat in one of the turquoise leather chairs and crossed her legs, her dress riding up her thigh. She must've been a real looker twenty years ago, Alex thought, although now she was a little too thin, her bony knees protruding. He opened the refrigerator. "What'll it be?"

"A diet anything. I have a Redevelopment Committee meeting at three this afternoon. So unfortunately this will have to be brief."

Maybe I can drag this out, he thought, run her up against her deadline. He clenched his jaw, as he handed her the can of Diet Coke. "Glass?" he said.

"Oh, I think I can handle it straight out of the can."

Alex twisted the top off a bottle of beer and it hissed at him. "You know, we ever get caught at this, some clown from one of the condos spots you...."

"Relax, Alex. This isn't my District. These people wouldn't recognize the Council president if I knocked at the front door. They're too busy making drug deals and polishing their boats." She winked at him. "Present company excepted, of course."

She reached for a bowl of mixed nuts. "So how's the winning team doing on the bid?"

Alex sat in the matching chair across the table. "Shouldn't even be bidding this thing. You could have sole-sourced it to us. We're the only real qualified company with the whole package and you know it."

She threw her head back and laughed. "Sole-source a $500 million contract? What an ego."

"It's not about ego. It's about politics."

"There are fourteen other Councilmembers and I can't control everything. I did what I could with the heavy bid bond, the living wage and insurance requirements. But some of my colleagues still think this is the land of equal opportunity. Besides, I'd hate to eliminate good, small businesses like that competitor of yours, Pacific something or other? The young woman I met at the composting demonstration?"

Alex brushed his hand along the table like he was sweeping off a fly. "When it's over, we'll tear down that junkyard and recycle it, too."

He leaned his forearms on the table and sighed. "We've got a problem."

Barbara Miller's eyes flared for a second. "Let's take a cruise and you can tell me all your troubles," she said, running her fingers through her hair.

"I thought you were short on time?"

"Just to Venice Beach. We don't have to paddle for Chrissake."

Alex glanced at his watch and drained his beer. As he walked out on the deck and cast off the dock lines, he heard her yell, "I don't suppose you have anything decent to eat here?"

"Sandwiches in the fridge," Alex shouted back. He climbed up to the flying bridge and started the engines. With a guttural roar, the big boat pulled away from the dock, the wake causing the other boats to rock in their slips, the halyards of the sailboats clanking against the masts.

The phone rang next to the wheel and Alex grabbed it. "Yeah," he said.

The voice said, "I want to go over the deal. So we're clear."

Alex hesitated and his expression soured. Even over the phone, he could feel the quiet menace of Jack Oseppian. "How'd you get this number?"

"Two hundred thousand when Pacific Rim loses the bid, plus a dime a ton at the landfill for ten years. That's $500 a day-"

"I know what it is."

"I just don't want any bullshit to come up after. I'm putting my life on the line for this."

Alex checked to make sure Barbara wasn't on her way up the companionway. He kept his voice down. "Your life was already on the line, remember? I told you I'd cover you on the gambling debt, and I did. Same holds here. You just get me the information."

"You'll get it."

Alex hung up, and stretched his jaw where he'd had it clenched. It not only helped to have friends in high places, he thought, but low ones as well. One thing about Pacific Rim, they were close knit. This would be the dagger he needed to strike to the heart of Nazareth Agajanian, and in more ways than one.

But Jack could be a problem. Alex made a mental note to think of an end game, after the bid was over. Make this guy disappear. He heard Barbara climbing the companionway ladder. She glanced at Alex. "You all right?"

"Yeah, everything's great."

"Relax, Alex. Let's not get boring."

As they motored up the marina channel toward the open ocean, Barbara put the sandwiches and drinks on the steering console. "By the way," she said, "that was a nice touch."

Alex noticed she was barefoot. She had taken off her pantyhose. "What was?" he asked.

"Endowing the chair at the USC Business School."

"I felt like I should give something back to the educational institution that has given me so much."

She smiled.

The boat cleared the breakwater as Alex gunned the engines and turned north along the coast. The bow rose and the stern dropped as the props bit into the water. A great V-shaped wave formed behind the transom.

"The endowment was your idea," Alex said.

"I suggested only that some type of gift to the University would look good to the Council when this bid comes up, at least to all but our two esteemed colleagues from UCLA."

"Actually," Alex said. "I remember it as more of a threat." He watched the shoreline of Marina Del Rey passing by, the blue green of the water. Clumps of kelp slipped by.

"I just want to make sure you win, Alex."

She was such a smooth one, Alex thought. The more he saw of the City Council president, the better his girlfriend, Julia, looked. At least she was honest, from what he could tell anyway.

He powered the boat parallel to the shoreline about a quarter mile beyond the breakers. A groundswell coming in off the Catalina Channel lifted and dropped the boat in long heaves. He cut the engines back about a half mile short of the Venice Beach pier. The boat drifted, bow to the waves, the stern facing the shore. He could see the joggers and skaters, bike riders, muscle men, and the rest of the zoo that was Venice Beach.

Alex helped Barbara down the ladder to the afterdeck and they sat in the catch chairs. Barbara put her hat on to shade her face. "I just hate this sun and wrinkle thing. Can't even get a tan anymore."

"You should be Armenian," Alex said, taking a drink of beer. "Built in tan."

"We all can't have everything." She cleaned her sunglasses on a napkin. "So...what's the big problem you were going to tell me about?"

"The landfill's leaking."

"They all leak. At least that's what the Environmental Coalition tells me."

"We detected landfill gas in one of our downstream groundwater monitoring wells."

"The point being?"

Alex stood up. "All this crap is blown way out of proportion. A little gas isn't going to hurt anyone." Alex wadded up a piece of bread crust and threw it overboard. He watched a seagull sweep down and snatch it out of the water. "We need to cover it up till we get the bid, then I can fix it."

"But in the meantime?" she said.

"The inspector. Bureau of Sanitation. She supervised the installation of the wells in the first place."

Barbara walked to the rail and gazed down into the water. The sunlight reflected in waves off her face.

"She's a nit picker," Alex said. "Overkill. You know the type."

She turned to face Alex. "And you want me to fire her?"

"Just transfer her out of our area. Put her in waste-water, or something. Make it look like a promotion. But if she comes out for her monthly inspection of our monitoring system, we're in trouble."

Barbara Miller crunched a potato chip. "Your food selection is blowing my low fat diet."

Alex stared at her, waiting for an answer.

"Of course I'll do it," she snapped. Then she smiled. "But I'm putting it on your tab." She walked over and put her hands on his shoulders. "You know, I can't back a loser, Alex. As much as I like you, I wouldn't want to be forced to end our little win-win situation."

Alex pulled away. He watched a pelican soar by, inches above the waves, never flapping its wings, just coasting. And at that moment, he would have given anything to be that bird—soaring over the waves, riding the wind and looking for a school of mackerel. No cares, no worries, no Barbara Miller.

"OK. I'll have her promoted," Barbara said. "But your landfill's leaking. Your merger's leaking. You're like a sieve, Alex. You're full of holes." She rubbed her hands against his chest. "Better plug them up before you run all over the ground."

She guided his hand under her dress, up between her thighs, and held it against her.

"Jesus Christ, Barbara. Someone might see us out here."

She grabbed her hat off the deck and pulled it low over Alex's face. "There," she said, "I doubt whether they'll recognize the rest of you."

Alex closed his eyes and started rubbing harder and faster, trying to get it over with.

She grabbed his hand. "Someone would think you're in a hurry to finish." She took him by the jacket and backed up to the catch chair, and slowly sat down. "Strap me in, would you?" She pulled her dress up over her hips.

Alex walked around behind the chair and cinched the harness around her waist and chest. He wanted to rip the chair out of the deck with her in it and throw it over the side.

"Not so tight! I need to breathe to enjoy it." She grabbed Alex's arm and pulled him around in front of her. She tugged at him until he began to kneel, then she placed her hands on his shoulders and brought him all the way down. Her tongue ran over her lips as she sank her hands into his hair. She raised her legs up and draped them over the arms of the chair, and drew his head forward, her breath quickening, the glare of the sun washing out the world.

In the distance, the white line of breakers rushed toward the beach, and the wind carried muffled sounds of conversation.

*   *   *

Carina closed up the office at Pacific Rim and stepped out into the yard. The evening commute was just beginning to taper off on the freeway overpass. Under her arm she carried a black binder with the latest draft of the bid documents that Denny had put together for her review. She noticed Charlie unlocking his shipping container, Black sniffing the dirt at his heels. He turned to her, hesitating.

"Ms. Agajanian?" he said. "I, uh…sorry. I was wondering if I could show you something I been working on."

"Uh…."

"It'll only take a second. I need some advice."

"Gee, Charlie. I really got to get going."

"Please, just for a second."

"…Sure, OK, Charlie." Carina was jarred. Charlie guarded this container with his life. "Wait a minute," she said. "It's not filled with kinky weird stuff is it?"

"Who do you think I am, anyway?"

"That's why I asked."

"Well, it ain't nothin' like that."

Charlie opened the lock and swung the door. Black bounded in and Carina followed, swallowing a brief moment of panic, feeling the walls closing in on her. She could smell the alcohol on his breath, but that was nothing new. She thought she knew Charlie pretty well, and on occasion he would try to do something nice for her, give her a bouquet of oleander sprigs he'd picked off the neighbor's property. He seemed harmless enough, but….

Charlie squeezed past her and led the way to the back of the container. As she inched between the rows of junk, the smell of decay was strong, and she hoped breathing the stagnant air in there wouldn't kill her. Charlie turned on the construction light that hung over his workbench. The shelves seeped into view as Carina's eyes adjusted to the light.

"My God, Charlie. These are beautiful!" Carina carefully picked up one of the metal bonsai trees and turned it slowly in her hands. "Where'd you get these?"

"Made 'em," Charlie said.

"You made these?"

"Yep. Here's my workbench, soldering iron, cutting torch, acetylene. Been makin' 'em for over two years."

Carina was dumbstruck. The trees were delicate and beautiful, like nothing she had ever seen. This seemingly good-for-nothing derelict was an artist, and nobody knew.

"Charlie. You've got to show them to someone. An art dealer or something."

"That's what I wanted to ask. Do you know someone who could look at one and tell me?"

"Well, it's not exactly my area of expertise, but I could ask my mother. She collects frogs. You know, statues, not real ones."

"I don't want to cause no trouble." Charlie took the piece from her and put it back on the shelf.

"It's no trouble."

"I don't want your Dad to know. He might think it's weird or something."

Carina said, "Sure, Charlie. Just between you and me."

Carina noticed a tattoo of crossing anchors and a name peeking out from under Charlie's rolled up sleeve. "Who's Fletcher?" she said.

A pained expression flickered across Charlie's face, and he glanced at his arm. "USS Fletcher. Destroyer."

"You were in the Navy?"

"Yeah." Charlie started rummaging through his tools.

It always amazed Carina when she found out about the old men who had fought in WW II. It just never occurred to her. Uncle Vahan had been an engine mechanic on a submarine. Sank three Jap ships, depth charged seventeen times, or so the story went. And now, here was this derelict, Charlie, on a destroyer.

"Did you fight in any battles?" she said.

"Only one…." Charlie gazed off into space, his hands running an oiled rag over a strange metal shaft that he had pulled from under his workbench.

"You know, that's OK, Charlie." Carina glanced at her watch. "I should get going."

"We were in a convoy. Three days out of Halifax. North Atlantic run to Liverpool. The U-boats hit us." Charlie grimaced and closed his eyes.

"I'm sorry," Carina said. "I didn't mean to…."

"I was in the engine room. We caught a torpedo. Water rushing in. I knew my job! The bulkhead door. A hundred times—drill after drill!" Charlie yelled.

Carina leaned away and glanced down the passageway for the door. "Look, Charlie, it's OK." But she could see Charlie was not OK. He was back in the engine room….

"But the water. I panicked. I didn't think I could reach the door. The water rising, cold. So I climbed up and up. The deck—air. But the door! I should've secured the door."

"I'm so sorry, Charlie. I'm sure you did the best…."

"Twelve men! Compartment flooded."

"Things happen. It wasn't your fault."

A sad, wild look veiled his eyes. "The rest of them wouldn't talk to me. Like I was invisible. But they weren't down there! They didn't feel the water up to their necks! The alarm screaming! The men screaming!"

"Shut up," Charlie yelled, his eyes wild, swinging around, brandishing the apparatus at Carina—a spear gun. She jerked back in reaction and stumbled into a pile of cans that crashed to the floor.

Black barked.

Charlie froze, his body twitching. His eyes blinked. He tilted his head to the side, a perplexed look on his face. His arms relaxed and the speargun fell to his side. Charlie sagged against the workbench, breathing hard, his hands trembling. He tried to speak, but nothing came out.

Carina lurched for the door, banged it open and stumbled out.

"Sorry," Charlie yelled as he walked unsteadily after her. "I didn't mean nothin'." He looked down at the weapon as he stood in the doorway. "I found it in the trash."

Carina yelled back over her shoulder. "Better get rid of it before you kill somebody!" She jumped into her car. As she swerved out of the yard, she saw Charlie and Black still standing by the open door of his container. He waved feebly.

*   *   *

"And out of the cocoon, the beautiful butterfly spread

its wings for the first time and flew off into the moonlight." Jack closed the slim book and pinched the bridge of his nose. His eyes were burning.

"Please, Daddy, one more time," the little voice said.

"Daddy's tired. It's time for bed."

"But I'm not sleepy."

Jack Oseppian pulled up the blanket with the teddy bears on it. He kissed his daughter's forehead. "Maybe tomorrow." He rose from her bed, paused at the door and looked back at her, then turned off the light.

"Leave the door open," the little voice said.

Jack eased the door back open.

As he walked down the hall, Jack heard his wife Sophie, Naz's sister, on the phone. She always shouted into the phone like she had to pump her voice all the way through the line. Jack turned away and plunged into his workshop off the garage. He pulled a bottle of scotch out of a drawer and poured a couple inches in a water glass. He took a swallow and tried to think of where it had all gone so wrong, but his thoughts swirled like a maelstrom, and he couldn't fasten on the torn pieces as they rushed by.

He could hardly believe it himself, that here he was—cutting a deal with the Harts to bring the Agajanians down, the family that had embraced him like a son. But he had a right to protect his own family, didn't he? An obligation to his girls and their future? Where was his future at Pacific Rim, anyway? Carina was clearly the heir apparent. Naz was sure as hell covering his family. And besides, their chance of winning this bid was virtually zero. Although Jack was the trusted lieutenant, he would always be the outsider, the son-in-law, not the son. Jack grimaced at the thought, sometimes something has to die, so that something else can live. This time, he would be the one left standing and that would have to be back up north, maybe in Madera County, where he could raise his daughters and live out the rest of his life in a quiet backwater. God help me, he thought. He drained his drink and poured another—the bottle clinking against the lip of his glass.

8

With less than a week till the bid, Carina felt she had better things to do than go to a meeting of LARRA, the Los Angeles Refuse & Recycling Association. But Naz had reminded her that it was mostly the smaller hauling companies; many loyal customers of Pacific Rim, delivering loads of trash and recyclables for years. And maybe she could win over a few more converts to replace the 400 tons a day Zaven and some of the others had pulled out. They needed to generate cash flow any way they could, and if that meant she had to put on her mascara and eat a rubber chicken dinner, then so be it.

The group of thirty or so trash guys sat at a cluster of tables in the back room of the restaurant in Pico Rivera. Carina tossed down the last of a glass of cheap Merlot, and set her fork down. The prime rib, or whatever it was, was so bloody it was making her gag. She looked up and unexpectedly locked eyes with Zaven Petoyan a couple tables away. He nodded to her and shoveled a hunk of meat into his mouth.

Carina shifted her gaze, pretending to focus on the speaker who droned on from the lectern, but her heart was racing. She could feel his gaze from across the room.

Her first instinct was to bolt for the ladies room, climb out the back window, and run for her car—get far away from the gaze, the meat-cleaver hands. But in her next breath, she felt disgusted with herself, embarrassed to call herself an Agajanian. Goddammit, she wouldn't be afraid, or at least she wouldn't show it.

She straightened in her seat, picked up her steak knife and looked back at Zaven. Ignoring the twinge of fear that gripped her, she cut a piece of prime rib and slowly put it in her mouth and started to chew. She shot a smile at him. Eat your heart out, you sonuvabitch, she thought, trying to buck up her own courage.

The speaker finished to a splatter of applause, plates were cleared, and some god-awful chocolate pudding was served with whipped cream and a maraschino cherry. Carina wolfed hers down. The bravado of before had evaporated, and she just wanted to get out of there.

The association director finished with a few final announcements and an admonition to get their membership dues in. Carina exchanged cards with a couple young men at her table using her best smile to pitch one last time the virtues of Pacific Rim, all the while knowing they were more interested in the virtues of Carina Agajanian. Whatever it took. A ton of trash was a ton of trash—no matter how it got to the plant.

Out of the corner of her eye, she saw Zaven circling

toward her. She grabbed her purse and buried herself in the flow of men pressing for the door. Swept down the hall, she glanced around, but Zaven was gone.

In the parking lot, she shook hands with admirers, received shouts of encouragement about the bid, and took a hug or two from some of her father's friends. Then she climbed into her car, the throng evaporated. Her driver's side window was stuck in the down position, some short in the electrical. She had decided to just put up with it until the bid was over.

Suddenly, a shadow blocked the streetlight, a hand grabbed her side view mirror, heavy gold bracelet hanging down.

"Good prime rib, huh?" Zaven said.

"Good enough," she answered. Fumbling with the ignition, she dropped the keys on the floor. He was so close, she could smell the horseradish on his breath.

"The problem I got is with your old man, not you," he said. "I might be persuaded to bring back my tonnage, we was to talk about it. You know, you and me."

Carina turned and stared back at Zaven and said in a clipped monotone, "Please, take your hand off my car."

"You're going to be left with nothin' when the dust settles."

"Great, I'll take the dust." Carina jabbed the key in the ignition, the blood pulsing in her head. She turned the key and pumped the accelerator. The engine cranked over and over.

"You flooded it," he said.

Carina prayed for the engine to start. Come on, please. She felt his hand brush back a strand of her hair, his fingertips touching the skin of her neck. She shivered and pulled away. The engine caught, and she jammed it in gear, the transmission grinding.

"I'll show you how to drive sometime," he yelled over the roar of the engine.

Carina punched the accelerator, squealing out the driveway and rocketed up the street.

Her father could go himself to the next fucking association meeting.

She flew up the freeway on-ramp, letting the power and roar of the engine wash over her. Blowing through the red merge control light like it was a Christmas tree ornament, she was fifty yards beyond and hitting the freeway at full throttle when it turned green.

*   *   *

The early morning rush hour traffic was jammed by a trash truck accident, garbage strewn across the lanes. Naz hoped it was one of Zaven's, but as he crept by the accident, he saw that it was one of the little guys, Topaz Disposal, one of his customers at Pacific Rim. Jermag Avoyan brought in only forty tons a day, but good commercial loads from the garment district. He only had a couple trucks, and half his fleet was laying on its side on the freeway, no insurance. Such was life. No one knew that better than Naz.

It was 6:20 a.m. when Naz pulled into the restaurant parking lot, not far from Pacific Rim. A low fog sucked the light from a neon sign above his head that read, "Cafe – Good Food."

A heavy-set, uniformed cop was walking toward his

car in the parking lot. Naz accelerated in and swerved into a parking space, just missing the officer, and causing him to spill his coffee. Naz leaped out of his car beaming.

"Naz, you sonuvabitch!"

"Jesus Christ, Joe. You eat any more of that shish kabab you're going to explode."

"It's irresistible. Besides, it's healthier than the cheeseburgers you eat."

"You go easy. I don't want you conking out of a heart attack or something. I might need you."

"What, find a body in a dumpster? A knife fight at the scalehouse? Charlie's dog eat someone's Chihuahua?"

"Hey," said Naz, "Just trying to get some goddamn service from the city for all the taxes I pay. Or don't pay as the case may be."

Joe's radio squawked from the car, and he bolted into the driver's seat. "You stay out of trouble, Naz."

Naz just held up his hands, palms out, as Joe squealed out of the lot.

Sergeant Joseph Andrzejek Kowalski. The guy who puts flowers on the pedestal of that statue of the Polish general downtown. The guy with the big heart and the heavy night stick. Fifteen years on the Boyle Heights beat. Would've made detective long ago, but for that time he beat that drug dealer senseless, and got nailed with excessive force, or some bullshit. Over the years, Naz couldn't even calculate how much Armenian string cheese and flat bread he had given Kowalski. Better than one of those stickers in your car window saying you gave to the Police Academy or whatever. And the Sergeant had already saved Naz's ass on a couple occasions.

Altercations in the local bar, shit with his car registration.

But it all evened out and then some the night Naz came upon Joe's Bonneville up against the lamppost, grill smashed and radiator hissing. And Joe, off duty and hammered out of his mind. Naz drove him back to Pacific Rim, pumped him full of coffee, and got him in the shower in the employee's locker room. Naz finally called the police station, to report the accident, but only after Joe had sobered up. Naz even went to the Police Commission hearing and lied his ass off. The Sergeant never forgot.

What little comfort Naz felt from the world, what little help he could count on outside his own abilities, a good chunk of it came in the form of Joe Kowalski.

Naz smiled as he walked into the one-room restaurant that steamed with the aroma of baking bread, frying bacon, coffee, hot sauce and sweating bodies. The traditional round bread was stacked on the counter top. It came straight from the ovens in the back that not only baked the bread, but heated the restaurant. Naz could see the other early morning regulars...truckers, metal salvage guys, and workers getting ready to go on shift at the Sears warehouse across the street. They huddled over tables, hands folded around cups of coffee, voices low in mumbled conversation.

"Good morning, Ronnie!" Naz said to a large woman behind the counter.

"You're late, Naz," she hollered back over the din from the tables and the hiss of a truck's air-brakes outside.

"Traffic was a bear," Naz said. "It's a cemetery out there. Cal Trans is burying people in their cars."

"Sure, sure, Naz." Ronnie laid her fat hands on top of

the counter. Her face glistened with sweat and she lifted up her apron and wiped her forehead. "What you want this morning, hon', the usual?"

Naz nodded. She turned and yelled to the kitchen. "Double cheeseburger, slice of onion." She poured Naz a cup of coffee and handed it to him.

He ambled over to the table in the corner. It had a red Formica top with cigarette burns around the edges, and chairs with red vinyl cushions. He sat, poured sugar in his coffee, and stirred it, his mind preoccupied.

Ronnie plopped the cheeseburger down in front of him, and Naz lathered Tabasco all over it. He took a bite and the fire made his eyes water—perfect.

She leaned over to warm up his coffee.

Naz said. "Lemme borrow your pencil, I gotta figure something."

She pulled the pencil out of her hair and handed it to him. "Don't forget to give it back. You got a hundred of mine already."

Naz clipped off the soggy end of his dead cigar, and stuck the fresh end in his mouth. He rolled it slowly with his fingers, moistening it all around. He pulled a pair of plastic reading glasses out of his pocket, bent them back to near straight and put them on. They were pink. He kept losing the prescription ones Mayda bought him, the ones that cost $300 each. So now, he bought twelve pairs of the two dollar kind at the drugstore, and stashed them everywhere, so there was always one within reach, even if the color didn't match the occasion.

He doodled on the napkin, starting to work the bid numbers in his head. Time was running out. He needed to nail his number. But it was a process that couldn't be rushed, he had needed to let things percolate. And he knew it had reached the level of obsession when he even thought about the bid immediately after making love to Mayda. If she felt him drifting at that critical time, there would be hell to pay. Definitely, time to get it down on paper. It had percolated enough.

Despite his half a high school education, and even that questionable, Naz was a natural with numbers. He'd been running figures like these since he was nine, calculating the value of the small bales of cardboard he picked up from the grocery stores. Revenues, costs, time, where to cut a nickel, where to exact a dime. Here he was, nearly fifty years later, the junkman at the top of his game. And in this case—a $500 million game.

Naz picked a piece of tobacco off his tongue and wiped it on the edge of the table. He stared at the blank napkin for a moment, then pulled a second napkin out of the metal holder. Across the top of the first one, he scrawled "COSTS" in a messy mix of small and capital letters; on the second, "REVENUES."

His mind dissected the L.A. bid like quartering a lamb. The costs fell into four sections: processing the trash to recover recyclables; loading the residue into the eighteen-wheel trucks, hauling that residue to the landfill, and the landfill dump fee itself. Over the years, Naz had honed jobs like this to the penny per ton. He began to throw numbers down on the napkin, stopping occasionally to take a bite of cheeseburger. The toughest number was the sorting cost, labor intensive and dependent on the quality of the trash. He thought of the loads coming in, the residential waste contaminated with food, grass from the lawns, other junk. Then the cleaner commercial material with more cardboard, office paper—the main focus of his recovery effort. He pictured the men on the sorting line, the river of trash flowing by on the conveyor belt, the hands moving, the material falling to the bunkers below.

It was easiest for him to think of costs per ton of trash. He'd done it his whole life. Naz scribbled a number down—forty dollars a ton.

Then the other costs clicked in his mind, like the tumblers of a lock. Loading the transfer trucks—five dollars a ton; hauling to the landfill, 250 miles, 10 Freeway east through Palm Springs, the high desert—seven dollars a ton; and his secret ace in the hole, the Rainbow Ridge landfill tipping fee. Although he had yet to meet officially with his cousin who ran the landfill and the Indian tribe who owned it, he had some preliminary indications that it would be in the range of eight dollars a ton. That sweet, low number, like a gift from God, or more accurately in this case from Cousin Armand, was twelve dollars under the HIA landfill, easy, maybe thirteen dollars, if those asshole merger partners squeezed them for more profit.

"Ronnie!" Naz yelled over the general hubbub, holding up his coffee cup.

"Keep your shirt on!" she yelled back, grabbing a pot and heading his way.

She poured scalded black coffee into his mug, noting the scribbles on the napkins. "So you can write after all."

"You want to run away with me to Ensenada?" Naz said, his eyes shining, intoxicated by the numbers burning in his brain.

"Honey, I love you, but I wouldn't run across the street with you."

As she walked away, Naz hollered after her, "Even Boyle? Look they got a crossing guard." She waved her hand without turning around, but Naz knew she was smiling. He grabbed the second napkin, the revenue side, the "up" side. He had two revenue streams on the L.A. bid—the sale of the recyclable materials, and the avoided disposal cost for that same stuff. Every ton he recycled was one ton that he didn't have to pay to load, haul and bury at the landfill. Depending on the landfill fees and market prices, sometimes the avoided cost was worth more than the material itself.

He plugged in the twenty-five percent recycling rate mandated in the bid, estimated the value of the recyclables, going heavy on the cardboard and paper from the commercial tonnage; and newspaper, glass, plastic, and-steel and aluminum cans from the residential side. Even a little for Carina's dirt and rock.

The recyclables markets were fickle, but Naz had charted their seasonal swings, their highs and lows, their tendencies, weaknesses, strengths—almost like a living thing, a migratory beast. He jotted down a number—sixty dollars a ton for value, plus the twenty dollars for avoiding the transfer truck loading, hauling, and disposal.

Naz did the math long hand. He never used a calculator, trusting his mind more than any machine. His mind was a great crap detector, and knew when something was off. No machine could do that. Punch the wrong button and you're fucked. And if he was going to get fucked, he'd rather fuck himself than have a calculator do it.

Naz added up his costs, multiplied some stuff, shifted a number over here, subtracted revenues and came up with a net cost of thirty dollars a ton. Twenty percent on top of that for profit before taxes made thirty-six dollars. That's what he would charge the city for every ton they delivered to Pacific Rim. A damn good number. A killer number.

The Harts, who didn't know about his looming backroom landfill deal with his cousin, would figure him to be paying the county landfill fee of twenty-six dollars a ton. Sure the long truck haul to the desert ate into that difference, but still, he was low.

Naz gobbled a chunk of burger, staring at the thirty-six dollar number. He closed his eyes, grimacing, not from the hot sauce that was at that instant devouring the lining of his stomach, but at what he was about to do.

He crossed out the thirty-six dollars and wrote in thirty-four dollars. Two bucks a ton off his bid. That was a loss of $6,000 a day, five days a week, fifty-two weeks a year, over $1.5 million a year—right off the bottom line. The thought took his breath away, but in his gut it felt right.

It killed him to leave that much money on the table, a fortune in its own right, but it would kill him more if he lost the bid. He had to be low bidder. Then it would be his deal to lose. He thought of his traditional tactic of low-balling to win and then trying to bump up the fee during negotiations, throw in some extra services, in other words—create some shit, the Agajanian mantra.

But there would be no shit creating on this one, not with the Harts and Barbara Miller hovering over him like jackals. No, this bid had to be low, but not so low that he lost his ass. No use winning the bid just to watch the whole company go down a rat hole.

He drew a circle around the thirty-four dollars.

He had his number. He would live or die at thirty-four dollars a ton. Over the twenty year contract, that was a bid totaling $530,400,000. He remembered his dad telling him when he was just a boy that all deals were the same, just a matter of zeroes, but this one was a shitload of zeroes. Now he would sleep with it, eat with it, live with it—alone. Nobody would know his number. Not Denny. Jack. Carina. Harry. Not even Mayda. Too much at stake.

Naz dropped a twenty dollar bill on the table and flew towards the door.

Noticing his high spirits, Ronnie sang out, "You win the lottery or what, Nazareth?"

Naz shot her a boyish grin, his blue eyes dancing, and pointed his cigar at her. "Not yet. But when I do, it's you and me to Ensenada!"

She just shook her head and waved him away, but he was already out the door.

* * *

Soft music drifted down over the polished mahogany table in the HIA conference room, where Alex, Kail, their CPA, and a couple stiff-looking men in dark business suits poured over *pro forma* spreadsheets. Crystal glasses of ice water sweated in front of them, making wet rings on the marble coasters.

The CPA, a guy who looked like a great blue heron with a tie, said, "Based on our favored landfilling rate, required recycling, virtually zero haul cost, and average material value with forty percent going domestic and sixty percent shipped overseas, we show a seventeen percent net rate of return."

One of the stuffed shirts said without looking up from the document, "We won't go after anything less than twenty percent."

Alex said, "The problem here is the companies bidding against us are desperate. We need to protect ourselves on the low side." Alex turned to his father. "You know who I mean, in particular."

Kail replied, "I suggest we worry less about what our competition is doing, and more about what we are doing."

One of the Global men drilled Alex with a cold look. "Why would we cut profit for some pissant competitors? I thought you had this thing wired?"

"It's being wired," Alex said, a belligerent look on his face. He couldn't stand these holier-than-thou assholes from the East Coast. They had gotten big by buying out smaller companies with pumped-up stock options—all paper value. Sooner or later, the balloon was going to break, and Global Waste Enterprises was going to have to actually perform. Alex and his father had built HIA on solid ground, centered on their billion-dollar landfill, and a dozen city collection franchises, with "evergreen" contracts, so-called because they rolled out year after year into the future and never died. Real money, not Wall Street hype.

Alex hated this merger deal, orchestrated by his father, the Chairman of the Board, the one who would walk away with the lion's share, while Alex would be left to work with these piranhas. When his father had sprung the merger deal out of nowhere, negotiating behind his back as if he didn't exist, that had shaken the ground under Alex and spun him off in a new direction. Now, Alex had his own plans for the merger deal and the Chairman, but he needed this bid first.

Kail said to the CPA, "What are you showing for our internalized landfill cost?"

"Sixteen dollars a ton."

"What if we made it say, eighteen?"

The CPA nervously punched numbers into his calculator, jotted some numbers down. "That would increase the rate of return to slightly over twenty percent."

"Yeah," Alex said, "And add over thirty million dollars to our bid."

Kail lined up the spreadsheets in front of him. "What's the county landfill rate, the one Pacific Rim will have to pay?"

"Twenty-six," the CPA said.

"I don't see the problem, Alex," Kail said. "He's still eight dollars over us in disposal cost alone, plus he's got hauling. Even if he pulls in all his chits with the mills, even if he pulls something unexpected, even if he thinks he's low—let him believe it. In the end, the numbers don't lie. We've got him." Kail fixed his son with a cold stare. "And if you need extra assurance, you can reduce your cost elsewhere, medical insurance for the workers, for example."

Alex swirled his water glass, the ice clinking in the silence. Maybe his father should deal with Barbara Miller. Then the two barracudas could go at it, taking bites out of each other, see who would eat who in the bloody water.

But then his father was just carrying on the family tradition from the days of the genocide, when Alex's grandparents had collaborated with the Turks, bribed the right officials and survived. His father was still looking out for number one and always would. And Alex knew that number one for Kail Hartunian extended no further than the tip of his own tongue.

"If we're all agreed then, I suggest we make the change," Kail said, smiling and nodding at the two men at the other end of the table.

They nodded back.

9

Alex stepped out of the car into the glare of the sun setting across the athletic field. His mind was still back in the boardroom, his father, the merger—and most of all, the bid number. Thank God, he'd made the deal with Jack Oseppian. Desperation was such a beautiful thing. It could move mountains. Jack was going to help move this one.

The crack of shoulder pads snapped Alex back from his thoughts. He started off across the field toward a group of young boys in football gear. Their white practice jerseys and helmets glowed in the twilight.

"Hey," a pretty woman yelled, as she shoved the passenger door shut and jogged to catch up with Alex. Julia Walker, Alex's girlfriend, was a cute blond with cover girl looks and a body-fat count in the single digits. Her shorts fit tight and her light yellow blouse matched a scarf that tied her hair back in a ponytail.

She caught up with him. "What's the hurry?"

"It's late. Looks like they're finishing up with tackling drills." Alex could almost taste the grass, the dirt, the leather of the ball. It took him right back to his days at USC, linebacker, big man on campus.

Alex stopped a few yards from the boys. Julia slipped her arm through his, but he didn't notice. He was watching his son, who gave him a slight wave, without lifting his arm. Alex nodded back. Johnny Hart was smaller than most of the others, not having started his growth spurt yet. But Alex knew the boy had good genes and would develop in the next few years, at least that's what he hoped. He had enrolled Johnny in a special spring football league to toughen him up against more advanced players.

"All right, Hart," the coach grunted. "Keep your legs pumping. Break the tackle. You hear me?" The coach shoved the ball into Johnny's gut.

"Yes, sir!" Johnny grunted back.

"D'ya hear me, gentlemen?"

"Yes, sir!" shouted the boys, their young voices still high and light and sounding out of place behind the face masks.

The coach turned to the tackler on the other side of two markers on the field, a big kid with a dark purple visor over his eyes. "And Thompson, I wanna see you hit! Knock 'im on his can! What're you, tired?"

"No sir!"

"All right then. Now come on! Get ready!"

The boys crouched. Johnny wrapped both hands around the ball and clutched it tightly to his chest.

"Come on, Johnny. You can do it!" Julia yelled.

"Ya! Come onnnnnnn Johnny," the other boys cried, "you can dooooo it." A smattering of laughter broke out.

Alex whispered to her, "Don't say shit like that."

"Sorry," she said. "This is supposed to be fun?"

"Phweeet!" the coach's whistle screamed, and Johnny Hart, all five feet and seventy-five pounds of him, ran as fast as he could between the markers.

Crack!

The Thompson kid hit him high on the shoulder. The power of the bigger boy carried Johnny off his feet and with a whoooomph he hit the ground. The ball bounced free.

"Fumble!!!" the boys yelled. Thompson dove on the ball, while Johnny rolled on his back gasping for breath.

Julia cringed and tucked her face into Alex's shoulder. Alex wasn't even aware of her. His eyes were black and wide open.

"That's the way to hit, Thompson!" the coach yelled. The coach hovered over Johnny. "Next time Hart, don't slow down when you hit the hole. You're gonna get hurt."

Johnny limped to the back of the tackling line, head down. Alex forced a smile and folded his arms across his chest. "Living with his mother's going to ruin him," he said to Julia. "She ought to watch him getting the crap beat out of him, then maybe she'd understand. You've got to be tough on them."

"He's trying hard," said Julia.

"Jesus, you women."

They watched for another twenty minutes as all the boys took turns running and tackling. Johnny again drawing a much bigger kid, trying to tackle him, but ending up being dragged five yards hanging on desperately to one of the runner's legs.

It was getting dark, and the coach called the boys to huddle. They gave a couple rebel yells, and the practice ended. Julia walked up to Johnny and, although she wanted to hug him, she punched him on the shoulder pad instead.

"You shouldn't punch with your thumb inside your fingers like that," Johnny said. "You'll break it."

"Thanks. I'll remember that, next time I get in a fight," she said, walking along beside him toward the car, where Alex was already waiting. "I thought, for a second, your Dad was going to tackle that kid himself."

"Dad was All-Conference. I'll never be that good."

"You don't have to be him. You just be yourself. Besides, now all he's got to show for it is a broken nose."

"That's not from football."

"What do you mean?"

"Nothing."

"He told me it was football." Puzzled, Julia glanced at Johnny. But the boy just picked at the lining of his helmet.

As they walked up to his father, standing by the car, Johnny's head dropped. "Sorry I fumbled, Dad, I...."

"Let me show you something about tackling."

"I'm tired, Dad...."

"You want to get your ass run over every time? Now, come on, this'll only take a second." Alex moved about five yards off. "The key is to watch my belt buckle. No matter what kind of fakes the runner throws at you, his belly goes in the direction he's running. You ready?"

"Yeah, I'm ready," Johnny said half-heartedly. He crouched and stared at his father's mid-section.

Alex ran at the boy and as he dodged, his foot slipped on the gravel. Johnny lunged at him and his shoulder pad caught his father right in the groin. Alex groaned, limped over and leaned against the car. Julia tried to suppress a laugh but it burst out.

Johnny hid a smile. "Sorry, Dad, I didn't mean...."

"Don't say you're sorry, for Chrissake. That was a good hit...goddamn gravel."

"Are you going to be all right?" Julia said, trying not to laugh.

"Let's get something to eat," Alex said, straightening up with a grimace. "How about Carl's Jr.?"

Johnny pulled his jersey and shoulder pads over his head and tossed his equipment onto the back seat. "You just like the free Coke refills," he said.

"Nothing wrong with saving a little money," Alex said. "Besides, Julia can eat the salad special, while you pound down two or three of those double-bacon cheeseburgers."

"Yeah, right."

"Don't listen to him, Johnny," Julia said. "You eat whatever you want."

Alex said, "Another ten pounds on you would make a hell of a difference."

"I'm not that hungry."

"Sure you are."

"Alex, would you stop it," Julia said.

They climbed in and drove off into the dusk.

*   *   *

Carina licked the salt off the frosty rim of the bowl-size glass, and took a gulp of the best margarita in Los Angeles, in her opinion, anyway. There might be no finer combination of flavors in the world—lime, triple sec, salt, and tequila.

The Villa del Gato was her favorite Mexican restaurant. In the warm, close air, she could smell the grilling chicken, green onions and cilantro. Everything was red—red carpet, red Naugahyde booths, red bulbs in wrought iron lamps. All trimmed with bright turquoise. The room itself seemed to be screaming and drumming its heels on the floor.

Naz had been in one of his stressed-out moods earlier in the day, popping Tums like candy, and had suggested in no uncertain terms that she find out where the hell Denny was on the bid package. It was her intention to meet Denny here after work and go over his progress, make this a work session. But after a couple slurps of her margarita, she realized why she had picked this particular spot...she was tired from pressing on all fronts and needed the break.

Her father would understand this kind of meeting, after all, he'd had more than his share over the years in the bar at the Dal Rae. Between he and his pals they must've thrown down an Olympic size swimming pool of Jack Daniels over the years.

The Villa del Gato was a one-room affair. To the right of the door, also red, was a U-shaped bar packed with patrons; to the left, a cluster of tables. The front door swung open and Carina watched Denny enter, lugging his three-ring binder. He stumbled over the threshold. She smiled. There was something noble about how hard he tried, his "org charts" and all the rest tucked under his arm.

"Hi," he said, plopping his binder on the seat, eyeing the half-finished "Grande" margarita sitting in front of Carina.

"You want a margarita?" she said.

"Uh...."

"Waitress!" Carina flagged the young girl in her homemade dress and ordered the drink.

"I'm making good progress on the corporate experience section," Denny said, sliding into the booth. "I'm even...."

"You know, I'm not sure I can handle the bid yet. I haven't eaten all day, one of the loaders went down...."

"Sorry," Denny said. "I'm a little wired."

A moment later, the waitress set down Denny's grande margarita.

"Cheers!" Carina said, lifting her bowl-sized drink with both hands.

"Uh, yeah, cheers!"

They clinked glasses and Denny took a short slurp. Carina took a long one. They grabbed the hot tortilla chips that came right from the oven and dug into the guacamole, served in a bowl carved out of volcanic rock.

Carina knew the best dishes so she ordered for both of them. An appetizer of albondigas soup, then chile rellenos, chicken tacos al carbon, and another round of margaritas. They were both ravenous, and said little as they ate.

Carina sucked the last sweet green liquid out of her glass until the straw snorkeled with air. "One more?" she asked.

"Shouldn't we get started on the bid?"

"Waitress!"

Denny squinted at his watch. A moment later, the waitress hustled over with the next round.

Carina rubbed her finger down the side of the icy glass. "So, Mr. DeYoung...tell me. How'd you get to be a solid waste consultant? I mean, I was born into trash. I didn't realize anyone volunteered."

Denny took a small sip of margarita. "When I got back from the Peace Corps, this big environmental engineering firm hired me."

"You were in the Peace Corps?"

"Three years, Angola. Africa."

"Say something in African."

Denny blushed a little and shook his head.

"Come on. Impress me."

Denny hesitated, then shot out a line in fluent Bakongo dialect.

"Whoa! That was awesome. What's it mean?"

"Cut the water buffalo shit."

Carina burst out laughing and put her hand on Denny's arm. "I guess I had that coming." She laughed again. God, those margaritas were good.

"It was a time in my life. That's all." Denny stared into his drink.

"I didn't mean to pry...well, I did, actually."

"Anyway," Denny went on, "I learned a bit about lagoon systems over there when I was teaching fish farming, and when I came back I started out in waste-water. That segued into landfill leachate collection and treatment systems, and that led to...."

"The amazing world of trash."

"Exactly."

"Well, here's to trash!" Carina said, lifting her glass.

"To trash," Denny replied and they clinked glasses, looking at each other as they drank.

"You know my Dad always said consultants couldn't grab their ass with both hands, but then he hired you...."

"Yeah?" Denny smiled. "I guess I better start practicing in front of the mirror."

Carina shook her head and laughed. The room was beginning to move in her eyes.

For dessert, they split an order of flan, their spoons clicking in the custard till they were scraping the glass clean.

Denny sat back. "That was some working session. Couple more like this and either the bid'll be done, or we will."

Carina said, "There's more to life than bids."

"Tell that to your father tomorrow."

"We'll be all right. Trust me."

She paid the bill over his objections. "You'll just bill us for it anyway," she said.

"Plus 15% markup," he said with a smile.

"You are such a deal."

Denny held the door for her on the way out, and this time she walked right through. Boy, I could get used to this, she thought.

Then she looked to the street and screamed, "Hey!"

Carina started running toward a tow truck that had

just winched her El Camino up on its back. "Hey! That's my car!"

The tow truck driver pointed. "See that sign?" Carina glanced in the general direction and even a blind man could see in big red letters "No Parking. Violators will be TOWED!"

"What sign?" she said.

"You parked in a red zone, lady. In front of a fire hydrant."

"The lot was full."

"Once I hook up, I've got to take it. You can pick it up in the morning. Sorry."

"Wait! Come on. Here's twenty bucks...."

The driver scrambled into his truck, fired up the engine and roared off with Carina's car.

"Shit!" she yelled.

"Red zone?" Denny said.

"Goddammit! Yeah, I know. Bad habit I got from my Dad. He says everyone's entitled to a parking space, and he'll take his right in front. I know it sounds dumb, but it nearly always works."

"Come on," Denny said. "I'll give you a lift."

"Can you imagine that job?" she said, as they walked toward the back of the restaurant. "Spend all day towing people's cars away? Bad karma, that's for sure."

"Just about as bad as parking in a red zone."

Carina wasn't paying much attention as Denny walked up between a car and a motorcycle and she started walking around to the passenger side of the car.

"Wrong one," Denny said.

She poked her head around and saw Denny strapping

on a motorcycle helmet. Her jaw dropped. "This Harley is yours?"

"No. We're going to steal it." He stuffed the bid binders in the saddlebags, then handed her a black helmet. "I always carry a spare for emergencies...like you."

Carina was momentarily stunned. Her brain was having a hard time connecting the dots.

"I know," he said, motioning to the helmet. "It messes up your hair."

"No...it's, uh...yeah, right."

Carina slid the helmet on, grimacing as it pulled her hair, then she struggled to fasten the chinstrap.

"Here," Denny said. "Let me help you get that."

She could feel his hands against her cheeks, tickling along her jawbone, and under her chin. Denny's face was only inches from hers, and while he focused on the chinstrap, she studied him, the straight nose, light blue eyes. He glanced up for a second and caught her staring at him. He cinched the strap tight.

"Ow," she said.

"It's got to be tight, or it tears your face off if we crash."

"How exciting."

"You ever been on a bike before?"

"Only in my dreams."

"I'll get on first, then you slide in behind me."

Denny hopped on the bike, turned the ignition key and punched the starter button. The bike roared to life. She swung her leg over and slid onto the seat behind him, the whole front side of her pressed up against Denny's back. The sudden intimacy cut her breath short.

"You OK?" Denny said, turning his head.

"Yeah, sure."

"Put your feet up on these pegs, and keep them there, even when we stop. Don't worry, we won't fall over."

"That's what they all say," she said.

Denny laughed. "OK, wrap your arms around me and just hold on."

Carina hesitated, then slid her arms around Denny and hugged herself gently up against him. Her heart was pounding and she hoped he couldn't feel it through his leather jacket.

"Where to?" he said.

"Montebello."

Denny eased out the clutch, rolled on the throttle and they roared out into the night. They passed body shops, taco trucks set up on blocks, gas stations, and neighborhood carnicerias. Carina closed her eyes and felt the rush of cool wind against her face. The guttural roar of the Harley's engine vibrated up through her pelvis.

They pulled up to a stoplight next to a 1962 Chevy Nova low-rider nearly scraping the pavement. On the other side of them, almost near enough to touch, an old pickup stuffed with rakes, lawnmowers, weed whackers, and four Mexicans, belched exhaust.

Denny revved the motorcycle. The men in the pickup whooped back at the sound, and the driver gunned his old Ford, sending a blue cloud of exhaust into the air. Not to be left out, the low-rider revved his engine in reply.

Denny turned his head toward Carina. "Hang on."

She hugged him, her face over his shoulder, her heart thumping. She wondered if his was thumping too, but if it was, she'd never know. He sat quiet and calm as marble.

They all watched the opposing light turn from green to yellow. Then their light flashed green.

The Harley dug in and roared across the intersection. Carina felt the acceleration in her gut. She couldn't breathe.

The old pickup sputtered and fell behind, but the lightweight low-rider was quicker off the line and had a short lead. Denny shifted into second and took the Chevy about 75 yards out. Then he decelerated quickly, turned left and dropped down toward the lights of the freeway.

Twenty minutes later, Denny pulled up Carina's driveway, bouncing over the hump where her car usually bottomed out. He killed the ignition and held the bike as she slid off.

Her entire body was one warm, tingling vibration. The exhilaration of the speed and power left her feeling like she'd just gone five laps in her stock car, or better. She took off her helmet.

"I should get towed more often," she said softly, the words feeling almost foreign in her throat after the deep, bone-rattling vibrations of the motorcycle.

Denny smiled and patted the gas tank. "Yeah, the old knucklehead'll do that to you."

Light as a butterfly, Carina leaned over and kissed Denny on the cheek.

"See you tomorrow," she said, then turned and jogged up to her front door. She heard the motorcycle accelerate up the sleepy street. Carina closed the front door and leaned back against it, heart racing.

10

Denny shot Naz a cheery smile from across the desk. Naz knew that glassy-eyed look only too well.

"So," Naz said. "You and Carina get a lot done last night?"

"Yeah," Denny replied. "We were at it for hours. Reviewed the, uh...corporate experience section and, uh, the org chart...."

"Oh, the org chart." Naz glanced at his watch. "Our girl's running a little late this morning."

"She had a little problem with her car."

They heard the unmistakable sound of Carina's El Camino roar up outside, then the office door bang, and she appeared in the doorway. Although all the pieces of Carina were there, they were slightly askew. She hadn't had time to blow dry her hair and it had developed a life of its own. Her eyes were bleary, jeans wrinkled, bottom shirt button undone.

"Sorry I'm late. Those bastards at DMV charged me $200."

"Expensive dinner," Naz said, without looking up from his paperwork. "The way you two are working on that org chart, it better look like the fucking Mona Lisa."

Carina remembered her alcohol-induced statement to Denny at the Villa del Gato that she would handle her father. Now, with no salty rim in sight, she wasn't quite so sure.

Naz continued. "Denny was just telling me all the work you got done last night. Seeing as the bid is due in, oh…." Naz checked the wall calendar. "Five days!"

Carina stumbled for words, her head still a little fuzzy, "Well, we, uh…."

Quickly, Denny spread out his binder on Naz's desk. It looked fantastic. In fact, Carina could swear that was a new cover page and the color-coded table of contents matching the fifteen section tabs. Denny must've worked on it last night, after the dinner and motorcycle ride, while she was trying to recover by downing three aspirin and soaking in a hot bath.

As Denny flipped through the sections, giving Naz a concise overview, Carina sat dumbfounded. At one point, Denny said, "And Carina came up with this idea, breaking out the equipment by year and beefing up the preventative maintenance section."

As Naz looked at the crisp chart, for once in her life, Carina was speechless. Denny had not only showed up on time, prepared, and apparently under no ill effects of the night before, but now was actually covering for her.

She almost felt like crying.

Grudgingly, Naz leafed through the document.

Denny jumped in. "We'll have a complete first draft for you within a day or so."

Through the cigar smoke, Naz eyed them both with the 'Don't give any more of your bullshit' look, and they both heard it loud and clear. "All right. Back to work. And with you two in charge, may God help us."

Denny grabbed his binder. "I didn't get the impression you were religious, Naz."

"I believe in anything that'll help us win the bid. God comes right after the baler company. Now get out of here!"

"Yes, sir," Denny said, ushering Carina out as if escaping from the executioner.

Outside the office, Carina grabbed Denny's arm. "Thanks for saving me in there. I'll pull those final references together and call you."

Denny reached out and shook her hand. "It's been nice working with you, Ms. Agajanian."

"The pleasure is all mine, Mr. DeYoung." Carina watched Denny get in his Jeep and drive off. Suddenly, she was feeling a lot better.

*   *   *

The wind kicked sand through the arms of the Joshua trees and sent it skittering across the freeway as Naz drove east on Interstate 10 through the Coachella Valley, past Palm Springs and Indio, paralleling the Union Pacific railroad main line. He exited the freeway and turned south across the open desert. Thirty minutes later, he could see the landfill up against the foothills.

Naz didn't like his position going into the meeting.

He had to make this landfill deal; the whole bid hinged on it. His father had told him from the time he was a boy to deal from strength, go in with options, fall back positions. His fall back position on this one was to haul to the county landfill, pay a monster tipping fee and watch his L.A. bid go down a rathole. On the other hand, out here in the desert virtually overnight the L.A. tonnage could transform the Indian's anemic landfill in no-man's land, into a mega landfill. But even at that, he needed them a lot more than they needed him. Tonnage or no tonnage, they still had assets...namely, the casino. He had a ten-year-old Lincoln with 200,000 miles on it, a house with two mortgages, and Mayda's fishpond with a few over-stuffed koi swimming around in it.

The hot desert air baked into him off the asphalt. The only consolation Naz had in regards to negotiating from a position of weakness was that he'd had a lot of practice at it, the history of the Armenian people, and his family in particular—the eternal underdog. Naz clamped a new cigar into his mouth. If he were going in as the underdog, he'd at least look like a confident one.

He walked into the trailer that served as the landfill office and a blast of air conditioning raised goose bumps on his arms. Naz's cousin sat in a chair, seeming to fill half the cramped waiting room. At five-eleven and 300 pounds, Armand Savoyan had never met a doughnut he didn't like. He wore a pair of khaki shorts and a Hawaiian shirt big as a tablecloth.

Naz smiled, remembering the early days. Most people thought Armand had been staring at the desert sun too long when he dropped a couple hundred grand on the Indians for the rights to operate a landfill on their reservation, a patch of high desert about one hundred miles east of San Diego and two miles short of oblivion.

What are you going to bury in your landfill, they would ask him, jack rabbits?

But Armand knew that sooner or later the big municipal landfills would fill up and all that trash would need some place to go. When that day came, he would be ready. And now, because of the L.A. bid and Naz's excommunication from the HIA landfill, that day had come a lot sooner than expected. Although Armand had rights to the operation, the tribe still owned the land and had final say on critical landfill matters.

Naz shouted at his cousin, "Why can't you do a landfill somewhere nice, like La Jolla?"

"You sonuvabitch, Nazareth! How are you?" They hugged, each man with an unlit cigar shoved in his mouth. Armand held Naz at arm's length, which meant his belly was still touching him, "You look good."

"What'd you expect?"

"Big city life must agree with you."

"Better than eating sand out here."

"I wouldn't say that to the Chief," Armand said. "He's kind of partial to sand."

A secretary opened the door and as she lead them to a back room. Armand said, "Let me do the talking for once."

"Hey, you know these Indians. I'm just here to shake hands on the deal."

Armand surveyed Naz with a jaundiced eye. "Yeah, and I'm Marilyn Monroe."

"Besides, these guys kicked the shit out of Custer, right?"

"Naz, I'm warning you...."

Naz just smiled and patted his cousin on the back. Although he was all smiles on the outside, Naz could feel the first pangs of heartburn.

They entered a small office where two men sat at a table. One was in his late twenties, impeccably dressed in a western suit with turquoise belt buckle and string tie with silver medallion—the tribal corporate attorney. Naz noted that he didn't look the least bit Indian, but that didn't seem to matter anymore. If you were one-eighth Indian blood, you were Indian. The other was a heavy-set old man, his moon face, deep brown complexion, high cheek bones and straight gray hair marked him as the real Indian, and as it turned out, the Chief. He wore a white cowboy hat.

The thought flashed through Naz's mind that maybe he could marry Carina off to the attorney. Overnight, he'd be part of a sovereign nation. Make your own rules. Free booze. But the attorney didn't look like he'd be much fun, and probably not a very good dancer, so Naz let the thought drift away.

Armand introduced them and they shook hands.

Naz said, "Great place you have here."

The Indians said nothing.

Armand launched into it. "As I told you last week, my cousin Nazareth here is bidding on the City of Los Angeles trash contract. Three thousand tons a day, twenty years. That's fifteen million tons, give or take a little recycling. And he wants to bring it all to us. Right, Naz?"

Naz nodded, "That's—"

"Now," Armand said, "Naz is up against stiff competition and if he's going to win this thing, he needs to come in with the low bid." Naz noticed that his cousin was sweating like he was in a sauna, and figured that probably wasn't helping their negotiating position.

The young Indian looked right at Naz. "You must realize, Mr. Agajanian that our landfill may be small, but it runs to the highest environmental standards. Many unenlightened people believe erroneously that we can make our own rules, circumvent the process, including the California Environmental Quality Act, the Integrated Waste Management Board permit, and the Federal EPA regulations."

Naz smiled weakly. That was exactly what he had thought.

"Nothing could be further from the truth," the young man continued. "In fact, we require each of our clients to also operate to the same high level. Is that a problem?"

"That's no problem," Armand cut in. "The Health Department inspectors are all over Naz's ass everyday. Right, Naz?"

"Every time I turn around. I go to take a piss, they—"

"Have you ever had any Notices of Violation from the Local Enforcement Agency, or the Regional Water Quality Control Board?" the tribal attorney said.

Naz glanced at his cousin, beginning to wonder just how wired this deal was, and had a bad feeling maybe it was chicken wire.

Armand said, "I can assure you that—"

The young man said, "Given what you have told me about Mr. Agajanian, I'm sure he is on top of his operation and can answer for himself, Mr. Saroyan."

Unfortunately, Naz was a little foggy on the violations

issue. Carina seemed to have better luck dealing with the inspectors. Naz tended to challenge their judgment, and failing that, their intelligence, and well, things usually went downhill from there. But he felt fairly confident that over the years they hadn't been hit with more than say, forty violations. Looking across the table at the deadpan face of the young man and the Chief, who to this point had not said a word and sat solid as wood, Naz had the sneaking suspicion that forty was not a good number.

Naz cleared his throat, "We may have had a couple a few years ago. Small stuff, you know, pigeons in the rafters, hole in a muffler...."

"You see, Mr. Agajanian, we cannot afford a violation. It would reflect poorly on our operations as a whole, our tribe, our people. I'm sure you understand."

"Absolutely," Naz replied. "We feel the same way at Pacific Rim." In fact, Naz couldn't care less about how anything "reflected", as long as he won the bid. When he was sitting on that fifteen million tons, everybody could reflect his ass, as far as he was concerned.

"You see," the young man said, "We don't really need...."

The Chief placed his hand on his associate's arm, then looked across the table at Naz. "Do you know John Wayne?" he said.

Naz started running through all the names of industry guys in his mind. "I know a Joe Wayne at Crown Valley Disposal."

"No, Mr. Agajanian," the attorney said. "He means the actor."

Naz's first thought was, what? His second was that

these guys were good. Throwing him off. Using some kind of weird negotiating tactic. "Sure," Naz said, smiling. "I think he's Armenian."

"That's funny," the Chief said. "We think he's Indian."

They all smiled, except the attorney.

The Chief continued, "John Wayne once said, I think it was in Red River, 'There's right and there's wrong. You do one, you're living. You do the other, you might be walking around, but you're deader than a beaver hat.' What do you think of that, Mr. Agajanian?"

"My wife would never let me wear a beaver hat," said Naz. "She's one of those animal people."

The Chief stared at Naz, then smiled, seeming to have made up his mind. "My wife, same thing."

"Well, now that that's settled," Armand said, "Can we talk numbers?"

*   *   *

One hour later, Naz emerged as the newest sponsor of the Little League, a gold-tier donor to the new wing of the Tribal Health Clinic, a mentor in the work/study curriculum, an "angel" in the reservation electricity grant program, and an honorary and contributing member of the Library Booster Club. Between the tag team of the young attorney and the John Wayne fan club, Naz wasn't sure when the meeting ended if he was the "booster" or the "boostee."

Armand walked Naz to his car, the wind and sand whipping at their pant legs. Naz said, "Hey, why didn't you warn me about the John Wayne thing?"

"How the hell am I supposed to know some goofball thing like that? The Chief may be smoking peyote in his peace pipe. Anyway, you got your deal."

"Some deal," Naz said. "They should erect a statue of me out here for all the goddamn contributions I'm making."

"You win that bid, I'll put up the sonuvabitch myself." The two cousins kissed each other on the cheek, and Naz climbed into his car.

As he drove west on I-10, Naz ran the calculations in his head. All his "charitable" donations, and the per ton royalty to the tribe and his cousin were eating into his margin, as slim as it already was. But it was worth it if it made the difference in winning the bid.

Naz had his landfill deal...and all the booze he and any other Agajanian could drink at the casino for perpetuity. And better yet, no one would know, not HIA, not the city, not even the jackrabbits.

11

Mayda stood over the cutting board in her kitchen. "So," she said to Carina, her hands sticky with stuffing and tomato sauce, "Your father tells me there is a new young man who works with you." She laid the rolled grape leaves in a pan. They looked like short cigars.

"Just a consultant," Carina said, standing elbow to elbow with her mother. "He's helping on the L.A. bid." She sliced another piece of raw steak for *kabbe*.

"Armenian?" Mayda asked.

"Everyone in the world isn't Armenian, Mom. And what difference does that make anyway? Give me some grape leaves."

Mayda chopped tomatoes, stopping to wipe the sweat off her forehead. She'd been up since 6:00 a.m. preparing the traditional dishes. "Is he handsome?"

Carina looked up at the ceiling, picturing Denny, rolling a ball of stuffing in her hands. She couldn't help smiling. "He's not bad—for a white boy!" And she laughed.

Mayda giggled. "Maybe he should come to dinner, this white boy of yours."

"Would you stop!" Carina said. "He's not *my* boy. What's Dad been telling you?" Carina splashed some lemon and olive oil over the stuffed grape leaves.

"He says you are having meetings. Business meetings."

"You two kill me."

"You know your father will never approve."

"There isn't anything to approve! Jesus Christ! Can't a person have a life around here?" Carina took a solid gulp of her red wine, the preferred drink for the women. She starting mashing up garbanzo beans for the hummus.

Mayda said, "You can have plenty of life. I'm just telling you, that's all. Pour me some wine, will you? You are making me thirsty."

Carina took her mother by the shoulders. "Don't worry. I'm a big girl now. Besides, I can handle Dad."

Suddenly, Naz's voice boomed out, "Who can handle me?" He walked into the kitchen, opened the refrigerator and pulled out a bowl of marinating lamb.

"Your daughter says she is marrying the consultant," Mayda said.

Carina screamed in surprise and tried to tickle her mother.

Naz said, "This is not something to joke about." But the two women were giggling and poking each other.

Later that evening, warm light spilled out of the windows of the home and onto a cluster of cars parked haphazardly in the drive. It was Sunday, family dinner night at the Agajanian household, and four days before the bid. As usual, the gathering included Naz and Mayda; Harry and Armi; Carina; Sophie and Jack, and their two young daughters. Although the dinners often included a menagerie of uncles, aunts, cousins (first, second or third), godparents and friends, tonight it was just the inner circle.

The thought of cancelling this dinner because of the looming bid never occurred to Naz. He knew in his bones that the family was everything; that the reason Pacific Rim existed at all sprang from the family. Besides, everyone needed a break from the constant stress. Like in those Shakespeare plays he heard about in high school, the part he went to, anyway, where Shakespeare would put in a funny scene to relieve the tension. Shakespeare did it with words, Naz did it with shish kabab and *oghi*. To each his own.

Naz and Mayda lived in Glendale, the growing city that was becoming the Armenian hub of California, even the whole U.S., eclipsing Fresno the original sanctuary for those escaping the genocide. Naz and Mayda's home sat on the side of a hill surrounded by palm trees. The driveway curved around a pond where six koi swam. Naz had paid $200 apiece for the exotic carp. The whole thing was Mayda's idea.

Naz had said, "What do you know about fish?"

"They look good," Mayda had replied.

"Maybe it's not all about looking good," Naz had said, "Sometimes it's about making some kind of sense."

Mayda had looked at him as if he was crazy, "It's always about looking good."

To Naz, it was an insane waste of money. A fish was a

fish. They all looked the same cooked. So it was a measure of his affection for Mayda, or perhaps an example of choosing his battles, that he had gone along with the fish deal.

The first night after he stocked the fish, raccoons got in and ate $400 worth of carp. Not only did Naz end up buying two new fish, but he shelled out $500 for a raccoon-proof metal screen over the pond to keep the little bastards out of there.

An ancient wisteria vine climbed over the sheltered entryway and coated the night with its sweet fragrance. Inside the house, mounted just above the heavy wooden door, was an opaque blue stone, the *Gabouid Atchk*, the "The Blue Eye," to guard the entry and keep evil spirits away. It was a larger version of the blue stone charm Naz had pinned to Carina's wrapping right after she was born, and on her crib as well.

*   *   *

The sun sent lengthening shadows across the backyard patio as Naz stood over a well-worn cutting board next to an industrial-size, built-in grill. He worked calmly as in a ritual, his hands lifting two-inch cubes of tenderized lamb from the bowl of marinade and running them onto skewers. He hummed an Armenian folk song as he squinted through the smoke from his cigar. Occasionally, he looked up to where his two young nieces played, splashing each other in the shallow end of the heated pool, their giggles drifting in and out on the cool evening breeze.

Cooking on the grill felt like a dance with a beautiful

woman—well, maybe not that good, but similar. Warm, familiar, expectant. He let all his worries drift off on the breeze, at least for the moment. He wore one of his Hawaiian shirts with the tail hanging out over a pair of old blue jeans and battered cowboy boots. The coals were turning from red to white hot. The sound of a mandolin floated out from the living room stereo.

Harry stood next to Naz, skewering quartered onions and green peppers. Naz felt his father's calm energy, like a warm blanket wrapped around them, as much a part of the night as the shish kabab, as constant as the stars.

Naz said, "Remember that time before we moved to L.A. you let me go with you to Dinuba with that load of tin cans. That '39 Plymouth flatbed with no shocks. Pound your guts out. We got behind a cattle truck on Highway 99 and I thought it started to rain. You turned the wipers on."

Harry smiled, setting a full skewer on the grill.

"Then that ammonia smell hit me and I realized those cows were pissing on us."

"Not last ones to piss on us," Harry said. "At least then, we got windshield."

"When we win this bid, you and Mom should buy a new car."

"What I want with new car?"

"They got these cars with leather seats, with heaters in them. When it's cold in the morning, you just turn that heater on. It's like your ass is in warm butter."

Harry thought for a moment, "Maybe you're right. I could use new car. New ass, too. You know, the what you call...."

"Hemorrhoids."

"Hot butter sound good."

"I told you to go see Dr. Halajian."

"No doctor stick hand up my ass."

"Fine. You better eat a shitload of fiber."

Harry took a gulp of white liquid out of a water glass and licked his lips. "*Oghi* do same thing and taste better."

"Throw the rest of those onions on the fire. Jesus Christ, I hope I never get old."

Harry patted his son on the back. "I get more *oghi*... for asshole."

Naz watched his father limp away on his cane. He looked up through the smoke of the grilling shish kabab at Jack, reclined in a lawn chair eating from an hors d'oeuvres platter of string cheese, black olives, and cucumber. Jack was on his third drink of the night, a heavy dose for his brother-in-law, who was normally not much of a drinker. But these weren't normal times. Everyone was feeling the stress. To Naz, Jack's heavy drinking was just another sign of their bond, their brotherhood in desperate times. Naz took a slug of his own whiskey in tribute.

Anoush, Naz's cat, was perched on Jack's lap, her little white paws perfectly aligned, her eyes staring into oblivion. In her whole life, Anoush had never cozied up like that to anyone, except Jack. And as he watched the two of them, Naz realized how alike they were, the cat and the man—they loved you most when you left them alone. There was a part of each that no one would ever know. Jack Oseppian was Naz's fellow trench fighter and had been since they were kids. Forty years. The fact that Jack had married Naz's sister just formalized a bond that was there all along.

As he turned the skewers, Naz remembered the time

a tough kid in high school had cornered Naz, accusing him of ruining his sister, then slugging Naz in the mouth. When suddenly, Jack was on top of the kid, beating him half unconscious and not stopping until Naz and two or three others managed to tear Jack away. The kid had a broken jaw, busted nose and a concussion—and he was lucky.

Naz knew better than anyone that Jack could be a tough bastard at times. But he's our tough bastard, Naz thought, and that's exactly what we need. Naz thought of himself as the lightning, flashing across the sky. But Jack was the thunder, and could rock you to the bone.

Jack looked to the swimming pool and yelled, "Hey, girls. Back in the shallow end. Come on."

"But we can swim. Mom lets us."

"Back in the shallow end! Or you have to come out."

Naz thought Jack was overly protective of the girls. He had them late in life, maybe that was part of it, but Naz had a daughter too, and knew how fathers could be.

"Jack," Naz said, as he lifted a skewer of shish kabab off the fire. "See if it's done."

Jack walked over and pulled a chunk of sizzling meat off the skewer with his callused fingers, tore off a bite and chewed, a drop of juice falling into his neatly trimmed beard.

"Better'n dog meat," Jack said, in their traditional response to shish kabab perfection.

"Fuckin' A," said Naz.

"How's the bid coming with that consultant?" Jack said, nonchalantly, his eyes on the girls in the pool.

"Good, at least that's what Carina tells me. But the way she looks at this consultant guy, I don't know."

"She'll forget him when it's over."

"I don't know, Jack."

Jack grabbed another chunk of lamb and said while chewing, "What about our number? We gonna low-ball it?"

Naz squinted through the smoke. "I been workin' on it. Can't screw it down too far or we lose our ass."

"Figure about forty dollars a ton?"

Naz swallowed the last of his drink. "Thirty-four," he whispered. "And we walk away with this thing." Jack just nodded.

"Jack!" a woman's voice yelled from the house. Sophie appeared in the kitchen doorway, squinting into the growing dark. "Jack...you out there?"

A large, horse-boned woman, Sophie walked toward them with a momentum that parted the seas before her. She wore a flowing, one piece black dress, that hung from her shoulders to the tops of her sandals. "Jack! Get the girls out of the pool. They were supposed to be out twenty minutes ago."

Jack grabbed a couple towels and walked toward the pool.

"Let him relax, Soph'," said Naz. "He's been working his ass off at the plant. You know, the bid and all."

"Yeah. Well, maybe that's it. He's acting quieter than normal, which is pretty hard to do."

"He's probably just trying to catch his breath, you yelling' at him all the time."

"Who's yelling?" she yelled.

"Here," he said to Sophie, as he pulled several skewers off the fire and laid them across a platter. "Take these in."

Sophie took one more glance at the pool, where Jack was toweling off the girls, then walked off toward the house. Harry walked over to Naz.

"She's my little sister," Naz said to his father. "But sometimes I don't know how Jack does it."

"He like rest of us. Do what must do. Jack a good boy." Harry picked up his cane.

"Yeah, he is." Naz watched his brother-in-law lead the girls into the house, holding their little doll-like hands in his thick paws, followed by his father's slow shuffle. Naz thought about being married to Sophie. If forced to choose between going ashore with the Marines in the first wave of the D-Day landing, or the first wave in the front door to face Sophie after a night out binging with the boys, he would have to think about it.

Naz pulled the food off the grill and as he headed toward the house, even Sophie's cackle, blasting out of the kitchen, couldn't dislodge the warmth of feeling he had for this night and this family.

Naz set the platter of shish kabab and vegetables on the table, every available surface occupied by some dish, surrounded by the family sitting in high-backed chairs. The table was covered with a crocheted tablecloth that Armi had made for Mayda when she and Naz had gotten married. A large mirror in a gold frame hung on the far wall. The cut glass chandelier overhead picked up a million sparks of red carpet and hurled them into the mirror. The room bloomed red and gold.

There were sacrosanct rules for seating at the Armenian dinner table, similar to a corporation. Everyone always sat in the same assigned seat based on their relative position in the patriarchy, which determined their status and power in the family. And so it was that night with the Agajanians.

Harry as the patriarch sat at the head of the table, flanked by Naz on one side and Armi on the other. Anyone could still see the beautiful face behind the 75-year-old wrinkles; the piercing blue eyes that she had passed on to Naz and the hawk-like nose that gave her granddaughter Carina part of her fiery look. Armi's silver hair was tied up in a bun on her head, and she sat straight-backed in her chair. Sophie came next, who even though a female, ranked higher than Jack, who sat next to her but further down the table, because she was the daughter, whereas he was just the son-in-law. Across from them sat Carina and Jack's daughters, and then Mayda at the foot of the table—and closest to the kitchen.

Naz spoke to the six-year old. "Lena, would you please say the blessing?"

Embarrassed, the young girl looked to Carina, who squeezed her hand. They all bowed their heads and Jack's daughter began to recite the Lord's Prayer in Armenian.

"Hayr mer, vor hergeens...."

At one point she stumbled and Carina joined in. They finished and all said, "Amen."

Then the table squirmed with activity. Serving bowls were passed with pilaf, warm yogurt soup with doughy meatballs, and cabbage rolls and tabouli, peeled and thinly sliced eggplant sprinkled with tahini and lemon. Pita bread was torn and smeared with hummus. Red wine was poured all around, and for the men, more *oghi*, the clear, anise-flavored liquor that turned white as milk when water was added. Silverware clanked on the plates, the clock on the mantel chimed seven o'clock. Over it all, the conversation ran and bubbled like warm oil, the lighter sounding English floating on top of the throaty Armenian. Mayda never seemed to sit, scurrying around, serving, running to the kitchen and back, passing platters.

Naz said to his father, "I hear Seg Oganesian sold out to those guys from up north. Made a bundle."

"So now he fart in silk underwear," said Harry with a smile. Jack's daughters giggled and Carina rolled her eyes.

Naz found the *oghi* tasted better than usual. His mood brightened with each glass, and Jack and Harry weren't far behind. The night wore on, the platters passed around a second, then a third time. They talked in revered tones about the Governor, who had just won his second term, George Deukmejian, one of their own. How could something this marvelous be real? Then, whether drunk or sober, high or low, rain, snow, fire or flood, the topic of the men's conversation eventually turned to Pacific Rim, their home away from home.

"403's got that punctured radiator," Jack said. "I don't know how long that sealant's going to hold."

"When I start in Fresno," Harry said. "One wagon and one horse. No problem with radiator."

"Oh, God. Not the horse again," Sophie said, shaking her head.

Armi, waved her hand in front of her face as if it would let her swallow faster. "I remember horse. He was happiest one when we buy first truck. I think horse try to kiss me, he so happy."

"That was Dad after a long day on the route," Naz said. "He just looked like the horse."

They all laughed, except Sophie. "Do we always have to talk about trash?" she said.

"What do you want to talk about?" Naz said.

"Shopping at the Galleria."

"OK, fine. Let's talk about the Galleria. What do you say, Jack?"

Jack thought for a moment. "Didn't I see one of Garo's roll offs over there, behind the May Company?"

"It's hopeless," Sophie said.

"Come on, Aunt Sophie," Carina said. "Just think of all the shopping you can do when we win the bid."

"And you!" said Sophie. "Such a beautiful young woman. You should be married and raising children…not recycling garbage. What kind of influence are these three on you?" Sophie nodded to the men's end of the table.

"What are you talking about?" said Jack, banging an empty *oghi* glass on the table. "How many women you know can change the oil in a Cat D-8."

"How many men want to marry a woman with oil under her nails?" Sophie said. "Huh, Jack? You tell me."

Carina checked her nails, frowned, and folded her hands in her lap.

Mayda appeared carrying a platter overflowing with the traditional sugar and spice cookies with the hole in the middle. "Here," she said, "Armi made *mahlab*." Hands reached out, and soon all were munching. The smell of espresso boiling wafted in from the kitchen.

"That new consultant didn't seem to mind her nails, from what I could see," said Jack.

Carina shot her uncle a glare, but he just ate his cookie.

Like a heat-seeking missile, Sophie turned toward her blushing niece. "What's this? I didn't hear anything about a consultant."

"You're the one doesn't want to talk about trash," said Naz. "Besides there's nothing to talk about."

"What, Nazareth?" Sophie said. "You should be excited for her. After Galen...."

Sophie caught herself. The room fell silent. Even the girls, noticing the adults go quiet, stopped chewing, staring at the frozen faces.

"Look everyone," Carina said, holding her hands up, palms out, as if surrendering. "Galen is gone, all right? I loved him. You loved him. We all loved him. But that won't make him come back. It's time we all moved on, and for God's sake, stop this morbid fascination with my love life, such as it is."

Stopped in her tracks for once, Sophie said quietly, "This is serious...this consultant?"

"No, it's not *serious*," Carina said.

"And it never will be," said Naz.

"Ohhh," said Sophie with a knowing nod. "Not Armenian, our consultant."

"Is this right, Carina?" said Armi, a worried look on her face. "Odar?"

Carina sighed. "I hardly know—"

"I think Carina can be with who she wants!" Mayda said.

"Who's saying she can't?" Sophie said.

"I'm saying she can't!" boomed Naz.

"More *oghi*!" cried Harry, his gold tooth catching the light.

Carina looked at the ceiling, beseeching God.

"I'm going for the coffee!" yelled Mayda. She turned to her nieces. "You girls want to be excused from the table? You can go watch TV in the living room."

They nodded and started to push their chairs back.

"Uh, uh," Naz interrupted. "What do we say first?"

"*Pak asczzou* (Thank you, Lord)," the girls replied, and scampered away from the table.

"I think I'll *pak asczzou*, too," said Carina, tossing her napkin on the table and heading for the kitchen.

Mayda walked in after her and picked up the tray of small cups, steaming with sugary espresso. "You don't want coffee?" she said to Carina.

"Nah, I'll start on the dishes."

Back in the dining room, Jack got up and began clearing the table.

"You don't have to do that, Jack," said Mayda.

"Don't spoil him, Mayda," said Sophie. "I just got him trained." Sophie handed her plate to Jack like he was the butler, and turned to her coffee.

"No problem, Mayda," Jack said. "I need to get Harry his *oghi*, anyway."

Naz passed Harry a cigar. The sound of the TV droned in from the living room.

Sophie said to Carina, "Don't you ever worry, living alone?"

"Maybe you should move back in here!" Naz yelled out. "Think of all the rent you'd save."

"And have to listen to you all day, and have all my

clothes smell like cigar smoke? No thanks," Carina said, and then in a faux southern accent, batting her eyelashes and patting her hair, "I'll just have to find some big handsome man to take care of me. Maybe even one of those Armenians. I hear they are rich and uh...very well endowed."

Harry stuck his forearm up on the table making a fist.

Armi hit him with her napkin and they all laughed.

Naz got up and punched on the stereo, and the mandolin band struck a rollicking folk song. He held out his hand to Mayda, then Harry joined the line, and Armi, and finally Sophie.

Carina and Jack looked up from loading the dishwasher. She held out her hand to him and said, "As long as you'll hold hands with someone who changes oil on a D-8."

They joined the line that snaked around the dinner table, laughing, regal, triumphant.

"Hoopa!"

*   *   *

Later that night, when everyone had gone, Naz and Mayda retired to their bedroom. Even though his face was now lined and his hair thinning, she could still see the high school boy with whom she had fallen in love. He was tall and gangly and not as handsome back then as some of the other boys that floated around her like bees to an almond blossom. She had developed early and was buxom in 8th grade, like Naz would joke years later...she looked like ten pounds of mud stuffed in a five pound sack. And she would use those breasts, the curve of her hip to supreme advantage when she decided to go after Naz. Even then, he was consumed with the scavenging business his father had started, the local junkman. He would just as soon go through an old barn looking for copper fittings, than go to the senior prom. But she took care of that one night in one of those same barns, in the hay loft, the two of them, both new to the adventure. She had had enough sense to maintain her virginity, but just barely. She would give it to him, but later.

And all these years later, they had survived, the good, the bad, the times of turmoil and loss when all seemed to hang by a single thread. But now she knew that it was a very strong thread, like that metal from the space rockets. And no matter how mad he got, how much grief he caused her, she knew that she was not just in Naz's inner circle, she was the inner circle. She defined its boundary.

Naz flicked off the light and they lay in bed with only the moonlight shining through the window. She curled up against him.

"I love our family," she said.

"Me, too."

"I wish this bid was over."

"Me, too."

"Tell me it's going to be all right."

"I'm not God, you know."

"Tell me anyway."

"Jesus. It's going to be all right."

She kissed the corner of his mouth. "You are such a liar."

He smiled.

Outside the window, the palm fronds clattered in the wind.

*   *   *

Zaven Petoyan sat in the dark at a booth in the back of the strip club, sipping his second beer, his eyes riveted on the woman dancing under the hot pink lights on the stage, making love to an aluminum pole that ran from the floor to the ceiling. She was Asian, black hair cut in bangs over her dark eyes, and falling in shimmering sheets along the side of her face, over her shoulders and across her breasts. Her body was supple and muscular as she moved in the pulsing lights.

He had been thinking of Carina since the haulers association dinner. God, he wanted her, the thoughts of her, running his hand over the soft down of her perfect thighs, her sweet, full lips, the long black hair.

He waved the owner over, said something to him, and handed him a couple twenties. When the girl's dance ended, he saw the owner motion to her. She glanced over to his booth, peering into the shadows, nodded and headed his way.

She came up to him in a loose chiffon shift, purple with lace at the throat and along the fringes high on her hips, a hint of G-string underneath. She wore pink lipstick and makeup with fake diamond glitter on her eyelids.

He felt her hands on his shoulders and then the rush of desire as she straddled him in the chair, her thighs over his, the warmth and sweetness of her, the pressure of her against him.

He closed his eyes and floated in a smoky dream world. He could feel the power returning, the pounding of his blood, her sweetness grinding against him. Suddenly, he grabbed her; rubbing his face in her breasts, shoving his hand up under her G string.

The girl screamed and fought to squirm off him, but he held her with one arm around her, the other prodding to get inside her. The girl punched his arms, pulling away, screaming at him. A fist clubbed him on the back of the neck, a pair of hands ripped her away. He threw a punch at a shadow and felt a nose crunch under his knuckles. All turned to chaos, punches rained down on him, something hard and heavy crashed into the side of his head.

The gravel stuck to his sweaty hands as he raised himself up in the parking lot where they had thrown him. He tasted blood where his tongue was cut. He stumbled to his pickup and grabbed a tire iron from behind the seat. He turned to face a group of them still huddled at the front door, yelling something at him, their faces contorted.

He'd show them who they were dealing with. You didn't throw him out, like a nobody. Like some loser. There would be a reckoning. He heard the siren and could see the red lights of the cop car glinting off the power lines a couple blocks away. He tossed the iron through the window of his pickup, hopped in and drove off. He would get her later. That bitch, that fucking, cunt bitch.

*   *   *

Over at Pacific Rim, Charlie crouched behind a bin and watched Manny back into the tipping area with another stolen HIA roll-off container. The loads had been coming in for a couple weeks. His stash was growing. Once again, a mountain of cardboard and clean office paper tumbled out of the roll off. And this time, something else, glinting at the bottom of the pile.

After Manny drove off, Charlie kicked some paper aside, and there it was—an ingot of dull, silver metal about the size of a fireplace log. The first flicker of fear caught in Charlie's belly. Thinking it was aluminum, Charlie reached in and tried to lift it out, almost pulling his shoulders out of their sockets—this bar was heavy. He pulled a magnet from his pocket and tapped the ingot, no pull. Not ferrous, but not aluminum either, and obviously not copper or zinc. In fact, it was no metal he could think of, but his gut told him is was something.

Charlie glanced around. Not a sound, not a movement. He dragged the heavy ingot onto a busted wooden pallet, then climbed onto a forklift and started it. As he pulled forward, he adjusted the height of the forks. The old skills were coming back to him. After he left the Oklahoma oil fields, he worked a summer in the potato sheds in Bakersfield, shunting pallets of spuds with the forklift. The pay was piecemeal and he got real good at driving forklifts.

The forks slipped smoothly under the pallet. He feathered the controls and carefully lifted it. Keeping the lights off, he drove across the moonlit yard to his shipping container. Black crawled out of the car, stretched, sniffed the air and trotted over.

Charlie pulled a lanyard over his head with a key dangling from it and unlocked the door. He whacked a flashlight against the palm of his hand, and a weak beam came on. He swept the light around, illuminating his treasures.

Quickly, he rearranged a few items to make room, then wrestled the ingot off the pallet and onto the floor of the container. If it was what he thought it might be, he had struck something big. Visions of his little bonsai tree shop danced in his bloodshot eyes.

Standing in the door, he looked around the yard for any sign of movement. He heard a thud and jumped, only to see Black scratching his side with a hind paw that whapped the ground as it followed through.

Charlie locked the doors, parked the forklift, and walked over to his hearse. He rummaged around under the seat and came out with a bottle, and a chunk of rawhide bone. He looked at that bottle of Old Overholt like it was home. Snuggled up in the front seat of the hearse with Black and his bottle, it was as if the booze itself covered him in a warm blanket.

Charlie thought not only about the "treasure" he had just found, but about what might be hidden in the next HIA load, and the next. As a kid, Charlie had never been on an Easter egg hunt, but figured this was how it must feel. Except what he was hunting now was a whole lot better than colored eggs. Being the hoarder he was, Charlie usually liked to hang on to the stuff he salvaged, to savor it. But this ingot was different. This time, he would move fast, before anything could go wrong.

Black grabbed the bone, as Charlie lifted his pint. "Here's a toast, Black. To Pacific Rim." He took a long belt.

"And here's to Naz. Long may he reign supreme!" Another blast from the bottle. "And here's to Charlie. Shit eater, no more!" Black gnawed on his bone. "And here's to Black, the Black Beauty!" Charlie rubbed behind his dog's ears.

12

"Two hundred, Charlie," the man said, fanning the twenty-dollar bills on the counter.

"Come on, Luis!" Charlie yelled. "It weighs over a hundred pounds! Look at it. You're the one supposed to know this shit. That's precious metal! Probably from one of them aircraft plants. It's worth a thousand, easy."

Luis folded his thick hands, his fingers bent and scarred from boxing down at the Olympic in his younger days. "It's zinc alloy, Charlie, from some plating shop making auto parts. But for you, amigo, I'll go two and a quarter. Take it or leave it."

Charlie grumbled. He'd already sold Luis his shopping cart full of aluminum cans, unfortunately, they'd found the ones he'd filled with sand, and that transaction had netted him eighteen dollars and a tongue lashing. Two hundred and twenty-five dollars was more money than he'd seen in one shot for longer than he could remember.

He knew this metal had value. He had watched Luis's face when he'd hefted the ingot onto the scale, and he had seen the telltale flash in his eyes. A flash that quickly clouded over again.

Charlie ran his tongue over his lips. Boy, he could use a drink. But he was not going to sell himself short. Not this time. Not like he had his whole life. He started to drag the ingot off the scale. "Let's see what All American will give me."

"Sure, go ahead," said Luis, turning back to the cash register. "It's a free country."

"Bet your ass it is." Charlie muscled the ingot back into the shopping cart, straining his back and pinching a couple fingers in the process. He didn't really want to push this cart another half mile. The sun was unusually hot for a spring day.

As if reading his mind, Luis reached into a small refrigerator behind the counter and twisted the cap off a bottle. "A beer for the road, Charlie?"

Charlie looked at the sweating bottle, and rubbed his hands on his pants. He needed to keep his head clear, but maybe a beer would actually help, replenish his fluids. He reached for the bottle and poured half of it down his throat. He closed his eyes, the cool bottle in his hand. He belched.

"I'll tell you what I'm going to do, Charlie. Because you're one of my best customers. I will take this at a loss. I will go $275. For you, Charlie." Luis laid the additional bills on the counter.

Charlie hammered down the remaining beer and set the bottle on top of the cash register. "And another beer."

Luis popped another beer. Charlie grabbed the bottle, swiped the bills off the counter and marched out the door, grumbling. All right, he thought, so I didn't get a thousand. Got that bastard up from two. Won that battle. Didn't sell short, or all that short. He took a swig of the beer.

Behind him, Luis Vasquez ran his hand over the ingot and smiled.

* * *

Naz swayed into the Queen Mary banquet room. This would be a good night and he needed it. There was nothing more he could do on the bid. It was all in Catrina's and Denny's hands now. And their bid package looked good to him, even Mt. Ararat would be proud.

He had just gotten off the phone with Denny. There was some last minute deadline on notifications for minority and women owned businesses. God, he hated this city bureaucratic crap. He spent more time and money on red tape than the bid itself. If Armenians weren't minority businesses, who the hell was? The Mexicans? Shit, there were more of them than anyone else. How the hell could they be minorities? And the Asians? They ran half the banks in L.A., and the billion dollar paper mills he sold to in Taiwan. They need a helping hand, too? Where was the government when his dad was eating dirt in Fresno? He lifted a drink off the tray of a passing waitress and swilled it down.

This was the Hall of Fame Banquet. The Armenian event of the year, at least as far as the male contingent was concerned—five hundred Armenian men and male

guests. The ultimate celebration of prosperity and gen-
erosity amid the volatile mix of testosterone, booze, and
family bragging rights. No women allowed, except of
course for the quintet of Los Angeles Ram cheerleaders,
who sailed around the room like cruise ships among the
dark islands of tables. Their sequined uniforms exploded
like sparklers, igniting their hair and high-cupped
breasts. The men ogled and teased them, peeling off rolls
of money in exchange for strings of raffle tickets that
waved from the cheerleader's hands like kite tails.

As usual, Naz had shelled out $1,500 that he couldn't
afford for a table. He had to do it. All the money went to
the Armenian Senior Citizen's Home in Fresno. But more
importantly, he had to show he was on top, to throw the
money around like it was wastepaper. Especially now,
with everyone knowing about the bid.

But most of the talk this night was of the Harts and
their four tables. Naz gazed across the room and saw
Alex shaking the hand of one of his guests, the Chairman of the Los Angeles County Board of Supervisors.
Naz recognized the Director of the Bureau of Sanitation
sitting with Kail Hart at another table, and two L.A. City
Councilmembers. God, he wished he had more money.
He'd buy eight tables and show that asshole. He jerked
the cigar out of his mouth and knocked the ashes into his
water glass.

Harry with his gold-handled cane and Jack in his
typical lumberjack garb sat on either side of Naz, and
across from Naz's uncle Vahan, who owned a fleet of
tank trucks that ran milk in from the dairies in Chino
and further out in Riverside County. Rounding out the

table were his heavy equipment supplier; and an old friend from the liner board mill in Oxnard, one of Pacific Rim's biggest cardboard buyers. They had no pull when it came to the bid, but they'd give him an above market price for his bales, an offer they would never give to HIA.

Up on the stage, the emcee was introducing athletes of past or present fame. Old football players with gimpy knees, a couple of pitchers from the Dodgers, a Heisman trophy winner from twenty years back at USC, the baseball coach from the local State University, on and on. The crowd applauded lightly, a few hollers and catcalls rang out as men in the crowd recognized those crossing the stage, especially the old Armenian athletes.

Out of the corner of his eye, Naz saw one of the cheerleaders approaching. To him, this was the only part of sports that made sense. Any moron could tackle or throw a ball, but these cheerleaders, now that was real talent. With one arm, Naz encircled her waist. He raised his glass in the other, "To the Rams!"

"To the Rams, yeah! You bet, Naz." The men at his table tossed their drinks down, their eyes never leaving the girl.

"Whoever the hell they are!" laughed Naz.

The cheerleader whacked him on the shoulder with her roll of tickets. "You're going to pay for that," she said.

"I hope so, honey," Naz replied, and the men guffawed and elbowed each other. Naz reached into his wallet, pulled out a twenty dollar bill and gave it to her.

"Now that's more like it," she said, as she peeled off a streamer of raffle tickets.

Naz watched the motion of her breasts in the low-cut

cups of her uniform. "That all you selling?" he said, eyes twinkling.

"All I'm selling to you, my friend," she said as she turned and spike-heeled her way to the next table.

"Boy, you really impressed her," Jack said.

"Hey! She called me friend, didn't she? Besides, the night is young."

"And you are old," Jack threw down a gulp of whiskey. His eyes were already glassy and his heavy fingers played with the empty glass.

Naz beamed and rolled his cigar around in his mouth. This was living. Someone else in his place might've spent the night worrying over the bid package, but Naz let the others worry. He knew his bid price and he knew his team. And most of all, he knew his pattern. He knew the anxiety would come in the morning with the first light. But tonight was all his. He got up unsteadily and weaved around the table.

The paper mill manager broke in. "How're you guys doing on that City of L.A. bid? That could mean a lot of supply for our plant."

"Hey, who said you're gettin' it?" Naz shot back with a grin on his face, patting the short, ruddy man on the shoulder.

"Knowing you, Naz, you'll pull something out of your ass and win this thing."

"That's what scares me." Naz signaled the waiter to bring another round of drinks to the table. "Cause then we've got to pass the performance test."

"Hell, Naz, you were never short on performance," Uncle Vahan said. "How many you got to fuck in one night, anyway?" He laughed and elbowed Harry.

"I wish it was that easy, Vahan," laughed Naz, as he ambled off toward the restroom.

Standing at the urinal, Naz sighed. One of the waiters had thrown a bucket of ice cubes in the bowl, and they clicked and clattered as they melted. He closed his eyes and sagged against the cool porcelain, letting a momentary weariness seep in. From behind the marble wall that separated the urinals from the sinks, Naz overheard two men talking while they washed their hands. He recognized the voices—two small haulers and both clients of Pacific Rim.

"You think Naz is dead?" one said.

"HIA owns the landfill, the biggest recycling plant in the Country, and the City Council. You do the math."

"I can't stand those assholes."

"Progress, Sammy. Better ride the horse in the direction it's going."

Naz heard the door close and he stood there all alone in the silence, his bravado, buoyed by the booze, ebbing away. But he wasn't really surprised. Everyone on the street could figure the odds. He needed a victory now, no matter how small, something, anything to show them that he wasn't dead, not yet anyway.

Back at the table, Naz poured whiskey into an empty wineglass, and took a swallow. Harry looked at his son, aware that something had changed. "What Nazareth?"

"Nothing."

Harry put his hand on Naz's forearm, as if comforting a boy.

The emcee bolted back up to the mic. "Before we get to the raffle, there are two gentlemen here who I want you all to recognize. Two of the founding members of the original association in Fresno. The only reason we are all here tonight is that these men and a few others had the guts, the fortitude, the vision to create this wonderful organization that supports our culture, our success, our future as Armenians and Americans."

A volley of applause and cheers rose from the crowd.

"I'd like the two legendary founding fathers of the association to rise, please: Mr. Kail Hart of Hart Industries of America, and Mr. Harry Agajanian of Pacific Rim Recycling."

Kail rose and waved. Harry had trouble with his hip and Jack grabbed his elbow and helped him to his feet.

Harry gazed across the room at Kail. The elder Hart's gaze swung back and meet Harry's. A slow grin spread across Kail's face. A confident grin. Harry just leaned forward on his cane.

The two sat back down, and the emcee started the raffle, calling out winning numbers as one of the Ram cheerleaders pulled ticket stubs out of a bowl. Four tires from the Armenian discount tire store, a dinner for two at the Ritz in Newport Beach, a foursome at the L.A. Country Club, home of a PGA tournament the MC boasted. On and on the prizes rolled out. Then finally, it was time for the climactic event of the night—the live auction of sports memorabilia.

"All proceeds to the Armenian Senior Citizens Home, and for the homeland earthquake relief fund!" cried the emcee. "Dig deep, gentlemen for a worthy cause!"

And they all knew what that was. Not only the cause

of their people and their homeland, but the cause of their own pride, their family's standing in the Armenian community. All in the name of charity, of course.

A Kurt Rambis Laker jersey went for $150, then Jack Youngblood's football helmet, a perennial All Pro, the emcee reminded everyone.

"Let's go. Bidding starts at $200. Who'll give me 200?"

And so it went through baseballs signed by Tommy Lasorda, a poster of the Ram cheerleaders signed by all the lovely ladies. That brought $250. Obviously, the girls were Hall of Famers to this crowd.

Then, the piece de resistance, a football from this January's 1985 Rose Bowl, signed by all the members of the winning University of Southern California Trojans.

Naz glanced over at the Hart table and saw Alex whispering to one of the city councilmen while his eyes never left the football. Naz knew Alex had been a star player at USC. He twirled the cigar in his mouth.

The bidding started at one $150 and quickly went to $250 then $300, as Alex dueled with the owner of a bakery and another guy who sold truck fleet insurance.

Naz could see that Alex was gloating. His bid was high. The politicians at his tables were laughing, and toasting their glasses to him. Half of them had gone to USC, too. The old boy's network was fully-lubed tonight.

Yells cascaded across the room, encouraging one bidder or the other.

But finally, there was no more from the other bidders.

"A Rose Bowl ball!" cried the emcee. "Signed by all the Trojans. Twenty to seventeen over the Ohio State Buckeyes—one of the greatest games of all time! Come on!"

"Why don't you bid on it, Jimmy?" someone shouted to the emcee.

"Hell, I think I will. Three hundred fifty dollars!" the emcee blurted into the mic. Applause rattled the tables. "Four hundred!" Alex yelled as he raised his fist in the air.

A roar went up. One of the tables started chanting, "Al-ex! Al-ex! Al-ex!"

No other bids rang out.

"What the hell," Alex yelled over the din. "Make it $475...for the senior citizens!"

"Four seventy-five it is!" screamed the emcee waving the ball over his head. "Alex Hart is bidding against himself! Four seventy-five once! Four seventy-five twice!" He looked across the room, gavel upraised.

"Five hundred!" Naz yelled. The gavel hung in mid-air. Whispers and murmurs crossed the tables. The men glanced around the room. Who? Five hundred dollars?

"Five hundred dollars!" Naz's voice rang out again and all heads turned to his table. His own people stared.

"Jesus Christ, Naz, are you crazy!" Jack whispered.

"Five hundred dollars from Mr. Agajanian," the emcee said, and he turned to the other side of the room where Naz could see Alex Hart crushing a napkin in his hands. The men starting clapping in cadence. "Go! Go! Go!"

"Five twenty-five," Alex yelled.

Now the focus turned back to Naz. He took a bite of green onion. "Five fifty!"

"Naz?" Uncle Vahan said. "You can't win this thing. He'll eat you alive!"

Naz barely heard him, like some gnat buzzing

around his ear. He toyed with the cigar. He knew there was no love lost between Alex and his father, and was betting that the older Hart wouldn't step in to help him. For all his wealth, Alex was a notorious tight wad. Naz hoped this would hold true tonight.

Naz glanced at Harry and saw the light glint off his gold tooth. A twinkle in his eye.

"Six seventy-five!" yelled Alex, jumping the ante and not even waiting for the emcee.

"Seven hundred!" said Naz. He had $400 in his pocket that he had ripped out of the scalehouse till. He was flying on scotch and fumes.

Hands grabbed for drinks. Men stopped their conversations in the hallway and flowed into the room, standing along the walls.

Naz noticed that one of the haulers he had overheard in the john was edging back over to his side of the room. He watched Alex take a slug of his drink, then stare at Naz.

"Eight hundred dollars!"

A roar went up from the Hart side. A murmur spread through the Agajanian ranks. Blurry eyes were sparkling, even the white guys. Naz seemed to surface from some deep reverie. He looked around at the screaming mouths, the fluid faces.

The emcee said, "Eight hundred, going once!'

Alex reached around and grabbed the hands of celebration reaching out to him.

"Eight hundred twice!" The Agajanian camp slumped in their seats. Harry tapped Naz on the shoulder with his beautiful cane then laid it on the table. Naz smiled at his father and nodded slightly.

"Two thousand dollars!" Naz yelled.

The entire room gasped. Two thousand dollars! This was unheard of. This was insanity—and they loved it. In a mass, the Agajanian men exploded from their chairs with a roar. Fists punched the air, drinks spilled.

"Two thousand once!"

Naz stole a glance at Kail Hart. The smirk on the old man's face told Naz that Alex was alone.

"Two thousand twice!"

Alex's breath was coming in short bursts, his eyes wide. Agajanian's a fucking mad man. No one would pay two grand for a football! And he'd probably go higher. His guys would understand. You can't bid against a lunatic. He threw his napkin on the table and headed for the door.

"Sold, to Nazareth Agajanian for $2,000!" The emcee grabbed the ball and cocked his arm. A perfect spiral swirled under the chandeliers.

Jack caught the ball. He held it out to Naz, but Naz just nodded toward his dad. Jack gave the ball to Harry and the old man raised it slowly and triumphantly above his head.

Harry handed his gold-headed cane to Naz. "For the ball. I use other one now. This one get back later."

*   *   *

Late that night, Alex drove up the access road at the HIA landfill, past the fountain glowing in the dark with its pattern of colored lighting. He pulled up to the black, glass-fronted recycling building that sat off to the side. His heart was still pounding, the adrenaline only now wearing off. Agajanian might have the football, but Alex had something a lot more precious—he had Naz's bid number. Jack had called earlier in the day. At the height of the bidding for the football Alex had felt like screaming out "Thirty-four dollars a ton! You goddamn sonuvabitch!"

His deal with Jack had been worth every penny, and with a few adjustments to their number, Alex knew they would win the bid. Fuck the football. He'd pull it out of the wreckage of Pacific Rim.

Alex saw the roll-off bin from the catalytic converter company on the truck at the scale, and pictured the ingot buried inside. Once per week that bin came in, an ingot in every one. What a haul. With a hiss, the truck released its air brakes and pulled into the building. A twenty-five-foot high mechanical door slid down behind it.

Alex walked into the tipping area and watched as the load tumbled out. Immediately, he noticed something was wrong. Instead of the normal recyclable cardboard and paper, this load was mostly garbage. He remembered that his recycling foreman had mentioned that quite a few of the loads from some of their best industrial recycling programs were dropping off badly in quality. But Alex had been focused on the bid and hadn't paid much attention. He stepped back in the shadows as his worker methodically raked through the trash. After several minutes, he hadn't found the ingot, and Alex knew he never would. The man looked up at Alex and shrugged his shoulders.

Back in his office, Alex jerked the phone off the desk, and dialed. That ingot of industrial grade platinum was worth over $20,000.

"North American Catalysts," a voice answered.

"Pritchard in custodial services," Alex said.

"It's after hours, sir. If you could please call back."

"This is important, a family thing. Can't you page him?"

"Oh, OK. Just a moment please."

Alex tapped a pencil on the blotter, wondering what the hell could have gone wrong. He couldn't afford a screw up. Not now.

"Pritchard," a tired voice answered.

"What happened to the last load?"

"Who is this?"

"Who do you think it is?"

"I thought you weren't going to call me here."

"What the hell's going on over there?"

"What do you mean?"

"The load's full of garbage and the ingot isn't there."

"Look harder. It's there," the janitor said in a whisper. "And that load was all cardboard and high grades. I know 'cause I filled it."

"Either you're full of shit," Alex said, "or…. Are you sure no one saw you?"

"Not a chance."

"Could someone have screwed with the bin?"

"No way. I saw your truck pick it up last night."

"Last night!" Alex shouted. "The driver just brought the bin in fifteen minutes ago. Goddammit! What color was the truck you saw?"

"Gray, I think. Maybe yellow trim. Hard to see."

Alex closed his eyes and groaned. He knew those trucks. Goddamn Agajanian. "Don't do anything for a couple days, till you hear from me."

"You said there'd be no problems."

"Just be ready." Alex banged the phone down. He crossed to the wet bar, poured a shot and slugged it down. He poured another one. His mind was racing. What the hell had happened? How had Agajanian caught on to him? What about his other special accounts, were they in jeopardy too? Suddenly, he felt vulnerable, the ground under him shifting. There was just no way Agajanian could be on to his scheme. But there was no doubt that somehow he had grabbed that load.

Alex thought for a moment, his jaw clenched. He had to move fast. Get some intelligence. Find out what was going on at Pacific Rim, what they knew, what they had, maybe even recover the ingot, if he was lucky. He would send his best man to check it out. He'd worked for Alex several times before, difficult collections, "salvage" work, that type of thing, including the little truck episode with the bleach and ammonia.

For a moment, Alex thought of his bigger weapon, Jack. But if by some freak of nature, that he couldn't imagine now, Naz won the bid, Alex would be glad he'd saved Jack for a more crucial moment, when the damage he could inflict on Pacific Rim would be fatal, not just crippling.

Alex picked up the phone.

13

Carina idled in the morning traffic, her car a red jewel in the chatter of dilapidated pick-ups, bruised sedans, and other road-weary vehicles. She pulled the visor down, looked in the mirror, and ran lipstick around her mouth. She thought about what she had to do that day on the bid package, the assignments Denny had given her. It all tied in to the presentation and site tour for the pre-qualification inspection that was coming up the next day. It was the usual scramble, but this time the stakes were so much higher. If they failed the inspection, they would be disqualified from even submitting a bid. It was the city's way of getting rid of the riffraff and eliminating unwanted competition. It worried her.

She was thinking about Denny when the traffic eased ahead and out of the corner of her eye, she saw a homeless man drooped against the signal light with a dog curled up next to him. Nothing new. They were everywhere. The figure suddenly came to life, the disco music thumping out from a car ahead seeming to pump life into the scarecrow of a man. He waved his Dodger baseball cap in the air and danced to the beat. Carina let out a gasp. Oh, no.

Charlie was flying high now. As he wobbled out into the street, Black ran out after him, barking. A delivery truck nearly clipped Charlie with its side-view mirror.

"Get out of the road, you jackass," Carina heard the driver yell. She saw Charlie wave his hat and bow as the truck sped off, Black barking. Charlie tipped a bottle to his mouth but it was empty. In disgust, he hurled the bottle to the curb and it smashed. Then the wind blew his hat off. Horns honked. Black continued to bark, swirling around Charlie's legs. Another car swerved past, brakes squealing, and Carina realized Charlie could get killed. Half of her wanted to let him, especially after that episode with the spear gun in his shipping container. But then there was the dog. She couldn't let Black get hit.

Carina turned onto the side street. Charlie was struggling on his knees trying to pick up his cap when she stepped into his line of vision, such as it was.

"Jesus Christ," Charlie whispered in reverence, his breath shortening, his gaze fixed on the shapely calves.

"Come on, Charlie," Carina said, lifting him by the arm.

Charlie staggered up against Carina. He stunk of booze and stale sweat. They lurched to Carina's car. Charlie tapped the side of the bed of the El Camino. "Black," he slurred. The dog jumped into the bed.

Suddenly, a cop car pulled up and seeing it, Charlie

struggled to get free. "Oh shit," Carina muttered, until she saw the big bulk and the wide smile of Sergeant Kowalski climbing out of the car.

"It's OK, Joe. I got him," she hollered.

"You sure? I could load him in the squad car."

"Naw. Guys at the plant see your black and white, half of them will be over the fence before you hit the scalehouse."

The Sergeant helped Carina dump Charlie in a rumpled heap in her front seat. Using his nightstick, Joe shoveled Charlie's dangling foot in, then closed the door.

"Vice-President of Security doing a little partying," Joe said.

"Lucky he didn't get killed," she said.

"You alright?"

"Yeah."

"Say hi to your dad for me."

"Thanks, Joe. I owe you another one."

"No one owes anyone anything." Joe smiled and walked back to his squad car. Carina slid into the front seat. "So, Charlie. What's the occasion?"

"Huh?"

"I said, what's the occasion?" Carina hollered as she pulled the car back onto Boyle.

Charlie was fixated on her breasts that were filling out the pockets of her work shirt.

"Oh, just a little, uh," Charlie belched, "celebratin'!" He sighed then giggled, and slapped his thigh.

"Oh, yeah?" Carina said. "Hey, that's nice, Charlie. You hit the lottery or what? Come on, Charlie. Sit up!"

Charlie broke his gaze off Carina's chest and stared

blankly out the side window, his head wobbly. They drove past the hubcap salvage yard, where the sun reflected off a thousand hubcaps fastened to the fence. Charlie threw his hand up in front of his eyes to fend off the glare. That seemed to jog his memory. "Naw, no lottery but, uh, lemme tell you a secret," he whispered. "Don't, don't t-tell anyone, OK?"

"Scouts honor," she said.

Charlie coughed a hunk of phlegm up out of his lungs and caught it in his mouth, stupefied.

"Shit," Carina gasped. Reaching quickly to the console, she buzzed Charlie's window down. With a look of relief, she watched him spit into the breeze. If there was one thing Charlie was good at it was spitting, and Carina was fairly certain that Charlie had cleared the side of her car. The whole episode had her close to gagging. God, what a way to start the morning.

Charlie dozed, his head nodding to his chest.

"So, Charlie!" Carina said. Charlie's head snapped up. "What happened, anyway?"

"You won't tell?" Charlie slurred, his tongue like a wad of cotton.

"No, I won't tell. Jesus."

"I found somethin' in the trash. An ingot."

"A what?"

"Metal," Charlie struggled to speak. "You know." Charlie belched. "Heavy fucker."

"So where is this thing?" she shot back. Why am I talking to this guy like he's normal, she thought, as she drove up the access road to the plant.

"What thing?" Charlie said groggily.

"The 'heavy fucker' you found in the trash!"

"Sold it." Charlie looked pale. Carina hoped he wasn't going to puke.

"Great," she said, blowing off his rambling as just more Charlie lunacy. He was always finding "treasures" in the trash. He was worse than her *Babig*. She pulled past the scalehouse. The scale attendant stared at them, his coffee mug frozen at his mouth.

Charlie snickered. "Ol' Luis tried to put one over on me. But I got him up to 275!" Charlie giggled and went to punch Carina in the arm. She swerved and Charlie hit his head against the door frame with a thunk. Black skittered around in the pickup bed.

"See what you made me do," Carina said.

Charlie moaned and grabbed his head. Carina pulled up next to Charlie's hearse. She climbed out and walked around to open Charlie's door. Black bounded out of the back and woofed for Charlie. Carina saw Jack across the yard. "Hey Jack! Can you give me a hand?"

Jack walked over as Carina opened the door, and he grabbed Charlie to keep him from falling on his face.

"Hey, Jack!" Charlie spat the words out. Spittle foaming at the corner of his mouth.

"Almost home," Jack said, as he caught Charlie under the arms and started dragging him out of the car. "What happened to him?" Jack asked Carina.

"Hell if I know. I found him like this wandering in the middle of the street."

As Jack lifted the limp body, Charlie's foot got caught behind the gearshift and he let out a yelp. Carina reached down and twisted his basketball shoe till it came free, then looked around for something to wipe her hand on.

"Fuckin' ingot," Charlie whispered. "Alloy my ass!" he screamed

"Easy, Charlie," Jack said, gripping him under the armpits and dragging him to his car.

"OK, Charlie," Jack said. "Here you are."

Carina pried open the rear door of the hearse. They deposited Charlie in the car, and Black jumped in beside him. Charlie mumbled too himself, laughed, and fell asleep.

Jack closed the car door.

Carina said, "The day hasn't even started and I need a shower."

*   *   *

Denny lived in an old iron works compound that had been converted to a maze of artists lofts just north of downtown. He had spent most of the day hunched over his "desk," an old door he had sanded and varnished and set across two saw horses. He was working out the final details for his big day at Pacific Rim the following morning—the Pre-Bid Inspection. Naz had put him in charge of leading the opening presentation, and although he was confident, he was feeling the pressure. Given what he had seen of Alex and Barbara Miller at the composting demonstration, he knew the city staff would be looking for any reason to disqualify them. Failure tomorrow would eliminate Pacific Rim from the competition, a catastrophe beyond imagining. He grimaced.

As he polished his work boots, he checked the notes on the desk, and ran over the presentation in his head. Outside, the sun had gone down and the lights of the adjacent rail yard shone in through his windows.

The loft was one large room with red brick walls, open ceiling crossed with structural I-beams and a sloping corrugated tin roof. A bank of small paned windows looked over the rail yard. African rattles and masks, spears, seashells adorned the walls. A large wooden drum sat by a leather couch and a wood-burning stove stretched its stovepipe up through the roof. On a side-table, sat a rectangular Warri game board, its twelve "cups" or depressions in the wood worn smooth over countless years by fingers moving the stones from one cup to another.

The phone call shocked him, the sound of her voice on his home line seemed out of place. She knew it was late, she said, but she was just leaving Pacific Rim and thought maybe they should go over the details of tomorrow's inspection. There would be little time at the plant in the morning, and it would be even more chaotic than normal. She didn't want to impose, but could she stop by? Would he mind?

No, of course not, he had said.

As usual, everything in the loft was in its place. Denny couldn't stand chaos, and in his case, chaos represented a dirty dish in the sink. He found freedom in order. He did the only thing left to do: he flossed then brushed his teeth.

Although it was a cool night, it felt stuffy in the loft, the heat from the day slowly discharging from the brick walls. Denny walked past the wooden scrim that separated the living room and kitchen from the bedroom, and pulled a rope connected to a pulley that ran to a section of tin roof over his bed. A rectangle of metal hinged up and opened to the night sky. Denny felt the cool air pour down over his face. It was a feeling that took him back to Africa and the nights sleeping outside. He had cut the roof section, and now found it hard to sleep without it open.

In the two years since he'd been back from his Peace Corps stint in Angola, no woman had been in the loft and he wondered how it would feel. Denny looked around the room, at all the artifacts from Africa, and remembered another day, back in Angola, the feel of the teacher, Mimsala, her hand on his arm. He had met her digging out one of his lagoons, where he was teaching the natives fish farming. She had taken him to a ceremony where a pregnant woman, channeling the spirit of her unborn child, sang a song to the tribe gathered around her. The song was the baby's expression of its own soul, of its purpose in coming to this earth and this village.

As the mother sang the song over and over, and the tribe learned it and sang back, Denny was moved almost to tears at the sense of the family and spirit that connected the village. Here they were, these poor people, struggling to stay alive, and yet so connected to what was really important. Then, Mimsala had explained to him, as the child grows and throughout its life if ever that person forgets who they really are, the village gathers around them and sings that person's song as a reminder of where they came from and why they were there.

At the time, Denny couldn't help but compare that village to his own back in Southern California, with its sea of matching Spanish tile roofs, the hissing of the automatic irrigation systems, the twenty-eight cubic foot refrigerators with ice makers, the Beemers and Mercedes, wealth beyond imagining, and yet to him, a desert of spirit. Many times since then, Denny had wanted to hear his own song, so he could remember who he was and what he was supposed to be doing. But there was never anyone around him to sing. At least, not yet.

Now Carina was coming to his private world. He had heard the tension in her voice, the need to review the work, to be certain about the critical steps tomorrow. Or maybe just to sense the human connection with someone on the team before going into battle, a fellow warrior. He knew the feeling. Pacific Rim in its funny little way, was more of a family than he had ever known. But he also knew that the Armenian families were tight-knit. There was a bright line around each of them separating the "in" from the "out", as clear as sun and shade. Inside, you were protected, given the benefit of the doubt, defended, loved. Outside, you had to earn everything, and then still, you were not blood. No matter the sacrifice or years of faithful service, you may never be invited over that line.

About Carina herself, he didn't know what to feel. There was something familiar and alluring about the territory, yet he wasn't sure he was ready to go back there. Then he heard her footsteps ringing up the spiral metal staircase. He realized he was in his stocking feet and felt oddly vulnerable. He crossed the room, and opened the door.

Carina stood there in her brown leather jacket and worn jeans, steel-toed work boots, dark and beautiful, tiger-eyed, breathing from the long climb up the spiral staircase, and for a moment, just a moment, Denny felt a tightness in his chest—an exquisite ache he hadn't felt for a long time.

"Can I come in?" she said, seeing him hesitate.

"Oh, yeah, sure, sorry."

Carina stepped into the loft and into another world. She was momentarily stunned by the exotic beauty, so different from what she expected driving up to the industrial complex in the heart of the city. She walked slowly into the open space of red brick walls, steel beam bracing. She laid some file folders on the coffee table, an egg crate with a piece of glass on top.

"Here, let me take your jacket," Denny said.

She hardly heard him.

She shrugged out of the sleeves, her eyes still studying the walls, the artifacts. "This is beautiful, Denny. I... had no idea."

"I was lucky to be able to bring some of this out of Angola. I had friends."

Carina noticed a picture, almost hidden on a shelf, of Denny deeply tanned with a young native woman leaning against him, her hand on his chest.

"Yes. I imagine you did," she said, a momentary flutter of sadness brushing her, like the wings of a small bird. "Who's the beautiful lady?"

"Just a school teacher," he said, a slight catch in his voice. "She died of cholera."

"I'm sorry."

Denny nodded.

Ever since the ride on the motorcycle, she had felt the conflict, the confusion. The ghost of Galen stalked her, not maliciously, but more as a guardian, there to protect her, and remind her of what can happen to a heart. Even though part of her would have gladly hung on forever in her pain and sweet solitude, she knew she had to let go. Sometimes, you have to trick your own mind, she thought. Tell it you want to approach the fire just to get warm, and then when you are close, throw yourself in. Maybe that's why she had grabbed the phone in the spur of the moment earlier that evening.

She walked to the bank of small-paned windows. She noticed a wall of clouds moving in over the towers downtown, the advancing mist rolling into the rail yard; a distant grumble of thunder. "Union Pacific?"

"Santa Fe," he said. "Marshaling yard. You want something to drink? Tea, water?"

"Tea would be nice."

She watched Denny, his shirt hanging loose, his movements unhurried, almost graceful, filling the kettle, setting it on the burner. The pilot light clicked as it struck and lit the burner.

Carina realized in that moment that everything would be OK tomorrow. That their destiny lay in the calm hands of the man who lived here, in this ordered room overlooking the rail yard, with his books and masks and drums, his teakettle, his motorcycle and his mind.

She watched a freight train snake out of the yard, its headlamp a beacon in the foggy night illuminating the track ahead. And she saw her life and the moment and her body standing there at the window, all wrapped up in the bid. And behind that, like a movie, the journey of her family, how the tracks were laid decades ago, stretching out before each of them in turn, invisible and true as longitude. There was a magnetism to it. She felt it most every time she came near her *Babig*. Her compass would swing—and there he was, her grandfather.

And even more startling, she felt it now.

As Denny took his sleeve and wiped one of the panes, Carina looked at the curve of his throat where it disappeared behind his button-down collar. In the background, the teakettle hummed.

He glanced at her. "What?"

"Sorry. Just that thinking thing, you know?"

They looked at each other. Denny reached for her hand. They moved closer.

The teakettle screamed.

Denny ran over and turned off the burner, and the whistle died. "You want cream and sugar?"

"Sure."

Carina heard something, so soft she wasn't sure. She pushed the window and it swung out on its hinges. She stuck her head out and saw a scrawny cat, not much bigger than a kitten, crouched on the metal roof that jutted out below. A mask of white covered its nose, its tawny, mottled fur balled with foxtails.

"Here, kitty," Carina said, scratching the roof with her fingernails. She saw the cat's little pink mouth move, but the meow was so soft she had to imagine the sound.

Denny came over with the tea in mugs.

"Who's your friend?" Carina said.

"I call her Timbuktu. Timmy. She's a stray. I feed her at night." Denny set his tea down and picked up a can of cat food from a stack on the floor below the window. At the sound of the top popping, the little cat meowed and snuck closer, crawling low, cautious, ready to fly. Denny wedged the can in the metal brace of the window, and touching Carina's arm, lead her back a step. The cat moved up slowly, sniffing the air, eased up to the can and started to eat, glancing up every bite to make sure all was still safe.

"That's a girl, Timmy," Denny said in a whisper.

"Sometimes my hair feels like that," Carina said, and they laughed. The sound in her throat, the relief, cracked the final caution that held her.

Denny reached up and brushed a strand of hair off Carina's forehead. "We should go over my outline for tomorrow," he said, voice trailing off.

Carina ran her fingertips across Denny's shirt, along his collarbone. "Yes...I suppose we should."

They fell into the kiss so hard their teeth hit.

Carina lost herself in lips, tongue, chest. Denny's hands pulled her by the small of her back, she hugged him under the arms, grabbing him by the shoulder blades. She rubbed one leg against the outside of his. She couldn't find enough places to touch.

He swept her up off her feet in his arms, and carried her to the bed.

A frantic groping, unbuttoning, moaning, rubbing, writhing, her back arched, breasts, belly, shoving, pulling, she bit his shoulder, he kissed her neck. She pulled her shirt over her head and threw her hair back. He unfastened his belt. She fell into him. He pulled her on top of him, full length touching from lips to toes.

Carina kissed his chest, his belly, felt his hands in her hair, his breathing.

Suddenly, a flash radiated the room in blue-white light. Then, a sharp crack and dark rumble, the air trembled, electric.

She stopped, crouched over him, the rain hitting her back, cold. She rolled off him. "Oh, God." The rain hit her face and breasts and she heard him scramble up and run to the wall.

The roof closed, the last drops dripping from the beams overhead.

She returned to her body. The spell lost. A voice of reason—what are you doing? And suddenly, she wasn't sure. And then the vision of Galen rose up again, the guardian, his muscled body, dark hair. She felt weak, drained as if her blood were running out on the floor. She reached for her shirt.

Denny stood beside the bed, bare chest, pants sagging from his slender hips, panting. "Let me get you a towel...."

"I should probably be going," someone said, she thought maybe it was her.

He opened his mouth, but nothing came out.

She eased off the bed. Brushed her hair back with her fingers. She got up, buttoning her shirt over her wet skin.

"I'll, uh, get your coat," he said.

In a cocoon of numbness, Carina finished dressing, pulled on her boots, walked toward the door. His hands held out her jacket. She slipped it on.

"Don't forget your files," he said.

"See you at six?" she said.

"You have the site plan?"

She held up the folder, then turned and walked out

the door. She heard him say, "Be careful, the stairs are slippery."

It's all slippery, she thought, as her steps dropped down the spiral, around and around and around.

14

Denny checked his watch as he drove past the gate at Pacific Rim. The city's pre-bid inspectors would be arriving in thirty minutes. He hoped everyone was complete on their tasks.

He stuck his head in at the scalehouse to make sure the attendant had the new Geiger counter up and running, supposedly to scan loads for radioactive waste. The tall, skinny albino was holding the meter up to his mouth.

"I think my breath is nuclear," he said.

For some reason, that information did not surprise Denny.

It was still dark in the yard as Denny unloaded the easels and display boards from the trunk of his car and carried them to a cleared area of the tipping floor. The offices at Pacific Rim were too small, and Naz and Denny had decided to set up in the plant, with the equipment as a backdrop.

Denny noticed Carina hard at work making a final adjustment to the sorting line conveyor, Naz over at the compactor, running it through a couple cycles, probably jacking up the pressure on the hydraulic pump. The machine couldn't function long at that elevated pressure, but it would speed up its cycle time, and make it appear that they could pack trash into the transfer trucks faster than they actually could on a consistent basis.

Denny focused on his part of the inspection—the opening presentation. Naz had told him that it had to look polished, professional. Even if the plant itself didn't measure up to HIA's, their presentation could.

Denny had commissioned a blown up aerial photograph of the neighborhood, highlighting the site and the truck routes leading to it. Since there were no existing drawings of the plant, he had to take painstaking measurements and prepare a Site Plan himself. The plan was color coded, showing the property lines, paved areas, structures, future landscaping, and onsite traffic patterns. The latter were somewhat theoretical, clean arrows showing miniature trucks lining up at the scales, pulling into the yard, backing into the tipping areas. A real traffic pattern would have looked like a bowl of spaghetti, which would reinforce the city's preconceived notion that Pacific Rim was a terminal of chaos, from which an entering truck, once past the front gate, would never return.

Denny set a third board on an easel depicting the floor plan with the plant's three main processing systems—the heavy screen and elevated sorting line, the baler for recovered recyclables, and the compactor to load out residual trash.

To provide stronger visuals, Denny had also commissioned a rendering of the facility depicting it with a new paint job and adorned by new landscaping—Bird of Paradise plants, jacaranda trees—all to be installed once Pacific Rim had won the bid, of course.

Other boards covered company personnel and responsibilities, the so-called org chart; bullet points highlighting Pacific Rim's sixty-year history, starting with Harry in Fresno; a short-list of end-user markets— the companies that bought Pacific Rim's cardboard, newspaper, aluminum, glass, steel, plastic, and rock and dirt.

In short, Denny was ready to paint a picture for the city, a picture of a small but competent company with a long and honorable past, with capable management, and experienced, hard-working staff. A no-frills company with character, integrity and above all—the ability to get the job done. And in his own mind he added, "no matter what", because Pacific Rim was a "no matter what" kind of place.

Carina walked up and straightened the legs of one of the easels, not looking at Denny.

"Hey," she said.

Denny smiled. "Hey."

"Looks nice. You done good." She yelled to a worker to give the area one final sweeping, then turned back to Denny.

"Look, about last night...."

"Don't worry about it. Not the first time I've been all wet."

She touched him on the arm. "My fault. I just have some things...."

"I know the feeling," he said.

"Next time, I'll bring my Gore-Tex PJ's."

They both laughed, and part of the wall that had sprung up the previous night, tumbled back down, maybe most of it.

"Hey!" Naz's voice boomed out. They turned and saw him charging across the yard, a cigar bobbing in his teeth. "Denny, you got everything ready?"

"Yep."

Naz turned to Carina. "What about you?"

"Six feet a second on the line. By city standards, that'll give us twenty tons an hour through the system. Even HIA can't do that."

"Neither can we, for long. All right, they'll be here any minute. Remember, Denny starts short and sweet, no State of the Union message. Carina follows with the site tour, scales to tipping floor, to sorting, to baler, to compactor. Got it?"

"Yes, Dad. I got it."

"And no tour of Grandpa's cucumber patch!"

"What?" Carina said, a look of surprise on her face. "The only part of the plant that always produces?"

Naz patted Carina on the cheek, Denny on the shoulder. "Carina, you get out there by the scale house to greet them. First thing I want them to see is that Agajanian smile. Denny, you give 'em hell." He turned and yelled. "Mrs. Avakian!"

"What Nazareth?" her voice echoed out from the office.

"Where's the goddamn coffee?" Naz stormed off.

"He's a little on edge," Carina said.

"He's not the only one," said Denny. "I've got a flare gun in the trunk of my car. If we don't pass, I'm going to shoot myself."

"Save one flare for me."

Denny smiled at her.

"I better get my smile ready," she said. She touched his hand, then walked across the yard.

Denny thought how beautiful she looked. Beyond her, he spotted the plain white sedan with the city logo on the door pull up the access road and stop in front of the scalehouse. He saw Carina flash them a smile that could have melted a glacier, but couldn't penetrate the hardened faces he saw in the front seat of the car. Clearly, they had their marching orders and were going to carry them out with grim determination. Carina's smile would only go so far today.

The four Bureau of Sanitation inspectors climbed out with their clipboards, stopwatches, Polaroid cameras, and mechanical pencils in their plastic pocket holders.

Naz, too, had watched the inspectors arrive. He clipped off the soggy end of his cigar, then he rushed out of the office to welcome them, shaking each of their hands as if they were Bedouins coming to his oasis after a long journey over the hot sands. Naz led them over to the tipping area where Denny would launch the day, then moved to the back to watch things unfold. Although he had to fight the urge to take control and run the whole thing, he knew they had to look like a team, not just a one-man show. Denny had told him that from the beginning, and he had to admit his consultant was right. He couldn't do it all himself, no matter how hard he wanted to. Naz would have crawled to New York on his knees, if it would win this bid. But it wouldn't.

He needed to give up the responsibility, let his crew face the fire, build confidence. And as he listened to Denny give his presentation, he knew he had done the right thing. Up there with his white shirt, blue blazer, and wing tip shoes, he looked just like the city people. Tapping the presentation boards with his telescoping aluminum pointer, sounding as if he had designed the plant and run it for years, using words like "strategic" and "innovation" and "compliant," something was "reflective" of something else, "derived from," "contingent upon"—words that had never been uttered at Pacific Rim, and as far as Naz knew, may never be again, but right now he was all for them. Yeah, bet your ass, "contingent upon"—whatever the hell that meant!

Near the end of his talk, Denny introduced Naz and Jack and Harry, with their titles, CEO, Facility Manager, and Founder. And all three nodded, a little embarrassed.

Then Denny turned it over to Carina, introduced as the Chief Operating Officer, first time Naz had ever heard that. Sounded good. Maybe he should check out this org chart of Denny's. Carina started in. She looked confident, poised, knowledgeable and so tall and beautiful. Naz was stunned for a moment. Maybe he had never looked at her like this before. A critical situation, everything on the line. Maybe he had just been too busy being on the line himself, covering everything himself, listening to himself.

Naz smiled. Not so bad, this daughter. He tossed his

cigar butt in the trash pile and plopped a fresh cigar in his mouth.

And behind the scenes, there was Jack, never seeming to hurry, yet handling all the little things, wire caught around a pulley, a paper jam on the heavy screen, a dust mask for a sorter, all the shit jobs—never a complaint. He looked over at Jack and smiled. Jack nodded back.

Naz tagged along at the end of the group, as Carina lead them up the steps to the sorting line, talking with that loud, husky voice, her hands expressive. He looked down the conveyor at the workers, for once arrayed with matching hard hats and safety goggles, ear plugs, orange reflective vests, and gloves. The city inspectors checked the conveyor speed and the furious action of the workers on the line, pulling off the recyclables as the stream of trash flowed by. Carina winked at Naz.

Jack moved up quickly behind Naz and whispered. "We got a problem with the compactor."

Naz whirled to face him, this could be bad. The compactor was the backbone of the operation, the machine that loaded out all the residual trash. Without it, they would fail the inspection and be prohibited from bidding. "What's the problem?" Naz said, jerking the cigar out of his mouth, his face lined with worry.

"Got a pinprick leak in the hydraulics. I'm afraid when we crank her up to that new pressure you set, could burst the line."

"Where's Charlie?"

"Hiding in his container where you told him."

"Get him over there. Tell him he's got five minutes to seal that hole."

As Jack ran off to get Charlie, Naz rolled the cigar

in his mouth. In Naz's life of unimaginable happenings, one of the hardest to believe was that Charlie was the best welder he had ever seen, trained in the Navy or something. Sonuvabitch could drop a spot weld on your wedding ring and not burn your finger.

A moment later, Naz saw Jack hustle Charlie and his acetylene tank over behind the compactor. Luckily, the inspectors were still honed in around Carina and the sorting line, noting the new signs Naz had put up at Denny's insistence, "Hearing Protection Required" and "Safety is Job One." Then, they were down and measuring the tipping floor square footage, frowning, punching calculators. Naz watched Denny answering questions, taking an inspector into his confidence, holding the end of the tape measure, describing the process as they fired up the baler, spitting out a large bale of newspaper. Naz saw the sparks still flying from behind the compactor where Jack and Charlie were going at it.

Naz pulled Denny aside and whispered. "Don't look now, but we got a problem with the compactor."

"What?" Denny said, a concerned look on his face.

"Take the city to the scales. Show them the system, weigh a truck, weigh Carina. Do whatever you got to do. Buy us ten more minutes."

As the baler demo ended, Denny grabbed the arm of the lead inspector and detoured the group away from the compactor across the yard to the scales.

While that was happening, Naz hustled over to Jack and Charlie. "How's it going?" he said to Jack, careful not to look directly at the brilliant arc of Charlie's welding torch.

"Touchy," Jack said. "The piping's corroded. Charlie's

having a tough time finding solid metal to hold the weld." The sparks were burning tiny specks in the sleeves of Jack's shirt, landing on the backs of his hands as he held the welding rod in place.

"Jack! Listen to me. I'm going to hold them off as long as I can. Just give me one good cycle, that's all she's got to do."

Naz looked up to see the group heading back across the yard toward the compactor and leaped out to intercept them. Perhaps sensing from the urgency in Naz's step that the compactor wasn't ready, Denny stopped the group in the middle of the yard and launched into what Naz would later recall as one of the best five-minute bullshit jobs he'd ever heard.

Denny pointed out features of the stormwater drainage system, that basically weren't there, described the new landscaping that would screen the view from the freeway. When he finally started faltering for ideas, Carina stepped in, talking about how the facility could accommodate busloads of school children for tours. Naz had never heard that one before, but it sounded pretty good right then.

Finally, Jack waved to Naz and gave him the "thumbs up" sign, then scooted off with Charlie. Naz walked up to the group and said, "OK, now for the big finale. The compactor."

The crowd gathered around the compactor. Naz glanced at Jack, who glanced at Carina, who glanced at Denny, who glanced at Naz, who nodded to his loader operator. The loader rumbled forward with a bucketful of trash and dropped it in the compactor hopper. Manny activated the packing cycle. The inspectors hit their stopwatches.

Naz positioned himself between the crowd and the ram hydraulics. The huge compactor ram groaned and crushed the trash into the semi-trailer, Naz glanced at Charlie's bright, gleaming weld. Hold you beautiful sonuvabitch, he prayed. Hold.

Ten seconds to go,

Nine....

With a final moan, the ram stopped and retracted.

Victory.

The amped up hydraulics had raced through a packing cycle in forty-five seconds. Naz breathed a sigh of relief and shot a quick smile at Jack. The bastard had held.

Walking back across the yard for the final wrap up, Naz had to admit that Denny and Carina had done a terrific job, better than he could have done himself, well, close anyway. However, now that the pressure was off, something else was bothering him. He couldn't help but notice the growing familiarity between the two of them. How they looked at each other. How Denny was always there at her shoulder. He felt a slight vertigo and realized he may be losing her. It was one thing with Galen, the son of a good friend and childhood playmate, almost part of the family from the beginning. This was another matter. A virtual stranger. A white boy.

This would not, could not, be tolerated. Naz had seen outsiders ostracized by the Armenian community, and not just the outsider, but the Armenian family itself. Although they weren't his proudest moments, he had at times been one of the accusers. There was a reason for it. People were better off with their own, where they were understood, where things were expected, where everyone knew their place. Otherwise, the family lineage would be diluted, the history lost, the traditions abandoned.

Naz saw Carina signaling him.

Denny said, "And now, some last words from the CEO of Pacific Rim Recycling, Nazareth Agajanian."

Denny stepped back, and Naz took the stage, such as it was, making a point of standing between Carina and Denny. Naz pulled himself together quickly. He was, after all, CEO.

"I personally want to thank the city for coming out today to see our facility," Naz said. "We take none of this lightly. This bid is the most important one in the history of our company. As Mr. DeYoung told you, my father started with a horse and wagon in Fresno in 1925. What you see here all comes from his dream, or as Denny would say "from his strategic positioning."

The group laughed. Naz looked to the back, where Harry sat on a bale of cardboard, pretending not to listen.

"I know this isn't fancy. We're not fancy people. I know it doesn't even look like much, especially compared to some of our competitors. But this job isn't about fancy. It's about hard work. Years of trial and error. Hell, you're catching us at the right time—we already made every mistake. Right, Jack?"

"Personally," Jack replied from off to the side, wiping grease off his hands with a rag.

"All we do is get the job done," Naz said, "for a small fee, of course." The city folks smiled despite themselves, and Naz thought that perhaps Pacific Rim had won them over, or at least moved them to neutral. "So now, we only have one question," he said, "How'd we do?"

A couple of the city staff conferred, then a large, gangly man, Larry Smith, Deputy Director of the Bureau of Sanitation, stepped forward and said, "It's not official until we go over all the details back in the office. But at this point, Mr. Agajanian, and baring something unforeseen, you look reasonably good."

Naz smiled and popped the cigar in his mouth. "That's what all the girls tell me."

Naz saw Carina roll her eyes at Denny. Ah, what did she know. He just couldn't resist playing a little with the city. He watched their car drive off, and cringed when he saw Charlie waving at them, Black at his heels barking. He'd hidden Charlie's hearse behind a stack of bales and warned him about making an appearance. But then again, the old derelict had saved Naz's ass with the compactor. Naz didn't know whether to wring Charlie's neck or buy him a bottle of Old Overholt. Jack walked up and Harry tapped along on one of his spare canes.

"Now all we gotta do," Naz said, "is win the bid."

"I think I get some *oghi*," Harry said.

Naz said, "I think we all get some *oghi*!"

The sun broke through the morning overcast and dowsed the plant in gold as the five of them walked across the yard toward the office and the bottle in Naz's lower desk drawer.

*   *   *

Naz couldn't believe it. Here it was the night after the inspection and two days before the bid, and he felt like there were fifty things he should be doing, and not one of them was this. But in a moment of weakness he had promised Mayda, so…in frustration, he swung the hammer just a little too hard. It glanced off the nail and clipped his thumb.

"Goddammit!" he yelled, sucking at the blood oozing under his fingernail.

Mayda put down the corbel for the shelf, and headed for the kitchen. "I'll get some ice."

"Forget the fucking ice! Just give me the scotch." Naz gazed at the glass shelves it had taken him two hours to install. They were already lined with frogs—glass frogs, ceramic frogs, frogs with bow ties, mother frogs with baby frogs, frogs playing the violin, frogs in boats. The only one he didn't see was the one he had given Mayda a year ago with a huge pink erection and the caption, "Frog This!" He thought it was the best frog he'd ever seen.

"Hey!" he yelled to the kitchen. "What happened to that frog I gave you for your birthday?"

Mayda came out with a plastic bag of ice. "Please, don't insult me."

"Guy at the store told me it was an exact life-size replica."

"Here's for your thumb." She threw the ice at him. "I hope it's broken."

Naz caught the bag off his chest and put it on his finger. They sat on the couch.

"So," Mayda said. "How is the consultant?"

"Don't start."

"What start?"

"Aren't the frogs enough? Now we have to talk about the consultant?" Naz said.

"I saw Carina a couple days ago for breakfast. She looks good."

"She always looks good." Naz rummaged in his tool-box with his good hand, muttering.

"I mean good, good."

"I had a pencil in here. One of those thick ones."

"I think she likes this boy."

Naz lifted the ice pack and checked his thumb. "It'll never work." He shifted the ice and stuck his thumb back in, wincing.

"I think it's already working. Did you see the color in her cheeks?"

"Lots of things can do that. Tequila, for instance."

"In the morning?"

"It's springtime. Maybe her hormones are out of control. That happens to women, right?" Naz reached over and pinched Mayda on the thigh.

She slapped his hand away. "You should be so lucky."

"Besides," he said, "everything's a little crazy because of the bid. It's like a time warp or something. After this whole thing's over, we'll get back to normal. He'll move on to his next thing and that's that."

"And what if she loves him?"

Naz got up from the couch. "I'm not talking about this any more!"

"But if she loves him and he loves her...."

He pointed at Mayda, "You know what it's like for them, the outsiders and the families. They will put an "X" on her. I will not allow that for my daughter!"

Mayda got up, too. "No one will put an "X" on her! You sound like your father. The world is changing."

"And who says this changing is good?" Naz yelled.

"It is what it is."

"Not in my house. In my house it is what I say!"

"Even in your house, you cannot say what is love!"

Naz poked Mayda on the shoulder, his eyes flaring. "If I say the sky is red, the sky is red! If I say Carina will not love the consultant, she will not love the Goddamn consultant!"

"Don't touch me!" She knocked his hand away. "If you break her heart...."

"Better her heart is broken quickly, than every day for the rest of her life!"

"You are not God! You cannot hold on to her forever."

Naz yelled, the veins puffing out in his neck, "Who's holding on!" As he threw his arms in emphasis, he jammed his thumb on the edge of the bookcase, and screamed in pain.

"See? That is a sign for you," she said, her voice softening a bit.

"You want to see a sign? I'll give you a sign...."

"There is no need to talk like that."

Naz closed his eyes and shook his head, hoping when he opened them, he would be somewhere else. "Let's just finish the goddamn shelves, before I end up a cripple." He hobbled around, holding his hand.

Mayda took a deep breath and watched him. A tiny smile spread across her face, but she didn't let him see it. She turned to the shelves crammed with frogs. "Three or four more and the collection will be complete."

Naz looked at her like she was insane. "Forty isn't enough?"

"How many of those cigar clippers do you have?"

"I use those! They have a purpose. What purpose does a goddamn glass frog have?"

"They're collectibles. Don't you ever hear of that?"

"It's only a collectible if someone else wants them. I never seen anyone with even one."

"Mr. Aloyan at the import store says they are the new wave. I am, what does he say? 'Ahead of the curves'."

Naz shook his head. The years of inane conversations if stretched end to end..."It's curve. Ahead of the curve."

In his heart, Naz knew that if it ever came down to it, he would die for Mayda. It just hadn't occurred to him that it might be tonight, because about five more minutes of this and he was going to blow his brains out.

"All right, hold up the corbel again," he said. "And this time, don't move it."

"I didn't move it."

Naz tapped the nail in, then a couple more. Done. He set the last glass shelf. Mayda quickly started placing the remaining frogs on it. Naz picked one up and set it on the shelf.

"Let me do it," she said, moving it about half an inch. "There." Mayda clapped her hands and jumped. "This calls for a toast!"

"We should've started with the goddamn toast," Naz mumbled as he kneeled to put away his tools. If he never saw another hammer, it would be too soon. He checked his thumb. It was swollen and throbbing.

Mayda dimmed the living room lights and turned on the lights in the display. The frogs shimmered. Naz got up and plopped his tool box on the coffee table. He looked to the kitchen where Mayda stood under one overhead light that draped shadows over her shoulders and breasts, the calves of her legs. She looked like a watercolor.

Mayda walked into the living room carrying two brandy snifters. She handed one to Naz and clinked his glass. They each took a sip.

"Look," she said, pointing her glass at the shelves. "Aren't they beautiful?"

"My thumb is killing me."

Mayda grabbed him. "Nazareth, would you look?" She turned him to the display.

Naz didn't look at the display, he looked at Mayda and how happy she was, then glanced at the frogs. "I have to admit," he mumbled, "that is the best display of frogs I've ever seen."

Mayda ran her fingers through Naz's hair, and pressed her hip up against him.

"I've got to put the tools away."

Mayda slipped into Naz's arms and started to dance with him, humming. Naz took another gulp of brandy. This train that was Mayda was running down the track, as it had a thousand times before. And he knew that all there was to do was get on board for the ride, because she was as persistent in her own way as he was—maybe more.

He pulled her close. He felt her body against him, and as they danced in the kaleidoscope of frog light the thought occurred to him that maybe this frog thing wasn't a total waste of time after all.

15

On her way home from work, Carina had stopped for groceries and now, as the red El Camino flew up the on-ramp and merged onto the freeway, she hit cruise control and kicked off her construction boots. As she nudged a cassette into the player, she didn't notice the black pickup accelerating a few cars behind her. The sound of applause grew in her speakers, then the organ riff, the drums, and finally the driving bass of Van Halen's "Jump" rocked the car. She accelerated, flowing with the energy of the cars, the music, the cadence of the freeway lights streaking by.

It was then that she noticed the headlights gaining on her, not always right behind but threading through the traffic, and closing. Another macho man, she thought, trying to prove he had big cojones. Real men didn't need to prove it in their cars.

Suddenly, the lights were right on her tail, and she

felt the jolt as the car banged her rear bumper. Adrenaline flashed and she instinctively tromped on the accelerator and swung over to the fast lane, her heart pounding. She passed a string of cars caught behind some trucks. A moment later, she caught the headlights again breaking out of the pack and coming on.

She punched off her stereo and gripped the wheel. All right asshole. She gritted her teeth and accelerated, trying to keep some distance, but the other car was flying, must be near a hundred. Out of the corner of her eye, an exit sign flashed by, and just as the headlights were closing on her she veered across two lanes of traffic and off the freeway. The car, maybe a pickup truck, flew by and disappeared under the overpass and into the night.

She fought the wheel, barely re-gaining control as she weaved and braked from shoulder to shoulder down the off ramp, her stock car training serving her well.

"Goddamn weirdo!" she screamed out the window, her heart thumping. Goddamn asshole, she whispered, trying to calm down.

After taking surface streets for a mile or two and constantly checking her rearview mirror, Carina turned up her street. She looked for suspicious parked cars, but all seemed normal in the quiet residential area. For once, she wished there were streetlights. She pulled into her driveway too fast, scraping the rear bumper on the concrete. "Shit," she blurted.

She reached across the front seat and grabbed her bags of groceries. She peered into the dark backyard. "God," she thought, "get hold of yourself." She remembered when she used to scare herself as a child, riding her bike back from the neighbor's a few blocks away, thinking there was something after her, pedaling so fast, but never being able to get away from the monster's hairy hands reaching out for her..."

Carina shivered. Balancing the bags on her knee, she fumbled to unlock the dead bolt in the back door. The sound of the keys seemed loud in the still night. Since Galen had died, she felt more exposed, more vulnerable, although she didn't exactly know why, since she had never lived with him. She remembered the handgun Galen had given her, even taking her out to the range to learn how to shoot it. She hated guns, but had kept her promise—the weapon still lay in the dresser drawer in her bedroom—loaded, a scary thought in itself.

The last rain had swelled the door and it stuck. She threw her hip into the door and it flew open with a grating noise that set her teeth on edge and her heart pounding again. She controlled the urge to rush for the light switch, and instead, walked to the butcher block in the middle of the kitchen and set the bags down. One of the bags started to topple and as she grabbed it she didn't hear the man who quietly slipped into the kitchen behind her.

Carina reached for the light switch.

Something exploded. She screamed and reeled against the counter. The lights flashed on and a man stepped out of the shadows.

"Oh God," she moaned. Her knees sagging. Her mind numb.

"Surprise!" Denny said, standing there, a grin smearing his face, holding a champagne bottle overflowing with foam.

She stared at him in disbelief, her heart roaring in her ears.

"To celebrate! Passing the inspection!"

"You fucker!" she screamed. She grabbed a handful of walnuts out of a bowl on the counter and threw them at him.

"What?" he said, squirming backwards, dodging the hail of nuts.

"You crazy...! You scared the shit out of me!" And with that she rushed him.

"Hey!" was all he got out, backing up into the living room. He was still holding the bottle when the first punch landed right in the center of his chest. The bubbly liquid sloshed out and drenched the front of Carina's shirt.

"Carina! Hey! Sorry!"

She said nothing, panting heavily.

He sat on the couch with a groan, reached down and felt the golf ball size lump on his shin where he had run into the coffee table. He held up the bottle. "Champagne?"

She let out a sigh and brushed the hair off her face with her hand. "Some asshole, I think it was Zaven, chased me on the freeway. I thought you were him for a second."

Denny passed her the bottle. She took it by the neck and raised it to her lips. It burned as she swallowed, and the carbonation shot up behind her nose making her eyes water. She passed it back, and Denny took a long swallow. Then slowly, he leaned over and fell to the carpet. As his back hit, he raised his legs up stiff, like the dying cowboys in the old movies, and let them flop down.

Carina smiled. She took a deep breath and let the adrenaline die down. She took another sip of champagne, and passed him the bottle. Denny sat up on the floor, his back against the couch, Carina sitting above him. He hefted the bottle and as he swallowed, gave the top of her work boot a squeeze.

She reached over and put her hand on his shoulder.

They each took another swallow of champagne.

He slid his hand up under the cuff of her jeans, cupped his hand around her calf, and passed her the bottle. She tipped it up and took the last swallow.

"Most of it's in the carpet," he said. "Sorry."

She slid off the couch and sat next to him, put her arm around his shoulders. "Kiss me, stupid."

He kissed her on the forearm.

"Would you stop it," she laughed. Gently, he kissed her on the mouth. She opened her legs and easing herself down on her back, pulled him on top of her. She reached around to put her hands on the small of his back.

This time there was no wild hunger to devour his body like there had been in his loft. Now, she was just willing to drift where the current was taking her. She held his face in her hands and kissed his cheeks, his chin, his lips, his nose. She rubbed her hands down his back and hugged him hard to her, feeling his muscles flex through his shirt.

As he kissed her neck, her collarbone, she could smell the spilled champagne, see the moonlight in a pattern on the wall, sense his urgency, and it made her tremble.

Denny raised himself up and gazed at her face. She could see the softness in his eyes. He started to speak, but she whispered, "Shhhh." And touched his lips with her fingertips. He kissed them.

"I could make love to you forty times tonight."

"I'll settle for one good one."

She saw him smile, feeling the effects of the champagne and the warmth between them.

"Hold on a sec," she said, rolling away from him. Carina unbuttoned her soggy shirt and let it drop off her shoulders, then stepped out of her jeans and panties. She stood naked, except for her white socks. The champagne was hitting her and she felt like flying. She spread her arms and whirled, feeling like the air itself, translucent, buoyant and free.

Denny raised himself up on his elbow, watching her. "You are the most beautiful thing I have ever seen."

Carina smiled as she gently lowered herself on top of him.

*   *   *

Beyond the west perimeter of Pacific Rim, the river pulled a veil of mist along the channel. Charlie shivered in his sleep beneath a ratty blanket in the back of the hearse. Snores rose softly, and every now and then Charlie would moan in his sleep. Black's big body lay curled in a perfect ball in the crook of Charlie's knees.

Suddenly, Black's head jerked up and he snorted, trying to home in on the sound. His coat glistened like metal in the purple light. Lifting his nose, he flared his nostrils. Then he let out one soft woof.

Behind the main building, the man swore under his

breath, checking the cuff of his shirt where he had torn it coming over the barbed wire fence. He got his bearings and listened. Nothing. Edging up to the building, he eased through a gap in the corrugated siding and dropped silently to the floor. Alex had given him the instructions. Metal ingot. Heavy. Two feet long.

Back in the car, Black flopped back down on the seat and rested his head on his paws. The sound had not come again, and the still air carried only the familiar smells of the trash, and the sounds of the rats scurrying around the corners of the tipping floor. But now he didn't sleep. He waited.

The man searched the tipping area methodically. He checked the baler and the compactor area. He let his gaze drift out across the yard, wandering over bins of broken glass, piles of scrap metal and stacks of wooden pallets. A car on the freeway threw shafts of light that swung above like a searchlight. He saw the dim outline of a junk car under the overpass, coils of copper wire, and a shipping container—with a lock on it.

Quietly, he circled around the yard, slipped up to the container and lifted the lock.

This time when Black's head came up there was no hesitation. Black jumped to the front seat and slipped out the window. Charlie rolled onto his back, still asleep.

The attack came with no warning. Only at the last instant did the man sense the dog coming. He turned and caught the blow on his shoulder, and let the force carry him over. As he went down, he could feel the hot breath close to his face and the jaws clamping down on his forearm that he had thrown across his neck. As his back hit the ground, he punched up with his knees and arms enough to toss Black over his head.

The man picked up a short piece of pipe as he got up, and stood lightly in a crouch. Black came in again. The man's blow missed the dog's head and caught the ribs. Black went down with a cry of pain.

Charlie woke at the sound and bolted out the rear door of the hearse. He saw the man by his container and Black on the ground struggling to get up. Without hesitating, he charged the hulking form. It wasn't much of a contest. The man clipped Charlie with the pipe, and the old derelict went down hard, and stayed there.

Black was hurt, but he wasn't through. Slowly, cautiously he edged forward. The hair down the center of his back stood up, and he growled soft and low. The man glowered back and the two animals faced each other. Black feigned a lunge. The man shifted his weight, and Black took the opening. This time the dog went in low and managed to tear into the man's left ankle before the pipe came down and the white pain exploded against Black's shoulder. He let go and crawled away, limping on a front leg that had gone dead.

Preoccupied by Black's suicidal attacks, the man hadn't noticed Charlie, who had crawled off into the shadows. Charlie wobbled to his feet, his head pounding, his vision blurred. He tasted the blood from his nose, and he heard Black cry. He knew the dog would not stop and that the man would kill him. Charlie ducked behind a bin loaded with glass cullet, jumped into the seat of a forklift, and started the engine.

The man turned his head at the sound. At that

moment, Black made a final desperate attack. But as he lunged, his left front leg buckled as the injured shoulder gave out, and he rolled heavily into the man's legs knocking him down.

The man scrambled back up, dazed and winded. Only half conscious, Black too was trying to drag himself up. The man raised the pipe over his head. The last thing he ever saw, was a glint of light out of the corner of his eyes. He turned instinctively toward it.

The heavy blade of the forklift stabbed clear through his chest and skewered him up against the wall of the container. He wriggled and grabbed at the metal as if the hand of God were tickling him.

Charlie climbed down from the forklift, and walked to Black. The man's body gurgled and twitched just beyond him, blood running down and dribbling off his boots.

Charlie stroked Black's head. "That's OK, boy. That's OK. Take it easy, boy. Good job, Black. You got him. You got him, boy." With tears in his eyes, Charlie slipped his arms under his dog and lifted the ninety-pound animal. Black whimpered. Even though it hurt, he didn't try to bite Charlie.

Charlie laid Black in the back of the hearse and brought him some water in his bowl. The dog made a feeble attempt to drink. Then he groaned and his head sank onto the mattress.

"Good boy, Black. That's a good boy."

Black's tail gave one feeble flop in response.

Gingerly, Charlie checked Black's shoulder, moving his leg slowly, feeling the joint. The dog cried softly, but all the bones seemed intact.

"Nothing broken, boy. You're a tough one, aren't you, Black. Tougher than steel."

Charlie noticed blood oozing from a cut over Black's eye. He dabbed it with his shirt tail. Picking up a pint of whiskey, Charlie poured a little on his shirt. "This is gonna sting a little, but we gotta disinfect it. Hold on."

As Charlie cleansed the wound, Black yelped but Charlie held him.

"There we go. Killed them germs. Goddamn expensive disinfectant, Black." Charlie took a drink of it, then reached over the back of the front seat into the glove compartment and pulled out his jar of Vaseline. He smeared a glob over Black's cut.

"Just like the fighters, huh, Black?"

Charlie looked at his crippled dog and ran his fingers over one of his ears. Charlie's eyes teared and he wiped them with the back of his hand. "You're gonna make it, Black. You just take it easy. Now, I'm gonna fix the guy did this to you."

Charlie pulled a blanket over the dog and climbed out of the car. A coldness came to Charlie's eyes as he looked up at the body, now limp and lifeless. He walked over and shifted the forklift into reverse. The fork screeched as it pulled out of the container wall. The body hung by the bones of the rib cage from the steel fork. The arms and head flopped around like a scarecrow as Charlie drove across the yard and headed toward the compactor.

Charlie bobbed the forks over the compactor hopper but the body was stuck. He climbed up on the forklift and pushed the body off with a 2x4. It thumped into the hopper. Charlie punched the power on the feed conveyor and it piled trash on top of the body. He activated the compactor ram, and the blade moved forward, crushing the body and trash into the half-filled trailer. In the morning, the crew would unknowingly pack in more trash, burying the body in the middle of the load.

Back at his car, Charlie patted Black on the head. The dog looked bad. "There's one asshole you'll never have to worry about. He's taking a one-way, all expenses paid trip to the county landfill. Worms'll be pickin' his bones." Charlie raised the bottle of whiskey and drained the remaining inch of liquid. He dropped the empty bottle out the window of the car.

Charlie put his hands on the steering wheel and gazed out through the cracked windshield at the mist crawling along the river. He had the bad feeling that his luck had suddenly run out. That thug was looking for something, and Charlie had a pretty good idea what it was. He decided he better let things cool off for awhile, keep a low profile, not that his was high in the first place, but, you know, lower.

But his dog was alive, that's what counted. His best friend would make it. Maybe a little gimpy, but so was Charlie. They could gimp into old age together. Yessir. Charlie curled up around his dog.

16

The sound of chainsaws buzzed like angry bees behind the rumble of the dozers working trash on the active face of the HIA landfill. Down in the arroyo below the cutoff wall, majestic eucalyptus trees were falling to the saws. The migrating landfill gas was killing them, leaves turning brown, bark sloughing off.

Alex stood on the wall and watched. The tree line stood like a red flag eighty feet high. If the regulators see those trees, Alex thought, he could kiss the L.A. bid goodbye. Luckily, Barbara Miller had come through with the transfer of the troublesome inspector, so he was clear on that front for now. Maybe she was worth that ten grand a month after all.

Before anyone noticed the missing trees, the bid would be over and he'd figure out how to fix the gas problem. Then he'd plant new trees, some kind of California native variety, drought-tolerant, maybe even "endangered," the kind the tree-huggers were always clamoring about. Bring in the local politicians, the Sierra Club and one of those non-profit groups with the school kids for a day of celebration and tree planting. They'd love him.

He looked down the canyon to the Eagle Heights housing development. They'd been nothing but trouble from the start, complaining about odor, seagulls, dust, noise. They had moved in next to a landfill—what did they expect? Laguna Beach?

He had developed a closure plan and a model of the high-line development that would crown the landfill when it was filled: ball fields, a golf driving range and championship eighteen-hole course, riding trails—the works. Sure it was a hundred million tons of trash from now, but people needed to see the long-range picture. Delayed gratification they called it. So in this case the delay was twenty-five years. What's the problem? Their grandkids would be hitting golf balls up here, with condors flying overhead, trout in the streams.

Alex smiled. Most people were such morons.

And of course there was his ex-wife and son, Johnny, living down there. She actually had the gall to show up at the last public hearing about the landfill expansion and even go on record with her complaints. She of all people. Where did she think the $15,000 a month in child support and alimony was coming from? She should be down on her knees thanking God every day for that smell and noise and dust, and praying that it never ends.

Alex turned at the sound of one of the company pickup trucks pulling up. He watched his father emerge in his starched white shirt and the immaculate boots he wore for "field work." Alex turned back to the tree slaughter, as Kail walked up beside him.

"New landscape project?" his father said, looking down into the arroyo with the phony, know-it-all smile that Alex knew so well.

"The trees were getting old," Alex said. "Thought I'd bring in some oaks or maybe a stand of coastal redwoods. Give the folks in Eagle Heights a better buffer. They'll wake up and think they moved to Monterey."

"Those were hundred year old eucalyptus."

"Price of progress."

"Price of stupidity, Alex. I told you before we started filling this cell that the bedrock was fractured. We could have sealed it, first. But you wouldn't listen and now that gas is migrating. You saved $200,000 that meant nothing, at the risk of millions, at the risk of jeopardizing the bid and the merger. That's not good business."

Alex turned to his father, a hard set to his face. "You taught me to do whatever it takes, and that's what I'm doing. A hundred years from now, every goddamn tree out here will be a hundred years old. So what's the difference?"

"The difference is your decision has made us vulnerable."

"You worry too much."

The elder Hart opened the door of the pickup, then turned. "By the way," he said. "I assume you have the *pro formas* together for the merger team?"

"Like I said, you worry too much."

"I'm not sure that's possible in the present

circumstances." Kail pulled away, leaving a cloud of dust swirling around Alex's head.

*   *   *

Carina jumped on the gas and powered out of the turn of the dirt track oval raceway. The Camaro street stock car came loose in the rear and started to fish tail, but she caught it quickly, steering into the skid like they had taught her and leveling out a foot from the wall at ninety miles an hour. She accelerated to 140 down the straightaway the sun glinting off the hood, then dropped down to hit the low grove in the next turn. When she had first started racing, the speed had overwhelmed her, the world would blur and she'd back off too early for the turn. But over time, her mind had caught up.

Some people did yoga, some meditated, some listened to Japanese flute music, or even floated on brine in those sensory deprivation chambers. But now, all the soul-soothing Carina needed came from a 450 horsepower engine and a half-mile dirt oval. She downshifted and braced to fight the centrifugal forces in the next turn. She still felt the tingle and soreness in her body from the lovemaking with Denny the night before. She smiled. That part of her life was coming back.

As lap after lap rolled by, the vibration of the engine soothed her. She began to even out, the pressures of the day at Pacific Rim easing, her moves flowing one to another in a natural rhythm of power and speed. She felt the car as an extension of her hands, her legs, even her mind. She thought turn, and the car turned; she thought acceleration and the car ate up the straightaway.

Twenty minutes later, Carina rolled off the track into the pits. She climbed out through the driver's window, took off her helmet and headed for the gate. She glanced up in the empty stands and froze at the hunched figure seated there. Her father had never come down to the track before, and in fact, had never shown the slightest interest.

"You drive pretty good...for a woman," Naz yelled out.

Carina smiled, climbed up into the stands and sat beside him. "Coming from you, I'll take that as a compliment."

They watched a couple cars careen around the oval.

"You just in the neighborhood and decide to drop by, or what?" she said.

"This the place Galen brought you?"

Carina nodded.

"Do you miss him?"

"This isn't about Galen, is it?"

"But you don't miss him like you used to?"

Carina hesitated, thinking of the night before with Denny. "Of course I miss him."

Naz took the cigar out of his mouth and sat forward, resting his forearms on his thighs. "You remember the time you were twelve, I went to your soccer game?"

"You mean the time you tried to kill the referee?"

Naz smiled. "The sonuvabitch had it coming. Letting that bully on the other team foul you. Lucky for him he was a faster runner than me."

"I think I still have the scar on my shin where that kid tackled me."

"Your mother was so mad she wouldn't talk to me for a week. Then when she did, she said she was so humiliated that she would never go to another game, not with me, anyway."

"You didn't want me to play."

"You were a girl! Why did you have to play with the boys?"

The two stock cars roared down the straightaway.

After a moment, Carina said, "I know he's not Armenian, Dad."

"Who?"

"He's probably never even heard of Mt. Ararat, or the Association, or how to marinate lamb."

Naz put his hand on Carina's knee. "I'm just looking out for what's best for you."

She removed his hand. "Well, you can't just beat up the referee this time."

"You're being carried away in the moment, the bid…."

"You talk to me about getting carried away in the moment! Mr. 'Knee Jerk Reaction'!"

"Who's reacting?" Naz said, his voice rising. "I'm talking about your future!"

"Dad, things change! This isn't Fresno in 1915!"

"What about the family? What about your people!"

"What people?"

Naz stood up. "You know damn well what people! Think of *Babig*! What he has done for us, for you. Would you throw all that away?"

"I can't talk to you about this." She started to walk away.

Naz yelled after her, "You think only of yourself! I'm telling you, you will never marry him!"

Carina turned, her eyes flashing, "I will marry him

if I want, when I want, and where I want! With you or without you! And do me a favor," she screamed. "Don't come here again!"

Naz watched his daughter storm off. He sat down and ran his hands through his hair. What was it with the women in his life? Why did every conversation end up this way? Why couldn't they for just once listen to reason?

He looked up to the sky and said, "God, you know I am right. I know I am right. Please, get it through her stubborn head that I am right. That is all I ask, for now. Amen."

Naz watched the stock cars bang into the turn and circle the track. Around and around they roared, spewing exhaust, like angry metal beetles. And after all the miles, really going nowhere.

It looked a lot like his life. He had to admit he had made plenty of mistakes, and maybe this was one of them. You just hope that your children can forgive you, and that you can forgive yourself, which is harder.

Enough of that.

Naz plopped the cigar into his mouth and walked out of the stands.

* * *

The leaves of the trees rustled outside the bedroom window, but Alex was oblivious to everything but the feeling rushing up inside him. He pulled Julia roughly to him, her breasts pressing into his chest. He kissed her, his tongue in her mouth, then rolled on top of her. He grabbed the headboard and crushed her down on the bed, groaning with each thrust.

When it was over, Julia forced her legs together and heaved, rolling him over on his back. Alex moaned in a whisper, like air coming from a cave. And for a moment, he felt empty and calm. No bid, no Nazareth Agajanian, no Chairman of the Board—nothing.

The sun was just coming up when the ringing of the phone woke him. Alex stirred and groaned, but didn't get up. Julia walked over to the bedstand wearing a silk bathrobe and toweling off her hair still wet from the shower. She picked up the phone. "Yes?" She listened for a moment, then bent down and jabbed Alex in the ribs. He grunted.

"It's Steve from the plant," she said.

"Huh?"

"It's Steve!"

"All right. All right."

She dropped the phone on the bed and walked away. Alex picked it up.

"Yeah?" Alex said, then listened for a moment. "So what, they find bodies at the county dump all the time. Some drunk falls in a trash bin, gets packed in a truck and that's it."

Still listening, Alex eased himself up and sat on the side of the bed. "You sure they got a positive ID...Yeah... Yeah. Through the chest? Right."

Alex hung up the phone and said, "Pour me a drink, will ya?"

"Pour it yourself," she said and walked through the sliding doors to the deck.

Alex stared after her, then got up and poured a drink. As he swirled the ice cubes around the glass, his mind raced. What the hell had happened? This guy was good. Had done a hundred strong arm jobs, clean, professional.

Calm down. Think. So, Agajanian found out about the smuggling scam and got hold of the ingot. I send my guy down to Pacific Rim to investigate...somehow they kill him. He must've got careless. Bad time to get careless.

Dammit! He had underestimated Agajanian. That sonuvabitch was clever. Sooner or later, this thing could blow wide open. No way he could keep his contacts quiet. The police would follow the trail of smuggled material and he'd be dead. He needed to button this up, and in a hurry. Find out who at Pacific Rim knew about his smuggling scheme and eliminate them. He better get to Jack. Jack could point the finger, Zaven would pull the trigger, and somebody would fall.

Alex tossed down the rest of his drink. He picked up the phone and dialed.

A few minutes later, Julia wandered back into the bedroom like a zombie, put her half-finished drink on the bar and sat on the edge of the bed.

"You never finish your drinks," Alex said. He picked up her glass and chucked what was left into the sink. The cubes banged against the metal. "Pour yourself half a drink. Saves us on the bar bill."

She didn't respond, just laid back on the bed and opened a novel. "It's only orange juice."

"I don't care if it's water. What's eating you anyway?"

She dropped the book in her lap. "You've got to be kidding?"

"What? We make love, and the next thing I know you jab me with the phone."

"That wasn't making love. That was you getting your rocks off, pure and simple."

"That was part of it."

"That was all of it."

"Listen Julia!" He pointed at her with his empty glass. "Seems to me, you got it a lot better than when I found you with that dipshit kid playing at record producer. What a joke."

"I'm beginning to feel old, Alex."

"Welcome to the crowd."

"Think I might go out. Get some fresh air for awhile."

"Good idea. Why don't you go for a jog. Run a marathon. Get those endorphins going or whatever it does."

Tears welled up in her eyes. "What's happening to you? I don't know you anymore. Where'd the other guy go?" She started to pull on a pair of sweat pants. "The guy who could laugh, who wanted to be together, do things. Even brought flowers a couple times."

"It's not flower season," Alex said, staring into his glass.

"You may win the bid, but when you do, you're going to be all alone." She pulled a sweatshirt over her head. "But then again, maybe that's the way you like it." She walked out the door.

*   *   *

Jack sat at his workbench. He grabbed a coffee can of screws, popped off the lid, and pulled out the plain envelope. He counted the bills again, his first payment from Alex, seventy-five grand. He would start replenishing the girls' college fund, pay the pool man whom he'd been avoiding, take care of a dozen other nagging obligations, maybe even buy Sophie some jewelry. He fought down the sudden urge to stuff the envelope in his pocket and head for the casino. Tomorrow at the bid opening Pacific Rim would go down in flames and the Agajanians with it. But he had a firewall, and would survive the conflagration. The thought of the whole ugly affair made him close his eyes for a moment, and grab a deep breath.

And now this other issue, the call from Alex. This smuggling scam or whatever it was. Naz was up to something again. Stealing HIA bins. As soon as Alex had mentioned the word "ingot" it had all flashed back for Jack. The morning a couple days ago, when Carina had brought Charlie in drunk. His babbling. It was Charlie. The ingot man.

So now, Jack had sealed the old derelict's fate as well, fingering him to Alex. The only other one who probably would have survived the collapse of Pacific Rim. Well, not now. But Charlie had brought all this down on himself. If he'd left the trash alone, this wouldn't be happening.

Jack stared out the window at the branches of the nectarine tree, swollen with buds. He too was ready for a new beginning. He just never could have dreamed it would be a nightmare like this. He slipped the envelope back into the coffee can.

*   *   *

Low-hanging clouds swept in off the ocean and darkened the moon. Pacific Rim lay quiet. Charlie creaked opened the back door of the hearse and checked Black, sleeping on his blanket. The dog was recovering slowly from his battle with the intruder. Charlie felt the wrapping he had placed on the injured leg. The dog whimpered softly, and tried to get up. "No, no, boy. You stay. That's OK. Old Charlie can handle this one on his own. You rest. Good, boy. You stay." Black hunkered back down.

Charlie closed the door and slung an empty burlap sack over his shoulder. He was heading for one of his best accounts, a Radio Shack store that occasionally threw out real electronics. Sure, maybe they were busted or defective, but stuff could be fixed, and anyway everything had some value. He walked toward the river.

Charlie liked this part of the river where the tall grasses and willows grew from the natural bottom. Where among the rusted shopping carts and Styrofoam packing, the ducks flipped upside down to feed on algae and white egrets perched in the trees and preened their feathers. It was a hidden oasis that most people never knew existed.

Charlie crawled under the chain link fence, and angled down the concrete embankment. He approached a large outfall pipe that gushed treated sewage into the river. Suddeny, a hand grabbed him on the shoulder, another by the neck and jammed his face under the wastewater. He struggled for breath, choking, fighting to get free, but the hands were like a vice. Finally, they jerked him out. He sputtered and flung his arms about, but the man punched him once in the gut and Charlie crumpled to the pavement, gasping for breath.

"You been busy, huh?"

All Charlie could see was the man's boots. He glanced up. Something was pulled over the man's face, a hood or a mask, he couldn't see. But there was something about the voice, the sheer bulk of the man. Charlie lunged to get away, but the man was quick and on him again. Forcing his head under the water. "We can do this all night!" he yelled over the cascade.

"Help!" screamed Charlie, gagging and spitting up water, trying to catch his breath. The man pulled him out of the flow. "Let me go!" Charlie screamed. "I didn't do nothing."

"There was a little altercation at the plant, couple nights ago. Now I'm thinking, who would've been around?"

Charlie's brain was burning. He couldn't place the voice. "I don't know what you're talking about."

"I'm talking about the guy they found at the county dump with half his chest crushed in."

"What guy?"

The man jerked Charlie under the water again, nearly drowning him, and pulled him out. The words burst out through gritted teeth, "Now I'm going to kill your sorry ass if you don't give me the straight shit."

"All right...please," Charlie said, holding up his hands. "What do you want to know?"

"The body in the dump," the man said.

"The sonuvabitch tried to break into my container. He got my dog."

"Yeah, life's a bitch sometimes. And the other little item, the ingot? Know anything about that, Charlie?"

How did this guy know so much? What the hell was going on? The man gripped Charlie by the neck, strangling him.

"Yes, yes!" Charlie gurgled. "I salvaged it." The man relaxed his grip just enough so Charlie could breathe.

"Where is it?"

"Sold it. To Louis, at the metal yard."

"Probably got a whole pint of whiskey for it, too."

Charlie stared at the pavement. "Okay," the man said. "Who knows about this? The ingot. Who knows?"

"No one. I don't tell no one about this stuff."

"Charlie!" the man said.

"No one! I swear!"

He grabbed Charlie by the scruff of the neck, and jerked him off the ground, inches from his face.

Charlie cried. "I don't know. I was drunk."

Holding him up with one arm, the man punched Charlie in the face, again and again. He kneed Charlie in the groin, and the little man collapsed to the concrete and vomited. The man grabbed Charlie by the hair and wrenched his head back. "Who knows?" he screamed.

Charlie couldn't see with the blood flowing into one of his eyes, couldn't stand, the pain in his groin felt like he'd been castrated. He realized the man would beat him to death. He hung his head and croaked, "I don't remember, maybe...."

The man put his head down by Charlie. "What was that, Charlie? You say something?"

"Carina," Charlie whispered.

Charlie felt the hands tighten on his throat and played the only card he had left. Just before his head was rammed under the water, he caught a breath. Charlie flailed against the arms that pinned him under the outfall, the hands that crushed his neck, cutting off his wind pipe. He lashed out with his legs.

Ten seconds went by. Still, Charlie fought.

Twenty seconds.

Charlie relaxed for a moment, then fought with everything he had. It wasn't enough. Charlie's body shuddered and fell limp.

The man felt the life drain out of Charlie, but still held the choke hold, held him under water.

After another fifteen seconds, the man hauled Charlie's body out, the derelict's face ash gray, limbs lifeless. He dragged the body into a cluster of bushes by the flowing water and walked away.

As soon as the man disappeared over the rim of the embankment, Charlie's body convulsed in a gurgling gasp. He vomited water. Groaned. Slowly, he eased himself up to his hands and knees. In shallow, panting breaths, he let the air back into his racked lungs.

Charlie cleared his throat and spit, then with a grimace, rolled into a sitting position. Water dripped off his scruffy chin, mixed with blood from his nose and the cuts above his eyes. He dabbed at his eyes with his shirt tail. He looked up and saw a black cat with haunted yellow eyes staring back at him. He flinched, thinking it was real, then realized the face was painted on the cover of a flood control gate across the river.

Charlie struggled to his feet and limped up the river toward Pacific Rim. He would get some food, water, blankets, his money, Black's towel and rawhide bone, then carry Black into the shipping container and throw the locking bar.

As he walked, Charlie started pulling himself into a familiar dark and inner place. A place where no one could find him, no one could hurt him. And he thought of the man who did this to him, trying to place the voice. Maybe a little Old Overholt would jog his memory.

17

Naz's team walked briskly up the stairs of City Hall, their breath puffing in the cool, misty morning air. Fifteen minutes till the bid opening in the City Council chambers.

Their heels clicked over the tiled city emblem in the foyer, and down the marbled hallway. No one talked. Naz led and the others spread back off each other's shoulders like a flock of geese, Carina, Denny, Jack, and tapping along at his own pace in the rear, Harry. Denny carried the box with the black binders in it.

Before they had started out that morning, Naz had slipped their $100,000 check for the bid bond into its envelope. His mortgage re-financing had come through in the final hour. Thank God, for the potent real estate market in LA. Naz had also gathered his team and told them the bid number as he inserted his cost page into the binders. $530 million and change over twenty years he had said, all from his magical calculations on the napkin in Ronnie's café.

The number was etched into each of their minds as they approached the Council Chamber. They were a strange-looking crew who turned heads as they entered; the tall, blue-eyed Armenian fidgeting in a long sleeved shirt and slacks; the statuesque young woman in high heels; the lanky white guy in the blue blazer and red power tie; the muscular freedom-fighter look-alike in his construction boots; and the stooped, old man tapping along with his cane.

Denny strode to the front of the chambers and presented the box to the Clerk of the City Council, who sat at a desk in the middle of a large horseshoe-shaped table that wrapped around him. He stamped a receipt with the time, handed it to Denny, and slid the box over next to the pile of other submittals.

Naz surveyed the crowd as his team wedged into a cramped space at the outside of one of the front pews. Across the aisle, in the first row were the Harts. They stared straight ahead, not acknowledging his presence. Behind HIA, was a Korean company that was also bidding. They could be tough competition. But Naz felt secure with his "cut to the bone" price. A consortium of local trash haulers sat near the back of the room. They jointly owned a waste transfer station out in the San Fernando Valley. He was always amazed that they could agree on anything, let alone put together a bid. He knew their costs would be high as each partner grabbed for a bigger share. He smiled as he saw a couple of them arguing already and could envision the blood bath that would break out when they lost.

Naz looked around at the crowd of over 300 packing the pews and spilling over into the aisles and up against the walls. Most of them were connected with one or another of the bidding teams—trucking companies, PR firms, lobbyists, shipping agents, guys from the local paper mills, equipment reps, trash haulers, recyclers, reporters from all the local media, kids from some third-grade classroom, and the normal assortment of City Council groupies.

Naz watched as the fifteen city councilmembers slowly filtered in, filling the high-backed leather chairs around the horseshoe on the raised platform. The Council president, Barbara Miller, sat at the apex of the curve slightly above the others. She looked gaunt. An American flag hung on one side of her, and the Bear Flag of California on the other.

The gavel came down with a boom, carrying the sound of judgment. In the back, the cameras of the local TV stations whirred to life. The air was electric, as if the slightest friction would detonate the room.

A local pastor rose to the podium and gave the invocation, asking for God to grant guidance to the Council, and wisdom and justice in their deliberations. Good luck with that, thought Naz.

"All rise for the Pledge of Allegiance!" Barbara Miller said into the microphone. The crowd spoke in one multi-colored voice. Naz Agajanian, hand over heart, mumbled the words, his eyes vacant, "...with Liberty and Justice for all." Benches creaked as the crowd took their seats. Amid hushed voices, coughs hacked the air.

Denny nudged Naz and nodded toward the Hart contingent, all dressed in dark blue suits. Between Alex and Kail, sat a heavy man in his early sixties whispering to Alex. Acne scars were visible on his face, even from a distance. The man finished what he was saying and smiled. Alex nodded and they both looked to the chair at the head of the Council table. The Council president gazed back over the crowd.

"That's Eddie Furillo," Denny whispered to Naz.

"Who?"

"The guy sitting next to Alex. Eddie Furillo. Big lobbyist. Ran Barbara Miller's re-election campaign. But I don't recognize the red-haired guy sitting next to Kail."

"I'm guessing that's the CEO of Global Waste Enterprises, the merger guy," Naz said. "Come to watch his new partner win the prize."

Naz noticed Denny slide his hand along the bench and hold Carina's hand. For once, he wished Mayda were there with him. She'd be touching up her lipstick. Might help him relax. Besides, he too felt like holding someone's hand.

The Council moved quickly through some old administrative business: a concept proposal to transform the L.A. River channel into a freeway, a twenty-five-year service award to a City Hall secretary, and a dispute regarding the issuance of a new liquor license to a restaurant on Vermont Avenue.

The Councilmembers and the crowd were beginning to fidget, glancing at the pile of bid proposals on the center table. Finally, the moment arrived. Barbara Miller adjusted her microphone.

"The last item for today is the opening of the bids for Waste Management Services for the City of Los Angeles."

She looked out over the crowd. "As you may be aware, the city is facing a landfill crisis. Our own landfill is due to close in less than eighteen months. To try to extend that life, the city has adopted an aggressive recycling goal of twenty five percent. We are also seeking a long-term contract with another landfill to secure our waste disposal needs for the next twenty years. Our Bureau of Sanitation tells us that the best way to achieve these goals is to award a franchise contract to a private waste management company with requisite experience and facilities."

"This morning is the bid opening," she continued. "With the award going to the lowest-priced qualified bidder. This project is extremely important to the citizens of Los Angeles and will establish our city as a leader in the recycling field. It will also help safeguard the environment for future generations."

Naz glanced over at Denny and rolled his eyes. What a crock. Politicians. He stared up at the ceiling with its mural of blue sky and clouds. Denny hunched forward and picked at his fingernails. Carina bit her lower lip and rummaged nervously in her purse. Jack sat ramrod straight, his heavy hands resting on his thighs. Harry leaned forward on his wooden cane.

Barbara Miller's voice rang out. "Would the Clerk of the Court read the list of firms that have submitted bids this morning?"

"There were originally seven bidders," the Clerk said into his mike. "Two were disqualified during the pre-bid inspections. The five remaining qualified bidders are Advanced Waste Systems, Golden State Industries, the Padasian Group, HIA Corporation, and Pacific Rim Recycling."

He continued reading the instructions in a monotone. "These bids are for a twenty-year contract for 3,000 tons of municipal solid waste per day, five days a week, fifty-two weeks per year. The bids include all costs associated with the guaranteed recycling of at least twenty-five percent of this total, and the transfer, hauling, and disposal of the residue waste at a permitted Class III landfill."

"Thank you, Mr. Hawkins. You may proceed to open the price bid envelopes, please."

The City Clerk carefully opened the first box of proposals, like there was a bomb in it.

"Anytime, Mr. Hawkins," Barbara Miller said.

"Yes, Madam President." He pulled out the top document and read. "Advanced Waste Systems bids $573 million!"

The sound of his voice reverberated off the stone walls, and lost itself in a moan of awe from the crowd. The third grade kids poked each other and giggled. 573 million! The TV cameras whirred and cameras flashed. Naz glanced over at the HIA contingent. They continued to sit like lumps of stone.

In turn, the clerk read the next two bids. $560 and $549 million. Only the HIA and Pacific Rim bids remained.

Naz saw Alex lean over and whisper to Eddie Furillo. Eddie laughed and glanced back at the Agajanian team.

"The next bid please, Mr. Hawkins." Barbara Miller's voice carried an edge of impatience.

The Council Clerk opened HIA's bid envelope and said, "Hart Industries of America bids...$525 million!"

A murmur rose like a wave around the room. The low bid so far! The HIA group smiled and whispered among themselves.

The Pacific Rim team looked like someone had sucked the air out of their lungs. How could it be? They were five million over HIA's bid. They had lost. Denny gave Carina's hand a squeeze as she closed her eyes and let her forehead rest on the pew in front of her.

Jack stared at the floor.

Naz twirled the cigar in his mouth.

"And the final bid, Mr. Hawkins," Barbara Miller said.

The Council Clerk tore open Pacific Rim's sealed bid. He hesitated, staring at the form.

"Well, Mr. Hawkins?"

"The bid from Pacific Rim is," the clerk cleared his throat, "$523 million."

The room exploded in a roar.

Pacific Rim had won!

Reporters ran for phones. The air rang with cheers and curses. Some people moaned, a few sat stupefied. The consortium of haulers who had bid as a team was screaming at each other.

Carina raised her head unable to comprehend what she had just heard. She and Denny stared at Naz as if he had somehow magically reached into the bid box from their pew and changed their number. Harry put his hand on Naz's knee. Jack sat dumbfounded, then glanced at the Hart's pew. Alex was staring right back at him.

"Dad!" Carina yelled above the din. "You said 530!"

Spotlights hit the Pacific Rim team as camera crews jockeyed to get shots of the winning team. Naz squinted into the lights. "Oh, yeah. Last night, I dropped our bid another fifty cents a ton."

"You what?" Denny said.

"I forgot this morning. I told you the old number." Actually, Naz hadn't forgotten. With all that had happened over the past thirty days, with his gut feeling that HIA might somehow be on to him, Naz had decided to withhold his real bid number from his own team, his own family. They'd find out when everyone else did.

Jack slumped back against the pew. "Goddammit, Naz. You sonuvabitch." He forced a smile, but his face was pale.

Carina screamed in delight, and threw her arms around Denny who, losing all decorum, let out a yell and slapped Naz on the back, nearly knocking the cigar down his throat. One of the largest bids in the history of the City of Los Angeles had just come down—and it was an upset.

Alex Hart's face darkened and he clenched his fists. Jack had betrayed him in the end. Either that or he had gotten bad information. Goddammit.

Eddie Furillo leaned over to Alex. "How can Agajanian bid that low with the county landfill price?"

"Can't pencil out," Alex said. "Get his bid. Check his numbers. He's low-balling it. We'll get the city to throw it out. He just shot himself in the head." Alex ran his hand across his mouth that was suddenly dry. He glanced down the pew to see his father in serious conversation with the CEO of Global, and neither of them looked good. Alex felt like he'd been punched in the gut, but he knew this was just a temporary setback. He'd get Barbara Miller to throw out Pacific Rim's bid on some technicality. But even if by some miracle Agajanian had actually put a bullet-proof bid together that even the Council president couldn't pierce, there was no way Pacific Rim would ever pass the performance test. No way. He'd make sure of that.

But still, this was bad.

Alex flashed back to the body at the landfill, Agajanian's discovery of his smuggling scheme, now this. He could feel his world unraveling. He looked up and locked eyes with Barbara Miller.

She took a deliberate sip from her glass of ice water. He watched her let the emotion in the room play out like a discharging battery, then pound her gavel down and pull her microphone forward.

"All right. All right. Order!" She hammered the gavel down again. The sound echoed off the marble columns. "I'm instructing the Bureau of Sanitation senior staff to review the low bidder's technical proposal immediately upon the adjournment of this meeting. Now, should the low bidder meet all the technical qualifications, the city's team will meet at 6:00 a.m. tomorrow morning at the Pacific Rim Recycling facility to conduct the performance test. Mr. Hawkins!" The little man jumped at the sound of his name. "Would you please read the requirements for the test so everyone in the room is clear on what performance needs to be demonstrated. Quiet, please!" She pounded the gavel again, harder, upsetting her water glass. She swore under her breath.

The Clerk read:

"Section III.2.5 of the Request for Bids states, 'The low bidder must pass a twenty-four hour performance test demonstrating the capability to 1) receive 3,000 tons of mixed municipal solid waste from the city's north and south central refuse collection districts; 2) recover a minimum of twenty-five percent by weight of recyclable material; and 3) load out all residue waste for transport to landfill disposal.'"

"And if the low bidder fails the test, Mr. Hawkins?"
"Section III.2.6," the clerk read:

"Failure to pass the test will cause the city to initiate negotiations with the next qualified lowest bidder, who will then demonstrate the performance delineated in Section III.2.5."

"And for the record, who would that be Mr. Hawkins?"
"The HIA Corporation, Madam President."
"Thank you, Mr. Hawkins," Barbara Miller said. "This meeting of the Los Angeles City Council is adjourned." The gavel came down with a thud.

HIA's team was up and moving. Alex grabbed Eddie Furillo's arm. "Go find Barbara. Tell her we want a copy of Pacific Rim's bid. I want you to go through that piece of shit line by line, word by word, like you were a gorilla picking gnats off your ass. Find something wrong with it. Anything. Get it thrown out."

"Don't worry, Alex. If they made a mistake, we'll find it."

"No if, Eddie. Agajanian is a walking mistake. Find something! And don't forget your fee is tied up in this."

The lobbyist stretched his jaw in a nervous reflex. "No problem, Alex. We'll get right on it."

Alex watched the Global CEO walking out of the Council chambers. Kail Hart turned to Alex with a tight-lipped smile. "You're making them very nervous."

"Agajanian low-balled it, and you know it."

"The point is...he's winning."

"He's just delaying the inevitable. He's digging his own grave."

"I thought you had their bid number?"

"So did I."

"I expect you to turn this around, and quickly, Alex! I'm not going to let you jeopardize the merger with your failures. Whatever happens, Pacific Rim cannot pass that performance test. Do I make myself clear?" Kail patted his son on the shoulder, and walked away.

Alex stood alone as the room emptied out.

*   *   *

Carina's car sped along Fifth Street through the back streets of central Los Angeles. Denny sat beside her. "I still can't believe it!"

"Look," Carina said, holding up her hand. "My hands are shaking."

"Assuming I didn't screw up something in the bid," Denny said, "in which case your Dad will turn me into shish kabab, it looks like it's down to the performance test. I know we've talked about it, but can we actually recycle twenty-five percent?"

"Most we've ever done is about fifteen. I've pressed Dad a hundred times, but he just gives me the 'We'll cross that bridge when we come to it' speech.' They fell silent as they drove over the L.A. River. They exchanged a nervous glance.

Tomorrow was D-Day.

* * *

Naz sat at his desk, chewing on a cigar. Carina and Denny burst in. Naz looked up from a piece of paper on which he had sketched a crude diagram. He peered at them over the top of his reading glasses and motioned to the seats arrayed around his desk.

"How does it feel to be winners?" he said.

"Scary," Carina said.

Denny said, "Good, scary."

Naz eyed Denny. "Your work here is up, you know. You prepared the bid package, and a damn good job, too. A winner. But you don't owe us anything more."

Denny glanced at Carina, then said. "I'd like to stay on for the performance test, it it's OK. On my own nickel. I want to see it through…bad habit of mine."

"Yeah?" said Naz. He played with the match book in his hand. He was torn. On the one hand, he was more concerned than ever about Carina's growing relationship with Denny; on the other, he needed every able body he could get, and he had to admit, Denny wasn't just any able body—he had proved himself in the line of fire.

"OK, you asked for it," Naz said.

Jack and Harry walked in and they all pulled up chairs. Naz was quiet for a moment. He walked over and stared out the window. "The easy part's over. It was just a number," he said. "Even now, a lot of people wouldn't give a rat's ass for our chances." Naz started pacing and waving his cigar. "Dad always said to me, 'Don't let the bastards grind ya down.' Right, Pop? Well, they been grinding and grinding." Naz was picking up steam. "They screw us out of our tip fees. They throw us out of the landfill. They stick the IRS on us like a leech to bleed us dry. They bribe City Hall. They leave us for dead." Naz re-lit the butt of his cigar. "But we didn't die. We showed 'em today. We showed the whole city."

Jack sat like a bear on his stool. He picked at the calluses in the palm of his hand. Every now and then his bearded chin would lift and his eyes would follow Naz's pacing form.

"So now, we're going to give it back to them," Naz glanced out the window toward Charlie's container, where all was unusually quiet, no Charlie, no dog. "We're going to pass this performance test no matter what it takes. And I mean no matter what!"

"Jack!" The wide brown eyes rose. "Tell Rodrigo and the rest of them," said Naz. "Check again, make sure their cousins and everyone else is certain for tomorrow. Everyone works, everyone gets paid. We pass the test, they're hired, all of them. Full medical. And call Uncle Garo and get the loader, bobcats, and forklift over here tonight. You got to push the shit out of the sort line tomorrow."

"I can push," Jack said. "But we'll never get 25% recyclables out of the lousy garbage the city brings in. Even if the sort line was 500 feet long."

"We can make it, Jack, but we got to believe we can. Who thought we could win the bid in the first place?

Nobody. That's who. So we got about the same number thinking we can pass the performance test. What's the problem? Now they're playing to our strength—the recovery side. We're recyclers, remember?"

Harry waved his cane, "We win football, too."

Naz turned and pulled the ball off the shelf behind his desk and tossed it up and down. "That's right, Dad. We're on a roll! We're undefeated!"

Harry winked at Carina, and she shook her head and smiled. She leaned forward and said, "We've got a couple new pieces that haven't figured into the equation before—the thirty-foot extension of the sorting line, and the glass recovery system."

Naz said, "Don't forget the new outlet for textiles with that industrial rag company. I've added one sorter on the line pulling clothing."

Denny grabbed his calculator. "A base of fifteen percent recovery, according to Carina, add say three percent for the extra sorters on the extended line, four for the glass, three more for dirt and rock, and one for textiles...." Denny hit a button, and smiled. "Twenty-six...theoretically."

"Look at that!" Naz said, slapping the top of the desk. "Overkill!"

Jack said, "Believing is one thing, Naz. Doing it...?"

Naz threw an arm around his brother-in-law's shoulders. "The material will be there, Jack, you get it out."

Jack smiled, "OK, Naz. Whatever you say."

"Carina," Naz said. "You get Manny and go to work on the compactor. Flush the hydraulics one last time, and check that new weld that Charlie put on there. If it blows tomorrow, we've had it. We'll never get the tonnage out."

Naz walked to the window and looked out at the yard. "Anybody seen Charlie?" Everyone shook their heads.

Carina said, "You'd think he'd be poking his nose in here, telling us he'll drive a fork lift tomorrow, or something."

Naz twirled the cigar in his mouth. He knew HIA. They'd pull something tomorrow. Probably when he'd least expect it and where it would do the most damage. He could feel it starting. Something not quite right with Charlie. Naz vowed again, to play it all close to the vest, just like he had with the bid number, at least until he knew what was going on. At some point, he'd have to tell the team his last contingency plan, but not until he had to.

Naz turned to his consultant. "Denny, you try to find Charlie. I want him where I can see him. Maybe Hart got to him. A little money, a little threat. I don't know. Try his container. And Dad, you order two of those port-o-potties. Better make it three."

"I get old, I get the shit job," Harry said, with a smile.

Naz stuck a few extra cigars in the pocket. "I want everyone to get a good sleep tonight. We gotta go full bore for twenty-four hours tomorrow. We meet back here at five in the morning. All right?"

Then, his eyes twinkling and his stomach burning, Naz Agajanian pounded out the door.

A few moments later, Denny peered in the windows of Charlie's hearse. Nothing but the usual assortment of blankets and empty bottles, a musty sleeping bag, a faded poster of Marilyn Monroe, a jar of Vaseline. He walked over to the shipping container and pounded on the metal door. "Charlie! You in there?" Nothing.

Denny noticed the padlock was missing and tried to open the door. It was locked solid from the inside.

"Charlie!!"

Denny hammered on the door. "Big day tomorrow, Charlie! Performance test. We need you. Come on!"

Denny listened, but heard nothing, not even a woof from Black. He turned and walked away.

* * *

Back home, Alex grabbed the phone off the bar in his den and dialed.

"Hello," the woman's voice said on the other line.

"It's Alex. What about Pacific Rim's bid package?"

"It's clean."

"How could it be clean? My army of Ph.Ds can hardly meet all the red tape."

"We checked everything," Barbara Miller said. "Minority business outreach, living wage ordinance, insurance coverages, references. One of the best proposals our staff has ever seen," she said. "Apparently, that consultant of theirs knew what he was doing. Maybe you should have hired him."

"Instead of you, you mean?"

"I can't fix everything. At some point, Alex, you actually have to beat the other team. Anyway, now they're twenty four hours away from winning the bid."

"It'll be the longest twenty four hours they've ever seen. Believe me, they won't pass that performance test."

"You've been wrong about them all along, Alex."

"Just get your bean counters down there, ready with their little clipboards and calculators."

"I'll have a little chat with the chief bean counter. He'll have his priorities straight," Barbara said. "I assume you heard that Pacific Rim is proposing the Rainbow Ridge landfill on some Indian reservation in Imperial County."

"Eddie Furillo told me. Agajanian's cousin runs it. But even with a dirt-cheap dump, the trucking cost will kill him. That's why his low-ball bid is a joke."

"Maybe he's thought of something you haven't. It wouldn't be the first time, would it?"

"He can't bullshit his way through a performance test. I doubt that hotshot consultant can process 3,000 tons a day single-handed. Don't worry, Naz will plunge off the high wire tomorrow."

"Well, someone will, that's for sure."

Alex heard the phone click, then the dial tone.

Alex hung up. He was sure the bid would be back with HIA after Pacific Rim's disaster tomorrow. Once the contract was signed and the trucks were rolling, he'd figure out a way to jettison Barbara Miller. He was already thinking of which local politician had the best chance to unseat her in the next election. All it took was money. And after he won the bid, money would be no problem.

18

"Do you understand 'Act of God', Mr. Smith?" Barbara Miller said, facing the big, loose-jointed man across from her palatial rosewood desk.

"I believe I do," the Deputy Director of the Bureau of Sanitation replied.

"Good, because outside of an Act of God, and it better be a goddamn big one like the sky raining fire, nothing stops this performance test tomorrow. No grace periods, no exceptions, no excuses...nothing. Pacific Rim must pass every performance parameter. And from what I understand, the chances of that are quite slim. Do I make myself clear?"

"Quite clear, Ms. Miller."

She stood and turned her back to him, gazing out her office window into the twilight. "How long have you worked for the city, Larry?"

"Nineteen years, twelve in Sanitation."

The Council president turned, flipped open a file on her desk and perused a document. "Looks like you were passed over for Director…twice."

"I wouldn't call it passed over."

"I would, Larry. But perhaps the third time's the charm, huh?"

Larry Smith swallowed and nodded.

"Get some sleep, Larry."

"Yes, Madam President. Uh, and…thank you."

"Just do your job, Larry. That's all I ask."

"Understood."

He turned and left Barbara Miller standing at her desk. She closed the folder.

*   *   *

Denny ran up a sharp rise, pumping with a short choppy stride, working, feeling the burn in his thighs. The recent rains had brought out the hay smell of the under-brush, cut by the menthol of the eucalyptus. He crested the ridge and dropped down a rock-strewn trail, the setting sun throwing his shadow long against the trees below.

He had found this remote trail one day while cruis-ing through Griffith Park on his Harley. Now, he could feel the stiffness loosening, his breathing become more regular, the energy flowing. As he hit the dirt road that rimmed the hills, he lengthened his stride. He needed to move, to just let it all go after the tension of the bid open-ing, the pressure of another do or die situation. And still the hardest part to come.

The road dropped down into a darkening canyon,

and he felt the difference in the air against his skin. A cool sadness—the old zoo, the stains of the animals' still marking the concrete walls, the black metal bars of their cages. The animals had been gone now for years, but something remained and it was this something that drew Denny that made him run among the cages, in the deepening dusk. In his mind, he could hear the wail of a bobcat, the grunt of a lion, the cry of a bird.

Sometimes, after the rush of a victory, a feeling of loneliness would hollow him out, regret nibbling at the corners of him. And the emptiness of it all would stretch out before him like a giant maw.

Then he would run.

Run till his guts cramped.

Run till the pounding of the blood in his head shut off his mind.

Denny stormed out the far side of the zoo, past the last concrete ruin, over the ribbon gutter, and leaped up on the short stone wall. He hammered his way up the canyon, climbing, burning, sweat stinging his eyes.

Up and up he ran. Now scrambling over bare granite, finally reaching the lookout, 500 feet above the canyon floor. He hung on the fence at the lip of the sheer cliff, lungs grabbing for air. He felt his heartbeat pounding in his temples, his wrists.

He was back in his body, in his core. Not the fragments that he often carried around in one sack of skin, but one whole. It was a rare and fleeting feeling for him.

As he looked across the San Fernando Valley, he thought of Pacific Rim and the test ahead. There was peace in knowing that the die was cast. That if Pacific

Rim failed tomorrow, Denny would go down with Naz's ship. And going down to Denny would mean more than just losing the bid. It would mean losing his career, at least in the L.A. basin and maybe more. The trash business was an insular world, dominated by a few power players. With the bid in hand, Alex Hart would be invincible and could blackball Denny in the industry. Oddly, there was something freeing about that thought. The sense of pushing his last pile of chips into the center of the table, of putting everything on the line.

Maybe that was the risk that had to be taken to be part of something, something worth fighting for, not just a company, but a family.

Denny turned from the fence and started back down the mountain at an easy gait, and in the clearing of his mind, he saw a vision, a young woman dancing. Tall and dark, twirling a long scarf that wrapped around her. Like a cat she moved, effortless and powerful and full of grace. For a moment, he was back in Africa, but then she turned and he recognized her—Carina.

He sprinted down the hillside, running toward her as she danced away in the dark.

* * *

Across the city, Alex closed the windows of his game room against the cool of the night. A calmness had settled over his features, making him look almost tired. But he was far from tired. He was confident. He knew that finally the end game was near. All his planning, all his maneuvering, all his years of work would now pay off.

Within thirty hours it would all be over. Pacific Rim would be finished. Nazareth Agajanian and his family would cease to be an issue. Would, in fact, disappear off the radar. He had talked to Jack. With Pacific Rim winning the bid, Jack had missed out on his big payday. Alex knew the debtors were leaning on Jack, that he was staring down the barrel of the gun. Naz had outsmarted both of them on the bid, but the performance test was a different matter. Jack had come up with the idea, and the moment he heard it, Alex knew it was the silver bullet. Alex smiled as he lined up the cue ball, knowing that the stars too were aligning. He not only had Jack in his back pocket, but the majority of votes on the company Board, and with that, the fate of its Chairman. He would sit alone on top of the HIA mountain.

He stopped for a moment and thought of the final piece, the ugly piece. He grimaced and closed his eyes. He had no choice. He couldn't let Carina blow the whistle on his smuggling scheme. Not now, with everything on the line and the end so near. The derelict had fingered her and Alex was forced to make a move, but it made him wince to think about it. So he put Carina in a back compartment in his mind and closed the door.

*   *   *

Carina pulled into her driveway, and rummaged through her purse. She brought out a fistful of keys and opened the back door. In the dark she didn't notice the phone cord cut and dangling at the corner of the house. She stepped into the kitchen and flicked on the light, then closed the door and threw the deadbolt.

The pinewood of the kitchen glowed warmly around her, the crannies stuffed with cookbooks, the copper pots hanging from a rack over the chopping block. She popped a can of beer and took a sip, then another deeper one for good measure. She ripped open a bag of chips with her teeth, kicked off her shoes, and walked into the living room. She pulled out a Waylon Jennings cassette and slipped it into the tape deck. The first strains of "Wurlitzer Prize" followed her as she walked back to the kitchen. Another swallow of beer, the steel guitar and that bar room brawl of a voice. The tension that had gripped her through the day seeped out of her. Tomorrow was the performance test, but they were as ready as they would ever be. She swayed with the music.

Reaching up overhead, she grabbed a pot off its hook, filled it with water and set it on the burner. She sang a few bars of harmony, blending a husky alto to Waylon's lead. She pulled a bag of shrimp out of the freezer and dropped a handful of linguine in the boiling water. The shellfish she chucked into the microwave and punched defrost. She walked into the pantry and came out holding a bottle of extra virgin olive oil.

She didn't notice back in the shadows in the dining room that adjoined the kitchen, the large man, still as stone.

Carina dipped a fork into the boiling pasta and lifted out several strands. She blew on them, then sucked one into her mouth. Still a tad firm. She dropped them back in the water, walked over toward the dining room and reached up to lift the colander off its hook on the wall.

The big man shifted to his left and moved up along the wall behind her, just a few feet away. There was a knock at the kitchen door.

"Carina? Hey, Carina! It's Terry," a voice called from outside.

"Coming!" Carina cried out as she spun toward the door with the colander in her hand. The man slipped back out of sight as Carina unlocked the bolt and opened the door. "Hi, Terry," she said as she walked back to the stove.

The young, short, blond woman followed her in. "Ooooh! Smells good in here." Terry took a deep breath and plopped herself into a chair at the kitchen table.

"Want some shrimp linguine?"

"Naw, thanks anyway. I just came to borrow some non-fat milk."

Carina lifted another noodle to her mouth.

Terry looked around the room, checking the shadows. "Do you feel something?" Terry said softly.

Carina stopped chewing. "What do you mean, feel something?"

"You know, just something." Her eyes gazed down at the far end of the kitchen.

Carina pointed the fork at her; a couple of noodles fell to the floor. "Don't start. I can scare myself just fine, thank you."

Terry continued staring. Carina turned in the direction she was looking. "Eat something," she said. "You'll feel better." Carina poured the noodles into the colander nestled in the sink, and the hot steam shot up around her arms.

"Ow! Shit!" Carina screamed, dropping the pot into the colander. Terry's eyes snapped over to Carina. "You all right?"

The man slipped further back into the living room.

Carina ran some cold water out of the faucet onto her hand.

"Did you burn it?"

"No. Just a little red," Carina replied, wincing as she looked at the back of her left hand. Once again, Terry checked the room. It was quiet. She went back to the fridge. "Mind if I take this quart?"

"Naw. It's all yours."

Terry turned at the back door. "Thanks, Carina. Hey, take care."

The door closed and Carina got up and locked it. Her hand throbbed and her appetite was gone. She slopped the pasta into a plastic container and poured the seafood sauce over it. She threw down a few bites, popped the lid on and put it in the refrigerator, then turned out the light and started to walk upstairs. She could feel the dried sweat under her shirt and the grime from Pacific Rim on her arms, face and neck. A hot bath would feel so good. Forget about tomorrow and the performance test for at least a few luxurious moments.

Carina sang softly with the music floating up from downstairs. Suddenly, she stopped. The sound was so faint, just a flicker. She turned on another light and glanced quickly over her shoulder. Nothing moved. No sound. She fought down a flutter of fear, stepped out of her pants and walked into the bathroom. Just keep moving, she thought. Keep moving. This'll pass like it always does. She poured a capful of bubble bath under the rushing water and added a squirt of baby oil. Lavender steam filled the room.

She wrapped her hair up on her head, slipped out of her panties, and climbed into the tub. She lay back and closed her eyes. The hot, soothing water lapped up around her neck. She let her breath out slowly and felt her chest sink deeper in the water.

Her eyes flew open. A creak. A floorboard? A footstep? Her breath stopped. She heard her heart beating, the bath bubbles quietly popping, the tick of the clock in the bedroom, the drip of water from the faucet.

Someone was in the house.

Oh, my God. Someone was in the house.

"Denny?" she said. "That you?" No sound. Her heart raced. She sat up and crossed her arms over her breasts.

Slowly, she rose from the tub. Bubbles clung to her skin. She lifted her bathrobe off the hook behind the door, listening, her pulse beating in her throat. She slipped into the bathrobe, and pulled the collar up tight around her neck. Her limbs moved in slow motion, her vision a tunnel in front of her. She saw the hardwood floor, the door to the bedroom, her feet walking, her hand grabbing the phone on the nightstand beside the bed.

She had already dialed 911 when she realized there was no dial tone. She clicked the receiver. Nothing. Slowly she hung up the phone. Her knees sagged. A hollowness welled up in her throat. The gun! She turned and took a step past her open closet toward her dresser. She smelled a strange fragrance.

Her hanging clothes exploded out! The flash of a ski-mask—and he was on her. She turned, and he grabbed her bathrobe. She slid out of it and it fell to the floor. He dove for her and grabbed her leg, but her oiled skin was slippery and she wriggled free and lunged for the dresser. Ripping open the drawer, she grabbed the heavy 45 with both hands and whirled.

He rammed into her as the gun went off into the ceiling, knocking her down. But she held on to the weapon and fired again from her back. She saw his shadow fly out the bedroom door and heard him rumble down the stairs, then all fell quiet.

She got to her feet holding the gun, her hands trembling, her breath coming in short pants, blood pounding in her head. She threw on her bathrobe.

With the gun in front of her, she eased down the stairs, each creak magnified in the silence. Looking, watching. Her finger taut on the trigger. Her bare foot landed on the living room carpet.

She heard a noise.

She whirled with the gun.

A shadow burst toward the kitchen. She fired. Pans clattered to the kitchen floor. Carina heard the kitchen door bang open against the wall. She stood holding the gun, staring ahead at nothing.

Then she heard the familiar sound of a motorcycle pull up in the driveway. A moment later, Denny walked in. Carina sagged down on the couch, the gun dangling in one hand.

Denny leapt to her side. "What happened! You OK? Are you hurt?"

"Someone got in the house..." she said, tears welling in her eyes. "He had a mask. But I think I know who it was. Big. Aftershave."

"Zaven?"

Carina nodded, "I think he went out the kitchen."

Easing into the kitchen, Denny pulled a carving knife out of the butcher block. He checked the open door, peering outside. All quiet.

Back in the living room Denny lifted the gun out of Carina's hand and set it on the coffee table. He hugged her gently, one hand on the back of her head, the other patting her back. She sobbed quietly. He adjusted her bathrobe tighter around her neck and shoulders. "It's all right...all right." Denny said, "We should call the police. He might still be out there."

"No, I...no police."

"What are you talking about? This maniac breaks in...."

"Wait," she said, placing a hand against his chest. "I can't deal with it now. It's all right."

"How could it be all right? There could be fingerprints."

"Let's get through the test tomorrow."

"You sure?" Denny said. She nodded. "The city will say we rigged it, stalling for time. We'll get disqualified. We can't risk it."

Denny sat next to her and they held each other in the living room, as the country song on the stereo ended and the house fell quiet.

*   *   *

Naz sprinkled Tabasco sauce on the fried egg sandwich Mayda had just prepared for him. He was lost in thought and visions of the performance test that would begin with the dawn in a few hours, mostly things that could go wrong. He took a bite, and the hot sauce pulled him back.

The phone rang.

"Not Charlie again," Mayda said, as she reached for the phone on the wall in the kitchen.

Naz took another bite, then mumbling through the food in his mouth, "I don't want to talk to anyone, unless they're dying." He noticed Mayda's face go pale, the phone at her ear. She gripped the counter.

"What?" Naz said.

"Oh, my God," she said into the phone, tears welling in her eyes. "Are you all right?"

"Give me the phone," Naz said, reaching out. Mayda stood frozen. "Mayda!"

She said, "Here's your father." And handed the phone to Naz.

"What?" Naz said, his eyes wide open and darting, listening. "I'm coming over!" he shouted into the phone. "I'll find that bastard and kill that sonuvabitch!" He paused, listening. "No, it's not all right!...I am calmed down!!...You're at Denny's?" Naz took a breath, trying to regain his composure, although he felt like ripping up the counter top.

"Thank God he showed up when he did," Naz said. "You want to come over here for tonight?...You sure? You might feel better in your old bed. All right. Just tell him to make damn sure nothing else happens, OK? You sure you're OK? All right...I'll kill that sonuvabitch!... all right, yeah. I'll see you in the morning." He slammed the phone down, stormed across the room and pulled his jacket out of the closet.

"Where are you, going?" Mayda said.

"I'm gonna drive around over there and find that cocksucker and tear his fucking balls off."

Mayda grabbed him. "Nazareth, stop. She's with the consultant, right?"

"No sonuvabitch touches my daughter...."

"Please, Nazareth."

Naz pushed Mayda aside, and she slipped on the rug and fell. Startled by his own violence, he reached down for her.

She whacked his arm away and struggled to her feet. "You will not go over there! She is all right, Nazareth! This person will be punished, but not by you!"

Naz closed his eyes and rubbed his forehead. Red light flashed behind his eyes, his pulse pounding in his temples. He sagged.

"Come on. Sit down," Mayda said, leading him to the couch and sitting with him, holding his hand. "I am scared, too."

"It's HIA...."

Mayda squeezed his hand, rubbed his neck.

He said, "We got 'em on the run. They're scared."

"Then everyone is scared."

"We win this bid, I'm going to bury those assholes."

"She is all right. That is all that matters right now."

Naz sat for a few moments, breathing deeply, bringing himself back to the room. He picked up a picture frame off the coffee table. It showed the three of them, Naz, Mayda, and a baby Carina. He took a slow, deep breath. Mayda rubbed his back.

"I remember when she was born," he said. "She was all wrapped up in this blanket, like one of those Indian papooses. I kept trying to count her toes. I was worried that she would have too many toes. But through the tears,

I couldn't see, and I would lose count. It was driving me crazy."

Mayda's eyes welled up and she patted Naz on the hand. "She will be all right, Nazareth. I know."

"It's a crazy world, Mayda. Sometimes, I don't know how we survive."

"We survive because there is nothing else to do. Now, come. We must go to bed."

As they headed up the stairs, she reached out and held his hand.

* * *

Denny opened the window of his loft, and the cool air spilled in. Carina stepped up beside him and gazed out at the city. A few stars burned their way through the city lights and mist.

"You want something to drink?" he asked.

"You can almost see Pacific Rim from here."

"I'll put on some water for tea. Chamomile, just for you."

"Part of me feels like I'll never sleep again, and the other part like I could sleep for a thousand years."

Carina heard Timbuktu meow from somewhere on the roof. She wouldn't mind being a cat right now herself. So she could curl up in a ball in some safe, warm, cozy spot, maybe lick her paw and brush her face with it and then fall instantly to sleep, with no thought for tomorrow.

She felt exhausted. The most exhausted she'd ever felt in her whole life. Almost like dying. Without a word, she drifted over to Denny's bed, and slipped under the covers.

When Denny turned around with the tea, she was already asleep. He stood there a moment with the cups in his hands, looking at her face. He wondered how anyone so beautiful could have ended up in his bed, and vowed that he would never do anything to hurt her. If someone's heart was going to be broken, he prayed it would be his.

As he crawled in bed beside her, and curled his cool body up against her warm one, each second felt like an hour, and tomorrow and all that it held, one way or the other, seemed light-years away.

*   *   *

Jack flicked on the light in his garage. It was cold, or maybe it was just him. He popped the trunk of his car and pulled back the blanket that lay over the steel cylinder. He checked the gauge, even though he knew it was full, and tightened the valve. Didn't want a leak, blow himself to kingdom come in his own garage.

It was one thing to smuggle out information, another to do this. He pulled the blanket back over the acetylene tank and closed the trunk with a soft click. He tried to think of a happier time, but in each one, the Agajanians were there. So he tried to think of no time at all, but his mind kept churning. He opened the car door and sat down behind the wheel, gripping it as if to keep himself from floating away. Thank God, this would soon be over.

When he could no longer stand being alone with himself, he left the garage and walked to his youngest daughter's bedroom. As on every night, he had left it ajar for her. He peeked in and saw her all twisted in her blankets; she was a restless sleeper, just like he was. Jack walked quietly to her bed and pulled the blankets from under her. She moaned and rolled over. He tucked them around her.

In his mind, what he was about to do, the lives he was about to shatter, was all for the future of this little one and her sister. Jack thought the odds were good he would get away with it. They would never suspect him, and in the chaos that would ensue, fingers would be pointed at Charlie, not the loyal lieutenant. Once the Agajanians went down for good, it would make sense for him to start over in his old stomping grounds north of Fresno. He would create a new beginning with the payoff from Alex. And even if in his heart, Jack knew that one way or the other he would ultimately have to pay for these sins, his daughters would go on and have a good life. Sophie too.

* * *

Black lay on the old beach towel, his head nestled down on his paws. A ray of moonlight shot in through a hole in the roof of the container and lit his shoulder. He looked up at Charlie, who was scrunched up at his workbench. Black got to his feet, limped over to Charlie and sat next to him, as if waiting for the welcome pat on the head. But nothing came. Black nudged his nose into Charlie's thigh.

Charlie was welding. But it wasn't a bonsai tree. It was what used to be a bonsai tree, but was now just a ball of metal gunk. His lips were moving, but no sound came out. Black twitched his head from side to side trying to pick up the words, but the only one who could hear them was Charlie.

When no response came, Black nosed him again, this time pushing a little harder and then scooting his haunches up so his jaw rested on Charlie's leg. Charlie dropped a hand on his dog's head, and looked off as if gazing across the ocean. Then, he lifted his hand and went back to welding. Black ambled back to his corner, circled once and dropped onto his towel. Charlie reached to a shelf behind him and pulled down a bottle. He unscrewed the cap, his motions slow and deliberate, and took a swallow.

His mind was beginning to fog. Every time it would start to focus on the trouble, Charlie would turn his mind to an empty part of his universe, like a telescope in the desert swiveling to an empty quadrant of space, where there was only the background murmur of memories and a gentle halo of diffuse light.

Charlie took another drink. A dribble ran down from the corner of his mouth. He turned the ravaged sculpture in his vice and put the torch back on it. Drops of molten metal fell to the floor.

*　*　*

Harry limped up the moonlit path that meandered through the scrub to a small knoll beyond their condo in Montebello. Naz had bought the condo five years ago despite Harry's protests that it was a waste of money. He and Armi did not have to live in Montebello, Boyle Heights, the old neighborhood, was good enough. But Montebello was the Armenian dream and Harry knew that his son wanted that dream for him, and so had let him buy it even though he was leveraged to the hilt, as usual. But it was Harry himself who had told Naz as a little boy 'Once you owe more than you have, what does it matter?' So he had only himself to blame.

Harry sat down on a bench with a sigh, and hooked his cane over the back. Looking northeast, he could see across the San Gabriel Valley, past the glittering lights of San Dimas, and the towers of the Conrock gravel pits in Irwindale, to the dark foothills and finally to Mt. Baldy, snow-capped in the moonlight. It still seemed magical to him, that here in this desert 10,000 miles from his home, this mountain stood. Nothing could match Mt. Ararat, but this one was good enough, for now.

He came up here often to think and to listen. He sat perfectly still, hands folded in his lap. He heard the background hum of the traffic from the Pomona Freeway off in the distance. A mockingbird sang to him from out of the night, running through his repertoire of chirps and trills and shrieks, warnings and boasts, and pure exuberance.

Harry knew this bird. He had listened to him singing for two weeks now, staking out his claim to territory, to a mate, to a future—to a life.

Just like me, Harry thought. He had been singing his song all his life, and would sing it again tomorrow, the day on which everything balanced. The day on which they could not only seal the victory on the bid, but finally even the score, after decades of defeats, against the Hartunians.

The long river of his life had flowed to here, trusting in hard work and loyalty and dignity. He felt sure that his God would not abandon him now. Not after such a long journey. Not after he had survived "the Darkness."

He gazed out at Mt. Baldy, the mountain with the black rock base, the snow-crowned peak, and it carried him back to Armenia…and he is walking. Just a boy, walking. So tired his only wish is to lie down on the ground and never get up. He sees his feet, bleeding through torn shoes coming down the trail from their little town in the highlands. The back of his mother in front of him, her coarse red dress, mud-spattered, swaying with her step. The sound of a horse's hooves pounding, as the Turkish officer in his blue and red uniform, rides up and down the long line of families marching toward the horizon. The soldiers on foot with their rifles slung over their shoulders.

All muted as if encased in cotton, and none of it real. It couldn't be real.

But it is real enough when they take his father and the other men and march them off. He watches his mother run and grab on to his father, the other women crying and clutching at their men. His father looks at Harry, knowing, unblinking and then the soldiers rip him away and they are all gone over the hill. Gunshots. The soldiers coming back over the hill, alone.

He screams and attacks the officer on horseback, grabbing his boot. The man laughing at him and hitting him with his whip. Falling to the ground, weeping. His mother's hands lifting him, wiping the tears from his face. "Come, Haroush." Her face, he sees her face. No tears. They had all fallen long before, and she had no more to let fall in this life.

He stands and sees far in the distance, the river, placid and blue like it was painted on the brown plain below. .

When the soldiers had forced them to wade into that river, tied together in twos, they only had to shoot one, knowing that the dead one would drag the live one under. They had tied him to his mother. When they shot her, a piece of bullet deflected and lodged in his hip. But he was so terrified and exhausted at the time he hardly felt it. In the water he didn't want to let go of his mother, even though he knew she was dead. But when their tangled bodies caught on a snag and he managed to grab a breath, he knew he must leave her. Using the mud as a lubricant, he managed to slip his bony wrists out of the knots. Before he could kiss her, the current swept him away. It seemed like forever before the fisherman pulled him out miles away.

Now, it was seventy years since that day, a lifetime he had worked and waited. He had asked for so little, but now Harry asked God for one thing—to let them pass the performance test. Then he could work a happy man to the day he died, and he would never ask for another thing. Well, maybe a little *oghi* now and then, but nothing more.

Harry shifted on the bench to feel again the pain in his hip, where the bullet fragment had gone in. It was a good pain. He rose from the bench and with a last look at the mountain, turned and limped back down the hill, his cane marking a slow and steady cadence.

19

Clouds sailed over the Santa Monica Mountains and across the L.A. basin, reflecting the lights of the city in a cold glow. It was 4:30 a.m. Naz drove down from the hills on the Glendale Freeway past Eagle Rock and Atwater Village.

He chewed on a fresh cigar, deep in thought. Today was the biggest day of his life. It was as simple as that. And not only his life, but his entire family's life, the long ancestral chain that started generations ago on the small farm in Armenia and extended finally to this morning driving through the cold and dark.

If he failed today, that chain of struggle and triumph would be broken. They could not recover from a loss today. They would be buried and the family dream would be gone.

But he knew that if by some chance God smiled on Pacific Rim today, they could win a victory—a victory so good as to be almost unimaginable.

Naz buzzed down the window and spit out a piece of tobacco. He let the cold wind blow in his face for a moment. He knew he was as ready for the performance test as he could be. They all were. You just couldn't be certain of anything in life. He just wished he were a little more certain about Charlie. The old derelict's sudden disappearance still troubled him. Had the Harts somehow got to him? Was he lurking, waiting for some crucial moment to hit Pacific Rim, when they were vulnerable, and perhaps unable to recover? Naz thought he knew Charlie, as well as anyone could know a lunatic. But most people had a price at which their head could be turned, and for Charlie that price could be mighty low. A case of Old Overholt and Charlie would cartwheel down Wilshire Boulevard. A couple thousand dollars, he might do anything.

Charlie or not, Naz knew the Harts would not stand idly by. One way or the other, Pacific Rim would have to take a body blow, maybe more than one, and keep fighting.

And of course, stewing in his mind, pulling at his concentration was Carina and her ordeal of the past night. The intruder, and the attack. Naz gripped the steering wheel with white knuckles, trying to crush the breath out of a dark figure that he imagined in the shadows. But who? And was it connected to the bid, to the performance test? He could hardly believe the Harts would fall that low. But they too, had their ass on the line and needed to win to keep their merger deal on track. A loss on the bid could be a big chink in their armor, the first crack that starts the empire crumbling.

God, he hoped Carina was all right. She was tough, but how much could she take? He thought of Galen, the funeral, the devastation of the loss. And now, just when she was coming back...Naz shook the thought from his mind.

As he pulled through the gate at Pacific Rim, he noticed the lights on in the plant and Jack's car out front. He knew Jack would have already turned on the power, checked the fluid levels in the loaders, warming things up. Just the thought of Jack, good, tough Jack, gave Naz a lift. He wasn't alone. Not by a long shot.

Like a downhill skier at the top of the run picturing each gate and turn along the course, Naz wandered around the plant imagining the flow of the trucks, the trash moving up the lines, the screening and sorting, the baling, the compactor loading the big transfer trucks. He wandered into a back corner of the plant, lit his third cigar of the day and looked up at the rusted metal relief of the Virgin Mary that the men had salvaged from the trash. A halo of white Christmas tree lights adorned her head, and rows of mismatched and charred candles lined the crude alter at her feet.

Naz didn't mind that the men had built this shrine in their makeshift little break area, next to the Coke machine. Everyone needed to believe in something and Naz of all people was a big believer in believing.

He took a couple puffs on his cigar and touched the hot ash to the remnant of a candle. The tiny flame caught and Naz placed the candle at the Virgin's feet. He looked at her face for a moment, hands folded in front of him, then turned and walked away.

Denny and Carina pulled up in front of the office, the car windows steamed with the heat and moisture of a hundred Egg McMuffins, boxes of hash browns, five gallons of coffee, two gallons of orange juice, a dozen boxes of Winchell's assorted donut packs, and a pile of Armenian bread stacked like pizza crusts. Denny turned off the engine, reached over and squeezed Carina's hand. She squeezed back, a determined look on her face.

"I'm all right," she said.

"Yeah, I know," Denny said. "It'll get better if you just start to work. Power down a few donuts, you know."

Carina smiled. She liked that about Denny. He could make her smile, even now. "You sound like my *Manig*, my grandmother. 'Eat!' she says. 'Eat!'"

When they walked into his office, Naz got up and hugged his daughter to him. "You all right?"

"Yeah," she said.

"We'll get that sonuvabitch."

"Would've got him already, if I could shoot better."

"Charlie show up yet?" Denny asked.

"No," Naz said. He spit a piece of tobacco into the trashcan.

"I think something bad happened to him," Carina said.

"Who knows," Naz said. "He may just be on a bender somewhere."

"What's to stop Hart from planting someone, or maybe a few 'someones' in with the new guys Rodrigo and Manny are bringing in?" Denny asked.

"I already thought of that," Naz said. "Our men will know them, but there's no way to watch seventy guys.

We'll just have to wait till something happens and hope we can handle it."

"So what else is new?" Carina said. A smile slipped between her lips as she walked to her office. Denny raised his eyebrows and glanced at Naz, who showed the semblance of a smile. She was tough. She would be all right.

While Denny and Carina set up the food on folding tables in the tipping area, Naz pulled a sheet of paper out of his desk drawer, put on his reading glasses, and studied the crude sketch.

Outside, a stream of headlights snaked up the access road, over the tracks and past the scalehouse. Rodrigo waved them up to the temporary parking area under the overpass.

*   *   *

The car lights played through a crack in the shipping container and flickered above Charlie's head where he lay curled in a corner and wrapped in a blanket. Bruises like purple handprints showed on Charlie's neck as he pulled the blanket up against the damp. The odor of the Egg McMuffins had filtered over to Black and he was getting restless. Charlie hugged his dog and held out another half a dog biscuit. Black mouthed it gently from his hand. Charlie calmed him with slow strokes of his hand.

Over and over, Charlie played the scene in his mind, the attack along the river. The bulk of the man, the voice, the heavy hands. But he just couldn't place him. He wondered what might have happened to Carina after he had betrayed her to his attacker. Charlie could hear the activity in the yard and sensed that out there somewhere

the man was watching, and he knew he could never survive another encounter. No, Charlie would stay with his
strong suit and do what he had done his whole life when
heavy shit was coming down—lay low, very, very low.

They can't hurt you when they can't find you. He took
an old Swiss Army knife out of his pocket and began to
cut the lid off a can of Spaghetti O's.

*   *   *

As they pulled into the plant and parked, the worker's cars looked like entries in the world's largest demolition derby. Dust rose and sparkled like snow flurries.
Boom boxes thumped, brakes squealed, tires sprayed
gravel like grapeshot.

The men yelled out to one another as they jostled in
a throng toward the building. Besides Pacific Rim's normal contingent of fifty workers were another twenty-two
just for today, to add some more hands where help was
needed. Each was someone's cousin, or uncle, friend, a
sister's boyfriend, guys from the neighborhood and now
all part of the extended family of Pacific Rim—at least
for the next twenty-four hours. They huddled in groups,
some taking last puffs of cigarettes before squashing the
butts under their heels. The noise drifted down and min-
gled with the smell of the food and Naz's cigar.

A bloodshot sun peeked over the San Gabriel Mountains and cast a rusty hue over the station as Naz walked
out of the office. "Okay. Listen up you guys! Hey, listen
up!" he yelled. Rodrigo stood next to him, and yelled it
out in Spanish.

"I want to thank all you extra guys for coming out today. I know Rodrigo and Manny told you, but I'm going to say it again so there's no misunderstanding. We're going for twenty-four hours, two twelve-hour shifts. You guys are on from six this morning to six tonight. Breakfast and lunch are on us. You eat at your station. Each man, if he works hard, gets eighty-five dollars cash at the end of the shift. If you guys move 1,500 tons through here in twelve hours, every man gets a bonus of twenty-five dollars. We pass this test…" Naz paused for effect, "and every man gets a full-time job starting at seven bucks an hour, plus medical." A murmur went up from the men. Plus medical!

Naz turned to Rodrigo. "Break these new guys up into crews. I want five on the floor pulling big stuff, wood, white goods, metal. Three opening bags. Give Jack twelve up on the extension of the sorting line. He'll tell them where to go."

"What about the litter crew, Naz?" said Denny, his mouth muffled with a hunk of donut.

"Oh, that chicken shit. Put a couple guys on that, too"

"Okay, men!" Naz yelled over their heads. "Rodrigo's going to divide you up and tell you where to go. Then you grab some breakfast and get ready."

The men surged toward the tables.

"Not yet, goddammit! We divide you up first, then eat!"

By the time the official city crew arrived at 5:45 a.m. to monitor the test, the extra men were at their positions, being trained by the regular crew while they finished their food. Trays of Styrofoam cups, brimming with coffee, circulated down the lines and across the tipping floor. The building smelled more like a cafe than a trash processing plant.

The Deputy Director of the Bureau of Sanitation, Larry Smith, piled out of the car with his crew of monitors, the same group that had conducted the pre-bid inspection.

Naz noticed that they all wore scowls like someone had shoved a piece of rebar up their ass. He could imagine the marching orders Larry Smith had received, and Naz figured he wasn't the only one with his tail on the line today. Naz gathered Carina, Jack, Denny, and Harry, and faced the city forces, like teams at the coin toss before a football game.

Naz shook Larry's hand. "Nice day for a little recycling, huh, Larry?"

"I guess we'll find out," Smith answered in a tense, dry voice. He referred to his clipboard and addressed the group gathered around. "The city will have monitors stationed throughout the plant, but most importantly at the scales to monitor the weight of the garbage trucks coming in, the transfer trucks going out with residue for the landfill, and the semis carrying recyclable material heading for markets. In the next twenty-four hours, 3,000 tons of municipal solid waste must be received and processed. A minimum of twenty-five percent recovered for recycling and the remaining seventy-five percent loaded out for disposal. All recyclable loads will be observed and graded to make sure the station is doing a proper sorting job and that the material was of requisite quality. Is that clear, Mr. Agajanian?"

"What does 'requisite' mean, exactly?" Naz said, a

twinkle in his eye. Before Smith could answer, Naz patted the Deputy Director on the shoulder. "Just kidding, Director, just kidding."

Suddenly, a big Mercedes roared up the access road and pulled up in front of the office. Joe Kirby, Alex Hart's attorney, climbed out. Smith said to Naz, "The rules allow one observer from the second place team."

"Joe! Come to see how it's done?" Naz shouted.

"Actually, Naz, I've come to pick up the pieces from what will soon be a disaster beyond comprehension." Joe Kirby wiped some mud off his shoe with a white handkerchief.

"Don't count on it."

"Time will tell." Joe Kirby grabbed an Egg McMuffin off the nearby table and munched down on it. "You get an A for the breakfast, though. After this all goes south, you should look into the restaurant business."

Naz noticed a few of the city staff eyeing the hash browns and egg sandwiches and he gestured to the food table. "Larry, you and your people want some breakfast... coffee?"

"We've already eaten."

"Well, you let me know. We'll save some in case you get hungry later on." Naz wolfed down a slab of hash browns. "Keep your blood sugar up. Don't want any of your folks missing something."

"Oh, we won't miss, anything," Smith said. "Of that I can assure you."

"Wouldn't want it any other way, Larry," Naz said. "When we ace this thing, I don't want no questions."

As the city crew dispersed to their stations, Naz

drew his inner circle around him. "OK, this is it. You all know what needs to be done. The city will use any fucking excuse to disqualify us. No matter what happens, we keep running. You all understand?"

They nodded.

Naz went on, "I don't care if we're down to our last man, our last breath, we better be using it to pull out one more goddamn can, load one more transfer truck!"

With that, Naz's team headed for their respective areas, Carina to the compactor, Jack to the sorting line, Denny to the scalehouse. As the Pacific Rim workers threw down their last cups of coffee, Harry scurried around limping on his cane with a container to collect the cups. He tossed them into the Styrofoam recycling bin under the elevated sorting line.

"See, Larry!" Naz shouted across the yard, "The first pound of recycling, and we ain't even started!"

Larry Smith turned toward the scale as the first trucks approached and yelled, "Hold those trucks at the gate! Five minutes to start time."

Naz watched as the first of the city's collection trucks came in off the routes with their eight-ton payloads of garbage, and formed a queue at the scales, engines idling. Even with all he had riding on this, and with all he had to worry about, Naz loved the challenge. This moment they could never take away from him. He wanted to kiss every one of those Mexicans, well, in theory.

Larry Smith glanced at his watch. "Okay, Mr. Agajanian," he said. "Let her go!"

Naz waved the first truck forward, and it roared up onto the scale. The scale attendant gobbled his donut in one bite, recorded the weight, and the managed chaos that was Naz Agajanian's life, that was Pacific Rim's life, shifted into high gear. As the first truck pulled off the scale, the next one was already on. Within minutes, the yard was alive with trucks backing up, alarms beeping, dumping, pulling out—crawling like crabs on a dead fish.

Crews of men on the floor grabbed pieces of wood and scrap metal, and heaved them into roll-off boxes for recycling. The loaders roared into the piles and pushed mountains of trash to the feed point for the screen and sorting line. There, men slashed open any plastic bags and spilled out the contents. The conveyors tripped on, and the trash was dragged up onto the heavy screen. Dirt, rocks, and broken glass fell through the openings and into a dumpster below. This material would later be sorted through Carina's glass recovery system. The "overs," the larger material that tumbled off the end of the screen, fell onto the fast moving conveyor that rushed the material past the sorters. Without taking their eyes off the river flowing in front of them, the men grabbed their assigned recyclable material and chucked it into chutes beside them that led down to the bunkers below.

Cardboard came off first, then newspaper, high grades like computer and office paper, mixed colored paper, and junk mail, glass bottles with two men each picking brown, green and clear, tin cans, aluminum cans, PET beverage bottles, milk jugs, Styrofoam, textiles, rubber and leather. And finally, the last two stations for disposable baby diapers. Denny had told Naz that the City of L.A. waste composition study showed that three percent of the entire waste stream was baby diapers. He had found a composting operation that would take them for nothing, so out they came. Yard waste, too. It all counted towards the twenty-five percent they needed to recover for recycling.

Carina checked the experimental glass cullet recovery system. Shards of glass were already mounding in the bottom of the container.

Jack cruised the catwalk above the sorting line. The loads were actually better than they had expected. The cardboard and newspaper bunkers were already half-full and they'd only been going for thirty minutes. And the trash was heavy in steel cans coming off the drum magnet, and a lot of brown glass from the beer drinking barrios. They were pulling maybe thirty percent so far.

The residual trash that fell off the end of the sorting line dropped back onto a separate tipping floor where a Cat 950 loader shoved it into the hopper of the compactor. From the console above, Manny activated the ram. Each push of the big compactor blade packed another three tons of waste into the back of an eighteen-wheel transfer truck. As each truck filled, it pulled out and roared off for the 250-mile haul to the Rainbow Ridge Landfill on the Indian Reservation in the high desert.

Naz stopped one of the first transfer trucks heading out. He jumped up on the running board and shook the big hand that reached out the window. "Have a safe trip, Moses," Naz said.

"Be back in twelve hours for my second load," said the driver, a large black man with laughing eyes and a shaved head. "And Naz, thanks for bringing me on."

"Hey, I only did it because of the minority business

bullshit." Naz smiled, this guy was the best trucker he knew in L.A., and Naz knew a lot of them. "Drive like hell!"

The driver laughed, threw the rig in gear and pulled away as Naz leaped off.

20

The first hour had passed and Naz came up to where Denny was tallying the scalehouse log.

"How we looking?" Naz asked.

Denny punched numbers into his calculator. "Averaging a transfer truck out every twelve minutes. Five trucks, 120 tons an hour." Denny looked at Naz and raised his eyebrows. "We're making it."

"Fuckin' A."

Harry stood over at the loading dock, watching the baler spit out bales of paper, aluminum cans, PET bottles, and the forklifts running the bales into the shipping containers. He hummed an old Armenian folk song. Naz put his arm around his father's shoulders.

"What's the bale count?"

"Forty bale first hour," Harry replied. "Like you say, Nazareth, no problem." Harry smiled, his gold tooth glinting.

As Naz walked back to the office his mind was working. Things were going well. Too well. He knew the boom was going to fall. It wasn't the falling itself that bothered him so much, but the waiting was torture. One of the loaders backfired, and he jerked his head around so fast that he twisted his neck. Jesus Christ! He walked into the office and grabbed his bottle of Tums.

*　*　*

The hours passed. Pacific Rim cooked along like some primitive organism, taking food in, extracting the nutrients, and excreting the residue. And over it all, Larry Smith hovered like a praying mantis looking for something to kill.

There were a few burps along the way. Like when a shell from a 205-mm Howitzer showed up under a cardboard box on the sorting line, part of a load from the local Army Depot. One of the sorters was stupid enough to pick the thing up and hold it over his head, his trophy for the day. Everyone else dove for cover, and Jack hit the emergency stop button, which backed trash up all the way to the tipping floor. That brought Naz flying out of the office. The pulse of the station had changed, like a heart skipping a beat. Turned out the shell was only a dummy, made of wood and used for training; but it had set them all on edge.

And then there was the other episode. About three o'clock in the afternoon, Naz looked up from his desk to see the entire crew from the tipping floor, including his veteran loader operators, running out of the building screaming *"Saco rojo! Basura infeccioso!"*

Denny burst into Naz's office, panting. Carina glanced up from her work. "Infectious waste on the tipping floor! Pile of red bags."

"Holy shit," said Naz, leaping out of his chair. "Who brought it in?"

"Don't know. The trucks are coming in and out so fast." They ran for the tipping floor. Denny grabbed a binder off the shelf and followed.

The look on Larry Smith's face said it all—he'd found what he needed to shoot this whole deal down. The entire station crew stood out in the yard milling around and mumbling. But Naz was actually relieved. Maybe this was the HIA move he was waiting for. They had spiked a load with medical waste from some hospital. But this Pacific Rim could handle; at least he thought they could.

Denny opened the operations binder he had put together and pointed to the health and safety procedures. Isolate the material. Cordon off the area. Call the County Health Department, and then above all, keep moving the trash.

Then Naz saw Larry Smith kick a toe into the pile of medical waste, his face with a look of disappointment, and then Denny actually pick up one of the bags. Are they out of their minds?

They weren't as it turned out. It was just a pile of red plastic bags, stuffed with garbage from a promotion at one of the local shopping malls. That was good news for the moment, but the feeling of uneasiness fell back over Naz. He knew something was coming, and with each passing hour he would have less time to fix it.

* * *

The day wore on. The sun sank behind the neighboring warehouse throwing the station into shadow. Naz walked out to the tipping floor. The men were tiring, and Naz could feel the production dropping off, but it was past 5:30 p.m. and the second shift was already arriving. The numbers still looked solid. But the good loads seemed to be petering out. They'd have to really work to sort out that last 300 tons. And there was still the issue of Charlie. Where was that old derelict?

Naz walked into the office and found Mrs. Avakian slumped over her typewriter asleep. For twelve hours straight she had run the numbers, made coffee, kept up with them all. Gently, Naz shook her shoulder and she started awake, embarrassed.

"You go home now, Mrs. Avakian."

"I'm fine."

"No, you go home. We'll need someone fresh in the morning. God knows, the rest of us will be dead on our feet."

"I want to stay."

Naz patted her on the back. "You will help us more by getting some rest. We'll be all right."

Reluctantly, she turned off her Selectric and reached for her purse. "OK, but I'm coming back early. I don't want you celebrating without me."

"We'll keep the champagne on ice, just for you."

As Mrs. Avakian brushed past Naz, she leaned over and kissed him on the cheek. Naz smiled after her. Not only did he have to win this bid for his family and his company, he had to win it for people like Mrs. Avakian.

He watched his secretary drive off, then walked over to the parking area where Denny had corralled the second shift. As he pumped himself up for his second speech of the day, Naz saw his litter crew picking wind-blown paper off the perimeter fence. Denny had them covering all the bases.

One shift down, one to go.

* * *

The phone rang on Alex Hart's desk and he answered. "Yeah, Joe," he said, after listening a moment. "Twen-ty-nine percent? Like I said before, Agajanian's a vam-pire, he never dies. You've got to drive a stake through his heart. Luckily, we've got the stake." Alex listened, then said, "Don't worry. Just do yourself a favor and stay clear of the compactor—and Joe? Keep your hard hat on. Safety first, you know."

Alex hung up and smiled.

* * *

There was a short pause throughout the plant, as the first shift ended and the second began. The city crew also swapped out personnel—all but Larry Smith, who stayed on, looking haggard and frustrated, and drinking coffee in a steady river.

During this lull in the action and with fatigue already setting in, no one noticed back in the shadows of the transfer truck loading area, the glint of a metal cylinder lowering into the compactor chamber. The welder's tank clunked softly as it nestled down against the hydraulic ram. A man's figure dissolved back into the bowels of the plant.

Twenty minutes later, the second shift was in position and the first loads of the last twelve hours tumbled up the incline conveyors. Carina walked over to the compactor to check on the weld that Charlie had touched up on the hydraulic line. All looked good. The loader charged another bucketful of trash into the compactor hopper, and Manny engaged the controls that started the heavy ram forward. Carina turned and walked away.

She heard just the first split second of the blast, then the concussion knocked her to the floor.

In his office, Naz had settled back in his chair, the second shift off to a solid start. Jack sat in front of him, looking tense and haggard—like the rest of them. Denny was running projections of numbers in Carina's office.

Suddenly, the loud "whumpff" had rattled the office windows and shook the floor. Their first thought was earthquake. But the ground stayed firm. It was just one boom. Then they heard the men screaming from the load out area.

Naz dashed out of the office, Jack and Denny in tow. A group of the men were bunched in front of the compactor. He could see twisted metal sticking up behind them.

Naz broke through the crowd. Carina and a couple of the men had just picked themselves up and were checking to see if they were all in one piece. Naz grabbed Carina, a worried look in his face. "You all right?"

"Yeah, except for the ringing in my ears." She stretched her jaw and pressed her fingers into her jawline.

They all turned to the compactor. Its loading hopper and ram looked like grotesque flowers, the metal twisted up and out like petals.

"Jesus," Denny whispered.

"We're dead in the water," Jack said.

The men gathered around and Naz reassured them, patting them on the back. "Don't worry. It's all right. Go back to your stations," Rodrigo yelled it out in Spanish.

Naz stopped as Joe Kirby and Larry Smith approached.

The HIA attorney looked past Naz at the ravaged compactor. "You're lucky no one was killed," he said. "Two miracles in one day. That's your quota. But hey, thirteen hours! That's twelve and a half more than I figured you'd last."

Naz just glared back, as Joe Kirby headed toward the pay phone.

Larry Smith looked at Naz with a sense of relief. "Wish I could help you, but you know the rules."

"If there's one thing I know, it's the goddamn rules," Naz said, "But we still got twelve hours."

As Larry Smith walked off, Denny, Carina and Jack gathered around Naz, heads hanging, bodies slumped in despair.

"Forget the compactor," Naz said, twirling the butt end of a cigar in his mouth. "We'll move transfer trucks up next to the residue pile and top-load them over the side with the Cat."

"That top-loading will be way too slow," said Jack.

"Don't worry, Jack," Naz said. "I got a plan. You just keep loading that trash out as fast as it'll go."

As Jack walked off, Naz noticed something peculiar down in the compactor chamber. He grabbed a piece of rebar and climbed down in. He jabbed the bar into the debris, trying to dislodge something that was stuck behind what was left of the ram blade.

"What're you doing?" Carina shouted down at him.

"Looking for a souvenir." Naz grunted, the bar jerked, and he reached down and held up a charred chunk of metal.

"What is it?" she said.

"Looks like the top of one of those acetylene cylinders," Naz replied. "You know, the stuff for blowtorches. From the way the metal's blown out, looks like this cylinder was wedged between the top of the ram and the cutoff bar. Pretty hard for it to get in that position all by itself. When the ram came forward to crush that first load...."

"Charlie had a cylinder like that," Carina said.

"What?"

"Yeah. He showed me one day. In his shipping container. He welds little sculptures of trees with it."

Denny said, "He's probably five miles from here by now. Still running."

"It's hard to believe Charlie would do this," she said.

"I believe anything," said Naz, as he climbed up out of the hopper with a wry smile on his face.

"What are you smiling about?" she said. "It's pretty much over, isn't it? I mean, even if we hit the recycling target, we'll never get enough transfer trucks loaded—like Jack said."

Naz threw his arm around his daughter and they walked back to the office. "I got a contingency plan."

"Another one?"

"I knew HIA would try something. No way they would let us pass this test. This was it. They shot their wad."

*   *   *

At the sound of the explosion, Charlie had jumped and lunged for Black, who was trying to get up, his claws scraping on the metal floor. Charlie heard the screams, the panic outside. It sounded like someone was dying, and he prayed it wasn't Carina. Enough people had died because of him. He had cupped his hands over his ears and started humming, hoping it would drown out what he didn't want to hear. He rocked back and forth, eyes shut tight.

*   *   *

Naz walked into his office, chomping on an unlit cigar like it was toffee. His Achilles heel was the compactor. He knew it—HIA knew it. So, he'd started thinking of a back-up plan. In the industrial gut of LA, south and east of downtown, the rail spurs ran like spider webs. All connecting to the main line coming up from the harbor and then turning east for Colton, San Bernardino and high desert beyond, including Cousin Armand's landfill.

Weeks ago, with the data he'd gotten from the rail dispatcher on car lengths, he'd paced off the spur behind Pacific Rim and found it was long enough to hold ten open-top coal cars. The railroad was his answer, and he had them waiting in reserve. But he knew that if he exposed his plan too early, that it too would be vulnerable. To lose his rail option would be to lose all. So he'd held it back...until now.

Naz pulled a business card out of his shirt pocket. He cradled the phone in the crook of his neck and punched in the number.

"Hello, Mr. Taylor? This is Nazareth Agajanian... right. I need those coal cars...One in the morning? You said 11:00 tonight! Goddammit, what kind of railroad you running anyway?" Naz ran his fingers through his hair, trying to calm down. He needed this train, even if it was late. "Look, Mr. Taylor, this is life and death on this end! All right, yeah...midnight?"

Naz twirled the cigar in his mouth, as if the motion was turning the tumblers in his head, figuring how long it would take to load each rail car. "Yeah, OK. That'll work. But goddammit, those cars better be sitting on my spur at midnight! I'll load 'em by six...What?...Bet your ass that's fast. Then your eastbound coal train will pick them up, right?...OK. This works the way I think and we win this bid, we're talking a hundred-car train every other day for twenty years...yeah, I know. That is one shitload of trash."

Naz hung up. He walked into the restroom and looked in the mirror. Blood-shot eyes starred back at him. He splashed cold water on his face and the back of his neck and allowed himself one moan of exhaustion. Then he threw open the door and pounded out as it slammed against the wall.

* * *

Ten o'clock. Only eight hours to go. Naz knew he was running out of time, even with the maximum effort they were making to top-load the transfer trucks. He had seen the latest numbers from Carina and Denny, but he could just as well have read the result on their faces. They weren't close to making it. He just hoped that the Harts would become more and more secure with each passing hour that Pacific Rim's effort was futile. That they were dead. Then they would relax their guard, not cripple him again.

He was still worried about Charlie, and whoever else HIA may have planted among his work force, but he couldn't conceal his plan any longer. It was now or never—the final move.

Harry, Jack, Carina and Denny gathered around Naz in his office. "Okay, I'm going make this real short," he said. "Here's where we stand, and Carina, you've been running the numbers so tell me if I'm wrong."

"I've had plenty of practice," she answered.

"Don't need numbers, Nazareth," Harry said, pointing out the window with his cane. "Trash piling up."

"Yeah, I know, but just listen. OK? We've got the 25% diversion part knocked. We pulled almost thirty percent of the first 2,000 tons. And since then, we've been getting at least twenty or twenty two. Jack's got them kickin' ass up on the line. I'm not worried about that. What I am worried about…." Naz paused to light the stub of a cigar he held in his teeth "…is the load out. We ain't going to make it."

"I told you that two hours ago," said Jack.

Naz walked behind Jack and put his hands on his brother-in-law's shoulders. He could feel the tension in the muscles. "So...we're gonna make a little change to the load out plan," Naz said. They all waited.

"To what?" asked Denny.

"Rail."

"Rail?" said Jack, jerking around to look at Naz like he was crazy.

"As in railroad." Naz walked up to a flip chart, picked up a marker, and sketched a crude diagram. "We unbolt the sheet metal panels here, and open up the back wall, looking out on the old railroad spur."

Naz pointed at the board. "Here's our spur. I got a Union Pacific switch engine coming with empty coal cars. When it backs the cars in, they'll sit right at loading height off our floor. Remember, this used to be an old bulk storage plant. They loaded cars just that way. We push trash out through the openings in the wall and load those sonuvabitches with every thing we got. They hold a hundred-ton apiece. Eight or nine cars and we'll have it."

Nobody said anything. They just looked, incredulous.

"Well? Are you dead?"

"How do we get the loaded cars to the landfill?" said Denny.

"Union Pacific hooks them on the tail of the empty coal train heading back to the mine in Utah. The train passes right by the landfill and drops them on the abandoned spur. UP loves it. Pure revenue for them on a back haul. Cousin Armand can unload the cars at the landfill with a crane for now. Long term, I looked at a rotary coal car tipper he can buy from the Fontana steel mill that just closed down."

"I'll be goddamned, Naz," said Jack shaking his head, a frozen smile on his face.

Naz said, "We get our own cars, our own train, railroad will think they died and went to trash heaven."

Naz shot out commands. "Carina, you get the guys with the air wrenches and unbolt that sheet metal. Denny, you tell the city what we're planning. Use all those big words. They'll scurry around seeing if it matches the rules. Keep them out of our hair. My guess is they never thought of this—so we're good. Jack, you keep the top-loading going. Every ton in a truck is one less we got to shove into the rail cars, and it's going to be close. We're short on time."

"We're short on space, too" said Jack. "We're piled twelve feet high across the whole goddamn building."

Naz said, "Stack it to the rafters if you have to."

The group moved out and left Naz alone with Harry. Naz said, "Think we're going to make it?"

"Sound little crazy, Nazareth. But we give bastard run for money, huh?"

"I'm trying. Now, you keep those forklifts running. We got a couple hundred bales to load out before six a.m. You holding up okay?"

Naz took his dad under the elbow as the old man shuffled for the door.

"Sometime, I close my eyes little bit. That good enough." Harry glanced up at the picture of Mt. Ararat hanging above Naz's desk. Naz followed his gaze.

"I won't let you down, Pop."

Harry pinched Naz on the cheek and ambled away.

*   *   *

"Are you sure?" Kail Hart said, facing Alex across his desk.

Alex nodded. "Just got the call from my inside contact at Pacific Rim. Coal cars."

"The same inside contact that gave you their bid number?"

"He blew up the compactor. I've got him lined up for 200 grand. Believe me—it's coal cars."

Kail shook his head, then gathered himself. "Those tracks are coming up from the harbor."

"We'll backtrack from Pacific Rim south along the main line," Alex said, thinking out loud. "Stop the train."

A tight smile pulled at the old man's face. "I should never have let you handle this."

"His compactor's down for good," Alex said. "Once I stop the train, it's over."

Kail rose from his chair and threw his pen down. "You don't stop the train, it's also over! You had the bid wired, we lost that! He'd never pass the performance test, now he's passing! With all your reassurance we are hours away from losing the bid, the merger, everything!"

Alex clenched his fists. It was all he could do to stop himself from leaping over the desk. "I'll stop that train."

*   *   *

The switch engine and its string of empty coal cars

rumbled through the night along the L.A. River a few miles south of Pacific Rim.

The engineer turned his collar up against the damp air that blew in the window of the locomotive. He was reaching for his thermos of coffee when a red flare flashed on the tracks ahead, then a moving white light signaling. A man stood off to the side of a car stalled across the tracks, waving a flashlight at him. The engineer hammered on the brakes, the wheels locked and squealed along the steel rails. The cars behind banged into their couplings.

Finally, the train stopped just short of the car. The engineer slumped, trembling at the controls. He turned a moment later to see the huge man with the flashlight climbing into the cab.

"Sorry about that," the man said. "My car died on the tracks, broke an axle, I think."

The engineer reached for the radio-phone. "You're lucky I could stop."

Zaven Petoyan pulled out a gun.

"Hey!" the man yelled, backing away.

Zaven pointed the gun at the engineer's head. "There's a spur a couple hundred yards back. Just back up onto that."

The engineer turned white, slowly released the brake and started to back the train.

* * *

Pacific Rim steamed in the night. Vapors rose up from the mounds of trash, from the bodies of the men, from the engines of the trucks. The men were nearly done unbolting the back wall.

They were ready.

Naz checked his watch and frowned. It was after midnight. Six hours to go. Where the hell was his train?

*   *   *

Charlie heard the air wrenches over the normal din. Black was restless and woofed. Charlie quickly grabbed his muzzle.

"Shhh, Black."

Charlie listened. What was happening?

As many times as he'd fucked up in his life, he knew this was the biggest. He'd be lucky to get out of this alive.

He reached up and touched his neck, where the bruises where. His fingers trembled. Again, he played the attack in his mind, picturing the river, the hands, the voice, the man. And this time, a memory flitted at the fringe of his consciousness—still unrecognizable, but resolving, like a figure approaching through the mist.

21

"Union Pacific lost our train," Naz said as Carina walked into his office.

"What?"

Naz hung up the phone.

"I called the rail yard. The dispatcher told me the train was on its way, but he can't raise the engineer. He's calling the police and railroad security."

"That could take hours, right?" she said. "Can't he send another train?"

"Those are the only cars he has, and even if he could, it wouldn't be till tomorrow."

"How can they lose a train in the middle of L.A.?"

"Maybe someone wanted it to get lost," Naz said, weariness in his voice.

"HIA? How would they find out?"

"Maybe someone over heard. Maybe someone rifled my desk and found the sketches I made. Someone from the city? Maybe the room is bugged. Maybe Charlie's hiding under the floor. Who the fuck knows? I kept it under wraps long as I could." Naz slumped back against his desk.

"I better call the guys in," Carina said. "Maybe they can think of something."

"Yeah," Naz said listlessly. "Maybe."

As Carina left to round up the team, Naz walked out into the plant and sat on one of the catwalk steps. All of sudden, he felt as if he'd been underwater for hours, days, years, holding his breath, and now he was ready to take a lungful of water and drown.

Carina, Denny and Jack walked over. All the air seemed sucked out of Naz. The others had never seen him like this and didn't know how to react. Jack looked at the floor. They heard Harry's cane tapping across the yard and the old man shuffled up. It had just started to sprinkle and drops of rain were lit up like diamonds in the wisps of his hair.

Naz saw Larry Smith and Joe Kirby approaching. The HIA attorney looked freshly scrubbed in a crisp white shirt with the sleeves rolled up, his pleated slacks, thinning hair brushed back and blown dry.

Denny held up his hand in front of the two men. "Private meeting."

"You don't look so good, Naz," Joe Kirby shouted. "Can't say as I blame you, though. Seeing as it's past midnight and you've got...." he glanced at Larry Smith's clipboard, "...oh, eight hundred tons to go on the load out."

Larry Smith added, "You're walking a very fine line here, Mr. Agajanian. Although the test parameters don't stipulate the method of load out, the shift from compact-ing into truck trailers to top loading rail cars is unortho-dox to say the least. And as Mr. Kirby stated, it looks like it's just a matter of time now."

"Thanks for the encouragement," Carina yelled back. "We'll get back to you." She and Jack turned their backs to the two men, blocking their view of the huddle.

Carina saw Harry's eyes twinkling, a slight smile on his face. Her *Babig* had always been magical to her, like he was laughing at some cosmic joke that no one else could hear. She thought in that moment how much she loved him. His spirit never flagged, even when everyone else's did.

"Make new train," Harry said.

Carina said, "What new train?"

"There." Harry pointed with his cane past the scale-house and up along the access road that paralleled the river. Everyone looked, then turned back to Harry, confused.

Naz mumbled, "The rain is seeping into his brain."

"You mean the spur along the old warehouse?" Carina said.

Harry nodded.

"What are you talking about?" Naz piped in. "There's no train there."

"Are you talking about those abandoned flatcars?" Denny said.

Harry smiled and nodded. Carina turned to Naz. "We could piggyback them," she said.

"Piggy-back what?" Naz said.

"Roll-off containers." Carina started pacing. "If we could get enough of them, we could put them on the flatcars end to end, two forty-footers per car." She glanced at her grandfather who nodded back. "Then we push the rail cars down here, behind the plant. And top load, just like before."

Naz twirled the stub of a cigar in his mouth.

"Where we going to get that many roll-offs?" said Jack.

"Uncle Garo's." Carina said, her eyes darting. "He's got more than fifty in his yard."

"How do we get them up on the flatcars?" Denny said.

Carina started pacing, just like her father did when he was on to something. "The plant's abandoned. If I remember right, that loading dock is lower, for loading boxcars. We'll just drop the empty roll-offs onto the loading dock and use the Cat 950 to slide them off the dock and onto the beds of the cars. Then we push the loaded cars ahead to position the next ones."

"OK, so even if that works," said Jack. "How do we move the flatcars down here to our spur?"

Carina frowned in thought, then looked up. "We take the two big loaders, one in front pulling and one straddling the tracks behind pushing." She glanced at her father.

Naz struck a match and re-lit his cigar. He blew the smoke at the roof. ""It's a hell of a long shot, but goddamn, at least it's something!" Naz leaped up out of his chair.

Harry smiled and waved his cane in the air.

"Hey, what's going on?" yelled Larry Smith, seeing the meeting breaking up and the Agajanian team running in all directions.

"Just keep your clipboard dry and get ready to start adding," Carina hollered back, then she ran out after Naz. She was so amped up, she didn't even notice that it had started to rain in earnest.

Thirty minutes later, the first of Uncle Garo's roll-off trucks carrying their empty containers arrived at the abandoned warehouse and into the flurry of activity, where men yelled, engines roared and lights flashed. The dark sky filled with diesel exhaust and rain. Like a sheep dog herding his flock, Naz ran and barked and flagged the trucks on, through the muddy slop spewed up by the spinning tires.

Running on adrenaline and hope, the team loaded the flatcars, each with two open-top roll-off containers. Then Naz lined up the loaders one chained in front pulling, and one in back pushing the string of cars. With engines roaring, Naz watched with relief as the cars began to inch forward. Such a small thing—such a beautiful sight.

They were rolling again.

* * *

From an overlooking hill, Alex Hart watched the scene. He pulled the hood of his jacket up over his head against the rain, and peered through binoculars at the activity down at the abandoned spur. He picked up a walkie-talkie and clicked the mike a couple times.

Zaven Petoyan's voice came over. "Yeah?"

"We got a problem," Alex said. "Agajanian's loading roll-offs on flatcars."

"Where?"

"Down the main line track a couple hundred yards. Warehouse with an old spur. He's moving them to Pacific Rim. Where are you?"

"Sitting off the main line a few miles down."

"Maybe we should give Agajanian his train after all."

*   *   *

Goddamn this rain, Naz thought, walking along the track, watching the loaders slipping in the mud and rock. Their solid, smooth tires weren't made for this type of work. Still the string of cars was moving, edging out onto the main line that connected to the spur at Pacific Rim. The metal of the track, cars, and loaders glistened in the rain that was now a steady downpour.

Naz glanced at his watch and swore under his breath. They were almost home, but time was against them.

After what seemed an eternity, the first of the flatcars rolled off the main line and onto the spur behind Pacific Rim.

It was then that Naz heard the sound up the track in the distance, in the spaces between the squealing of the flatcar wheels. He shielded his face from the rain and peered down the main line. Out of the darkness, he saw it. Dim at first, just a dot of white light, then brighter and brighter. He realized it was the locomotive's headlight coming around a bend a half mile or so away and closing.

"Hey, look!" yelled Carina, jogging up to her father. "Could be our train after all! Now they show up."

Naz didn't reply. He just stared at the oncoming light.

In the locomotive, Zaven Petoyan pushed the throttle up and over-rode the deadman switch by tying down the power handle. Moments before Zaven had cold-cocked the engineer and cut the carotid artery in his throat. The engineer's blood was still pumping out and pooling among the dimples on the metal floor.

The train gained speed, hurtling through the dark rain. Thirty, thirty-five miles per hour. The locomotive rocked and clacked over the switches. Up ahead Zaven could see the lights of Pacific Rim and the string of flatcars trailing out the Pacific Rim spur and up the main line.

He opened the cab door and stepped out onto the ladder, saw an opening coming and jumped.

Naz scrambled up the embankment. "That train ain't stopping!" he screamed at Carina. "We got to get the cars off the main line and onto the spur! Now!"

He leaped to the cab of the big Trojan loader at the rear of the string of cars and told the driver to jump. He gunned the engine and butted the loader bucket against the last car and pushed. The cars were moving. Half of them were onto the spur, the rest still strung out along the main line.

Naz could see the locomotive coming toward them. Carina ran up to the loader and screamed at Naz. "You're not going to make it!"

Naz yelled back through the side window. "Tell the others to get off the track and run for it!"

"Dad!!" Carina screamed.

"Get out of here!" he yelled back, as she ran along side him.

The train was closing at 300 yards away. Naz kept pushing until another flatcar was clear of the main track, then another. He was gaining momentum, picking up speed and only two more cars to go.

He heard the roar of his loader, felt the vibration in the steering wheel, saw the light of the locomotive growing larger and larger, the switch for the spur approaching. He was almost clear, floating in a dream of light and sound and rain, and all that existed was the track and then a brilliant light.

The locomotive gored Naz's loader at the tail end of the string of flatcars, and tossed it fifteen feet in the air. It landed on its side and slid down the embankment. The force of the impact derailed the locomotive and its momentum carried it past Pacific Rim, trailing its string of empty coal cars. With a deep boom, it rammed the side of the derelict warehouse. The ground shook. Everywhere was chaos, raging metal. The night caught fire.

Carina and Denny climbed up on Naz's loader, pulled out the broken glass from the window, ripped open the door. Naz lay crumpled inside, his head cut and bleeding, legs bent under the crushed steering column. Denny got his arms under Naz's shoulders and dragged him out. They knelt down next to the lifeless form.

Jack came running up and froze at the sight of Naz, who looked like a rag doll sprawled on the ground. "Oh, God...."

"Help!" Carina screamed into the rain. "Jack, get help!"

But Jack just stood there. Carina leaped up and shook her uncle. "Jack, come on! He's hurt—bad!"

Jack closed his eyes. "I'm sorry. I...."

"Jack!" Carina shook him. "Get help! Call 911! Go!!"

Finally, Jack snapped out of his trance, turned and ran toward the plant.

Denny raised one of Naz's eyelids. He pressed his finger tips to the artery in Naz's throat and felt no pulse.

Quickly, he carried out the CPR training he had learned in the Peace Corps, pulling out the jaw, clearing the throat. Denny took a deep breath, sealed Naz's nose and blew into his mouth.

*   *   *

Up on the hill, the rain ran down Alex's face and over his hands, as he lowered the binoculars. Fire from the locomotive lit the metal walls of the warehouse, and he could see the crowd gathered around Naz's broken body; someone pumping on his chest. Smoke twisted up into the night sky. All around Pacific Rim was devastation. The air reeked of diesel fuel—and victory.

The call came in over Alex's walkie-talkie.

"I guess the train came in a little fast, huh?" the voice said.

"Where are you?"

"About a hundred yards up the track. Gonna finish that last little business."

"Make it quick," Alex said. "No reason for her to suffer."

"You want to do it?"

Alex grimaced.

"I didn't think so."

Alex closed his eyes and felt the rain hitting his head and shoulders. The cold. He had unleashed this animal and wondered if he could ever get him back in his cage. But he needed him now, and knew Zaven would get the job done, one way or the other.

"I'll be at home," Alex said. He heard Zaven click off the line. Alex picked up his binoculars and watched

Joe Kirby walk to his car down in the yard and drive off into the night, his work now over. Then, Alex rose and climbed over the hill, not even minding the mud that slopped up over his shoes. He slid behind the wheel of his car, eased his head back against the headrest and sighed with relief. Goddamn them all!

He had won.

*   *   *

Pacific Rim flashed with light as fire engines, squad cars, and ambulances packed the access road and poured down the embankment to where the adjacent warehouse and locomotive were on fire. Overhead, the blades of a police helicopter thumped the air.

Naz lay on his back on the gurney in the ambulance, the paramedics hooking up machines, jabbing him with needles. His normally olive skin was gray. Carina knelt on the floor, holding her father's hand. Standing at the open rear door, Harry had reached in and was touching Naz's foot that was clad only in a muddy sock. Tears trickled down the old man's cheeks.

Barely conscious, Naz tilted his head slightly toward Carina and whispered, "You all right?"

With tears in her eyes, she nodded.

"Good, good." Naz grimaced and looked down at the needles in his arm. He was having trouble breathing. "How much time left."

"What are you talking about?" she said, wiping dried blood from the corner of his mouth.

"The test...."

"Shhh. You be quiet, now. For once."

Naz gave her hand a little squeeze. It was all he could muster.

"How much time left?"

Exasperated, Carina glanced at her watch. "Three hours, but...."

"Still enough."

"Look, Dad. The test is over. Forget it. You're hurt bad. We're going to the hospital!"

"You stay. Finish the test." Naz coughed and grimaced, blood oozed from the side of his mouth from something broken inside. But he refused to let go of her hand. "You promise?"

Carina closed her eyes, took a deep breath, and let it out. She opened her eyes, nodded, and wiped a tear off her cheek.

Denny walked up and put his arm around her. Jack joined them. They watched the ambulance accelerate past the scalehouse, Harry sitting in the back with Naz. The swirling red lights singed the freeway overpass.

The cop walked up to the group, in his poncho looking like a blue black mountain. "How is he?" Joe Kowalski said.

"Alive enough to make me promise to finish the test," Carina said.

"What did you expect?" said Joe.

Jack just nodded and watched the ambulance disappear. There were tears in his eyes.

"Joe," Carina said, "I need a favor—a big one."

* * *

Charlie struggled keeping Black in check through the

Armageddon that surrounded his shipping container. All the dog's instincts screamed bark, attack, chase, anything but lay still and be quiet. But to his credit, and Charlie's, he did.

By now, the last of the Alpo was gone and Black had crapped in the corner. Charlie had lit a small candle and set it under a coffee can, punctured with holes. But the jasmine smell had just layered like oil over the odor of dog shit and Charlie was growing desperate for fresh air. The candle sprinkled the walls with dots of light, and the container felt like some voodoo festival of darkness and excrement.

Charlie eased up to the doors, still barred tight, and stuck his nose up to the crack. The air outside smelled of fire, diesel and chaos. The whole night had been so catastrophic beyond comprehension, that Charlie had lost sight of his place in it. He felt the living and the dead swirling around him.

And suddenly, Charlie had it. The man. Charlie's body convulsed. He sagged against the doors and gripped the locking bar. His hands were trembling. He saw it all clearly now, the attack at the river.

Charlie reached into his pocket for his bottle.

*　　*　　*

"You what?" said Larry Smith, having just thrown his clipboard into the trunk of his car where he was packing up with his city monitoring team.

"We want to finish the test," Carina said, pulling out the clipboard and handing it back to him.

"Forget it. It's over. Look at this place! This is the

definition of catastrophe." Larry Smith waved his arm around the debris-strewn site. Fire trucks jetted water over the smoldering locomotive. The Union Pacific's men crawled over the carcass of the train, and finally the news crews were setting up with vans on the ground and helicopters overhead.

Carina watched out the corner of her eye as Sergeant Kowalski grabbed a couple rookie cops who were heading toward Pacific Rim and redirect them back near the scalehouse where he had them stretch yellow security tape along the side of the Pacific Rim access road and down the embankment, in effect separating the crash scene from Pacific Rim proper, which he left alone.

"Look Larry, the crash is down there! Carina pointed to the smoldering warehouse. "Our walls are still standing. The men are still here, at least enough of them, and we are finishing the test!"

"You're out of your mind!" Larry Smith yelled. Then he softened for a moment. "Look, Ms. Agajanian, you've made a spectacular effort. We all admit that. But this test is over."

Carina stood right in his face, and spit the words out between clenched teeth. "Either you get your clipboard back out here or we are going to sue your personal chickenshit ass and the city for $523 million!"

"You can't do that."

"You want to bet your career on that?"

"You're out of your mind!"

"We're finishing the goddamn test!"

Larry Smith looked to the heavens and shook his head in disgust. "You're worse than your father, you know that?"

"I'll take that as a compliment. Now, if you'll excuse me, I've got to move 800 tons of trash in three hours."

"Just how in the hell to you expect to do that?"

Carina pushed past him and headed into the yard.

A reporter rushed up, breathlessly speaking into her microphone as her cameraman struggled to keep up. "Here we are at the epicenter of devastation, Pacific Rim Recycling. The air filled with smoke."

She grabbed Carina's arm. "Excuse me? Can you tell me what happened here?"

Carina lifted the reporter's hand off her arm. "Unless you want to get your ass run over, I suggest you get the hell out of here."

On cue, a truck roared past within inches of the reporter, and splattered her with mud. As the reporter scurried off, Carina walked up to Denny, who was gazing out over the tracks and the train wreck. Their flashlights threw circles of light on the ground.

"Got any miracles left?" she asked.

"I don't know if it's a miracle, but take a look." Denny nodded to where the flatcars still sat on the spur behind the plant. "They made it after all, the ones your Dad pushed off the main line before the train hit. The locomotive must've cut them off clean from the loader."

Denny watched Carina's eyes narrow and the muscles in her jaw tighten. She wiped a hand across her eyes and squeezed the bridge of her nose. She took a deep breath, then leaped up on a table.

"All right, goddamn it. Listen up," she yelled. The workers who had been milling in the yard gathered around. In the background the machinery hissed and groaned. The air smelled of burnt metal, and stung in their nostrils.

"It's now 3:00 a.m. We've got three hours to load 800 tons into the containers on those flatcars. And goddammit, we're going to do it." She seemed to swell up, as if the words pumped air into her. The men looked around in disbelief at the disaster. Maybe she was loco with grief.

"Everything we've worked for, everything we care about, jobs for all you men, real jobs, all of it comes down to this. Our flatcars with the rolloffs made it through," she said, pointed out along the spur.

The men looked at each other.

She jumped down from the table. "Manny! Get the guys on the loaders and start moving the trash into those rail cars. Move it!"

"Denny!" she yelled. "You know the rules better than anyone. Stick to Larry Smith. Make sure he doesn't try to disqualify us."

"Jack?" Carina said, grabbing her uncle by the arm, talking fast. "Organize the guys on the sort line. Run a hundred tons through. We need about ten tons more on the recovery side. Just have them skim off the good stuff." Carina noticed the tortured look on Jack's face. "We've got to finish, Jack. For Dad...you OK?"

"Yeah, yeah," Jack said.

"We can still do it, Jack!"

Jack nodded.

Larry Smith walked up. "So what's the deal?"

Carina turned to face him. "We're going to load those flatcars and pass the goddamn test."

"I'll believe it when I see it," Larry said.

Pacific Rim flew into action. Carina was everywhere, barking orders, urging the men on, everything but twirling a cigar in her mouth. The loaders shuffled back and forth like frantic beetles and the station reverberated with the sound of the trash thundering into the rail cars.

*   *   *

Jack wandered into a dark corner of the plant and vomited. He couldn't shake the vision of Naz crumpled on the ground. The blood, that's what had gotten to him. Naz's blood. His best friend. His brother-in-law. No amount of money in this world would ever wash his hands clean. He could never outrun this memory. He realized Madera wouldn't be far enough—nowhere would.

As Jack wiped his mouth, he heard a familiar "pop" from behind the back wall of the building. He walked out and saw a large man, his face shielded by a welder's mask, raise an acetylene torch and touch the flame to the conduit that ran up from the transformer, carrying the primary power into the plant. Sparks flew.

For just a second, Jack hesitated, gauging what he was about to do. But from the moment he had seen Naz's broken body, it had all shifted, and damn the consequences.

Jack plowed into the man, sending the torch flying and knocking off the man's mask. But the big man was quick and even as he went down, threw Jack off of him. Jack scrambled to his feet and faced his adversary, Zaven Petoyan.

He saw Zaven reach across his chest and under his coat. Jack charged him even as the gun with the long silencer came out. He never heard the shot that killed him.

*   *   *

Carina had walked back to her office. She sat at her desk amid a mound of documents and adding machine tapes, checking the tonnages one final time—and now, less than one hour to go. My God, she thought, we're going to make it. She stopped and said a little prayer for her father that he would make it, too.

Then, the lights flickered and went out. She felt the pulse of the plant stop. "Shit!" she whispered, feeling her way to the window and looking out. The plant lay in blackness. The old fear of the dark seeped up into her throat and her heart started pounding, but she couldn't worry about that now. She had to get the power back on or it was all over. She started towards the door.

A beam of light danced in the doorway. It flashed in her eyes for a second and she flinched. Then the beam raced back across the floor and up under the jaw of the figure holding it in the door, a large man with a welder's mask on.

"Jack?"

No reply.

"Jack, what are you doing?" she said. "The test! We've got to get the power back on!" Yelling and panic echoed in from the plant.

The man closed the office door behind him, then pulled out a gun and pointed it at her face.

Carina stumbled back against her desk.

He slipped the welder's mask off his head.

Carina gasped.

"One sound, and I'll blow your fucking head off." Zaven took a step toward her desk, the flashlight beam danced on the floor.

"Stay calm! Stay calm!" her mind screamed. Think! The paperweight, the letter opener, scissors.

She could see the shadowed lines of his face, the black holes of his eyes. She heard the sounds from outside, where all was still madness, men yelling.

She edged back toward her bookshelf, eyeing the piston shaft souvenir.

He said, "So, it's going to be you and me after all."

Carina could smell that hint of aftershave. The same one she had sensed in her bedroom the night of the attack.

"I knew it was you..." she whispered.

"You should've shown me some respect. I could have protected you."

Still facing him, she reached down and behind her, felt the piston and curled her fingers around the cold steel. As terrified as she was, she knew she had to let him get close. She would have only one chance, and as Zaven moved in front of her, the gun held loosely in his hand— she took it.

Carina swung the chunk of metal with all her might. Surprised, Zaven threw up his arm and caught the blow on his wrist. He yelled in pain and dropped the gun.

In a flash, Carina was at the door, but Zaven caught her by the hair and yanked her back and threw her on the desk.

She screamed.

He hit her hard with his fist. The pain shot into her head and she could taste the blood in her mouth. She clenched her teeth and struggled to clear her head. She would not quit, she wouldn't die.

She felt Zaven's hands clamp around her neck. His body crushing down on her, forcing her legs apart. She scratched at his neck, his eyes with her nails. She fought to get out from under him, but he was too heavy. She punched at his face and tried desperately to squirm out of his grasp. But he was strong and crazed.

His hands tightened. She gagged and gasped for breath, her lungs screaming for air. All turning dark.

Suddenly, Zaven's hands relaxed and everything stopped.

Through a blur of tears, she saw Zaven frozen above her. A gurgling sound escaped from his lips. Slowly his hands lifted to his neck, where she saw something glinting, a metal rod run through. Blood ran down Zaven's neck and over his arms. With both hands on the shaft, he tried to scream, but only a hiss came out.

He fell in one piece.

Carina rolled to her side, clutching her throat, gasping in air. She struggled to a sitting position on the desk. The flashlight that had fallen to the floor threw a circle of light on the wall. She saw a figure standing in the doorway, the arm extended with the long metal shaft catching the light.

"Charlie," Carina whispered. "Oh, Charlie."

The little man stood in the doorway and lowered the speargun, his eyes never leaving the body on the floor.

Carina slumped back against the desk. Denny rushed in, nearly falling over Zaven's body. Charlie backed away into the shadows.

"Carina!" Denny yelled, panic in his voice. He grabbed her in his arms. She started crying.

"Zaven attacked me." She pulled away, wiping the tears from her cheeks with her hands. "The lights went out. He came in...." Carina's voice trailed off.

"That's OK," Denny said. "Easy now."

"Charlie killed him."

Denny turned and noticed Charlie for the first time.

"I got that fucker," the old derelict said. "I remembered. I knew that voice."

"I'll get Sergeant Kowalski," Denny said. "He's still out at the train."

Carina grabbed his arm. "Wait. Just give me a minute. Got to think. We're so close. They'll stop everything." She sat on her desk, rubbing her neck, trying to clear her throat. Her whole body was trembling.

Denny stooped and checked Zaven. His eyes were frozen open, turning glassy. A gurgle rasped from his lungs. "I think he's gone."

Charlie cleared his throat. "It's my fault."

"How could it be your fault?" said Denny.

"Look, stop...stop." Carina eased off the desk and stood up. "Jesus Christ." She grimaced and wiped the blood from the corner of her mouth, checked her jaw. She reached out an arm and steadied herself against Denny. She could hardly stand, but she had to. She couldn't let her emotions run over her.

Denny held her. "Come on. Sit down."

She put a hand on his chest and gently pushed him away. "I'm all right." She wiped her nose on her sleeve.

"You don't look all right," he said.

"We'll worry about Zaven later. If we stop, they'll say we failed. Let's pass the test. Then the police can do whatever they want."

Denny read the determined look in her eyes and nodded.

"See if you can find out about the power," Carina said to Denny. "And get Jack, maybe he can fix it." Then she stepped around the body and walked slowly out of the office, leaning on the door jamb on the way out.

Denny came up to her on the tipping floor a few minutes later, their flashlights casting shadows. She could tell by the look on his face that something else had gone wrong.

"I found Jack," he said, grimacing.

"Oh, no."

"Zaven must've shot him. He's out back, behind a dumpster, where Zaven cut the transformer conduit."

Carina started to rush past, but Denny caught her. "He's gone, Carina. I covered him with a blanket. You don't want to see."

Carina slumped in Denny's arms and closed her eyes. She breathed steadily and deeply as if that alone would pump her up and keep her from collapsing.

"Oh, God," she said. "I don't know if I can...."

"Let's finish the test," Denny said. "There's nothing else."

22

The sky was still black as the wrought iron security gate rolled back and Alex Hart pulled up the driveway and into his garage. He checked his watch. In one hour, the Pacific Rim performance test would officially be over. He got out of his car, slipped off his muddy shoes and walked through the kitchen into the living room.

The long battle was over, the victory secure. He smiled and gave in to the sweet exhaustion. He felt light and free, as if barely tethered to the ground. Like he had felt after so many football games, battered, intoxicated, but serene. It was too bad about Carina. But business was like war and there were casualties.

He was just about to turn on the lights when she called out to him from the dark.

"About time, Alex."

He flinched and flicked the light on. Barbara Miller sat on the couch.

"Where's Julia?" said Alex. He was beginning to feel like a trapped animal. This woman had claws that could rip a plane out of the sky.

"Oh, a bit of bad news, I'm afraid." Barbara picked up a note from the coffee table. "Seems Julia got a call from the doctor. Her mother, poor thing, has taken a turn for the worse and...."

Alex snatched the note from her.

"...she had to leave for the nursing home."

"Jesus Christ! Is there anything you can't fix?" he said.

"Well, I've never been very good at horse races, but then people are so much more predictable than animals." Barbara crossed to the couch and sat down. "I heard there was an unfortunate mishap with our low bidder early this morning."

"Good news travels fast."

Alex grabbed a beer out of the refrigerator, and walked toward the bathroom. "Think I'll take a fast shower. Get out of these clothes."

"Let me know if you need any help," Barbara said.

* * *

At USC County Medical Center, Naz Agajanian's body lay on the operating table. The surgeons worked over him. Machinery breathed for him, pumped his blood, triggered his heart, fed him. Lines of brain waves and heart beats zipped across monitors. Alarms beeped. The doctors gave commands in soft, stern voices. He was slipping away.

Mayda sat in the waiting room, wrung out from crying, twisting a damp handkerchief in her fingers, whispering a prayer. Harry and Armi sat stoically with her, holding hands.

*   *   *

Just out of the shower, Alex toweled himself off briskly, as if scraping off an unwanted layer of skin. It was time to think of the future. And with the old derelict, Carina and Naz eliminated, his smuggling operation was once again secure. When everything had blown over, he could ramp it back up. And he'd have his men track down the ingot that the old junkman had stolen and get it back. How far could he have gone, pushing it in a shopping cart?

He had the power now. Once the contract was signed and the trucks were rolling, nothing could stop him. Not Nazareth Agajanian, not Barbara Miller, not even his father, the Boxing King.

He thought about Johnny. He would do it this time. Get his son back. Twelve-year-old boys want to live with their fathers, right? They could throw the ball in the backyard. He'd teach him some patterns—buttonhook, deep post, fly. Feed him real food. Put a little bulk on him. Johnny could do it, he had the talent, a second generation at USC. Men of Troy—together.

The phone rang.

Alex wrapped a towel around his waist, walked to the bedroom and answered.

"Yeah?" he said.

"Congratulations," the familiar voice said.

Alex's face tightened. "I told you, you worry too much."

"A little over-dramatic perhaps, but affective nonetheless," his father said. "I've notified Global. Their Board will ratify the merger contract later this week."

"Good," Alex said. "I'll see you later this morning at the office."

"It's a new day, Alex."

"It sure is." A wry smile crossed Alex's face, as he hung up. Tomorrow he would begin negotiations with the city. Pass the performance test in a cake walk. Within days, 3,000 tons a day of that beautiful L.A. trash, would be coming to HIA. All he had left to do was call the special meeting of the Board and dethrone both the Chairman and his merger. Those East Coast vultures could shove their ratified contract up their ratified ass. He couldn't wait to see the look on his father's face, when, after all these years, he finally hit him back. And this would be a knockout punch.

Alex walked back down to the living room wearing a black robe. He popped a second beer, took a long belt. God, he felt good, like the world was laid out at his feet. Barbara sat on the couch, one leg crossed over the other, the supporting foot up on its toe. He noticed the curve of her arch, the tightened calf. Her dress had slipped up her thighs, and her small breasts pressed out under her silk blouse. In truth, she was looking good tonight. Hell, Julia would never know. Time to celebrate.

He crossed the floor and held out his hand. She took it.

"Maybe we should toast Mr. Agajanian for providing us this wonderful evening," she said, kissing Alex on the cheek.

"Come down to the wine cellar with me. You can pick out a bottle for the occasion."

He kissed her forearm and waltzed her across the room. He turned on the light to the cellar and led her down the stairs. His bottles of fine wine were nestled in their cradles, and he patted them gently as he walked by. It was the only extravagance he allowed himself.

"What's that smell?" Barbara said.

"What smell?" Alex tried to breathe through his nose, but since the punch from his father it had been all broken up inside.

"Almost like rotten eggs," she said.

"It's a wine cellar, Barbara, nearly down to bedrock. It's just dampness, the smell of the earth."

"Weirdest earth I ever smelled."

"So what'll it be?" he said to her. "A Bordeaux? Pinot Noir?"

"You choose," she said, running her hand over his back.

Alex pulled out a bottle, blew the dust off it and set it on a small table with two glasses. He sat on the leather couch at the end of the cellar. He laid his head back, closed his eyes, let the relief pour over him.

"You look tired," she said.

Alex pulled a cigar from the breast pocket of his robe. He reached for his lighter.

"Here, let me," she said, taking the lighter. Alex pulled her onto his lap. He slid his hand up her leg.

The gold lighter shone in her hand, as she flicked open the lid. He watched her perfect manicured nails and long, elegant fingers.

She raised the lighter up off the end of the cigar. "Oooooh," she said with a little start, as he slid his hand up higher.

She rolled her thumb over the flint.

Nothing.

She flicked it again and Alex saw a tiny white spark just before the blinding flash.

* * *

The blast rumbled like an earthquake and lit the predawn sky with fire. The folks living in Eagle Heights stumbled out of their sleep, dazed. They poured out the front doors of their homes in their pajamas and blankets, kids carrying teddy bears and dolls. Men waved flashlights about as the families huddled together and surveyed their broken windows; the air filled with terrified birds and the screaming of car alarms.

Johnny Hart stood in the street with his mother, a blanket draped over his shoulders. He stared at the orange fireball over by the landfill. Then he heard the rumbling underground, like a locomotive coming through the rock. The first manhole at the end of the street blew, shooting a column of fire a hundred feet into the air.

It startled Johnny and he finally realized what was happening. "Dad!" he screamed and he started running up the street toward the landfill, but his mother caught him and wrapped him up in her arms. The boy's whole body was flailing and he screamed over and over. "Dad!"

"Johnny! Come on!" She grabbed his arm and joined

the whole neighborhood running down the street away from the fire. The air itself seemed to be roaring.

Then the house closest to the landfill detonated. The ground floor exploded, blasting out glass, wood and stucco. The second floor collapsed into the fire below.

Then the next manhole went up another fifty yards down the street, and a few seconds later, the next one blew and shot up a wild flare. The fire was licking its way along the vein of landfill gas that had penetrated the sewer.

The crowd panicked. Little kids stumbled, only to be snatched up by terrified parents. Cats scrambled up trees, dogs barked and snapped at each other, running in a makeshift pack.

A second house went off showering the sky with sparks and flaming debris. The trees caught fire and the flames and smoke rolled down the streets. The tiring crowd struggled to get past the next manhole.

And then behind it all, the wail of the first sirens.

*   *   *

Johnny Hart sat in the ambulance, his mother's arms around his shoulders. He sobbed into the blanket. They were bleary-eyed and ashen, their arms and faces bleeding where shards of glass had cut them. Everything smelled burnt, their hair, their clothes, the air. As the ambulance drove off toward the hospital, the siren whined above their heads.

The inferno at the landfill created a massive updraft of super-heated air. Gas that had migrated off the landfill deep into the fissures in the rock, the sewers and basements, was now sucked back by the powerful vacuum to feed the main fireball at the landfill.

The whole canyon was in flames.

* * *

Twenty miles from the blast, and unaware of anything beyond their immediate world, the crew of Pacific Rim raced for the finish line. Naz had wanted them to fight down to the last breath. Well, this was it. The whole crew was near exhaustion and running on fumes, just like the equipment.

Charlie stood in the middle of the yard like General Patton directing tanks at a muddy crossroads in Germany. He waved and flagged and yelled at the drivers as they positioned their cars to illuminate the plant with their headlights.

"Leave the engines running, you idiots!" Charlie screamed. "You'll kill the batteries!"

The loaders were going full tilt weaving in and out of the headlight beams, pushing trash into the last forty-foot roll-off containers that sat on the flatcars behind the plant. The mountain of trash that only a few hours ago had filled Pacific Rim to the rafters was down to a foothill.

Carina checked her watch. Only twenty minutes to go. Her face was bruised, body battered, and her hair seemed to fly with a will of its own.

The clock ticked down.

Ten minutes.

Then five.

The tipping floor was almost clear.

Carina flagged the loader drivers and they lined up abreast, lowered their buckets and pushed. A wall of trash roiled before them across the floor and thundered into the containers.

The tipping floor was clear.

From out in the yard, Larry Smith waved at Carina and drew his hand across his throat. He walked over, muddy, exhausted.

"You can call off the dogs," he said. "The confirmed weigh scale records show 3,000 tons received, 770 recovered and outbound for recycling, leaving 2,230 tons loaded out for landfill disposal. I wouldn't believe it if I hadn't seen it, but you passed. Congratulations, Ms. Agajanian. Hell of a job."

Carina hugged Denny. Her legs were shaky, and she felt him holding her up. She looked over his shoulder to the dock where Charlie was climbing off a forklift. She closed her eyes and the warm tears welled up. She wished her Dad was here to see this—to feel it, to savor the incredible victory. She also prayed silently, that he was still with them at all.

"Thanks, Denny," she whispered, "for everything."

"You did it," he whispered back and gave her an extra squeeze.

As Larry Smith traipsed toward his car, gathering his exhausted monitoring crew with him, word spread quickly around the plant. A roar rose up from the men. Whether they had worked there twelve years or twelve hours didn't matter. They all felt the victory. They had all been caught up in the struggle, the emotion—and they had done it.

As engines and equipment were shut down, Pacific Rim fell silent in the early morning mist, the only sound the hissing from the wrecked locomotive and the spray of a lone fire hose.

Denny handled the aftermath. He guided Sergeant Kowalski to Carina's office and Zaven's body, then behind the plant to Jack. He told him the details to the extent he knew them, Charlie mumbling beside him, head down, dirty, bone weary. Carina filled in the attack by Zaven, and Charlie's heroics. Sergeant Kowalski called in the crime scene investigators who started taking pictures, bagging evidence.

The detectives read Charlie his rights and drove off with him in a black and white with lights flashing for questioning down at the precinct. Denny promised Charlie he would come for him as soon as he could. Charlie looked defiant almost regal through it all, as if he were finally someone to be reckoned with—and he was. Black had sat at Charlie's heels, growling at the cops, then whining when they put Charlie in the car, and finally limping after the cop car, snapping at the rear tire as it drove away.

It was Rodrigo, whose arm still showed the scabs from the bite Black had given him in the fight over the jumper cables, seemingly a hundred years ago, who lured the dog back into Charlie's hearse and set him up with food, water, and his blanket.

When it was finally over, Denny jumped in Carina's car and drove. They fish-tailed past the scalehouse, raced down the access road, and out into the dawn.

*   *   *

Denny and Carina rushed into the intensive care ward, asked at the nursing station and were directed to Naz's room. The nurse had prepped them on what they were about to see, but still the sight took their breath away.

Naz lay in the hospital bed, hooked up to more solutions, monitors, respirators, and machines than they had ever seen. His pelvis was encased in a cast, as was one arm and shoulder braced up at a strange angle by wires from a frame overhead. Naz's skin was blanched of color, except where the bruises flowered. His eyes were closed and he appeared to be sleeping. The heart monitor beeped behind him, the telltale blip pulsing across the screen.

Arrayed around the bed, as if at a séance, were Mayda, Harry, and Armi, who fingered a silver cross in her old hands, and rocked back and forth. Mayda held Naz's limp hand and stared at his face as if her gaze alone could open his eyes. Harry sat within his own thoughts, holding his hat in both hands and resting his forearms on his knees, staring at the floor. Denny stood back, staring at Naz and thinking the worst. The great Agajanian looked like a corpse.

Carina hugged all of them, the tears flowing. Mayda looked at her daughter's face, her cut lip, bruised jaw. A pained look crossed her face. "What happened?"

"I'll tell you later." She looked at her father. "How is he?"

Mayda whispered, "He's in a coma. They don't know. The doctor says he is a fighter. His heart is strong, but…." She dabbed at her eyes with a handkerchief.

Carina moved to the bed and picked up her father's hand. "Dad, I know you can hear me. We passed, Dad. We passed the performance test. We won. We did it."

She squeezed his hand, but felt no reply. She tucked her father's hand under the sheet.

Denny whispered to Mayda. "Do you need anything? Coffee?"

"Yes, coffee. Maybe something to eat."

"I could use an *oghi*," Harry said.

Denny took Carina by the shoulders, and said, "He's going to be all right." Although by the look on his face, she sensed he didn't believe it.

* * *

On the way to the cafeteria, Denny corralled the doctor. "Tell me the reality."

The doctor set down his clipboard, took a deep breath and let it out. "I wish I had better news for you, but I'm afraid his chance of surviving is very low. We're going to try to operate again, but he may be too weak now even for that. His pelvis is broken and his spine received collateral damage. If, miraculously, he were to survive, he'll never walk again."

The doctor clapped Denny on the shoulder. "I'm really sorry. We'll do all we can."

Denny closed his eyes and grimaced, fighting back the tears. He just couldn't believe it, didn't want to believe it. Not after all that had happened. No, God, please not after everything. Just when he had found it, his family was being taken away from him.

As he walked down the corridor, Denny was conscious of the sound of his shoes on the linoleum, the light coming in the windows, the brush of the air, and the gut-wrenching thought that Naz wasn't going to make it.

23
(Ten months later)

They erupted in a standing ovation at the sight of him.
Nazareth Agajanian.

In the flesh and blood.

It had taken what felt like years, including a perilous bout with a staph infection that had just about done what all the broken bones and ruptures couldn't.

He had lost fifty pounds since the train wreck and his tall frame looked frail and gaunt, but his color was back and so was his attitude.

"I can do it!" Naz whispered loudly to Carina, as she tried to guide him up the ramp to the platform of the head table. He looked around. Pacific Rim had been transformed for the occasion. In his honor, the organizing committee had decided to hold the 42nd Annual Rubbishman's Ball at Naz's plant. The entire plant had been steam cleaned revealing surfaces of wall and floor that hadn't seen the light of day for years. New paint on the railings, bollards, sorting equipment. Luminarias had lined the access road on the way in. Red, blue and apricot bunting, the colors of Armenia, framed the large I-beam frames of the main building. The tipping floor had been "recycled" into a ballroom, with a wooden dance floor, tables covered with table clothes, and thousands of white lights strung from every rafter and beam. The pigeons thought they had died and gone to heaven, until the pest control guy had chased them away before the festivities started. But just in case, a large umbrella sprouted from each table, shielding guests and food from any party favors dropped from above.

Naz hated his damn walker, but at least he was moving under his own power, and that in itself was a miracle. He was proud of the fact that they'd put his case in the annals at the hospital. What the hell did those doctors know anyway?

Dead my ass!

Can't walk my ass!

Naz struggled into his seat and waved his hands for everyone to sit down—his family and friends, fellow trashmen and recyclers, guys from the mills and export companies, Rodrigo and Manny and their families, his banker who had rushed through the house re-financing, Sergeant Kowalski and of course, Mrs. Avakian. All here to celebrate not just Naz's return to the living, but the victory on the bid and the surge of optimism it had sent coursing through the L.A. trash community.

It felt good being back after the long road through intensive care, physical therapy, the hurting and healing. He was just beginning to feel his old self again, and he couldn't wait to get to work, especially with the new city contract. When he had first heard of the victory, he had nearly launched himself out of the bed and run down the hall, I.V. tubing and electrodes trailing behind him like streamers. But since he hadn't been at Pacific Rim for nearly a year, it was still hard for Naz to fully get it—they had won. It wasn't a dream.

Now here he was with his whole family arrayed across the front table: Mayda, his Mom and Dad, his sister Sophie and her two girls, and at the far end of the table, Carina and Denny. Only Jack was missing.

One by one, the guests came up and hugged Naz, or patted him on the hand. God was thanked a hundred times, and Saint Gregory the Illuminator, the patron saint of Armenia. Naz would nod in acknowledgment, blow them kisses across the table.

Naz nodded at Carina and Denny. He had to laugh at the memory of Denny in his suit coming to the hospital to ask to "pick a rose from their garden," the formal Armenian request to the parents to marry their daughter, even though they were only moving in together. And Mayda screaming in delight and grabbing his injured shoulder. That whole fiasco had almost killed him.

And as much as it had bothered him, Carina with an *Odar*, an outsider, he had to admit this Denny was all right. In fact, he was more than all right; he was terrific, well, for a white boy. Between the two of them, Carina and Denny had launched the whole L.A. project within the sixty-day deadline. Sure, they had consulted with him in the hospital, but what could he really do? Hell, for the first two weeks, he was unconscious. Yes, perhaps the Denny-Carina affair would all work out in the end. So it hadn't turned out exactly as he had planned. Could there be a larger plan at work? Well, who the hell knew. But regardless, Naz decided he would teach Denny how to marinate the lamb. That much was necessary.

Carina and Denny, with the help of Mrs. Avakian, had resurrected the plant, built permanent rail loading ramps, hired the workers, harassed the UP for an upgrade of the spur, fought the IRS and not only got the lien removed, but paid the back taxes with a loan secured by the contract.

Naz had even gotten used to it, over time of course, this delegation of authority. What choice did he have? He couldn't leave his bed. And it had all happened, somehow, without him. And good thinking, too—innovative, "ahead of the curves" as Mayda would say. Naz smiled. Maybe he didn't need to push so hard anymore...nah. He'd push till the day he died, but now he'd let the others push a little, too.

And now the trash train was rolling every other day, one hundred cars long, rumbling from Pacific Rim east through the San Gabriel Valley, along the main line to Colton, over the Banning Pass, through Palm Springs and the Coachella Valley, down the shores of the Salton Sea, and into the barren hills of Imperial County, the Indian Reservation and the Rainbow Ridge Landfill. Oh, it was a sight to see. The most beautiful train in the world, better than the Orient Express.

The meal was served, busboys scurrying around, carrying plates of food. The sound of clattering dishes spilled out of the makeshift kitchen set up in a tent in the parking lot. The air smelled of booze, lamb and smoke. Occasionally, the scent of floral centerpieces broke through.

Naz picked at his pilaf, pushing the rice around with his fork.

Mayda glanced at him, then put her hand on his forearm. "You should eat."

"Yeah," Naz replied and stabbed a piece of asparagus.

Mayda read the sadness on his face. "Nazareth, you must let Jack go. It's over now."

"I could have done more, brought him in even more, told him how important...."

Mayda took Naz's chin in her fingers and turned his face toward her. She kissed him on the corner of his mouth. "Don't do this to yourself, Nazareth."

"How could I be so blind? In my house, my family?"

"It was the gambling. He was sick."

Naz shook his head, and winced at the memories. The cops had dug out the logs of phone calls from Jack's home and the plant to Alex's office, right up to the last, during the performance test. God, the whole thing. The revelations spilling out like a toppled basket of rotten fruit, crawling with maggots.

Naz set his fork down on the plate, picked up his glass and pounded back a shot of *oghi*. And for the moment, he swallowed the feelings of guilt and anger and betrayal, and let the *oghi* do its job. After all, Jack had come back at the end and fought to save Pacific Rim, to undo at least some of the damage he had done. Jack had come back to the family in the end.

"You are alive," Mayda said. "We will go on now, and do what we can. The rest—we leave to God."

"You're right," Naz said. "From now on, any new shelves for the frogs—God puts them up. He can borrow my hammer."

Mayda smiled. "I don't joke with God, if I was in your shoes."

Naz took another bite of asparagus and smiled back at Mayda, the old familiar twinkle flashing for a second in his eyes. He glanced down to the end of the table, where Sophie sat, crushing her napkin in her hands, head bowed, thoughts a million miles away. She, too, had lost fifty pounds in the aftermath, which in her case was an improvement. Naz caught her eye and smiled. She came back from wherever she had gone and smiled back, but it was a sad smile. Naz realized that her life would never be the same either, and wondered if she would be able to pick up the pieces.

He poured himself another shot of *oghi*.

But all in all, life moved on, and so would all of theirs—even Kail Hart's.

Naz thought of the fallout over the blast at the HIA landfill that had rocked old man Hart just as surely as if he had been standing in that wine cellar. Everything he had worked for his whole life had been obliterated, including his son. And that was just the beginning of the unraveling of HIA. The landfill, or what was left of it, was now a "Superfund Site." There were endless lawsuits. And of course the merger was gone, and in its place a grand jury investigation. Then, too, when it had been discovered by tracing pieces of her car, that Barbara Miller had died with Alex—the whole connection with City Hall had flared up to the front page of the *Times*. Bank records, undeclared campaign contributions, cash deposits.

And in a final grim twist, the body of Zaven Petoyan, in all its bloody horror, had brought in the attacks on Carina and Charlie—and murder. Naz could picture Kail standing alone on the rim of the crater at the landfill, with nothing left of his life but the smoke rising up around him.

Naz shook his head at the one final irony—that so much of all that had happened, of the horror, the victory, could be traced back to Charlie and that stolen ingot. With Alex's records thrown open, the smuggling scheme was revealed, the "special" accounts, the payments to certain HIA Board members. And ultimately, the plan to oust his father. That would be the deepest cut of all to Kail Hart—and one that would bleed for the rest of his life.

Life was a strange thing, Naz thought. Best to take what's given you at the moment. Tomorrow? Who knows?

Naz finished off his *oghi*.

Seeing Denny and Carina talking, and thinking of all that had been accomplished in the past few months, Naz wondered again whether they still needed him. But then the Armenian folk band kicked off into a song and that thought evaporated. He cracked open an aluminum tube and pulled out his first new Cuban cigar since the accident, well, the first that Mayda knew about, anyway.

Mayda looked at him, incredulous.

"What?" Naz said.

"Doctor Halajian told you!"

"I won't inhale," Naz said, striking a match and lighting the cigar.

"This is what I get for praying for twelve days you are in a coma?"

Naz looked at Mayda with a sparkle in his eyes. She

knew that look, the sneaky smile, then under the table the touch of his hand on her thigh. "You just try it!" she said. "You'll be lucky you don't go into another coma, and this time I don't pray one second for you."

"Remember that night on the beach in Palos Verdes?" Naz said, inhaling his cigar deeply.

"Of course I remember, mostly the sand everywhere, my hair, and other places."

Naz leaned over and kissed her. "I promise tonight— no sand."

She pinched his cheek. Naz blew her a smoke ring.

The celebration roared along powered by the high spirits and high blood alcohol. With the demise of HIA and Zaven Petoyan, it seemed as if a heavy cloud had been lifted from over the Los Angeles basin. The light of the open market was shining again, new hauling companies were already springing up, recycling programs proliferating and the little guys from Pacoima to Orange County were rejoicing and most of them bringing their trash and recyclables to Naz. Over seventy-five of the families were here tonight, and for them it was almost as much a renaissance as it was for the Agajanians.

*   *   *

Finally, the night began to wind down. As great as it had been, one of the best of his life, especially considering they could have been celebrating his funeral, Naz was tiring and his pelvis was killing him. He reached for his walker, when unexpectedly, the lights dimmed. A hand-held spotlight lit the area by the baler. Heads turned to look.

Behind the baler, Carina said, "Come on Charlie, you can do it."

Charlie peered around at the faces. He was all cleaned up, hair trimmed—virtually unrecognizable from his old self. "That's more people than I seen in twenty years." He looked down at his hands sticking awkwardly out of a rented tuxedo. They were shaking.

"Well, Denny and I aren't going out there without you," she said.

Charlie rocked from side to side. Denny motioned over a passing waiter and handed a glass of champagne to Charlie. He jerked it down in two gulps. The waiter turned to leave but Charlie grabbed his coat sleeve, lifted another glass off the tray and drained it. "Now or never," he belched at Carina.

"I hear you," Carina replied, downing her own glass. "Let's go."

Carina and Denny lifted a six-foot board, draped with a black cloth, and walked out into the spotlight. Charlie ambled along behind, as if towed along by the edge of the light, his head down, hands gripped together in front of him.

The little procession wound its way through the crowd and approached the head table. Naz recognized Carina and Denny, but didn't have a clue as to the guy bringing up the rear. What the hell is this, he thought.

The spotlight illuminated Naz as they placed the board in front of him. Carina stepped behind the microphone. Naz reached out a hand to peek under the cloth, but Mayda gently slapped it away.

They had set him up. Goddamn, he whispered to

himself. He pulled the cigar out of his mouth and allowed a smile to crack.

Carina's voice boomed out, "As you all know, there's been a lot happening with us for the last few months. And for a while, well, we weren't so sure how it would all turn out...you know, the part with Dad...." She wiped her eyes. "Well, I'm just real proud to be his daughter," her voice quivered, "and to be part of this great family." She saluted her grandfather. His eyes twinkled back and he waved his cane in reply, the old gold handled one he had offered up for the football at the Hall of Fame Banquet. She also nodded to Sophie and the two girls, who stared back at her from some distant world of pain and shock. Carina swallowed, hesitated for a moment, trying to hold herself together.

Naz couldn't watch her anymore and lowered his eyes to the table, breathing softly.

"Boy," Carina continued, "this might be harder to get through than that performance test." She laughed and the crowd joined in.

"Tonight we celebrate!" she said.

Cheers and applause rang out.

"To the health and long life of the winner of one of the largest bids in the history of Los Angeles! Founder and CEO of Pacific Rim Recycling, my dad, Nazareth Agajanian!"

The crowd exploded in applause, cheers, and whistles. Naz looked up, embarrassed for one of the few times in his life, but soaking it in just the same.

"In commemoration," Carina went on, "we have something to present to Dad from all of us at Pacific Rim, and in particular, Mr. Charles Goodnight, who made it."

Naz thought, who the hell is Charles Goodnight? Then, his mouth dropped open. Charlie? This guy in the tuxedo is Charlie? Holy shit. He smiled at the strange sight of the old derelict in a tuxedo, his neck shrunk down into his collar. Charlie glanced up at Naz and smiled nervously.

"Okay, Charlie. Go for it," Carina said.

Charlie pulled the cloth away. On the table in front of Naz, glistened a five-foot long sculpture of a train. It was breath taking. The metal gleamed, every detail perfect in shape and scale. It was the most beautiful train Naz had ever seen, with the gondola cars carrying the Pacific Rim logo and the five engines at the front. The train sat on a curving section of track, complete with gravel roadbed. A silver plaque read:

"The Pacific Rim Trash Train
Chief Engineer
Nazareth Agajanian"

and on one corner of the model, written in molten metal:

"Built by Charles Goodnight,
Senior Vice-President of Security"

The applause rolled on. Finally, Naz stood up and raised and lowered his hands a few times, as if he were patting the heads of the crowd. They quieted and Naz, leaning on the walker, limped over to Carina and hugged her. He gazed out at the faces.

"You sonsuvbitches."

The crowd roared. Charlie beamed. While the attention was off him, he hammered down another glass of champagne. Naz stepped back and motioned the waiter over.

"A toast!" shouted Naz.

There was a frantic scrambling for glasses, filled with anything. Charlie nearly panicked. Here was an official declaration to drink and his glass was empty. A woman's hand shot out in front of him holding a brimming shot glass of *oghi*.

Without looking up, Charlie lifted it like a religious relic.

"Cheers, Charlie," Mayda said.

"Cheers," Charlie stammered.

Raising his glass, Naz proclaimed, "To all of us here tonight. To my family and friends. My parents, Harry and Armi Agajanian, my beautiful wife of thirty years, Mayda, to my wonderful daughter Carina and our consultant and Carina's fiancée, Denny DeYoung, to Charlie Senior Vice-President of Security, to all our workers, you trash haulers, and last to Pacific Rim Recycling—*Genatz Noot!*"

Every glass in the room was raised. "*Genatz Noot!*" echoed back.

They chugged as one and the empty glasses hit the tables. A mandolin began to play.

Down the table, Harry rubbed the handle of his cane. He felt the warmth of Armi's hand on his knee, and covered hers with his. She turned her blue eyes to him and in their teary depths Harry saw triumph and joy and love. He also saw forgiveness for the hard journey, for the dark nights when the morning seemed so far away. Harry squeezed Armi's hand and she squeezed back. He took a deep breath to keep from crying.

There is a road, he thought, not even a special road, or an important road—just a road. And all your life is only to walk down it and hold in your heart your family and your people and your work and your mountain and your God. Then at the end of the road, well, you come out here on this night with now a new road, maybe not long for you, but long and good for the family—who after all, is you. Harry looked at Naz, like an extension of his own arm, and felt as if it was he himself who rose from the table.

Harry watched as they made a path for Naz, shuffling behind his walker toward the dance floor. When Naz finally got there, he shoved the walker aside and pulled a white handkerchief out of his pocket. Slowly, he raised his arms above his head.

Then he began to dance.

*   *   *

Later that night, moonlight spilled across the Pacific Rim yard and onto a field mouse nibbling at a morsel of cake left over from the Ball. It fell off the table and the mouse jumped down after it.

At the faint sound, Black raised his head in the front seat of Charlie's hearse. He checked Charlie sleeping in the back, still dressed in his tuxedo, then slipped out the window and rushed toward the sound. The mouse scampered to safety under a dumpster, leaving the Assistant

Sr. Vice-President of Security panting in the cool night air.

Black gave one more look around the plant, and seeing that all was well, trotted back to the Coup de Ville. He peed on the tire, then leapt through the window, curled up on his blanket and went to sleep.

THE END

Acknowledgments

It has been an honor and a privilege to work for over forty years alongside some of the great family companies in Los Angeles and Southern California. Trash haulers, recyclers, composting operators, renewable energy developers—and most starting from virtually nothing. Many of these entrepreneurs are first or second generation immigrants building the American dream for their families.

Battling against all odds, some of these companies are now worth tens, even hundreds of millions of dollars. They have become visionaries and leaders in the solid waste and recycling industry not only in California but the entire United States.

I am grateful for the opportunity they have given me to establish my own engineering consulting firm and work with them on some of the most exciting environmental projects of our time.

In particular, I want to thank and acknowledge the following families and individuals, with apologies to any I've left out:

Kazarian	Matosian	Kardashian	Blackman
Balakian	Kalpakoff	Bath	Scopesi
Blackburn	Burr	Mohoff	Adnoff
Borgatello	Young	Agajanian	Petrosian
Huberman	Gasparian	Rosenthal	Shaw
Perez	Arakelian	Jones	Beers
Minasian	Fry	Arsenian	Ratto
Ware	Pellegrini	Guttersen	Briggeman

Also to be acknowledged are Armenian friends who helped me with cultural elements of this book: Valentina Matosian, David Balakian, and Tanya Keshishian.

Influential in development of the novel was the expert review, critique, and guidance of Terry Wolverton and members of her L.A.-based "Writers at Work" class, and Tara Ison and Gwin Wheatley who gave insightful comments and recommendations along the way.

Heartfelt thanks as well to Deborah Daly who did a masterful job of editing, book design, and production; and to friend Skip Harris for his wonderful marketing acumen and assistance.

And of course, kudos to my wife, Lois Fletcher, for her ever present support, encouragement, guidance, and most of all belief that I could do it, especially at times when it seemed nothing more than a pipe dream. We should all have such angels in our lives.

About the Author

Supported by an athletic scholarship and one of the first grants from the newly formed Environmental Protection Agency (EPA), Chip graduated from the University of Illinois with a Master's Degree in Engineering. After working for several years for environmental consulting firms in Los Angeles, he started his own company, Clements Environmental Corp.  Through the ensuing decades, the firm represented clients on critical solid waste and recycling infrastructure projects and programs throughout the State of California and beyond.

From the time he met his first family-owned business

in the "trash" field, Chip was impressed by their ingenuity, guts, tenacity, loyalty, and lust for life. He drew from his experience working shoulder to shoulder with them "in the trenches," from the truck yards, recycling plants, and composting sites to their board rooms and on to the marbled Council Chambers of City Halls.

When not writing his next novel or pitching his screenplays to the film industry, he is working on the development of zero carbon energy projects creating renewable energy from waste.

Chip lives in Los Angeles with wife, Lois Fletcher, and their twenty-year-old cat, Joie de Vivre. They have four married adult children living with their families in Southern California and Spain, and seven grandchildren.

Made in the USA
Monee, IL
28 May 2023

34846906R00215